When Shadows Walk

Rebecca F. Pittman

DEDICATION

For Michael John Wells, my big brother, who passed during the writing of this book.

You are a fellow author, orator, and adventurer. You always kept a towel in your car for me so that I could jump out and put my feet in the water at every ocean and stream we passed. You are greatly loved and greatly missed. Your shadow will always walk with me.

Michael John Wells

October 8, 1948 - December 5, 2023

CONTENTS

Contents

ACKNOWLEDGMENTS

The characters and events depicted within this book are entirely fictitious. Any similarity to names or incidents is entirely coincidental.

A work of fiction still relies on literal locations, culture, jargon, and research. I want to give a heartfelt 'thank you' to the following who helped me with some of the background needed for this book:

Steven Ballard with Scheels Sporting Goods in Johnstown, Colorado, for his invaluable knowledge of waterskis and their construction. Thank you for uninstalling the binding so I could better understand its makeup.
Nenita Pellegrino with Northern Colorado Catering in Fort Collins, Colorado, for taking the time to instruct me on the party catering process and clean-up. I so appreciate your invaluable input.
The Myrtles Plantation staff for their insight into all things haunted in Louisiana, and the area's jargon. There's a reason it is called the "Most Haunted Home in America."
Sonny Panzico with Panzicio's Garden Mart in Monroe, Louisiana, for helping me understand the local water vegetation and seasonality.
John Drzemala for accompanying me to Louisiana and helping with the research for this book. You are always up for an adventure.
Dylann Leal with the Glenn A. Jones MD Memorial Library for being my tech support for this book. Thank you so much for helping me with the formatting.

i

PROLOGUE

2023-

It was the feeling that someone was watching her. That tingling feeling of an energy shift as if your soft cocoon of privacy has been invaded by an unseen force. The room suddenly felt claustrophobic, despite its openness. Tingling along her arms and the small hairs standing on end were the first signs that something was happening. A sudden bone-chilling cold seeped into the sunroom, despite the thermometer showing 95 degrees. The sudden drop in temperature was at once numbing and impossible to describe.

Tulie shivered and shot a quick glance to her right. Her breath caught. It hadn't been there a few minutes before. It was only after the faltering rays of the sunset had been absorbed by the pines and lake water that she had first noticed what at first appeared to be a dark stain forming in the corner of the sunroom to the left of the fireplace. Evening was coming earlier in the fall month of October. It did little to soften the Louisiana humidity that wilted one's clothing and spirits well into the twilight.

Nervously, Tulie pulled her gaze away from the corner and looked quickly out through the mesh of the floor-to-ceiling windows of the screened-in porch. *It was her imagination. Nerves*, she reassured herself, even as she shivered in the glacial air. She looked at her mother seated across from her. Having tea with her Mama here was her favorite time of day. Her sweet perfume lay like a soft whisper around them. The sound of the lake water lapping against the boat dock sitting several yards away at the bottom of the sloping lawn had always been a sound Tulie found soothing—until that fateful day. Now it added to the sudden tension she felt as the room darkened, and lights could be seen coming on in her Aunt Margo's house across the inlet. The nocturnal rhythm of the trill of crickets and katydids rose and fell with the wind, abruptly stopping when a branch cracked or a pecan fell, ricocheting hollowly off the hard tree trunks.

Steam rose from her teacup, swirling in gentle mists that dissipated with the slightest breath. She reached up and hurriedly pulled on the small chandelier's chain dangling low above their heads. A soft effusion of light from the vintage tulip-shaped bulbs brought the long room's furnishings into focus. Tulie glanced at the corner of the room, expecting the shadow to be extinguished by the overhead light. It had instead grown, wavering slightly in the soft breeze coming in through the mesh screens of the sunroom windows.

Tulie looked across the table at her mother, who had her back to the corner. Should she ask her to look? Her mother was so different since Ryder's drowning, her

2

mind as fragile as a butterfly's wing. Tulie decided to ignore what was happening in the room. It was only the ghostly shadows this time of evening brought with the old plantation house. She glanced at a Mardi Gras mask hanging on the wall near her—its sightless eyes watching her.

Her mother, Rachel, had decorated the old porch area that had once served as the kitchen for the palatial family plantation house in what could only be described as New Orleans whimsy. Rachel had the old walls knocked out and replaced with screened-in windows that took in the inviable view of Lake Broussard, the Louisiana cypress and pines, and the soaring egrets that nested around the inlet. The room was filled with antiques, porcelain statues of fairies, and fantastic creatures. Tulie's mother's fondness for the colorful harlequin jesters that smiled from New Orleans store fronts was evident. They filled the room in various sizes and materials. Mardi Gras masks in myriad motifs grinned toothlessly from the brick walls surrounding the fireplace and from the surrounding support beams punctuated by mesh windows. Beads hung from the chandelier, plumes of feathers competed with house plants, and a checkered porcelain cat stretched languidly across the fireplace hearth that had once been home to copper pots, firewood, and various ladles.

Tulie's mother, Rachel Broussard Barrows, had always lived in a hazy realm of fantasy, reluctant to let the dictates of reality infringe too far into her carefully crafted pastel world. She had raised Tulie on strange tales whispered in the night in her soft southern cadence. Tulie fell asleep picturing the creatures and adventures her mother pulled from somewhere deep inside her fecund mind. As Tulie grew and discovered books, she found they never equaled the fantasies her mother spun in the shadows of her bedroom each night. Even now, at 25 years of age, she longed to have her Mama propped up next to her against the pillows of her bed, weaving her words into characters so real you expected them to walk through the door and sit down to tea.

Wind rippled across the lake's surface, sending the gentle lapping sounds into sloshing waves that sent sprays of green lake water up the dock pilings and over the tops of the rocks bordering the shoreline. A shiver ran up Tulie's arm. She stopped mid-sentence in her description of the new dress material she saw in Butler's at Wing's Bend. Her breath quickening, she reluctantly glanced at the corner near the fireplace to see the shadow had doubled in size. It swayed with the wind; at one moment a shape sputtering into form only to undulate into an undefined mass. It had spread out over several of the fireplace bricks and was tall enough to obscure the Mardi Gras mask that hung on the wall behind it, about four feet from the floor.

Tulie looked across the bistro table again at her mother, but she seemed oblivious to the miasma forming in the corner. Brenn, Tulie's stepsister, had gone into the kitchen to fetch some scones, leaving her tea untouched. Tulie grabbed up her own cup and took a long sip of the hot herbal concoction, alarmed to hear the cup rattle against the China saucer as she replaced it. Her mother did not seem to notice.

Why is she so quiet tonight? Tulie wondered. *Does*

she sense something strange here as well?

The wind whistled around the corner of the room, rattling the black leaves of a tall Mican Philodendron in the corner behind her mother. Tulie looked in that direction and caught something shining outside the mesh window. Her rapid breathing slowed as she realized it was moonlight striking the white marble of one of the tombstones in the family cemetery that sat fifty yards from the house. As the wind propelled the clouds across the lunar face, the tombstones and crypts would one minute sit in dark huddled forms, only to be thrown into stark relief when the moonlight pierced its way through again.

"So…," Tulie said shakily, picking up her thread of conversation, hoping the sound of her voice would shatter the fear permeating the room. "There was a lovely jacquard print that would make a wonderful summer dress, and there was a purple paisley…"

She felt it watching her—the shadow that was now filling the entire corner of the room. Her heart pounded as she glanced over at it, unable to look away. She felt compelled to look, as if it demanded her attention. *Was that an arm forming?* An appendage was jutting out from the side nearest the window. She couldn't swallow. Her breathing was coming in short bursts. Tulie was afraid if she stared at it long enough, she would begin to see the mad glint of an eye, or the outline of a jaw taking shape within the black mass. Yet if she forced herself to look away, would it choose that moment to fly screaming at her from the corner, skeletal fingers outstretched, with a guttural cry that sounded as if it were coming from the bowels of the

5

earth?

A sharp flash of light lit up the room, and Tulie screamed, knocking her teacup over. The hot liquid spread through the lace tablecloth in a burnt sienna stain. Tulie whirled around in her chair to face the direction of the light and found Brenn standing there, cell phone upraised in her hand, looking shocked at Tulie's drastic reaction.

"For Pete's sake, Tulie, I only took a picture! You and your Mama looked so peaceful sitting there with your lovely tea service, I thought you might like a photo of it. *Lawd!*"

Tulie's chest was heaving. Without looking at her mother or the corner by the fireplace, she leapt from her chair and rushed to the open door behind Brenn, knocking her to one side. Tulie stumbled into the kitchen and ran for the back stairs to her bedroom above.

The wind reached a howling crescendo outside, rushing in through the screened windows of the enclosed porch and sending tiny dessert napkins and the antique chandelier swirling, its dangling beads clanking against the swaying crystal prisms. A napkin fluttered to the corner where a shadow in the form of a young boy was moving away. In its place, a playing card, worn with time, lay against the weathered floorboards where dozens of servants had walked in eras gone by. The King of Spades, his face turned to the right with an enigmatic grin, fluttered in the wind. A brown stain discolored the linen weave of the card. Across its face was a name scribbled in pale blue ink—*Brenn*.

1 Brenn's Story

2006-

The forecast for afternoon thunderstorms had moved the party inside. Rose and pink-colored balloons were tied in bundles to the backs of chairs in the small dining room. Matching paper plates and napkins sat next to a lopsided birthday cake; its 38 candles arranged to conceal the drooping border of piped roses. Only a handful of guests were invited to attend the auspicious flipping of the calendar for Brenda Barrows. They waited anxiously as the guest of honor gazed down at the lit candles through a haze of antidepressants. Only her daughter, Brenn, could have forced her to be here in this moment.

The nine guests studied the guest of honor with curiosity and concern. It had been a long time since anyone had seen Brenda. The word "recluse" had been branded upon her, carrying all the stigma the word

7

implied. The closed curtains and neglected lawn were the signposts of a woman who had given up. Her dark brown hair was pulled back into a tight ponytail. It was clear someone else had applied her makeup. It had been overdone; her pale skin was almost translucent beneath the garish rouge. A freshly pressed dress in paisley print hung from her frame; two sizes too large now.

Brenda's closest friend, Margaret Topper, acted as hostess, passing out flutes of champagne. There were no appetizers...a distinct oversight in the southern tradition. Brenda's 15-year-old daughter Brenn appeared almost frantic in her attempt to welcome people and thank them for coming. Her mother's self-imposed exile from the world had taken her prisoner as well; the doors and windows of the small home were merely missing bars.

A tepid rendition of *Happy Birthday* was drowned out by the sound of crashing thunder that rattled the sliding glass doors near the dining table. Carol Landcaster jumped, her champagne spilling onto the paper tablecloth. Brenda stared at the amber liquid spreading through the crimson paper weave like an errant bloodstain.

"Mama, blow out your candles," Brenn said quickly, placing a steadying hand on her mother's arm. "They're dripping all over the icing."

Brenda turned her head slowly toward her teenage daughter, straining to recognize her. Her face softened as a sad smile formed on her trembling lips.

"Alright, Brenn," she said, using her pet name for her daughter, who had cared for her since the divorce. "Just for you, my Brendyl, my joy," she added quietly.

Brenda gripped the back of the chair she was standing behind and bent over unsteadily, rocking slightly to one side. Brenn placed her hand on her mother's back. The guests held their breath along with the birthday girl. Brenda puffed out her cheeks and blew. Only two of the candles went out. Brenn hurriedly leaned over and blew out the rest before her mother could straighten.

"Yay!" the guests yelled out in feigned celebration.

"Happy Birthday, Brenda," Margaret Topper exclaimed. "This is your year! You just watch!"

Brenda turned vacant eyes upon her best friend of 20 years. Her eyes watered, and she looked away.

"Let's cut the cake!" Margaret said with forced gaiety. "Brenn, you did a wonderful job making this! It's just lovely."

Rain pelted the windows as the guests ploughed their way through their slices of dry cake. The room smelled of candle smoke and Bridget Newman's heavy perfume. Nervous glances were thrown toward the guest of honor, who sat almost comatose at the head of the table, leaving her slice of cake untouched. They glanced at their watches and the wall clock, where the hands moved slowly against a magnolia blossom background.

"Mama? Do you want to open your presents now?" Brenn asked, the tense atmosphere around the table as thick as the Louisiana humidity outside. Tyler Jenkins uttered a subdued groan. He was anxious to leave this party, which felt like a wake. His wife, Denise, kicked him under the table. Brenn removed her mother's plate with the uneaten cake and replaced it with a small gift

9

wrapped in blue foil. "This is from Jasper," she said, looking over with gratitude at their closest neighbor.

"I can't take the credit," he said. "Joann picked it out. She...um...regrets not being able to come. You know how her sinuses get this time of year." He looked around him awkwardly, gauging whether anyone believed his feeble attempt to excuse his wife's absence.

Brenda stared at the present, her head lolling.

"Thank you all for coming," she said thickly, and suddenly pushed her chair back with a screech. "I'll feel better tomorrow." With that, she stumbled from the room, her hand grabbing onto furniture and walls as she went.

The guests looked at each other with various facial expressions, registering their surprise and relief. It was over. Brenn sat staring at the mutilated cake and fought back tears. She finally pushed back her chair and walked to the short hallway where people were gathering their things.

"She's going to be alright," Margaret said, placing an arm around the girl's trembling shoulders. "I know it's been rough on you, taking care of her after your father...well...you know. I'm here if you need me. Speaking of which, do you need help cleaning all this up?"

Brenn shook her head no. "It will give me something to do," she said sadly. "She'll be in her room the rest of the night."

The guests left the house in pairs, hunched over beneath umbrellas as the rain came down in torrents that swelled the street gutters to overflowing. Brenn stood in the open doorway and watched them navigate past the puddles along the sidewalk and front yard. Jasper turned and yelled, "Goodbye," as he dashed across the lawn to his house next door, head bent against the slashing rain.

Brenn looked out at the black sky from beneath the front porch overhang. She breathed in the fresh smell of rain. It had always reminded her of a wet baseball field. For just a moment, the memory of her father screaming at her from the worn metal bleachers came back to her.

"Run to third, Brenn!" he screamed, the other parents eyeing him with frustration. "Do what I told you to. If you see a chance, take it!"

How long ago was that? Seven years? The thought brought back the wave of panic it always did.

Brenn shut the door and walked into the kitchen, looking about her at the mess she had made concocting her first cake. There was flour, broken eggshells, and spilled vegetable oil covering the counter near the sink. Sighing, she picked up a kitchen towel and began wiping the mess into the garbage can at the end of the counter. She piled bowls of hardened batter and frosting into the sink, turning the hot water to full blast.

A loud thud sounded outside the kitchen. Brenn turned off the faucet and stood still, her ears straining. *What was that? It sounded like it came from the next room.* Wiping her wet hands on her jeans, she walked through the kitchen doorway and turned right into the dining room.

For several minutes, the scene before her froze. Time splintered, and the floor became a trap door beneath her. The rose and pink-colored balloons tied to chair backs moved and bumped into each other as the object above them swayed rhythmically back and forth. It wasn't until her mother's shoe fell from her suspended foot that Brenn screamed.

2 Letters

Margaret Topper sat on the worn couch, both arms wrapped around the teenager who was dry heaving after an episode of uncontrollable hysterics. The female police officer had been empathetic and patient with the young girl, but was getting nowhere in garnering the information needed to process what had happened.

"She can't talk right now," Margaret said again, wondering why it wasn't obvious to the officer.

"I understand that," Officer Payton said kindly. "I'm sorry, but this is necessary. Perhaps you and I could talk in the other room."

In response to the suggestion, Brenn clung tighter to her mother's best friend, and a fresh series of wailing sounds filled the air. Sighing, the officer walked from the room. Her muffled voice could be heard coming from the area of the dining room, but Margaret could not make out the words.

"I can't get the girl to calm down," Officer Payton said quietly to Sergeant Moray. "Anything in here?"

"She hung herself from that ceiling hook," he said, pointing to a large white hook anchored into the ceiling to the right of the dining room table. "It looks like at some point it was decided to move the dining table over to there and a new hook was put in place for the chandelier. They didn't bother removing the old hook."

Officer Payton looked up to where he was pointing. Hanging above the dining room table was a small chandelier with dusty bulbs. Five feet away was a large white hook, one that looked like it could hold a good deal of weight. She looked at the carpet beneath it and could make out four imprints from where a table once stood. A toppled dining chair now lay on its side in the same spot. She raised her eyes to the ceiling hook and sighed. She would never understand suicide.

"What did she use?" she asked quietly, glancing over her shoulder toward the opening into the living room.

"Looks like a thick cord you use to pull curtain blinds. One has been cut in the back bedroom, which I believe was hers. The ligature marks around her neck match. No other trauma. No signs of foul play. It looks like she stood on that chair and then kicked it out from under her. According to the dead woman's friend in the other room, this had to have happened within minutes of the guests leaving the party."

"I'll keep trying to get something from the daughter," Payton said, pressing her lips together. "This is hard. I hate this part of the job. Can you imagine? One minute you're having a birthday party for your mother and the next..." She looked over at what was left of the cake. The dirty paper plates and napkins still littered the table. A stack of festively wrapped presents sat in

14

macabre juxtaposition to the toppled chair beneath a bare ceiling hook. Payton picked up one of the champagne flutes and sniffed it. "I guess we wait for the tox report," she said, and set the glass down. "Her friend said she appeared drugged, but it was common knowledge she was taking a lot of pills."

Margaret appeared in the doorway, looking haggard and pale. Brenda's sister had arrived and taken over the care of Brenn, who was still huddled on the couch, afraid to move.

"Brenn's Aunt Susan is here," Margaret said, her voice husky. "She's close to Brenn. She's Brenda's half-sister. Probably the only one in what's left of the family that Brenn will let close to her. She has occasionally come over the years to help with Brenda, but she's got health problems of her own. Beginning stages of MS. Go easy on her."

Margaret looked past Officer Payton's arm at the dining room table and began to cry. "Why?" she sobbed. "I know she had a tough time when Randall left them. Dealing with a husband's infidelity is hard enough, but for him to just cut them off like they didn't exist..." Her face flushed with anger. "How is Brenn going to survive this? She's been locked up here with a mother who could barely function for seven years! How do you put that burden on an 8-year-old? I've tried to help wherever I could. I set up counselors, but Brenda wouldn't go. I paid to have one come to her, but Brenda threw a glass at the woman, barely missing her head, and that was that."

"Were there signs that Brenda was suicidal? I mean, did she ever talk about taking her life?" Payton asked.

"She never said the words," Margaret replied, wiping her eyes with a mascara-stained tissue. "But she had continually spiraled down over the years. She sat in that dark room day in and day out, obsessing over those damned letters. I tried to take them from her, but she became almost feral. It was scary!"

"Letters?"

"She found a stack of love letters that the woman having an affair with her husband had written to him. There were about six or seven of them. She read them over and over! Brenn managed to steal them once when her mother had passed out from pills, but Brenda found out and became unhinged. Brenn told me Brenda threatened to kill her if she didn't give them back." At the look of shock on Sergeant Moray's face, Margaret quickly amended her statement. "It was the pills!" she said quickly. "She was never like that before. She was a great mother and wife. But after, she became a total wreck."

"Where is the father?" Office Payton asked, bringing out a small notepad from her back pocket. "Randall Barrows, is that correct?"

"Yes. He lives with his new wife about an hour from here, in Orleans Parish. They have two kids of their own...twins. It's like he just created a new life, and there was no room for Brenn. His own daughter! She got birthday and Christmas presents, but that's all. Oh, did I mention that the new wife is the one Randall cheated with? Rachel Broussard—richer than Rockefeller. No wonder Brenda fell apart. He just threw her away. And the bitch of it is, Brenn will probably end up living with them." She excused herself and left

16

the room, fighting back tears and anger.

Officer Payton looked at Sergeant Moray with raised eyebrows. "What a mess," she said. "That poor girl. I guess we have to inform the ex. Do you know anything about the Broussard's?"

"Yeah. Wealthy family. Been around for centuries. Some weird stories about scandals and mysterious deaths, but what rich family doesn't have those?"

"Next, you'll be telling me they have ghosts," she grinned. "Ok. Let's get it over with. I have a feeling the ex and the new Mrs. won't be all that heartbroken. Let's go see how the wealthy Broussard's live."

3 LEGACY

Tucker Wingate Broussard was born pure South in 1942. His birth was hailed in true Louisiana fashion with a party consisting of gumbo, jambalaya, crispy fried okra, crawfish, King Cakes, and a flowing fountain of champagne. Libations flowed faster than the Mississippi River just outside the south gate. Trays carried by white-gloved waiters were passed among the guests, bearing such favorites from New Orleans as Milk Punch, Peychaud's bitters, Ramos Gin Fizz, the infamous Hurricane—that would knock a large man on his derriere on his third round—Vieux Carré, Southern Comfort, and Mint Juleps. The conversation and raucous laughter rose with the amount of liquor consumed as the late afternoon wore on. A Broussard male had been born, and it was time to celebrate.

Men and women separated into clusters about the massive plantation lawn. Ladies in soft chiffon fluttered fans and bent together in conspiratorial fashion as they bashed the latest parish pariah.

"Did you see what Denise Lawson was wearing at

the Spring Social? I *swear* you could see her bosom every time she bent over...and she bent over a *lot!*"

"I *know!* But *I* swear *I* was more appalled at Marcie Jackson's bread puddin'! She had so much bourbon poured all over it that I thought every time Dwight Carson went near it with his lit cigar, the whole booth was gonna go up in flames!"

"Well! It looks like the Broussard's are makin' a haul. Did you see the number of presents on the parlor table? Let the spoilin' of the new Broussard baby begin!" This was followed with a twitter of laughter, despite the fact that the same ladies enjoying the snide remark had contributed to the gift table themselves.

On and on it went as waiters were kept hopping with trays of drinks and canapes. Across the lawn, cigar and pipe smoke wafted on the breeze until the sickeningly sweet smell of cherry blend tobacco, mixed with the briny aroma of boiled crawfish, was becoming a bit nauseating. It didn't help that the proud Daddy of little Tucker kept the cigars coming in celebration of the day's event.

The late afternoon sun peeked between pine boughs and live oaks, glinting off flasks of whiskey and bourbon as the menfolk tallied up their fortunes or denigrated some newcomer Northerner's attempt to buy up parish property.

"Barker Barrett done sold that Yankee that worthless swamp he's been trying to unload for 12 years!"

"I thought the only thing you could grow there was gators!"

"Well, let's hope the fine gentleman from Montana knows how to operate a purse and loafer store!" The laughter exploded at the images of alligator bags and shoes.

It was one of many parties throughout the generations held on the vast lawn of the Broussard Plantation. Laughter and the happiness that comes with a child entering the world laced the Spanish moss swaying on welcome breezes. The guest of honor, along with the woman who had made this day possible, were noticeably absent. The newborn's mother, Lavina Broussard, had to enjoy the party through the master bedroom window where she lay in bed, nursing stitches from the C-section she received after 21 hours of unsuccessful labor. She was one of only 5 percent of the population in 1942 to receive the relatively new procedure. The Broussard money factored into it.

A nurse/nanny had been hired to help the new mother. Lavina insisted on nursing the infant. All other chores, including diaper changes and helping with her dressing and toiletry needs, fell to the capable Ms. Adriana Falstaff. The woman was built like a small tank, her midsection testing the endurance of the buttons struggling to contain her girth. She spoke in clipped staccato sentences and sniffed at the end of each proclamation in the form of a period. Adriana swayed back and forth in the mahogany rocker next to Lavina's tester bed with little Tucker blissfully asleep in her arms and unaware of the jubilation in his honor sounding through the open window.

Some of the ladies from the party sneaked up the massive front staircase and into Lavina's room to congratulate her and coo over the sleeping infant. Nurse Adriana was not enthusiastic about their intrusion and kept the baby to one side in a protective maneuver that made it hard to get a good peek at him. Undaunted, the partyers gushed over the tired mother and imparted the latest gossip—Denise Lawson's ample bosom display at the Spring Social served up as the first course. Several brought Lavina mint juleps and soggy canapes as their way of including her in the party. Their effusive well wishes lingered in the air, along with the heady swirl of floral perfumes, as they giggled their way out of the room, with promises of "getting together soon" left as empty farewell parting gifts.

Lavina looked dismally at the wilted food and the alcoholic beverages in which she was unable to indulge in due to her breastfeeding the baby. Adriana eyed the bourbon concoctions with the sprigs of fresh mint and offered to relieve the hapless new mother of them. She passed the baby back to Lavina and deftly downed four mint juleps. After a few minutes of bourbon-infused bliss, the nurse suddenly excused herself and stumbled to the door in search of the powder room, pressing her pudgy hand to her mouth. She closed the large oak door behind her with a bang.

Lavina shook her head, sighed, and cradled Tucker, delighting in watching his lower lip suck in and out as he slept on. Laughter from the party rose and fell outside the open window.

After ten minutes, Adriana appeared at the door, took a deep breath, and walked unsteadily into the room.

"Hand him here," she said authoritatively, holding out hands that trembled slightly. Before Lavina could object, Adriana's fleshy arms had enfolded the infant.

21

She plopped into a groaning rocker and planted Tucker against her left shoulder, patting him forcefully on the back. The baby burped loudly and became still. "Better out than in," the nurse nodded approvingly.

The evening ended with the fading sound of violin strings and drunken "Goodbyes" as Louisiana's finest teetered through the garden gate to their waiting cars out front. Hired valets helped effusive ladies into the passenger seats and managed to save several expensive gowns from becoming crushed in slamming car doors. The tips were sparse as the inebriated wealthy paid more attention to revving their Packards, Lincoln Continental Coupes, and Cadillacs, and maneuvering them out onto the roadway. Several near collisions were miraculously avoided as the departing guests bottlenecked at the driveway exit.

The celebration of the birth of a Broussard child had been duly attended with all the pomp expected, especially for a male heir to continue the wealthy family's lineage. This had been Broussard territory before the Civil War, when Winston Valmer Broussard built the main house and surrounding plantation in 1859. He was thirty years old and newly married to the parish beauty, Eveline Taylor, a wealthy woman in her own right. They poured their inheritances into the palatial, columned home and 170 acres of fertile riverbed soil. While indigo and cotton were working for some of the plantation owners farther north, Winston became one of the successful Sugar Kings of the state. Money poured in and life seemed unlimited, until 1861 brought the sounds of cannons and gunfire.

The Civil War ripped through the South and the

complacency of the Louisiana magnates. In only a few short years, their fortunes had plummeted, and their way of life was relegated to the history books. Only the jewels and heirloom antiques that had been successfully hidden from Yankee marauders survived. Some who had invested their fortunes elsewhere came out of it and rebuilt. Winston Valmer Broussard was one of them. While the South had built railroads in the 1800s, they had limited themselves to short lines linking cotton regions to oceanic or river ports for exporting their wares. Winston knew the future would be transcontinental railways. He sought out the Big Four in California and bought in. The returns made him a wealthy man.

Before the Civil War broke out, Winston built two other large mansions on his sprawling property, with the intention of continuing to expand his role as a prosperous Sugar King. These would become homes to his offspring. Many believed he built them to keep his family close while maintaining his control over them. It also ensured a labor force for his plantation empire.

Rumors and gossip in the South swept faster and with more tenacity than the invasive kudzu vine. One such tidbit persisted that Winston had been rum pals with the pirate Jean Lafitte, who, along with his brother, Pierre, operated a blacksmith shop in nearby New Orleans. The ramshackle wooden structure masqueraded as a legitimate business while the brothers distributed smuggled goods out the back door. As their smuggling operation was in its heyday in 1805 (and Winston wasn't born until 1832), it was doubtful the rumors were true, yet many believed old Winston had a stash of pirate bounty buried somewhere on his property; perhaps handed down from his Pappy.

Garrison Wayne Broussard inherited the plantation and its vast acreage from his father, Winston, when he entered the world on June 21, 1863. The wealth that came with his birth certificate ensured he would never have to work throughout his lifetime. He carried on the tradition of marrying the local beauty, Bonnie Constance Revere. She became known for her lavish parties, always ending the evening by handing out complimentary bottles of champagne as party favors to her guests. Life was idyllic in the plantation mansion.

Only one thing was missing: children. The couple's plans had always been to have a large family to carry on the Broussard name. An ornate room in the west wing had already been selected as the nursery at the first sign that Bonnie had conceived. She threw herself into the room's decoration with an open purse and heart, choosing pale yellow rose-covered rice wallpaper and blue curtains.

Three weeks after Garrison passed out cigars at the baby shower, Bonnie gave birth to Brett Tucker Broussard. A lavish party heralded the new Broussard prince. It seemed the golden couple's future would be one of seamless perfection. Yet, as it is when Fate is tempted, the tide turned during Bonnie's second pregnancy. The little girl was stillborn. The couple was devastated, but hope came in the form of a pregnancy a few months later. It ended in a miscarriage, as did the following two conceptions.

Bonnie receded into the darkness of her bedroom, draperies drawn day and night. Gone were the famous parties. The servants continued to light the plethora of candles throughout the cavernous rooms. When the Anton Harber anniversary clock chimed midnight, the candles were extinguished.

One year later, a plague of yellow fever swept through the lower Louisiana parishes. Bonnie Broussard took to her bed, beset with nausea, high fevers, and headaches. As the days passed her skin and the whites of her eyes yellowed. In the final stages of the disease, her liver, kidneys, and heart failed. She died from a mosquito bite.

Only Brett Tucker Broussard, born in 1911, survived to adulthood of the four Broussard children. He lived his life in the shadow of his mother's tragic death and his father's subsequent descent into a whiskey bottle. Garrison died of liver disease three years later.

As Brett grew, he managed the servants and oversaw the massive acreage surrounding the house. He later married Lavina Mae Taylor, and together they endeavored to bring the Broussard plantation back to life. Brett spent a fortune on a crew of men to painstakingly dig a massive trench at the base of his cliff to divert the Mississippi River closer to his fields. His plan was to expand an export/import business. The water gushed in, covering acres of ancient soil, and a new dock was built. His trade up and down the river flourished.

Not to be outdone, Lavinia ordered fresh coats of paint for the mansion—inside and out—and the creation of expansive gardens. New velvet draperies were added throughout the home. Furnishings from Europe arrived on over-laden carts at their front door.

Lavina's prize possession was a pianoforte she placed in the music room. She spent hours at its keyboard, learning the sheet music residing in the music rack: *Roses from the South*. The waltz by Johann Strauss II echoed throughout the main floor, encasing the home in a romantic rhapsody.

Lavinia and Brett began populating the house with children immediately, filling the large nursery that had sat empty since Bonnie Broussard's death. Lavinia was scarcely beginning to wear tight-fitting gowns again before she found herself in loose, unflattering maternity clothes. Four young Broussard's were born within six years. It was with these births that the mysterious deaths befalling the Broussard families began feeding the local gossip mills.

Forrester Broussard, age six, fell headfirst into a cistern on the property and drowned. A year later, his younger sister Cecily was teasing a large chestnut mare when the horse kicked her in the head. She died instantly. Eight months later, Thomas Broussard, age twelve, shot himself in the stomach while playing at a Civil War reenactment with friends behind some old slave cabins. He lingered for five days before succumbing to his wounds. The nursery once again sat empty, the house no longer echoing with the sound of children's laughter. Brett buried his pain along with his children and stayed away on business whenever possible.

With her husband's frequent absences, Lavinia would often play her piano forte into the wee morning hours, moonlight from the palladium window pooling across the polished rosewood piano top. The old anniversary clock on the mantle would chime at two o'clock as she settled herself on the hand-embroidered cushion before the piano. She found sleeping alone in the cavernous house unsettling. She would often hear the sound of rushing water, although she could never find the source of the noise.

To deal with the loneliness and loss, she began spending money with abandon. Acres of lush gardens were added with winding trails and ponds. Brett hired a young man, Hally Kingston, who was known throughout the area for his skill at gardening and creating beautiful outbuildings called follies. Brett selected a portion of land at the rear of the gardens and contracted Hally to build a folly: a capricious building with a Medieval feeling. It would be a good-sized room with tiled walls in glowing mosaics accessed by a rustic wooden door of intricate carvings and hammered iron accents.

While the folly was the envy of Louisiana, it served a clandestine purpose of which only a few were privy. The secret society included Brett, Hally, and a rum runner known only as Jamaica Joe. Prohibition legally hit the nation in January 1920. New Orleans was one of the main cities to feel the punch. The city was one of the nation's most important alcohol distribution centers. It was dubbed by some government agents as "the liquor capital of America." When out-of-town agents began descending on the city, bootleggers scattered and set up their own speakeasies and nefarious means of hoarding alcohol.

The Broussard's had never been averse to cashing in on whatever was trending at the time, and bootlegging was no different. Brett, only 20 at the time, hired Hally to build him more than just a folly. The Repeal of Prohibition was still a few years away. The Mississippi River flowed just outside his property line now, and he was well aware of the liquid gold traversing that mighty waterway. He instructed Hally to build a tunnel running from a secret doorway inside the folly down the slope of the small cliff his plantation home abutted. The other end of the tunnel would open near the mouth of the river. The riverside entrance to the tunnel was well hidden by rocks and well-placed hedges. Here, rum making its way up or down the Mississippi (which now ran up to his dock) could be secretly left in barrels and hauled inside the tunnel. It was then stored in a small room just outside the secret door into the folly. The dark earthen enclosure kept the rum cool, and Brett Broussard cleaned up in illegal sales of the finest quality Bacardi.

Other bootleggers were smuggling liquor into New Orleans via Lake Pontchartrain and through St. Bernard Parish. Much of this was homegrown alcohol, and it tasted like it. Brett became known as the go-to guy for top-shelf rum. Once again, a Broussard padded his coffers while others struggled to make it through the rough years of Prohibition.

Never to put all his eggs in one basket, Brett also planted two massive orchards of pecan trees for his future. Knowing pecan trees take at least 12 years to mature, it was an investment for himself and his heirs, he still hoped to have.

His prayers were answered when Lavinia announced she was pregnant. Her face showed trepidation rather than the thrill of a new life coming into the home. Her children lay in raised vaults across the pecan grove in the family cemetery. The months passed without incident, and she gave birth to a healthy boy who was given his father's middle name: Tucker. Lavinia coddled him, reluctant to leave his side for a moment.

It was with this living heir that a lavish party filled the massive back lawn of the plantation estate on that warm August afternoon in 1942. As Lavina cradled the welcome male heir to the family fortune, she could not have known the small baby would be her last and warrant the final entry of her name into the sprawling Broussard family tree.

It happened one evening after Lavina had sung little Tucker to sleep and was walking back to her bedroom. As she passed the massive front hall staircase, she heard the sound of rushing water. She stopped, her heart pounding. The crashing sounds of waves engulfed her, infused with earsplitting screams. A sudden blast of frigid air ran at her, and she plummeted down the staircase. Tucker was only two at the time.

The story told throughout the parish was that her heel caught in the hem of her flowing silk nightgown, and she plunged down the twenty-five steps of the sweeping front foyer stairway. Her neck snapped on the fifteenth stair tread, and she died moments later. She was only 38 years of age. Brett was devastated and never remarried. Tucker was raised in the mansion by a distant cousin, Bethany Rhinehart, a widow, who was grateful for a place to go.

It was with Bethany that the first rumors of hauntings inside the house and strange lights in the plantation gardens began. Brett was often away from home, delving into one business opportunity after another; a necessary escape from the house and the stairs where his wife had died. His absence left the 34-year-old Bethany alone in a six-bedroom mansion with massive rooms filled with dark draperies and flickering candles. Despite the widespread use of electricity in 1944, Brett insisted on candles in many of the rooms, including the library, ballroom, music room, and upstairs bedrooms, in memory of his wife. Lavinia had loved to light candles in the evening, and he kept her tradition going. Brett finally relented and allowed the intrusion of electric bulbs into the kitchen and dining room after the servants complained of darkened conditions while trying to cook and serve meals.

Brett also filled vases throughout the home with his late wife's favorite rose: Windemere. The creamy yellow beauty with the orange sherbet colored center bloomed everywhere around the plantation. Its cloying citrus aroma was sometimes overpowering in the humid summer heat.

Other than those few concessions, he seemed to take no interest in the house, staying away for longer periods of time.

Bethany took care of the abandoned two-year-old Tucker and filled his days with games and learning. The house was filled with the gaiety of his laughter. The staff adored him and spoiled him with sweet treats from the kitchen pantry and gallons of lemonade. These were the times Bethany felt needed and happy. She had no children of her own. Her husband had died suddenly of tuberculosis in their third year of marriage. Tucker was to her the son she would probably never have. Plump, with a profound overbite and given to nerves, she had accepted that a second proposal of marriage was probably not forthcoming. She poured out her love on the small boy, and he thrived in her excellent care of him.

It was when the bulk of the staff left each day at 6:30 in the evening, she began to feel the shadows of the great house close in around her. Only Old Bill and Maggie stayed overnight in the Caretaker's Quarters at the back of the house. Old Bill's hearing had departed along with his ability to hold his wind a few years back. Brett had kept him on as an estate overseer out of loyalty to the old man. Maggie, Bill's wife, was a jovial, obese woman who was constantly clad in a stained apron comprised of the juices of whatever berry pie she had whipped up that day. Her hair was a bird's nest of wiry gray that sprang from the bun atop her head like frayed whicker. The elderly couple turned in by 7:00 each night. Bethany was totally alone in the house when darkness fell.

The staff at the Broussard mansion began to notice a change in Bethany. She appeared edgy and tired. Brown-colored hollows punctuated her eyes. She befriended a young maid and asked her repeatedly if she had noticed the candle flame floating through the Windemere rose garden at night. Despite the maid's assertion that she had never seen anything like that, Bethany persisted. The autumn months, when darkness came early, seemed to frighten Tucker's nanny more than any other time.

As Tucker grew, along with the declining state of

Bethany's nerves, she was finally let go. She gratefully packed up her meager belongings. The pain of leaving the boy, who was now in his teens, was overshadowed by her fear of the house. Too many evenings, she had been awakened by soft tapping on her bedroom door when no one else was inside the house, except for a sleeping toddler caged inside an antique crib. Summoning all her courage, Bethany opened the door the first evening she heard the tapping. A shadow, tall and appearing to be draped in something long and flowing, was floating down the hallway. Her heart clenched along with her stomach as she watched it arrive at the head of the massive staircase. It turned in her direction and then flew down the stairs as though something had pushed it. It was the final time Bethany opened her door, although the tapping continued.

Piano music played in the wee morning hour of 2:15, wafting up the grand staircase from the music room. This happened three or four nights in a row and then stopped. It was always the same song: *Roses from the South.* The waltz swirled along the balustrade as it climbed the staircase toward the second floor. Bethany often sniffed the faint smell of abandoned roses. Though she searched, she could never find the source of the elusive scent. Brett had long since abandoned the need to fill the house with his wife's favorite flower. The sounds of a small child screaming and thrashing about in water had terrified Bethany the most, always sending her hurrying to Tucker's nursery, only to find the child blissfully sleeping.

The shadow figure returned the night before Bethany called it quits. It was waiting for her at the top of the

32

staircase as Bethany climbed the stairs to bed. Before she could scream, it flew down the stairway past the terrified nanny, disappearing on the fifteenth stair. Racing to her room, Bethany locked her door. She sat on the edge of her bed throughout the night, eyes fixed on her doorknob, praying it would not turn.

The following morning, Bethany breathed a sigh of relief as the taxi cab's tires left the Broussard plantation in its dust; her two suitcases and several boxes of personal belongings residing in the trunk. She was free.

As the taxi rounded a bend, a young boy suddenly ran into the street chasing a dog. He froze when he saw the advancing car. The taxi swerved wildly as the driver tried to bring the car under control after narrowly missing the child. With the sickening sound of smashing metal, the taxi plowed through a brick wall encircling a large estate. The driver and Bethany were killed on the spot.

Tucker Broussard spent his days with strangers inside the massive home. He felt his father's constant absence keenly. Young children of distant relatives from neighboring parishes were sent to play with him. Aware that their parents were being paid by his father for the use of their offspring, Tucker never formed any lasting friendships with the children. They seemed more interested in his hoard of expensive toys than in him. He was invited to their birthday parties more in the hope of the pricey present he would bring than in his attendance.

Tucker went through three nannies until his late teens after Bethany departed. They ceased being called nannies when the boy turned twelve. Their new label was "companion." They were there to keep the boy company during his father's ubiquitous absence. It was hard to keep the women for more than a year or two, although Tucker was an easy boy to raise. Each in their turn became nervous and jumpy, something Tucker never understood. They left candles in the hallway burning throughout the night and bolted their bedroom doors. With some hurried excuse of an ailing relative or a new lucrative job offer, one by one, they scurried from the mansion with their suitcases, books, and treasured photos.

Tucker inherited the family fortune when his father was found in a backstreet alley of New Orleans on a late September evening. He had been robbed and beaten almost to the point of unrecognizability. It was postulated that Brett Brousard was drunk and had passed out, or been "helped out," of a local bar known for its rough customers. Perhaps Brett had been caught selling watered-down rum, or had come to collect on a shipment, and the bar owner thought it easier to relieve Brett of his wallet and murder him. It was yet another tragedy in the Broussard lineage.

When Tucker reached the age of twenty-seven, he married Tamara Cleary, the reigning Queen of Mardi Gras. They had three children together: Margo Lavina Broussard bounced into the world in 1963, followed by Barrington "Barry" Broussard in 1964, and Rachel Valmer Broussard in 1966. The family and the pecan groves flourished.

Tucker fixed up the two additional mansions his grandfather had built on the Broussard property, which now surrounded a blind lake left behind when the

Mighty Mississippi diverted back to its original course years before, leaving behind a sizable body of water. The end of Prohibition had also ended the illegal rum running for the profitable Broussard enterprise, now leaving the secret tunnel, for the most part, unused—still hidden behind a rock outcropping and tangled brush. The secret mouth to the tunnel lay only a few feet from the lake, now aptly named Lake Broussard.

The two mansions Tucker's grandfather built were to be for his two daughters, Margo and Rachel, as part of the girls' dowries when they married. Rachel's home sat to the left of the main plantation house, separated by a sizable portion of the pecan grove. Her home and its acreage also contained the family cemetery, which she did not mind. Margo's house sat to the left of Rachel's and across the lake from the main house. It, too, was separated from Rachel's house by a large orchard of pecan trees. The two mansions still retained the old slaves' kitchens with their large open fireplaces, and the verandahs that overlooked the front and back of the houses. They were nearing renovation completion when yet another tragedy befell the Broussard heirs.

Tucker and Tamara were fond of hosting summer parties at their magnificent estate. Invitations to their catered events were coveted. The event was usually built around water sports, copious amounts of food and drink, a live band, and lawn games. The current summer party fell on August 21st, the anniversary of Lavina Broussard's tragic fall down the mansion stairs. The party was in full swing. Inebriated guests jumped into the lake from the boathouse pier to escape the cloying summer humidity—some forgetting they had not donned swimwear. Several small boats roared around the lake, the wakes bouncing the excited guests who were swimming or riding out the swells in inner tubes.

Tucker was at the wheel of his prized watercraft: *Rum Runner*, the name unabashedly scripted upon its stern. It was aptly named as the four guests aboard had drained several plastic tumblers of the dark overproof with an alcohol concentration of a numbing 75%. Tucker veered recklessly back and forth across the lake, narrowly missing the other boaters and not a few wayward swimmers. He had turned to shout something to his wife Tamara, who was holding on tightly to the boat's railing, when she screamed. Tucker whipped his head around in an alcoholic haze, the dizziness almost taking him down.

A dark figure, smoke-like and shimmering, skimmed across the water in front of them before suddenly vanishing. Moonraker Rock loomed straight ahead. It was too late to turn. The boat ploughed straight into the outcropping that spread into the lake from the east shoreline. Tucker and Tamara were flung from the craft, hitting the jagged rocks, where their bodies lay like bloodied ragdolls. The other two passengers were thrown into the water and rescued by one of the other boaters.

It would not be the last time the lake would claim a Broussard heir.

4 DARK WATERS

2006...

Screams of feigned terror rose above the band hired for Barrington Broussard's long-awaited summer lawn party. The heir to the Broussard fortune, Barrington "Barry" Broussard inherited his father's mansion and vast property holdings when Tucker and Tamara Broussard were thrown from their speeding boat and dashed upon the rocks of Lake Broussard. Barry inherited the pecan groves, railway shares, his father's collection of rare coins, and most of the household furnishings. His two sisters, Margo and Rachel, were given the two mansions built around the lake, as had been promised to them in Tucker's will. They had duly moved into their new homes with their husbands and offspring. Barry, who had never married, lived in the mansion alone except for a gaggle of servants.

At 42 years old, Barry was the favorite uncle of three of his sisters' four children. Margo had one son, Landon, age 11. Rachel had a set of twins: Tuleah

(Tulie) and Ryder—a girl and boy, respectively, both age 8. Randall, Rachel's husband, had brought to the marriage a daughter, Brendyl. Her name was a combination of her late mother Brenda's name and her father Randall's. She hated the name, and by the time her school years began, she demanded to be called Brenn. After her mother's suicide, she moved in with her father and his new wife Rachel: the woman Brenn felt responsible for the breakup of her world. Already ensconced happily in her stepmother's and father's home were his two new children: the twins Ryder and Tulie.

Uncle Barry's summer lawn party was a hit. Over fifty guests attacked the food tables piled high with barbequed pork chops, bowls of steaming crawfish, lobster claws, coleslaw, corn on the cob, potato salad, bacon-wrapped scallops, and hot dogs for the guests' younger children. The dessert table featured pecan tarts, meringues, strawberry shortcake, and beignets dusted with confectioner's sugar. Two punch bowls resided on a checkered tablecloth beneath a spreading myrtle tree: one was labeled "Leaded" and the other, "Unleaded." The former was refilled six times within two hours,' while the latter was topped off once in the same period.

A hired local band from New Orleans, Swamp Relics, performed from a tiered stage; their drumbeat alone knocking pinecones to the ground from the trees flanking the dais. Despite the throbbing sound of instruments and tortured vocals, screams dominated the afternoon as Uncle Barry chased Landon, Tulie, and Ryder across the yard, threatening to throw them into the lake. He was wearing the gorilla mask he had purchased at a costume company in New Orleans for a party some years back. It was his favorite, and the children squealed with delight and fear as he lumbered about after them, hunched over and rolling like a drunken sailor. Only Brenn refused to join in. She was 15 now. Much too old for such childish games.

Truth be told, Brenn was having a tough time warming up to her stepmother Rachel's side of the family. Her disdain for them was reciprocated. Uncle Barry had never taken a liking to her and teased her sarcastically whenever he could, deliberately calling her by the name she hated: Brendyl. She eyed him now with contempt as he scurried about the yard in his monkey mask, looking like an idiot. The guests, however, were highly entertained and encouraged him as he darted past them in hot pursuit of the screaming children.

Brenn looked around. Her Aunt Margo (Rachel's and Barry's sister) was flirting with Jackson Waingate, as usual. Why her Uncle Reed never seemed to mind his wife's overt actions always amazed Brenn. The woman was forty-three but tried her damnest to look 20. The amount of Botox in her face was evident in the arched eyebrows and frozen mouth that could only manage a half smile.

Brenn's father, Randall, and her stepmother, Rachel, were helping refill platters of food. Brenn noticed her father casting furtive glances in Margo's direction as she preened and giggled at Jackson's jokes. She felt a hot flushing along her cheeks and neck. He had cheated on her mother with Rachel. Was her father once again on the hunt? Brenn walked slowly across the lawn to the back patio, her mood black. She glanced over her shoulder and passed through the mudroom door into the kitchen.

The cloying smell of boiling crawfish filled the kitchen. Over a dozen women and men were busily cutting up fruit and wrapping bacon around scallops. She narrowly dodged a huge platter of raw pork chops headed out to the grill.

"Brenn!"

Brenn turned to see Rachel's cousin Angela standing there with a tower of napkins. "Be a dear and take these out to the table. Put them next to the plates, please."

Brenn arched her eyebrow and pushed her thick blonde bangs to one side.

"Do it yourself. You know the way."

Angela looked at her in shock. Her face turned red in frustration and anger. Children did not talk like that to their elders in the South.

"You get your smart ass over here and take these napkins out like I told you, Brenn Barrows. I'm not afraid to take a belt to your plump butt!"

Bristling with contempt over the reference to her weight, Brenn steadied herself and shook it off. She would not give her dumpy new relative the satisfaction.

"Plump butt?" she said acidly. "Isn't it lucky you can pull off wearing elastic band sweatpants on any occasion?" she shot back, deliberately focusing her gaze on the dull burgundy workout pants her cousin was wearing. Brenn shot her a look of amusement and walked out of the room.

Two maids standing next to the 48-year-old woman glanced at her nervously. When Angela swung her head in their direction, they hurriedly returned to shredding cabbage for the coleslaw. Angela took several deep breaths, licked her lips, and exited out through the screen door, balancing the teetering tower of napkins.

Brenn walked slowly through the long hallway of the first floor. Some guests were perched on expensive chairs and settees to the left in the massive double parlor, while others were admiring the exquisite paintings that seemed to adorn every wall. *Decades of Broussard acquisitions*, Brenn thought disgustedly, as she passed a couple exclaiming over a rare Vermeer glistening beneath a pin light.

Brenn smiled banally as people passed her in the hallway.

"Hello, Brenn," Mrs. Arnolds said sweetly, stopping the girl. "My, y'all get taller each time I see you."

"Really?" Brenn asked. "I only moved here six months ago. You're probably thinking of my stepsister, Tulie." The saccharin smile she gave the woman did little to dispel the sudden unease Mrs. Arnold felt.

"Yes...yes...I see your point," the elderly woman stammered, unsure of how to gracefully ease herself out of the conversation. She needn't have worried. Brenn smiled again and moved on.

"That girl is odd," Mrs. Arnold whispered to her husband as they walked out the parlor's French doors to the back patio. "That's the second time I've been around her. You're never sure if she likes you or not."

"Teenagers," Mr. Arnold snorted in reply, deftly summing up his reasoning for the actions of all children within a certain age range. "Needs a good spanking. My parents didn't spare the rod, I can tell you that. Nowadays, you get hauled into court." He snorted again and put the punch table in his crosshairs.

Brenn dodged a few other guests who showed signs of stopping to talk to her. Reaching the master staircase, she climbed purposefully to the second-floor bedrooms. Choosing the guest room to the right, she entered, glanced out into the empty hallway, and shut the door behind her. The purses of the women who had come early to help with the party were laid out across the bed, kept out of the way while they busied themselves with the decorations and party preparations throughout the day. Daphne Hobart's purse was easy to spot. Every accessory she owned had some sort of faux safari skin; this time it was leopard. Daphne had been put on beignet duty. That required messy flour and yeast concoctions, so Brenn assumed her rings would be in the purse.

Barry had finished his harmless harassment of the children and was helping himself to the "leaded" punch. The vocals from the band's lead singer filled the sticky afternoon as he belted out a local favorite he had composed, *"If Ya Think It's Hot Now, Wait 'Till the Sun Goes Down."* Spirited guests hoofed it in bare feet, yelling out the chorus in unison. Outboard motors competed with the music as several boaters who were guests at the party zoomed around Lake Broussard.

Barry smiled as he downed his drink. It would be time for his waterskiing contest in about an hour. He slapped an old female classmate's behind as he made his way to the patio door. She yelled something playful at him, and laughter erupted from the nearby guests. He stopped in the kitchen to check on things and then made his way along the long hallway, glad-handing guests and reminding a few of his male friends that the waterskiing contest was coming up. "Wait 'till y'all see this year's prizes!" he bragged.

Barry climbed the staircase and turned to go into his

bedroom at the end of the hall. He heard a sound coming from behind the closed door to the guest room behind him and halted. A grin crossed his face. "50 bucks says that Randy Andy is in there with Stacie," he muttered to himself. Tiptoeing, so he could catch them in the act, he reached the door, turned the handle gently, and burst in, his face beaming at their anticipated response.

Brenn screamed, turning toward him with her back to the bed. She hurriedly put her hands behind her as her cheeks flushed a ruddy crimson. It took Barry a moment to adjust to the new scenario. No naked revelers. Just his niece looking guilty about something. He glanced behind her to the bed and saw the purses.

"What are you doing, Brendyl?" he asked curiously. "What's behind your back?"

Quickly recovering her composure, the teenager squared her shoulders and looked at him defiantly.

"Aunt Margo sent me up to get her aspirin from her purse. You got a problem with that?" Barry paused uncertainly. "Aren't you supposed to be playing King Kong with the kiddies?" she poked, eyeing the quickest route to the door.

Barry crossed the room in two quick strides and grabbed her right wrist, jerking her arm from behind her back. A thin gold tennis bracelet with set diamonds fell to the floor.

"Ow!" she screamed, rubbing her wrist.

"You little brat," he hissed. "I've known for a long time you were stealing. Every time you come here, money is missing, or some item you thought you could pawn. You took my watch I left in the boathouse last week while I had the boat out. I saw you come out of there. I want it back!"

Brenn looked at him with the same haughty grin she had given her cousin Angela in the kitchen.

"How does it feel to want?" she asked smugly.

With that, he shoved her. She landed on the bed and recovered quickly, her eyes blazing with hate.

"You pig!" she screamed. "You're nothing but a lonely loser no one wanted to marry!"

She fled the room before he could retaliate and ran full tilt into Roger Henderson, who had come looking for Barry to ask him a question about the waterskiing competition. Barry exited the room as Brenn ran down the staircase. He would talk to her father after the party and tell him his daughter was a thief. It would be a moot point. Randall rarely punished her. She fed off his guilt about her mother hanging herself over his abandonment of them.

Brenn reached the bottom of the stairs, chest heaving and felt inside her pocket for the ruby ring she had stolen from Daphne Hobart's purse. Her face suffused in rage, she walked through the parlor and out the French doors to the patio.

Barry locked the door to the guest room. He would hand the key to Margo and let her know he had locked it to protect the guests' purses. Telling Roger to wait for him by the dock, he walked into the massive master bedroom that had been home to the mansion's patriarchs throughout the decades. He changed into his swimsuit, grabbed his boat shoes, and returned to the party. Brenn was nowhere to be seen.

Dawson Kingston watched as Brenn streaked across the lawn and disappeared up the path to the gardens at the side of the mansion. Her face was red, and she looked angry. Dawson was used to seeing her in some state of high emotion. He had seen the drama since she moved in with her father half a year ago. Dawson grew up with the Barrows twins and Margo's son Landon, although he was slightly older. Dawson was Hally Kingston's grandson: the man who created the folly and secret rum-running tunnel decades ago. The Kingston's took care of the property through the years. They lived in a small cottage behind the pecan grove. Dawson's father had split when he was a baby, and the 17-year-old lived there alone now with his mother. Helouise Kingston was known throughout the parish for her pies. Pecans lay like a blanket outside her cottage door, and she put them to good use. Margo, Barry, and Rachel were usually given a fresh pecan pie at least once a week.

Barry walked across the sloping lawn, heading for the path that would lead down through the pecan grove toward the boat ramp. He paused when he saw the boy and asked, "Dawson, did you see Brenn come out of the house?"

"Yes, sir," Dawson answered. "She headed for the garden. She looked mad."

"Yeah, well, she's gonna get a lot madder when I'm done talkin' to her Daddy," he said hotly. "Empty those garbage cans by the tables. They're overflowing," Barry barked and walked away. Dawson was used to being treated like a servant by the Broussard's. His family was just the hired help. He primarily took care of the pecan orchards and helped with minor repairs at the main house. He also did odds and ends for the two sisters at their mansions. Margo was succinct and condescending to him, but Miss Rachel was always kind and usually offered him a cold sweet tea when he was working around her property. Dawson walked toward the full garbage cans as Barry entered the boathouse.

Several of Barry's male friends were headed to the boat ramp, some shouldering their own waterskies. Family skis were provided for those who took the sport less seriously and didn't own their own. Barry himself had an expensive set of skis that he kept in the boathouse. He chose the slalom ski and an extra set of regular skis and met the others at the boat.

"Same rules," he blurted out importantly, as the other five skiers waited for instructions. "Twice around the lake. You must weave in and out through the buoys or it doesn't count. On the third turn, you attack the ski ramp. The one who completes the three turns and manages to land his jump cleanly wins. Questions?"

"Yeah," Roger Henderson said uneasily. This was his first time competing in Barry's annual contest. "Do you have to 'attack the ramp?'" It was the question he had hoped to ask Barry alone earlier outside the bedrooms, before he heard the argument between Barry and his niece going on inside. A few of the veterans sniggered. He chewed his lips in embarrassment but couldn't help glancing out across the lake at the massive ski ramp near Moonraker Rock. If you messed up on the ramp, you could come dangerously close to bashing your head in on the jagged shoreline.

"Two turns around the lake," Barry repeated as he turned to board the boat. "Last turn, ski ramp. Don't compete if you don't want to. You can be our wench and hand out the beers."

Roger flinched at the snide remark. He took a deep

breath and pulled himself into the boat. He would see how the others did. No shame in going last.

The other party revelers were gathered along the shoreline and cliffside, cheering the six competitors on. Several had brought along binoculars for the occasion. The ramp was at the far end of the lake. Six red and yellow buoys bobbed in the current about midway to the ramp.

Barry idled out into the lake a few feet, let out the ski rope, and tossed the handle to Daryl Fledges, who was treading water behind the boat. Daryl grabbed the handle, steadied himself over his skis, and yelled, "Hit it!" The boat roared to life, surging out into the water. Daryl deftly came up onto his skis and centered himself in the wake.

"You ski like my retriever!" Barry yelled over his shoulder at him. The remark was lost in the roar of the boat.

Daryl made the first two rounds of the lake cleanly, showing off as he jumped the wake and swerved back and forth across it. He weaved expertly between the buoy obstacle course and smiled broadly. Barry shook his head, grinning. "Hot dog," he muttered to himself.

He turned the steering wheel and looked back over his shoulder. Daryl was lining up behind the boat for the final turn. Barry brought the boat around and pushed it full throttle toward the boat ramp. Daryl clutched the rope handle and veered to the right, aligning himself with the middle of the ramp. Bending his knees, he hit the ramp dead center and was suddenly flying out over the top of it. He squatted just as his skis hit the water. Recovering from the jolt, he straightened up and waved triumphantly.

"Damn it!" Barry called. The others laughed...all but Roger, who felt like he was going to throw up. Meekly, he began handing out beers from the cooler. Barry laughed. "I'll take the Marauder's, *Wench!*" he called to Roger, referring to the local beer favorite. Roger's face flushed as he passed a bottle of Marauders to Barry.

"You can be a real dick," Jenson Colby yelled. Barry only laughed and dropped the boat into idle as he reeled Daryl in and allowed Samuel Weathers to slip over the side into the water.

Samuel, Jensen, and the next two skiers completed the two turns, but only one made the jump. Two of the men chickened out or weren't lined up correctly.

"Well, boys!" Barry chortled as he slid into the water and slipped his right foot into the front binding of his slalom ski. "Time for the master to show you how it's done!" He wobbled back and forth a few times as he aligned the ski beneath him, its tip pointing out from the growing current. The wind had picked up.

"You sure you don't want to wait for the wind to die down?" Daryl called to him. "I don't mind winning this year," he grinned. It was the wrong thing to say. Barry gripped the handle and signaled for Samuel to push the throttle over. The boat roared to life and Barry rose up onto the wake, placing his left foot in the binding behind the right one. He wavered for a moment until he got his bearings. The wind stung his eyes, along with the spray of water coming off the wake. He veered to his right and then his left as he made the first clean sweep of the lake through the buoy obstacle course.

The other occupants were feeling the beer in the heat and laughing loudly as the boat sped about the large lake and brought Barry around for the second lap. He was feeling the wear and tear the wind was putting on his body, but he felt confident in the stunt he was about to pull off to win the prize. Daryl had nailed his jump. He would have to spice it up a little.

He rounded the second turn and ran a hand over his eyes. Water from the wind was running from his wet hair and eyelashes. The ski jump loomed ahead, and he took a deep breath. Leaning again to the right and then to the left, he came about and watched as Samuel gunned the boat and veered off to the left of the ramp. Barry held the handle tightly and let the rope, pulling now from the left of the ramp, carry him up.

The wind howled around his ears as he neared the top of the ramp and let go of the handle with his right hand, still holding it tightly in his left. As he soared into the air, he did a full twist before grabbing the handle again with both hands. *Smack!* He hit the water hard but steadied himself and let out a whoop of triumph.

Just then, he felt the front binding of his ski slip sickeningly to the right. He looked down at it just as the screws anchoring it on the left to the ski came completely loose. The binding flipped onto its side, releasing his front foot, and he found himself flying through the air.

The horrified boaters and guests back on shore screamed as he hit the rocks, the nauseating sound of his skull cracking filling the air. His body went limp.

Margo, Barry's sister, who had been watching the competition through binoculars from the boat ramp, cried out. Confusion erupted as everyone broke into shouting.

"Call 911! For God's sake, get an ambulance over to the other side!" "He's dead!" one woman screamed unnecessarily. "He has to be dead."

The wind escalated, sending paper plates and napkins whirling like confetti through the air. Women battled their hair as they raced for the house. An ominous black cloud had moved suddenly into place above the lake. The members of the band scrambled to unplug their equipment and secure their instruments. They barely cleared the bandstand before the first large raindrops began pelting the lawn. Within minutes, piled platters of food were swimming in their own sauces, desserts melted into unrecognizable puddles, and the punch bowls filled to overflowing with the sudden deluge.

Fifteen minutes later, flashes of red and blue could be seen through the pine trees across the lake as the medical personnel began arriving. The drenched partygoers huddled inside the parlor near the massive plantation windows and peered out through running rivulets of water. They watched as silhouettes in rain gear made their way carefully along the rocks to where Barry's body lay. It seemed to take forever for them to finally load him onto a gurney and struggle to pick their way back up through the slippery rocks.

Margo's and Rachel's wailing echoed throughout the house as their husbands stood by helplessly. Women knelt beside them in the parlor, pressing glasses of bourbon into their trembling hands and rubbing their forearms, or pushing their wet hair from their faces. Their heartfelt admonitions of "This too shall pass," "God only takes the good ones young," fell on deaf ears. Their brother was gone. Smashed against the rocks that had killed their parents years ago.

Margo rose and watched helplessly from the window

as the final emergency vehicle departed across the lake by the home she had inherited. How could she live there now, so close to those cursed rocks? As she stared across the water at the front porch of her house, barely visible through the pines, she gasped. She pressed her face closer to the glass. The rain distorted the images outside, but she was sure she saw a figure up at the top of the rocks where the police cars had just departed. It was black, its shape too distorted to say if it was a man or a woman. It stood there for several moments and then disappeared into the towering pine trees.

She struggled to regain her composure. The fear and pain of the afternoon caught up with her. Against a loud peal of thunder, Margo suddenly screamed, "Tear it down! Tear the damn thing down...NOW!"

No one needed to ask what she meant. The following day, the boat ramp was dismantled by a group of local men. A week later, a small white wooden cross, with three names lettered upon it in engraved gold script, was pounded into place between two boulders on Moonraker Rock. Three Broussard's had been claimed by the jagged outcropping. If there was a curse hanging over the plantation properties and their owners, it seemed to have seeped into the murky waters bearing their name. Like an unseen hand pulling them down into its shadowed depths, the lake would lay claim to others in the Broussard family tree.

5 SUMMER'S LACING

Louisiana summers consisted of timing. One did chores outside in the early morning hours or late in the evening when the heat and humidity were bearable. Folks came out at dusk, like moles peeking out of their burrows. They sank into weathered rockers and shared sweet tea and lemonade, along with the local gossip. Their soft southern cadence blended hypnotically with the sound of bull frogs and crickets. Cicadas had their own rhythm: their buzzing filling the air like incessant white noise. When the men joined the ladies, the sickening sweet smell of tobacco smoke would lace the breeze. An occasional deep guffaw at some off-color joke would jolt the night, silencing the insects. As if on cue, the nocturnal song would start up again as soon as the outburst subsided.

Rachel Broussard Barrows, Tucker and Tamara's daughter and heir, rocked rhythmically in a white Adirondack chair. The tired boards of her back verandah groaned in unison with her rocking. She fanned herself with a magazine as she sipped her second glass of sweet tea and watched the moonlight cut a swath across Lake Broussard. Her daughter Tulie was seated on the boards next to her, her legs swinging idly over the side of the raised porch. She was making a doll out of fabric remnants and twine.

"Mama?" Tulie said quietly. "Is Uncle Barry in heaven?"

Rachel was startled at the impromptu question. While Tulie usually said the first thing that entered her mind, she was not prepared to discuss her brother Barry's death with her nine-year-old daughter. Last summer's waterskiing accident was still fresh in her mind.

"I'm sure he is, Tulie," her mother finally managed.

Tulie looked out over the water to the jagged rocks that pushed into the lake like pointing fingers. The small white cross marking the passing of three of her relatives was hidden from view by large boulders. Her Uncle Barry's house sat across the lake and above them, set back about a hundred yards from the cliffside. She still thought of it as her Uncle Barry's house even though her Aunt Margo had taken over the main house after her Uncle Barry died. Their cousin, Angela Peterson, and her husband, Calvin, bought Margo's old house on the other side of the pecan grove and lived there now with a mangy dog named Chester and an orange and white tabby cat: Beauregard.

"Mama?"

"Yes, Tulie." Rachel sounded tired.

"How did Cousin Calvin end up in a wheelchair?" Tulie asked, casting her gaze at the house a few hundred yards away.

"Goodness, Tulie," Rachel said, sounding more frustrated than she felt. "You're in a morbid state of mind this evening."

Tulie looked over her shoulder at her mother to see if she was upset with her. The evening shadows wrapped the porch like black gauze, but she could make out her Mama's face. Rachel softened, arched an eyebrow at the girl, and grinned. Tulie grinned back and returned to her doll.

"He was in a tractor accident," Rachel said finally, glancing past the pecan grove to her left to where Angela and Calvin were now living. It had taken some time to get used to her sister Margo not living there. They had worn a path along the lake shoreline between their two houses and usually spent a good amount of time together. After Barry's death, their visits had dwindled, once Margo moved into the large plantation house across the lake several months ago.

"What kind of accident?" Tulie pressed.

Rachel sighed. "He was clearing some acreage they had over in Shreveport. He got out of the tractor while it was still running. I'm not sure how it happened, but it ran over him while he was digging out a big rock or tree root or something. One suggestion was that he didn't set the brake, or something like that. It crushed his legs. It's all very sad. He'll never walk again," she said in hushed tones, cognizant of the fact that sound carries around water. She glanced again toward the house but didn't see Angela or Calvin outside. Chester was digging in the dirt under their front porch, his hunched back looking crablike in the moonlight.

"When's Daddy coming home?" Tulie asked, seemingly satisfied with her mother's explanation concerning their cousin's accident.

Rachel nibbled her lip and looked out across the water. "I'm not sure, pumpkin," she said. "He's been busy a lot lately. Some land developers are hounding us about building some new homes where the pecan grove is. I don't want to sell it, but Randall wants to hear them out. He'll probably be late again."

Tulie shot a look over her shoulder at the darkening form of her mother. She was no longer rocking. A heaviness hung in the air.

"Mama? I love you," Tulie said, trying to make out her mother's face in the shadows.

She saw the silhouette shift and her mother's head turn in her direction.

"I love you, too," Rachel said warmly. Tulie could always read her mother's moods. They shared a rare kind of connection. Rachel had it with her mother before she passed...a kind of sixth sense. They often knew when the other needed help and would show up without being summoned. Rachel missed her mother keenly. It was comforting to find the same type of connection with her daughter, even if she was only nine.

Suddenly, Tulie screamed. A bat dove toward her, skimming her hair. She jumped, arms flailing, and fell from the raised porch, landing hard on the packed soil.

"Gotcha!" Laughter filled the night as her twin brother Ryder appeared from the shadows, a fake black bat dangling from a piece of fishing line tied to a long stick.

"Mama!" Tulie shrieked, climbing to her feet and brushing dirt from her knees.

"That's not nice, Ryder," Rachel said, but her tone

held a hint of amusement. "You could have hurt Tulie."

"She's a baby," Ryder said with disdain. "It's just an old rubber bat." He climbed the two stone steps to the porch and took a long swig of his mother's tea. "The rope on the tire swing is comin' undone again," he said. "Gonna go work on my magic tricks." He slammed the screen door to the sun porch as he headed for the kitchen door. The bat and fishing line got caught in the closing door. He shoved it open, pulled in his torture device, and let the door slam again.

Rachel shook her head, sighing. "Are you alright, Tulie?" she asked. "Any blood?"

"No," Tulie said irritably. "He's a menace!"

"He's a boy," Rachel said.

"Same diff! He sawed my favorite doll in half for one of his dumb magic tricks *and* stole one of my shiny garnets from my rock collection to make "The Crystal of Houdini!" she screamed. "He's ruining my life!" She climbed dramatically up the steps and went inside, letting the screen door slam behind her.

Rachel took a deep breath. The smell of lake water hung in the sodden air. She let the cricket's song lull her into a state of calm. It was only when she glanced over to Moonraker Rock that her mood darkened. She had a sudden memory of the night her Daddy named the outcropping. It was an evening like this one: velvet and still. He had been clearing weeds from the graves in the family cemetery not far from where she sat now. He came to the porch for something cold to drink while several of the family sat here talking about the upcoming lawn party.

"Look at that moon," Tucker Broussard said, mopping his brow and looking across the lake to the huddled rocks. It was rising behind them, half of it hidden in the jagged crags. "It's raking the top of the rocks," he said dreamily. After a few minutes, he smiled and said, "That's what we'll call it: Moonraker Rock." He polished off his lemonade, looking pleased with his announcement, and sauntered off through the pecan trees, heading home. Rachel watched him as his silhouette made its way along the path through the pecan grove and finally disappeared beneath the short cliffside to the main house. Ten minutes later, the lights came on in the palatial family home.

The memory felt heavy. Rachel would prefer it if they tore the outcropping down. Never mind that it supported the cliffside on this side of the lake. Feeling a sense of panic coming on, she pushed the memory down. Another one floated into consciousness…one that brought a feeling of peace. It was her mother. Another summer evening, when the two of them sat rocking in a sweet, caressing breeze. A broken cobweb hanging from the porch support above them fluttered in the moonlight, humidity flecking it like small diamond studs.

"Summer's lacing," her mother said softly. With those two simple words, she summed up the magic of those Louisiana summers on the lake.

"Summer's lacing," Rachel whispered, and at once felt at peace.

The grating sound of metal against metal echoed from the pecan grove as Tulie sat on a ratty blanket, shaking an aerosol can of spray paint. The mixing ball inside the can clanged over and over as the young girl shook it to mix the metallic gold paint. Satisfied that it must be blended, she pried off the top and aimed the nozzle at a grouping of small rocks she had aligned on the blanket. Beginning at the left of the pile, she began spraying them gold. Within minutes, the acrid smell of spray paint permeated the grove.

Rachel came out onto the porch and looked out over the cemetery's crypts toward the grove.

"Tulie!" she yelled, wrinkling her nose as the unpleasant smell made its way to her. "What are you doing?"

"Making pirate gold!" Tulie shouted back. "Duh!"

"Where's your brother?"

"Pirate boat!" came the short answer.

Rachel turned and crossed to the front of the back porch. Ryder was sitting in the small fishing boat tied securely to the dock. His back was toward her. He had on a tattered pirate hat his father had given him from New Orleans years ago. Randall had also rigged up the small boat with a wooden pole and sheet. The makeshift sail featured an amateur drawing of the skull and crossbones in black paint that bled into the cotton weave. A small ship bell had been screwed to the boat beneath the sail. As Rachel looked out at the boy fondly, he turned to his right, and she saw he had a spy glass pressed to one eye.

"Any pirates lurking?" she called out playfully.

Ryder swung the eyeglass in her direction. "Just you!" he yelled. "Ye might want to be thinkin' 'bout bringin' a basket of goodies to the ship, Matey. And don't forget the rum!"

Rachel laughed. "Rum" was root beer, and she was used to the summer lunch routine.

"Aye, aye, Captain!" she called out, turning to go

into the house. She saw Dawson up on the cliff by the folly at the main house. She waved at him, and he waved back. She walked through the sunroom and into the kitchen to prepare sandwiches for the motley crew.

Brenn walked through the kitchen on her way to the back room where they kept extra food supplies, tools, and an assortment of junk. She was carrying a large piece of parchment paper covered in artwork.

"I need a black marker," she said, as she paused by the refrigerator.

"What are you doing?" Rachel asked her as she opened the bread bag.

"Tulie talked me into making a pirate map," Brenn said smugly, waving the parchment just long enough for Rachel to catch sight of some brightly colored drawings. "I just need to add one thing."

"Look in the shoe box in the cabinet above the boxes of canned goods," Rachel said. "I'll have lunch in a few minutes."

Brenn didn't answer her. She found the markers and returned to her room upstairs. For the next few minutes, she bent over the map she had worked hard on, marking locations around the lake. She was extremely pleased with the detail of the palm trees and sea serpents, although neither existed in Orleans Parish. Leaning back, she held the large, finished map up proudly. "It looks like something Blackbeard would use," she said aloud to the empty room. She rolled up the map and headed out of the room.

Rachel placed the thin slices of honey-smoked ham on a layer of lettuce and slathered mayonnaise onto the bread top. Ryder hated tomatoes, so she left one sandwich without them. She sliced them through an angle and wrapped them in plastic wrap. She included lunch for Dawson, who often joined in the summer adventures. He was closer to Brenn's age, but he had always been kind to the twins. He attended Ryder's magic shows with enthusiasm and was actually impressed by some of the 9-year-old's tricks. The Rising Kings was his favorite card illusion. Dawson had yet to figure out how Ryder did it.

Opening Ziplock baggies, Rachel filled them with potato chips and dill pickle spears. Two chocolate chip cookies completed the feast. The sound of the pirate ship bell clanging drifted up from down by the lake. Smiling, she began stacking everything into a picnic basket. She paused and drew an "X" with a red writing pen on each napkin.

Rachel opened the refrigerator and was taking out the "rum" when she heard screaming coming from the lake. She paused, waiting to hear if it was part of the pirate game. The screams became frantic. It was Tulie. Rachel dropped the bottle of root beer. It smashed against the floor, glass and amber liquid flying everywhere.

"Tulie!" Rachel screamed as she flew down the two steps from the kitchen into the sunroom. She could barely make out her daughter down on the boat ramp through the distortion of the mesh windows. Flinging the screen door open wide, she cleared the back porch and two stone steps, and raced down the slope to the lake. "What is it?" she yelled.

"What the hell is going on?" Brenn yelled. Rachel looked up to see her across the lake above the cliff at the edge of Margo's garden.

Ignoring her, Rachel made it to the dock and realized

the small boat was untied. It floated languidly on the water a few feet away.

"Where's Ryder?" Rachel screamed, grabbing Tulie by the shoulders and shaking her. The young girl was hysterical. "He's…he's…he's in the water," Tulie gasped, and pointed to her twin brother's pirate hat floating in the lake a few feet away.

Rachel looked frantically into the deep greenish blue of the water but saw nothing. She was about to get on her knees to look under the dock when she saw it. A flash of red slowly emerged from the water, several feet away, followed by matted auburn hair. He was face down. Ryder's bottom bobbed up next, clad in his jeans. His feet remained below the surface.

"Oh my God!" Rachel screamed and dove headfirst into the lake. In frenzied strokes she reached her son and turned him over. Brushing his hair from his face, she shook him. "Ryder! For God's sake, PLEASE, NO!"

Tulie was crying hysterically. She sank to her knees on the rough and splintered boards of the dock.

"Go call 911!" Rachel screamed at her. Tulie remained rocking and hugging herself on the dock, choking cries coming from her bowed head.

"Tulie!" Rachel screamed as she pushed through the water with one arm while holding Ryder under his armpit with the other. She reached the dock and the short ladder that was used to get into the boat. "Help me, Tulie!" she screamed. "Grab his arm!"

Tulie crawled to the edge and leaned as far over as she could. She took hold of Ryder's arm and pulled. It was hard going. His clothes were water logged, and his dead weight surprised her. When she finally saw his face, she cried out. He looked dead. A wave of dizziness and nausea overtook her. Rachel climbed up the ladder and reached over to pull her son up onto the dock. Lifting him from beneath his armpits, she heaved, finally lying him gently onto the boards. He lay there, not moving.

Dawson suddenly appeared on the dock, his running feet sending vibrations through the old boards.

"I called 911," he heaved. He bent, hands on his knees as he caught his breath. He could see the blue around Ryder's mouth and knew the boy was dead. He watched helplessly as Rachel performed CPR on her son, pleading with God between breaths and compressions. But God did not intercede that day. She had finally surrendered and was lying in a heap near her son when sirens split the afternoon.

6 THE RISING KINGS

Detective Archer Hilliard stood in the parlor of 27 Broussard Lane. Everyone knew the street: a private road that circled the lake and connected the three Brousard mansions. These were the calls he dreaded most: interviewing the grieving parents of a dead child. Despite his twenty-nine years in law enforcement, dealing with this kind of loss was outside his purview. A tall man who had once been an Olympic hopeful in basketball, Hilliard's competitive need to win remained with him throughout his life. Perhaps it was his position as point guard on the team that compelled him to always carry it across the line.

His social skills, however, were awkward at best. He would often avert his blue eyes when talking face to face with someone he was interrogating. His habit of pushing his thick brown hair away from his forehead was like a poker player's tell—he was nervous. The detective's affinity for making odd movements with his hands while talking, as if dribbling a phantom basketball, also made most people who met him uncomfortable. In short, he was more comfortable behind a desk looking at mug shots and forensic reports.

Which is why he selected a female officer to accompany him. After only a few minutes into the interview, he began to question his choice of Sergeant Adelaide Calvo.

A stocky woman with mocha skin, pocked with black moles, Adelaide stood with a poised notebook and pen, ready to begin the interrogation. Although 30 years Detective Hilliard's junior, she had an air of fierce capability about her. She had arrived on the scene in jeans, a New Orleans Saints sweatshirt, and a tattered ball cap. Black braids peeked out from beneath the cap. A delicate sandalwood scent wafted from her clothing each time she moved. This was Hilliard's first time meeting the officer. He would have preferred her to wear something more professional, such as a suit jacket and slacks similar to the ones he was wearing. The scent emitted from her clothing reminded him of incense burning in some hippy pad. He feared he had made a huge mistake in asking for a female back-up.

Detective Hilliard surveyed the room with a practiced eye. He was a hulking man of 6'6" whose clothes were crisply pressed. His green paisley tie clashed with his blue and white pin-striped shirt—a dead giveaway to his recent divorce. His hair was chestnut brown, the gray at his temples his only concession to advancing time.

Sergeant Calvo peered up at him, awaiting his first question to the group. Standing only 5' 3" tall, her best view of the detective was his armpit. The law enforcement odd couple stood in front of Rachel, who was hunched over on the embroidered settee, a shawl wrapped tightly about her. She was rocking softly, her arms hugging her trembling torso. She had delicate features and an oval face that cameras love. Her long, dark hair hung in damp waves, accenting her green eyes. Her daughter Tulie was curled into a ball next to her, her face hidden by her stringy strawberry blond hair.

Only Brenn sat upright in a chair across the room, looking on with an air of disinterest. Dawson sat in abject misery in a chair next to her. He fidgeted with a leather coaster he had picked up from the side table next to him, rolling it in circles between his two hands. Detective Hilliard watched him for a few moments and then turned his attention to Rachel.

"Mrs. Broussard," he began, in the reverent tones one reserves for a funeral parlor, "I am really sorry about your son. This isn't easy for us to bother you right now, but we have a few questions. I promise to keep this as brief as possible." The large man paused, feeling inadequate. His tall frame seemed to shrink into itself. He pushed his dark hair back from his forehead and looked helplessly at Sergeant Calvo, who was watching him with interest.

"Mrs. Broussard," the sergeant began, feeling the need to take over. A strange accent coated her words like warm honey on freshly baked rolls. Before she could continue, Brenn spoke up sharply.

"It's Barrows!" she said. "Not Broussard! She *was* a Broussard, but she married my father. Barrows!"

Sergeant Calvo looked at the teenager through the narrowed eyelids of a raptor. After a pregnant pause, she turned back to face Rachel's huddled form.

"Mrs. *Barrows*," she corrected, "I know this is tough, but you need to pull yourself together and give us some details, please. A child is dead..."

Rachel's head rose sharply. The pain evident in her swollen face and eyes was heartbreaking. It was quickly replaced by anger so fierce, Hilliard recoiled.

"The *child?*" Rachel cried; her voice choked. "The child's name is Ryder! *Ryder!*" She broke into fresh sobs, a keening wail rising to fill the room.

Detective Hilliard pushed past the sergeant, who seemed at a loss as to how to continue after the sudden outburst. He turned to the young teenage girl sitting upright in a bright red velvet parlor chair that belonged to another era. She was the only one in the room who lacked any sign of emotion.

"You are?" he asked her.

"Brenn...Barrows." She looked at the towering detective through brown eyes that held not the slightest hint of interest. Her face was full, as if reluctant to let go of the baby fat that had followed her into puberty. A section of her blond bangs stuck out to one side: the result of a stubborn cowlick that refused to be tamed.

"And your father is the young, deceased boy's father?" Brenn didn't answer him, so Hilliard chose a different question. "Can you tell us what happened today?" he asked, trying to keep his tone even and respectful.

"Not a lot," Brenn said succinctly. "We were having a treasure hunt...something the kids enjoy doing. I was in my room upstairs, making a pirate map for the game. I heard Tulie off in the pecan grove spraying rocks that they were going to pretend were pirate gold. The sound from the spray can was really annoying. They had this old chest, and Dawson,"—she jerked her head in the young boy's direction next to her—"was supposed to dig a hole for it. He told me where it would be, and I drew a map. Tulie asked me to."

Sergeant Calvo was scribbling down the account on her small pad.

"What time was that?"

"I don't know…around lunchtime, I guess, cuz Rachel was making sandwiches."

Hilliard paused, confused at the family dynamics. "You said your father married Mrs. Brous…sorry…Mrs. Barrows. Are you their daughter?"

"I'm *his* daughter. Not hers. My mother died almost two years ago. They divorced seven years before her… death, and I ended up living here. Rachel is my stepmother." It was hard to miss the blunt edge Brenn placed on the last word.

"Where is your father?" Sargant Calvo injected, her tone resolute. She didn't like this girl. And the girl clearly did not like her living situation.

"He's on his way," Brenn said neatly. "He was on business in the city."

"Has he been told of the…uh…situation here?" Hilliard asked uncomfortably. His right hand rose and fell as he spoke. Sergeant Calvo fought the urge to place a basketball beneath it.

Brenn shrugged. Hilliard eyed her. She showed no grief over the death of what the detective assumed was her stepbrother.

"You're making a map, the young lady over there is spraying rocks, and this young man (nodding toward Dawson) is digging a hole. Where was Ryder?"

"Sitting in his boat, playing with a spyglass," Brenn said. "I saw him from my bedroom window."

"Was he out on the water with the boat?" Hilliard asked. Sergeant Calvo scribbled away.

"No. He's not allowed to. The boat has to be tied to the dock always."

"How was it then that the boat was untied and several feet from the dock?"

Brenn shrugged again and the detective fought the urge to smack her.

"Do you know how he ended up in the water?" he pressed; his tone harsher this time.

"I wasn't out there," she countered, looking him defiantly in the eye. "When Tulie started screaming, I was checking my map points way up on the cliff in Margo's garden for the treasure hunt. Ask Tulie how he ended up in the water."

Once again, Hilliard's eye was drawn to the monotonous movement of Dawson rolling the drinking coaster in his hands.

"Dawson? That's correct, isn't it? Dawson?"

Dawson looked up at the detective and nibbled his lower lip. He stopped rolling the coaster.

"Yes, sir."

"Couple of questions, son. Where were you digging this hole for the game?"

He noticed the teenage boy shoot a furtive glance in Brenn's direction. The girl was staring at him with an intensity that was palpable.

"Um…I hadn't been at it long," he began. "It was going to be behind the pecan grove. Not the one out there," he nodded toward the grove to the left of Rachel's house. "That one," he said, nodding to the right.

"The one on the other side of the headstones?"

"Yes, sir," he said quietly.

"Could you see Tulie from where you were. She was in the grove earlier, correct?"

Once again, that odd glance in Brenn's direction. Hilliard stiffened but waited, his normally ice-blue eyes taking on a steely hue.

"No, sir. I could hear her shaking that can of paint, but the trees were blocking me from seeing her. I heard the bell on the boat clanging. I guess it was about ten minutes or less, I heard Tulie screaming."

Hilliard stared at the boy; his head cocked to one side. He wasn't telling him the whole story. Years of interviewing people had given him a sixth sense of when someone was withholding something. He chewed on the inside of his cheek and looked over at Rachel's and Tulie's huddled forms. Their soft sobbing sounds played like background noise in the sudden hush of the room.

Brenn had been studying Sergeant Calvo and suddenly blurted out, "Are you Cajun?" The sudden jolting question took both Hilliard and Calvo by surprise.

"Creole," Calvo said evenly, eyeing the smug 16-year-old with unveiled distaste.

"Yeah, I thought you had a funny accent. So, is it French, Haitian...what?"

"It's mixed," came the short answer. Calvo turned away from the girl and crossed over to Tulie. Hilliard stiffened. To his surprise, Calvo squatted to Tulie's level and spoke to her in softened tones.

"Miss Tulie," she said kindly, cocking her head to

peer under the cascade of hair covering the girl's face. "Can I talk to you for a minute, please? Just real fast and we'll get our ugly butts out of here."

Tulie looked up, brushing a section of hair to the side. The sergeant's unexpected comment had caught her off guard.

Calvo smiled, displaying perfect white teeth. Her green eyes looked at the girl with compassion, and she placed a hand on Tulie's knee.

"This is hard, isn't it?" she asked.

Tulie nodded, fresh tears streaming down her face. Rachel had moved closer to her daughter in a protective manner, her chest still heaving with shuddering sobs.

"Did you see your brother in the boat?" Calvo asked.

Tulie looked at the sergeant but said nothing. She seemed confused.

"When did you last see your brother?" Calvo tried again.

Tulie looked to the side, trying to remember. Her face twitched with emotion.

"I went to show him the rocks," she said slowly, choking on the words. "I heard the bell on the boat, so I went to show him." She stopped, and her face convulsed. "He wasn't in the boat!" she cried out. "He wasn't there! The boat wasn't tied up anymore. I could see at the bottom of it, and he wasn't there." She burst into fresh sobs.

"Stay with me, Tulie," Calvo said quickly. "Almost done! Where was the boat? You said it wasn't tied up anymore, but you could see into the bottom of it. Was it right by the dock?"

Tulie looked at her with pained eyes and shook her head no.

"How far away, Tulie? Like from here to that table?" she motioned to a coffee table about three feet away. Tulie shook her head. "To the fireplace?"

Tulie looked over to the hearth. She considered the distance and finally nodded.

"Ok…about six feet away? So, close enough that you could see Ryder wasn't in the boat, right? Where was he?"

Tulie's face convulsed. She tried hard to remember what had happened at the dock, but she kept pushing the memory down.

"I don't know," she cried out. "I don't know. I just saw the boat and then his hat floating by it."

Sergeant Calvo took a deep breath and leaned in closer. Rachel put a protective arm around her daughter and finally spoke.

"She answered your questions," she said brokenly. "This is a very traumatic thing for her. Ryder is her twin. They are…were…very close." She took a shuddering breath and looked at the sergeant with the eyes of one who had died inside. Calvo felt a wave of pity for the woman, but she had a job to do.

"Mrs. Barrows, your daughter seems to be the only one on the dock. Don't you want to know what happened? I'm trying to help, believe it or not. Did *you* see or hear anything? Your stepdaughter says you were in the kitchen making sandwiches. Did you see your son in the boat?"

Rachel looked at her, and Calvo wondered if the woman was capable of reason now. She looked like a corpse who was still breathing.

"He…he was in the boat when I saw him last. He was playing with a spyglass and asked about lunch."

The words were choked off as tears welled up again in her eyes. "I talked to him from the back porch railing, and then I went in and started lunch."

"Was anyone else out there?" Calvo asked gently, afraid of scaring her back into her shell.

Rachel blinked, sending rivulets of tears down her cheeks. She thought for a few seconds and finally said, "I saw Dawson up on the cliff...by Barry's...Margo's house. I waved and he waved back. I heard Tulie with the paint can and yelled to her, but I couldn't see her. She yelled back that she was making pirate gold. That's all at that time."

Hilliard glanced at Dawson.

"I thought you said you were in the pecan grove, digging a hole," Hilliard said, eyeing the boy keenly.

"I was up on the cliff earlier," Dawson said. "When I waved to Rachel, I was on the cliff, about to head down to the pecan grove. Rachel asked me to take some pictures of damage to her house from some past storms for insurance stuff, so I shot a couple from up there where I could see the roof better. I had been shooting pictures all around the property that morning. I could hear Tulie shaking her paint can, but I couldn't see her through the trees. I saw Ryder sitting in the boat for a minute before I headed down through the trees. It was when I was digging the hole in the grove that I heard Tulie scream."

"And Brenn?" Calvo asked Rachel, deliberately not turning to look at the girl. Brenn stiffened and pressed her lips together.

"Brenn walked through the kitchen and got some markers. I think she went upstairs to her room. I heard her walking overhead when I was making lunch. Later,

I saw her up on the cliff at Margo's. She was yelling, wanting to know what was happening because Tulie was screaming."

Hilliard noticed the girl relax and return to her defiant demeanor.

"How far is the top of the cliff from the dock?" he asked nonchalantly.

Dawson answered him. "To walk it from the dock, through the pecan grove and up the trail to the folly...takes about 15 minutes. It's a pretty steep trail up the side of the cliff."

"From the time you started digging a hole in the grove, to when you heard Tulie screaming, how long would you say that was?"

Dawson thought for a minute. "Probably, ten minutes...maybe a little less. I dropped my shovel and ran when I heard her screaming. By the time I came out of the grove, I saw Rachel pulling Ryder's body through the water. I ran into her kitchen and called 911, and then ran to the dock."

"One more question," Hilliard said. "From where you were digging the hole, you said you couldn't see the dock through the trees. Could you see the trail going up the cliff to the folly?"

"Oh yeah. I told Brenn I was going to dig the hole close to the trail so it would be easier for Tulie and Ryder to pace it off from her map. I was right next to it." Each time Ryder's name was mentioned, Rachel and Tulie broke into fresh sobs.

"And no one came along that trail while you were there?"

"No, sir," he answered quickly. But again, there was tension in his voice.

Calvo scribbled down the information. Hilliard studied the young man who refused to meet his gaze. He figured him to be around 18- or 19-years-old. Brenn sat with arms folded, her legs crossed, and her right foot jangling. Hilliard studied her for a moment.

"You were in your room making the map while your stepmother was making the sandwiches, but then, what I'm guessing was only a few minutes later, you were up at the top of the cliff. Neat trick." His eyes bore into her, all sense of awkwardness gone.

"I don't agree with Dawson that it takes 15 minutes to get to the top of the cliff," she said stiffly. "I had just barely gotten there to make sure I had the right images on my map when I heard Tulie screaming."

Calvo turned back to Tulie, who was her only witness at this time.

"Tulie? One last question, okay? Did you hear anything? On your way to the dock...to show Ryder the gold rocks... did you see or hear anything?"

Tulie looked helplessly at the rug beneath her feet. Her eyes traced the swirling jacquard pattern in a trancelike state. Suddenly, a memory erupted.

"Splashing," she said quickly. "I heard splashing, right after the bell rang."

"Splashing? Was it loud? It wasn't water against the boat, but splashing, like someone swimming?"

"He didn't swim," she blurted out, crying. "After Uncle Barry, Grandma, and Grandpa died in the lake, he wouldn't go in the water. He couldn't swim!" She was almost screaming at this point, and Rachel stood up, weaving as if she was going to fall.

"That's enough," she said, her voice broken but forceful. "No more now. You can talk to Randall when he gets here, but no more now." Just then, she looked down at the coffee table and cried out.

"Oh God!' she screamed, staring at a pile of playing cards strewn out across the table. The King of Spades was on top, his image looking off to the right. She grabbed Tulie's arm and pulled her to her feet. Sobbing heavily, she led Tulie from the room, each leaning upon the other.

Sergeant Calvo looked over at Brenn and Dawson for an explanation of the sudden outcry over the playing cards.

When the silence lengthened, Dawson said miserably, "Those are Ryder's cards. He does magic tricks. He puts on shows." Dawson refused to meet her eyes. Brenn stared at her with steely resolve.

"Did everyone in the family get along?" Calvo asked, taking advantage of Rachel's absence.

"Typical family stuff," Brenn said nonchalantly. "Ryder could be a brat. He was always teasing Tulie, and she got fed up with him. You know…kid stuff."

Dawson turned to her quickly with a look of annoyance on his face.

"Ryder wasn't a brat," he said. "He was a typical kid, and he teased his sister sometimes. They loved each other. They were twins. Playing pirate was one of their favorite things. Ryder loved the old stories passed down from his grandfather, that there might be pirate treasure buried around here. He would have done anything for Tulie, and she would have walked through fire for him." He shot Brenn a stern look.

"Anything else you two can add?" Calvo asked the pair, although she was confident of the answer. She glanced back down at the playing cards.

Dawson shook his head. Brenn began to shrug but thought better of it as she sensed Detective Hilliard's antipathy toward her.

"He must have fallen in," she said simply. "Stuff like that happens…especially around *that* lake." She looked at him meaningfully.

When Hilliard paused, remembering the other Broussard deaths, his sidekick chimed in.

"How did the boat get untied?" Calvo asked her smoothly.

"I guess it's a mystery," Brenn said, a twinkle in her eye. "Let me know if you solve it."

At that moment, the front door opened and closed, and Randall Barrows walked into the room. His face was a roadmap of pain, and it was clear he had been crying. He stopped in the entrance to the parlor when he saw the two officers standing there. It was then that the death of his son became real, and he crumpled to the floor.

The sound of cars arriving and doors slamming could be heard from the driveway. Sensing the house was about to become flooded with people, Detective Hilliard looked down at the distraught father of the dead boy.

"Mr. Barrows, I'm truly sorry," he said quietly. "If we can do anything for your family, please let us know. I understand you weren't here today, but if you would come down to the station this afternoon for a short statement, I would appreciate it. A ride can be arranged if you need one."

Randall looked up at him with pain-filled eyes. He nodded and pushed himself to a standing position. He leaned sideways, and Hilliard grabbed him, steadying the man who was a good four inches shorter. Randall Barrows was a handsome man, even in his grief. His hair was a strawberry blond, layered in tumbled abandon that looked groomed and untamed at the same time. His bloodshot eyes still revealed a deep blue. He had one of those chiseled faces that would age well, Hilliard thought. He placed a steadying hand on Randall's shoulder.

The front door burst open, and a cacophony of voices suddenly filled the foyer. Moments later, a tall woman with auburn hair and a figure that would rival most runway models hurtled into the room. She made a beeline for Randall and pulled him into her arms. A wave of gardenia perfume surrounded the couple in a cocoon as she purred over the man who clung to her fiercely. Hilliard wondered who she was.

Others began arriving, their sobs filling the room. Most were women. One man, older than the rest, walked in and stopped when he saw Randall engulfed in the female's embrace. She was rubbing Randall's back as she whispered into his ear. Hilliard couldn't help but notice the reddened face of the older man as he watched them.

Sergeant Calvo moved over to the detective and told him they were probably done here for now. Hilliard didn't react to his subordinate taking the lead. It felt like a wake in the room, and he was eager to get outside. As he crossed the parlor, it suddenly occurred to him that Brenn, the young, arrogant teenager, hadn't made a move toward her father. She was merely eyeing him, being soothed by the bombshell. She finally rose to her feet and walked out to the foyer, avoiding the sobbing arrivals. Hilliard and Calvo followed her out.

They caught up with her at the front door.

"Who is that woman with your father?" Hilliard asked, trying to sound nonchalant.

"Aunt Margo," Brenn answered, an amused tone in her voice. "That's her husband, Reed...the old guy staring at them. Cozy, isn't it?" She turned to leave.

"One minute," Hilliard said. She paused and sighed. "You made a comment about the lake out there...."

The look she gave him was unnerving. It was pregnant with meaning, but he couldn't decipher it.

"Do you believe in curses?" she asked him.

"No," was the flat response.

"So would you call four deaths in one family, all in the same lake, a coincidence?" She squinted at him and waited.

"Four?" he asked incredulously.

"Four...so far." She walked away, disappearing through a door into another room.

As the two officers walked out into the sunlight, Calvo asked, "Which one of us gets to slap her?" Hilliard didn't ask about whom she was speaking.

"Look up the past deaths in the Broussard family," he told her. "Check the circumstances. I do remember some headlines, but they appeared to be boating accidents."

The following day, some male friends of the family came and retrieved the small boat with the pirate sail and ship bell. Dawson helped them load it onto a boat trailer attached to a pickup truck. The police had released it after a thorough search.

Detective Hilliard and Sergeant Calvo oversaw the boat removal. The detective made a point of measuring the sides of the small fishing boat from the top to the bottom of its exterior. He made a note of the measurements on the back of a receipt from his pocket. The family was at the funeral parlor planning for Ryder's service. The house sat empty, and Hilliard took advantage of it. He and Calvo entered through the unlocked sunroom door. They crossed through the kitchen and into the front hall. Making as little noise as possible, they climbed the main staircase to the family bedrooms.

"You realize we don't have a search warrant," Calvo whispered.

"We're not searching," Hilliard said. "We're getting a lay of the land."

Calvo softly pushed open the second door to the right on the landing. It was a good-sized room with a king-sized bed. The décor, while tasteful, felt over the top. Everything was encased in peach brocade. A pair of men's jeans was thrown over a chair near the window, and men's sneakers were resting on their sides beneath them. Perfume bottles littered a vanity top, its mirror surrounded by peach-colored tulle.

Hilliard crossed to both heavily draped windows and peered out.

"Master bedroom," he intoned unnecessarily. "Next."

They passed into the hallway and walked to the next doorway, the one closest to the staircase. Inside was a room decorated in a blue motif. It had the air of not being lived in. There was just enough to make a guest feel welcome, but no personal touches. The closet housed empty hangers and a few guest towels. They closed the door and moved down the hallway to the third room. This door was standing open.

"Tulie's room, I would wager," Calvo said, noting

the dolls and a stack of books written for the juvenile audience. It was a happy room, with twinkling lights suspended from a tulip bulb chandelier. The bed fostered a canopy draped in soft pink chiffon. The bedspread and pillow shams were alternating colors of ivory and pink. A large porcelain doll reclined against a heart-shaped pillow in the center of the headboard.

Once again, Hilliard crossed to the window and peered out. He could see the lake but not the dock. The pecan grove spread out on the other side of the cemetery headstones. A large oak tree sat just outside the window, its large limbs reaching to the house. A tire swing hung from one of the branches. Across the lake and up on the cliffside sat the family plantation estate. He looked about the room from where he stood. He sensed the innocence he saw here would never be the same again.

The room sitting next to Tulie's was in complete contrast to the feminine retreat they had just left. This room was all boy. Small wooden sailboats were suspended by fishing lines from the ceiling, swaying from the current of air created when they opened the door. It gave Calvo a sudden sense of voyeurism and sadness: a boat's movement in the stillness of a dead boy's room.

Hilliard walked about the space, touching things with reverence. Magic tricks were strewn across the dresser top. A ragged stuffed rabbit hung limply from an upended top hat. Decks of playing cards were seen on multiple surfaces. A black cape was flung over the back of a small blue chair. Dominating one corner was a large pirate chest. Hilliard lifted the lid to find more magic tricks, some books on magic, jars of rocks and what appeared to be the skeleton of a frog. A well-thumbed book lay to one side. Its title brought a sad smile to his face: "Vanishing Acts for Amateur Magicians." He straightened and stared at the unmade bed where a young boy would never dream of pirates or magic again. He thought of his own son and walked hurriedly from the room.

The final bedroom was at the end of the hall, above the kitchen. The two opened the door and walked in.

"This must be Brenn's room," Hilliard said, noting the wall posters of the current TV teen heartthrobs. Magazines littered the unmade bed, most catering to teenage girls. Dirty clothes were tossed on the floor of the closet. The room had a musty smell and lacked any feeling of cohesion. There was no one color that dominated. The bedspread was a quilt that had seen better days. The detective pulled on the handle of the drawer of the small nightstand next to the bed and found it locked. He peered at the keyhole and felt tempted. Sighing, he turned away.

Calvo watched with interest as Hilliard once again walked to a window and pulled back the sheer. He narrowly missed knocking an empty soda can to the floor. Patches of blue lake water glimmered through the interlocked tree branches, bursting with leaves just outside the window. He stood there a moment looking out. Letting the sheer fall back into place, he glanced down at a small table and chair. Colored markers lay scattered about. Crumpled parchment filled a small trash can next to the table. Hilliard bent and pulled out the top one. Unfolding the creases, he looked down at the beginnings of what appeared to be a pirate map. Two other discarded attempts at a map were also crumpled in the can.

The two left the house and wandered down to the dock.

"It always feels strange to return to a crime scene after everything important is gone," Calvo said, looking out to where Ryder's body and boat had been found.

Hilliard glanced at her sharply.

"So, you think it's a crime and not an accident?" he asked, surprised at how eager he was to hear her answer.

"Don't you?" she asked evenly. "I mean, sure, Tulie could have pushed him in a fit of rage. Kids that age do it all the time. Their emotions haven't developed brakes yet. My nephew's friend hit him over the head with a bag of rocks when they were ten. Took eleven stitches. They were back playing together a week later."

In the end, Ryder's death was ruled a sad accident. No reason was found for why anyone would hurt the boy. He had seemed happy when the members of his family had last seen him. Somehow, the rope must have come untied, and when the boy leaned over to try and tie it back, he had fallen into the water.

While the answer satisfied the department forms that had to be filled out, it did not quell the feeling of unease in Detective Hilliard's mind. Something was wrong. He knew from the measurements he took off the side of the boat that someone of Ryder's size could have pulled himself back in. Then there were the statements from the family. One of those statements he now knew to be false, and other information had been carefully hidden. A thought came unbidden to his mind. *How do you account for four family deaths in one lake? What are the odds?* He didn't believe in haunted bugaboos or curses. Before the mysterious deaths surrounding this family were over, he would.

7 MESSAGES FROM BEYOND

Tulie heard voices beneath her bedroom window and looked out to see Detective Hilliard and Sergeant Calvo walking out of the pecan grove. They stopped near the cemetery and checked a stopwatch. She watched as the sergeant scribbled something into her ubiquitous notebook. As they continued on toward the dock, she lost sight of them, her view blocked by the house's situation.

Five days had passed since her brother's drowning. The funeral had been unbearable. Her mother insisted on a closed casket. It felt as if all of Orleans Parish had turned out. Strangers pressed her hands as she stood in the receiving line, trying to hold her mother erect.

"They've only come to gawk," her mother said huskily to her daughter during a pause in the flow of people. "Another Broussard death in the lake, that's what they're thinking. I don't know half of these people."

Tears flowed down Rachel's face, leaving track marks in the makeup she had worn to cover her paleness. The overpowering smell of lilies and roses was causing Tulie's stomach to churn. She looked out in the foyer at the wall clock. Only one more hour to go.

Now back at home, the house held the same feeling as the funeral parlor: sad, empty, and filled with the smell from the flowers that had been sent over by the funeral director after the service concluded. Her mother had not left her room; her plates of food Tulie brought her were left mostly untouched. Brenn had contented herself with organizing the copious dishes of leftover food that usually accompanied a funeral. The sympathetic guests left the burial service and spilled into the Barrows' home, laden with southern dishes and the appropriate offerings of condolences.

Tulie left her room and glanced down the hallway to the closed door to Ryder's bedroom. Her heart lurched, and she felt panic coming on. *This can't be real*, she thought. *He'll come out of that room with another dumb magic trick and ask me to pick a card.* The tears fell in torrents. *Would this pain ever end?* She headed to the staircase.

Brenn turned to see Tulie enter the kitchen, her face swollen and strained.

"You need to eat something," Brenn said tersely. "Look at all this food. There's no more room in the refrigerator."

Tulie looked dully at the island counter laden with containers of fried chicken, potato salad, and a bevy of various casseroles. Nothing felt real. The kitchen seemed alien, the floor merely an illusion beneath her feet. She managed to fall into a chair at the kitchen table.

Brenn filled a plate with chicken casserole, some kind of Jello concoction, and a roll.

"Eat that," she said, and slid into a chair across from Tulie, digging into her own filled plate.

"Mama isn't going to survive this," Tulie said, her voice sounding as if it were echoing through a tunnel.

Brenn stopped eating; her fork poised in mid-air. "Of course, she will," Brenn retorted, color rising in her cheeks. "You think I don't know what it feels like to lose someone your whole life revolves around? You think I don't know what that kind of pain feels like?" Her voice cracked as she fought to hold back tears. "You survive. You go on. You have to."

"She lies there praying he will come back," Tulie said, crying openly. "She didn't get to tell him goodbye. *I* didn't get to tell him goodbye." She hung her head and sobbed.

Brenn studied her for a moment. She quietly laid down her fork.

"But Tulie, you must have seen him," she said, her voice low and steady. "I mean, you went to the boat with your rocks, remember? Right after you heard the bell. If you heard the bell, he must have been in the boat then. Did you talk to him?"

Brenn waited, holding her breath. She had to handle the fragile girl carefully.

Tulie lifted her head and looked at her stepsister across the table from her. Her forehead was furrowed, and her eyes unfocused.

"Saw him?" she asked, her voice small and indistinct.

"Didn't you? At all? You said you saw into the boat. What did you see?"

Tulie studied the images of lemons that were

86

sprinkled across the tablecloth. Her eyes darted back and forth as she tried to recall arriving at the boat.

"It was untied," she said, her voice barely a whisper. "It was drifting farther away. The rope was dragging behind it in the water. He wasn't in the boat. But there was something…something in the bottom of the boat…"

Brenn leaned forward, her face ashen.

"What, Tulie?" she asked forcefully. "What was in the boat?"

Tulie squinted at the lemons and then raised her head suddenly, locking eyes with Brenn.

"A skull," she gasped, her voice filled with terror. She struggled to remember, but the effort was too much." I don't know!" she cried out and fled the room.

The days passed in a haze of summer heat and a feeling of isolation. Rachel and Tulie remained cloistered inside the house, ignoring doorbells and phone calls. Angela and Margo were the only visitors allowed inside. Margo became uncomfortable with the depressive atmosphere and departed after a few perfunctory words of encouragement. Angela stayed.

"You have to get out of the house," Angela said to Rachel, holding both of her cousin's hands in her own. "Come over for dinner tonight, you and Tulie. Calvin has found a new True Crime show on TV that he's addicted to. He won't bother us." Tulie, who was seated next to her mother, noticed the omission of Brenn's name in the invitation.

"It's too hard," Rachel finally managed.

"It's just a short stroll along the lake," Angela said and immediately regretted her words. Rachel recoiled at the word 'lake' and scooted forward on the couch cushion in preparation to rise.

"I can walk with you," Angela said hastily. "Or how about a car ride? Just get out into the sun for a bit?"

Rachel pressed her lips together to contain her emotions. She looked at Angela with so much pain that it forced her cousin to realize this kind of grief would take a lifetime to quell.

"If I could just see him one more time," Rachel sobbed. Tulie's tears began streaming to match her mother's. "Just hear him. Just tell him I love him, one more time."

"We all feel like that when we lose someone," Angela said, her own eyes welling with tears. "It's no good saying this will pass. It will hurt until it doesn't."

A movement in the hallway outside the parlor archway caught Angela's attention. She glanced in that direction just in time to see Brenn dart out of view. A flash of anger crossed her face.

"Be careful of Brenn," Angela whispered to Rachel, and then glanced at Tulie to include her. "I don't trust her."

"She's being kind," Rachel said. "She understands loss. I've seen her trying harder since... She's trying harder."

"Bringing you tea is one thing," Angela said, unmoved. "She's always listening at doorways. She's even turned me away a couple of times when I've come to check on you both. Just be careful, that's all I'm saying."

The following day, Tulie tapped on her mother's bedroom door. She waited a few seconds and then entered. The room was as dark as a closet, the air stale from lack of circulation. She made out her mother propped up against a pile of pillows on her bed, wearing the same clothes she had been in the day before.

"Mama?" Tulie said quietly, crossing the room to the prostrate form. "Mama, Margaret Ruthers is here from the church. She said she hates to bother you, but she has something to tell you that might be helpful."

"Helpful?" Rachel's voice came from the dark, huddled form on the bed. "I don't need someone to sit here and read me scriptures," she said bitterly.

"She says it's something that may help you find Ryder."

Rachel lurched forward from the pillows.

"What are you talking about?" she croaked. "*Find* him? How do you *find* him? He's *dead! We buried him!*"

A few minutes later, Rachel was seated in the parlor. She had put on a fresh summer dress with Tulie's help and run a comb through her hair. She sat perched on the edge of a parlor chair as if prepared to take flight at any moment.

"Rachel, dear!" Margaret purred. "I never got to tell you how beautiful the service was for Ryder." Rachel flinched. "I know how very, very, very difficult this must be. I came out of the goodness of my heart to offer something that I thought might help you through this trying time."

Tulie watched her mother from her chair next to her with apprehension. One wrong word from Margaret Ruthers and her mother would fall to pieces.

Margaret stared at Rachel's frozen face and

continued, her hands moving nervously as she spoke.

"Her name is Madam Sangers. She is a medium from New Orleans with the most extraordinary powers! I've gone to her many times myself, and the things she knows are just uncanny! I really, really, really believe she could give you news from Ryder."

She stopped and waited, her hands wringing together. Tulie moved to the edge of her chair, ready to keep her mother from attacking the woman. Instead, Rachel turned to face Margaret squarely.

"Talk to Ryder?" she asked, her voice full of hope. "She can talk to him?"

Encouraged, Margaret bobbed her head vigorously.

"Yes! I was at a séance a few months ago where she spoke to Emily Pointer's dead husband! It was the most amazing thing I've ever seen. She could come here. She prefers to be in the environment where the dead…uh…the beloved departed resided."

Rachel looked at Tulie, her eyes suddenly bright. "Tulie?" she asked her daughter hopefully.

"I don't know, Mama," Tulie said hesitantly, not wishing to offend Mrs. Ruthers. "I don't think you should mess with that stuff."

Rachel stared at her daughter, considering her words. Margaret took advantage of the lull and reached into her purse.

"Here! Here is her card! I promise you will not be disappointed! Tell her I said for you to call."

With that, Margaret rose abruptly. Tulie rose as well. Rachel remained in her chair, staring at the business card with the name Madam Sangers splayed across it in a purple scrawl. The image of a crystal ball sat above the phone number.

As Margaret turned to walk from the room, she suddenly stopped and flashed a bright smile in Rachel's direction.

"When you're better, I simply must have you make some more of your tea cakes for us! There's a church social next month. You should be your old self by then."

Tulie walked her to the front door.

"Thank you for coming," she said awkwardly, swinging the large door open.

"Oh, you can thank me when Madam Sangers changes your life! You'll see! Y'all need to open some curtains," she said, looking about her. "It's like a tomb in here!" She patted Tulie on the shoulder and exited down the sidewalk, stopping to straighten a small statue that was tilted to one side.

"I will need everyone to remain completely still."

The parlor sat in darkness, apart from one large pillar candle sitting in the center of the dining room table. The small flame danced on the small eddies of current that came through the open window by the fireplace. The moonlight had been shut out by storm clouds that threatened to erupt at any moment. The other window draperies were pulled closed.

Madame Sangers sat at the head of one end of the table, draped in magenta robes of shining silk. The fabric was covered with celestial spheres and stars. Her raven black hair was pulled atop her head in a careless bun; black pins protruding everywhere. Her hands rested on the black lace tablecloth she had brought with her, along with a tuning fork, a bell, and a gold goblet residing near her left hand. A carafe of water was the only other object on the table. To her left was a large, standing black chalkboard like the one used in old school rooms. Two pieces of chalk rested in its tray.

Rachel, Tulie, Brenn, Angela, and Dawson sat around the table, each bearing a different expression. Angela showed the most contempt, while Dawson and Tulie wore expressions of fear. Rachel bit her lips repeatedly, her labored breathing evident to everyone. Only Brenn seemed eager to have the show begin. The candlelight illuminated only a portion of each of their faces, leaving most of the room in shadows.

Rachel had elected not to tell her husband about the séance. He would have hated the idea, along with the $450 price tag attached to it. She also kept the clandestine meeting secret from her sister Margo. She sat now questioning her own resolve. In the darkness of the room, with only one sputtering candle and all those shadowed corners, could she handle what was about to happen?

Suddenly, Madame Sangers grabbed up the tuning fork and struck it forcefully on the side of the table. It vibrated with a high-pitched tone. She waved it in a circle before her and then replaced it on the table. She poured water from the carafe into the gold goblet and took a sip.

"Hold hands," Madame Sangers intoned. "She reached taloned fingertips out toward Dawson on her left and Rachel on her right. Dawson took hold of the medium's hand reluctantly. Rachel gripped it, feeling the warmth that underscored her own ice-cold fingers. Tulie, who was seated to Rachel's right, squeezed her mother's hand assuredly. She reached next to her to Brenn and took her hand. Brenn, in turn, reached out to

Angela, who paused before taking it lightly. She shook her head in disbelief and sighed elaborately as she took hold of Dawson's free hand.

Madam Sangers looked about the table with satisfaction. She took several deep breaths and lifted her chin to the ceiling, closing her eyes.

"Do not speak. Do not move. The spirits will not come if there is a distraction."

The group surrounding the table held their breath, all but Angela, who was glaring angrily at the medium. The psychic's jet-black hair, red lips, and purple eyeshadow were so patently overdone to achieve an effect. *How foolish could her cousin be?* she thought.

The candle's flame flickered, small sputtering sounds emanating from it like tiny fireworks. The smell of honeysuckle rode in on a breeze through the partially open window. A distant roll of thunder was the only other sound. As Madam Sangers sat in silence, the others shot furtive glances around the table, trying to make out each other's faces in the dim candlelight.

"I hear you!" Madam Sangers suddenly shouted. The group jumped; Tulie emitting a thin squeal. "You have come far to talk to us! We do not take lightly the long voyage you have made to be here!" she shouted.

Rachel felt her stomach drop with fear. Was it Ryder? Her heart was pounding, causing the bodice of her dress to quiver.

Madam Sangers began to moan and sway. Angela pressed her lips together, fighting the urge to halt the whole thing. Just then, the flame on the candle shot up to twice its height, illuminating the bulging eyes of those around the table.

"Yes!" Madame Sangers screamed. "You are here!

You must be thirsty after your long journeys. Please! Quench your thirst."

Before the startled eyes of the group, the water in the glass carafe began to lower slowly until about a third of it was gone. Tulie gasped and squeezed Brenn's and Rachel's hands.

"Good!" shouted Madam Sangers, "Now we can proceed. You will communicate by ringing the bell. Ring once for yes and twice for no. Do you understand?"

Silence followed. All eyes were on the bell in front of Madam Sangers chest. After several agonizing moments, one sharp bell tone sounded. Everyone jumped.

"Excellent!" the medium exclaimed. "Let us proceed."

Rachel felt faint and gripped Tulie's hand so tightly she felt the girl's bones. She could feel her daughter shaking.

"Ryder Barrows?" Madam Sangars intoned. "Are you with us?"

The group held its collective breath, including Angela, who had been trying to figure out how the water disappeared from the pitcher.

A vibrating bell tone filled the room.

"Yes!" Madam Sangers said jubilantly. "Excellent. Welcome, Ryder!"

Rachel was crying now, her head dizzy and her heart rate off the charts. *What was going to happen?*

"Ryder," the medium said in quieter tones, "your mother and sister are here. They miss you. Your stepsister and cousin are here, and your good friend Dawson. They all miss you. Will you answer their questions?"

The bell rang once without moving, its tone reverberating in the shadowed room.

"Thank you, dear boy," Madam Sangers said in a conversational tone. "Who will ask the first question?"

For several moments, there was silence. Finally, Rachel, in halting words, asked, "Are you happy where you are?" She burst into fresh tears but continued. "I'm so sorry I wasn't there to save you! I would give my life to have you back!"

"You must ask one thing at a time and not confuse the spirits with more," Madam Sangers scolded. "Ryder? Your mother wants to know if you are happy in your new spirit home?"

Silence engulfed the room. The ticking of the mantle clock from the parlor in the next room was suddenly amplified. After several minutes, Madam Sangers looked at the bell expectedly. She took a breath to repeat the question. Suddenly, the bell rang out in two sharp tones. The group gasped. The medium paused and looked about her at the worried faces. She let the silence linger for a few more moments and then continued.

"No? Ryder, repeat that, please. Are you happy where you are?" The bell suddenly rang twice, surprising everyone. "We must find out why you are not happy, Ryder."

Silence followed. The clock ticking thrummed in the stillness.

"Is it because of the way you died?" Brenn suddenly blurted out, causing Angela to jump.

The bell rang out once, and Rachel screamed.

"Silence!" Madam Sangers shouted. "You will

frighten the spirit away!"

Rachel wanted desperately to release the medium's hand and run from the room. The sound of thunder was coming closer to the house, making the atmosphere all the more threatening.

Dawson spoke out, his voice shaking. "Did you fall accidentally into the lake?" he asked. No one took a breath as they fixed their eyes on the bell.

The clock ticked. Then two sharp rings shot through the room. Tulie shrieked, let go of Brenn's hand, and covered her mouth.

"What happened?" Dawson asked, leaning forward.

"That won't work," Madame Sangers said. "These are yes or no questions. We must move to the chalkboard for this. Do not break the circle," she screamed at Tulie, who hurriedly grabbed Brenn's hand again.

All eyes looked to the large standing chalkboard. Madame Sangers leaned her head back again and moaned. She drew in several deep rattling breaths.

"Now," she said, sounding tired. "The circle has been restored. Draw upon all your strength, Ryder. This is harder than the bell. Take the chalk and write out short answers as your strength allows. Repeat your question," she said, bringing her chin down and focusing on Dawson. He shuddered, taking a moment to compose himself.

"What hap..."

Something suddenly attacked the open window. A shrill cry filled the room. Rachel and Tulie screamed, shoving their chairs back as they prepared to flee the room. Dawson jumped up, his heart pounding. Brenn and Angela turned in their chairs to face the window, their eyes wide.

"Beauregard!" Angela yelled, jumping up from her chair and crossing to the window where her cat was yowling with pain from outside the window. Its nail was caught in the mesh of the window screen. Angela pushed the nail back through the metal mesh. The cat leapt from the windowsill and ran off into the night.

"Good lord!" Dawson yelled from his chair. "What the hell?"

"He's afraid of thunder," Angela said defensively.

"You have broken the circle!" Madam Sangers yelled. "The spirit is gone!"

Angela looked to the medium, ready to unleash her fury on the woman she was sure was a fake. Something to Madame Sangers' right caught her attention, and she froze. The others looked at her in astonishment in the candlelight as the blood drained from her face. She was staring across the dining room table at the black chalkboard. Five words were glowing in a childish scrawl across its face:

Gold
Treasure

Torn
Secret Path
MURDER

Dawson recovered from the shock first. He pulled his camera phone from his back pocket and took a photo of the blackboard before Madam Sangers could object, its flash blinding after the prolonged darkness.

Suddenly, the bell near Madam Sangers began to ring. The clanging tones became frantic, ringing on and on. The small bell shuddered across the table with each vibrating tone. It swelled in pitch; the group of six people flinched as it pierced their eardrums. When it finally reached an earsplitting crescendo, the tone changed to one much deeper. *Clang, clang, clang.* The loud vibration of a ship's bell reverberated off the walls. The bell fell onto its side.

A sudden crack of thunder rattled the room. It shook the windows, threatening to shatter them into shards of glass. The candle flame leapt and swayed in the gusts of wind whipping through the room. It suddenly flared up, orange and yellow tongues of flame reaching for the chandelier. The crystal prisms clashed together as the light fixture danced crazily on its chain.

Something fell through the chandelier's metal arms. It caught on one of the crystals and then fluttered down, landing atop the candle flame. The fire licked at its edges, catching at the worn weave of the playing card. Before the startled faces of the six people in the room, the King of Spades curled in on itself and caught fire. Rachel fainted, banging her head against the back of Tulie's chair as she went down.

8 CANDLES

2023…

The jarring sound of hammering echoed across the lake water, scaring egrets into flight. Tulie came out through the sunroom porch door onto the back verandah carrying a large glass of iced tea. She walked to the end of the porch and peered up at the young man atop an extension ladder leaning against the side of the house near the cemetery.

Dawson Kingston, now 34 years old, was pounding one end of a birthday banner into the eaves. His chiseled biceps glistened with a sheen of perspiration in the hot June humidity and heat. Tulie stared at him for a few moments before he glanced down and saw her there. He pushed wet brown bangs from his forehead and smiled at her, his hazel eyes soft in the sunlight.

Tulie became immediately flustered and looked down. "I…I… brought you some tea," she stammered in her soft southern cadence.

Dawson descended the ladder, his work boots squeaking on the slick metal rungs. Tulie noticed how tight his jeans fit him and how snugly his tank top clung to his sweating torso. She thrust the glass of tea awkwardly toward him, keeping her eyes on her shoes.

"Thanks, Tulie-O," he said happily. "Just what I needed!" He polished it off in four long swallows and handed the glass back to her, running the back of his hand over his mouth. "Almost done. Just need to nail the other end up." He paused and smiled kindly at her. "So…whose big day is it today?" he asked her, flashing her a smile that made her knees wobbly.

"I didn't want the party," she said in a barely audible whisper.

Dawson stopped smiling and studied the young woman in front of him. No longer a child, Tulie still carried the vulnerable innocence of the little girl he had grown up with.

"I know you don't," he said kindly. "But it's been 17 years, Tulie. You should celebrate your birthday. Ryder would want you to."

Tulie felt the usual twitch in her stomach. "It's his birthday, too," she said brokenly. "He should get presents."

"I imagine being a twin makes this even harder," Dawson said. "We can celebrate him too, okay?"

Tulie smiled at him gratefully. He always seemed to know the right thing to say. Maybe he was right. She was 25 now. Time to move on. But life never seemed ready for her to move on. In fact, lately, she felt the memories of the past were closer, not farther away.

"I still feel him around," she said in an embarrassed whisper. "Sometimes, I think I hear him in his bedroom at night. I could always hear him through the wall practicing his magic show. 'Ladies and Gentlemen!' she said, mimicking her brother's voice. 'Get your tickets for the greatest magic show in Louisiana! The Great Ryderinski will perform marvels of prestidigitation that will baffle the senses! Step right up!' I know it sounds dumb, but it feels real."

Dawson was laughing. "I had forgotten the name he had for his act! 'The Great Ryderinski!' Where in the world did he come up with that?"

Tulie was laughing now, recalling the fun they had when Ryder turned the parlor into a magician's stage.

"He loved Houdini. He thought his name needed to sound more mysterious and have an 'i' at the end."

The smile faded from her face as quickly as it had come, melting away like a snow cone on a hot summer day.

Dawson put an arm around Tulie's shoulder and squeezed it. "I got you a cool present," he said coaxingly, hoping to distract her. "You'll like it."

Tulie's face flushed with color at his nearness. She could smell his perspiration. It wasn't unpleasant at all, she thought. He smelled of pine needles, earth, and soap. She felt herself tremble.

Suddenly, Brenn burst through the porch door and stood eyeing them, a look of smug satisfaction on her face. "If I'm not disturbing, Rachel wants you, Tulie," she said, her voice laced with sarcasm.

Tulie pulled away from Dawson, grabbed his glass, and hurried along the verandah, almost tripping when she reached Brenn, who was blocking the door.

"You're red," Brenn whispered, grinning. "Nice muscles, huh?"

Tulie pushed past her and hurried inside. Dawson, who had not heard Brenn's comment, merely eyed the girl who was two years his junior. He wiped his mouth again on the back of his hand, picked up the hammer, and the other end of the banner. Crossing the verandah, he brushed past Brenn who barely moved to make room for him. "You're in my way," he said to her, not bothering to hide his contempt.

"So, I noticed," she said snidely. When Dawson jerked his head in her direction, she playfully flipped her hair and entered the sunroom. The screen door smacked her backside, and Dawson grinned.

Brenn entered the kitchen to see Rachel slumped over the dinette table that sat in an alcove. Several women were scrambling about the kitchen making hors d'oeuvres, gallons of iced tea, cucumber sandwiches, crab dip, and cheese platters. A large cake sat in the middle of the island counter. It was surrounded with piped pink pansies of buttercream icing. "Happy Birthday, Tulie," was written in a delicate scroll across the middle. It was the first birthday cake made for the June 9th date in 17 years, and the first time Ryder's name was not part of it.

Brenn walked casually over to Rachel, who was nursing a cup of tea. The bags beneath her eyes and sallow complexion aged her beyond her 58 years. Strands of gray threaded her dark hair. She had one elbow propped on the table, holding her head with her hand.

"You look awful," Brenn said unkindly. "You need to pull it together, Rachel. People will start coming soon. It's just one day, and then you can go back to hiding in your room. I'll get you some more tea. It will help you sober up."

Brenn picked up the cup and walked to the cabinets next to the sink. She pulled down a square tin with garish red geraniums printed upon it. Popping the lid, she spooned two rounded teaspoonfuls of ground tea into Rachel's cup. Touching the kettle that was still steaming on the stove, she recoiled at the burn it caused, and poured the hot water into the teacup.

One of the ladies that Margo had sent over to help with the party preparations eyed her. "Y'all don't have a tea steeper? It's better when you let it steep," the large woman in a green apron said.

Brenn merely gave her a contemptuous look and walked back to the table, stirring the cup as she went.

"Here," she said, placing the cup back onto its saucer with a clink. "Drink it and get ready for the party. I can't babysit you. I've got stuff to do. I'll make you a hair appointment for next week." She walked from the kitchen, oblivious to the looks of disgust from the women who followed her from the room.

"You'd never catch me wearing shorts like that if my thighs were as big as hers," one of the women said, watching Brenn's thick legs disappear through the kitchen doorway.

Rachel stared into the cup of steaming amber liquid. She felt numb. Nothing seemed real. Nothing made sense. As she brought the cup to her lips, she seemed to become suddenly aware that there were other people in the room. She turned half-closed eyelids to study the three women who were watching her with worried expressions. Rachel looked back at the tea and took a long swallow. She had trouble placing it back into the recessed circle of the saucer before finally pushing her chair back with a screech and teetering unsteadily from the room.

"How people start drinking this early in the day is beyond me," one of the women commented in hushed tones.

"Maybe it ain't alcohol," another said in a conspiratorial manner. "She looked drugged to me. I hear she's been on sedatives since that boy drowned."

"They don't keep giving you sedatives for 17 years!" one woman scowled.

"They do if you got Broussard money," the other said defiantly. They nodded wisely in unison and returned to the food preparation. Tulie walked through a few minutes later, banging her hip painfully on the counter corner. She dropped the paper plates she was taking to the sunroom. It took several attempts to corral them all back into a neat tower. Looking embarrassed, she passed the women and made her way down the two steps to the enclosed porch.

"That's another one," one of the women said, motioning with her head toward the doorway Tulie had just exited. "Vague as vague can be! Like she's in some cloud world or somethin'."

"Uh-huh," the other nodded. "Like mother, like daughter, I always say."

At five o'clock, the guests began arriving. A sign had been tacked to a wooden stake in the front yard directing the partygoers to the back of the house. They rounded the corners with arms laden with presents and plates of food. Many of the church women had volunteered to bring a plate of something. They walked up the steps to the sunroom and deposited their offerings on the long tables draped with plastic, pink-colored tablecloths. Helium balloons of Tulie's two favorite colors of pink and ivory, bobbed in a light breeze coming in through the mesh windows. The smell of barbequed brisket laced the air as Dawson manned a large grill below the back porch.

Tulie stood awkwardly to one side, her gaze down. Most of the guests were relations: some close, some she saw maybe once every two years. She had only two friends from her school days there. Macy Struthers and Agnes Dehorney were as socially awkward as Tulie herself. Agnes's last name had caused her no end of teasing throughout her life. The three had bonded during those terrifying high school years when the school hallways between classes were an obstacle course of humiliation to be navigated. Their arrival brightened Tulie's mood, and the three moved away from the crowd to huddle together and giggle.

A hush fell over the raised voices of the party attendees. Rachel was standing in the doorway of the sunroom, looking out across the lawn and blinking in the sudden sunlight. She was leaning heavily on her sister Margo. It was clear she was sedated. The sundress of bright summer colors and the makeup Margo had applied to her pale face did little to brighten the frail woman swaying there. Her dark hair was pulled up into a stylish chignon with a matching bow. It was a look better fitted to someone half her age.

Margo forced a smile and said cheerfully, "Here's the birthday girl's Mama. We can start the party now."

Some let out a forced hoot of appreciation while most stood where they were, unclear of what to do next. Dawson called out from the yard, "Meat's on!" That seemed to break the ice. The guests picked up their plates and made their way down the verandah steps to Dawson, who began forking up brisket. He had been smoking it all day in the shade of a tall elm tree; it's mouth-watering aroma hovering in the air.

Just then, Tulie's father, Randall, appeared from

around the corner of the house. Margo led Rachel from the sunroom out onto the back lawn and placed her in one of the many folding chairs positioned around the cake table. A small, rented tent supplied the cake with protection from the sun beating down overhead. Margo had been careful to choose a chair for Rachel that had its back to the lake dock sitting just down the sloping lawn. Large patio umbrellas were strategically placed, offering the guests some respite from the early evening heat.

Several women, standing off to one side and shoveling brisket and fruit salad into their mouths, surreptitiously watched Randall's movements. He sat a large chest of ice on the porch and began shaking hands with a few of the male guests. He made pleasantries with the females and finally approached his wife. He gazed down at Rachel with the look of a man who had removed himself from his need to care about her. It was a wooden expression, devoid of compassion. Tulie walked over to him and touched his arm.

"Hey birthday girl," he said warmly, suddenly brightening. "You look pretty. Look at all these people who came to celebrate with you. Twenty-five-years-old! You'll be married and pregnant before your next birthday, you just watch!" he said, squeezing her shoulder.

The well-meant comment missed its mark. Tulie colored and shrugged out of his embrace. There was an awkward silence from those closest to the situation. Rachel looked up at him with pure hatred; the only emotion she had shown since joining the party. Randall sniffed and moved off. "Hit me up with some of that brisket, Dawson," he said a little too loudly and jovially. Dawson obliged him, and the party voices rose once again.

The afternoon wore on with the usual overtures. Most of the guests drank too much, and their voices floated over the lake in raucous laughter. Tulie had made it through cutting the cake, although there were tears in her eyes when they sang to her. It took her three tries to blow out the twenty-six candles…one to grow on. The presents were opened to the appreciative exclamations of the guests. There was an especially lovely cut-crystal egg resembling Faberge from her father. It was exquisite. The hinged lid opened to reveal a gold ballerina surrounded by crystal lily pads. It was nested in a flanged gold pedestal base.

"Thank you, Daddy," Tulie said in hushed excitement. She held it up for the rest to see. The sunlight caught the crystal, and it shot out prisms of color. Brenn was the only one standing near Tulie who looked on without appreciation. She glowered at her stepsister and then turned the same look of disdain to her father, who was beaming proudly at his gift and its effect on the birthday girl.

"You're welcome, Tulie," he said lovingly and hugged her. "Happy 25th!" He felt relieved that the gift might have covered for his recent mistake at mentioning marriage to his daughter. To date, Tulie had not had one suitor. She and her two friends were some of the few who had not attended Prom or Homecoming dances during their school years. What made him say it, he did not know. But it looked like his expensive gift had saved his butt.

Tulie took the egg over to her mother, who had not moved from the lawn chair during the entire party. She carefully placed it in her mother's cupped hands.

"Look, Mama," she said, sinking into a chair next to her. "Isn't it beautiful? Look at the little dancer. Just like you when you were a ballerina."

Rachel stared at the delicate gold dancer as her forehead furrowed in concentration. Then a small smile played across her lips, and she turned to look at Tulie.

"I danced," she said quietly, but there was pride behind the words. "I was a dancer. I was in Swan Lake, and they clapped."

Tulie brightened. "Yes, they did! They clapped loudly!"

Rachel looked at her daughter, and her eyes filled with tears.

"Happy Birthday, Tulie. I love you."

"I love you, too, Mama." The two embraced, and several people clapped.

Dawson pulled Tulie aside as the guests separated into groups on the lawn. He smiled and produced a small, wrapped present from behind his back.

"It isn't much, but I thought you would like it," he said.

Tulie blushed with pleasure as she unwrapped the gift. As she lifted the lid to the box, she bit her lip, and tears filled her eyes. Nestled in pink tissue paper was a framed photo of her with Ryder, standing near the lake. He was wearing a pirate patch over one eye and a bright red shirt with the words, "The flogging will continue until morale improves." You could see the small boat tied to the dock behind them as sunlight dappled the water.

"Oh…," she said, her voice filled with emotion. An image of Ryder's red shirt bobbing in the lake came flooding back. "When did you take this?" she asked in surprise.

"That day," Dawson said. "Rachel asked me to take some photos of the house and pecan grove for an insurance claim from the damage a storm did to the roof and some trees a few years before. I was taking a couple of pictures of the grove as I walked over to start digging the hole for the buried treasure. I saw you and Ryder by the lake planning the treasure hunt, and I took it."

"I do remember wearing that shirt," she said, her voice choked. "I picked the one with a parrot on it. The boat is still tied to the dock," she whispered, cradling the picture in her hands. "This was just before I started painting the rocks."

Dawson nodded quietly. "I hope it's not a bad idea to give it to you," he said. "I just thought enough time had passed and you would want a memory of your last day with him."

Tulie noticed the intricate carving in the wood frame for the first time. "Did you make this?" she asked.

"Yeah," he said sheepishly. "Nothing special. I do some carving in the tool shed sometimes. Happy Birthday, Tulie," he said. He squeezed her shoulder and moved away as he saw Brenn approaching.

"Love note?" Brenn asked mischievously.

Tulie walked away from her, still looking at the present Dawson had given her.

Sunset heralded the illumination of the colored party lights strewn between trees from the porch eaves. Many of the guests had departed. Several remained in lawn chairs, nursing their favorite drinks. A few women scurried about picking up paper plates with cake icing stuck to them, a few popped balloons, and wrapping paper remnants. The sleepy sound of waves licking the shoreline lulled the inebriated partygoers into that melancholic revelry that rears its head at this time of evening.

"'Member ole Jermiah Cobbs?" one man asked as he puffed on a cigar, blowing smoke rings into the air between sentences. "That fool knew better than to drive along Hillson Bluff at night. It ain't fit for cars during the daylight, let alone when there twern't no moon that night."

"You got it," another man said languidly. "At least he was dead before he hit the bottom of the cliff. They got a guardrail up now. It always happens after somebody dies, notice that?"

The men bobbed their heads and looked off bleary-eyed at the moonlight skimming the lake. Suddenly, Hallace Watman sat straight up, leaned forward in his chair, and stared down at the dock. The moonlight was bathing a few of the weathered boards in a whitewashed spotlight.

"What the hell is that?" he barked out. Several heads swiveled in the direction he was looking.

"What's what?" Dave Milliard asked him. "Nessie out there?"

Several men laughed at the Loch Ness joke, but Hallace was stone-faced. He suddenly went pale. "There's a boy on the dock," he choked, the hand holding his plastic tumbler of whiskey beginning to shake. "There's a boy there, I tell ya. He's…he's not real. I mean…" he faltered and then blurted out. "I can see through him!"

A couple of the men stood up and stared at the dock. Seeing nothing but a whisp of fog, they walked slowly down the slope, stopping before the boards that led out into the water.

"There ain't nothin' here," Dave yelled back, exasperated. He had fallen for one of Hallace's pranks. But when he turned to look back at the man, he could tell by his face that it was no joke. At that same moment, someone screamed. There was a rush of people who hurried to the center of the lawn. Rachel Broussard Burrows had fainted.

Hallace and Dave rushed up the lawn toward the crowd. Only Jiles Davison remained near the dock, his eyes transfixed at a spot near its end. He squinted, trying to bring a wavering shape into focus. It was shadow-like with minimal definition. He thought he made out short, thin legs protruding from what looked like shorts. There was a small head and scrawny arms. It was all black and floated a few inches above the dock. Through its transparent form, he could see the pilings at the end of the pier.

Slowly, it floated toward him along the weathered boards. Its arms passed in and out of view, as did the head. As soon as he thought he could make out some detail to the face, it evaporated again, like windblown smoke. It came back into focus, and to his horror, it was now at the mouth of the dock, only a few feet away. Suddenly, the small head jerked in his direction, and a hand reached toward him. Jiles stumbled back, stifling a scream. The shape wavered and suddenly sputtered out completely, like an extinguished candle flame, it was gone.

9 RYDER'S GHOST

Detective Hilliard stood in the parlor at 27 Broussard, a feeling of déjà vu pervading the room. Seventeen years had done little to bring the parlor's furnishings into the 21st century. Old-fashioned settees and Queen Anne chairs were arranged in cozy clusters. Hand-embroidered doilies rested on chair arms. A vintage sewing kit sat off to one side of a lapis lazuli crystal vase; a few wilting flowers draped over its mouth. The room smelled of old wallpaper, still plastered to the walls in the William Morris palette popular in the mid-1800s. Area rugs were faded and expensive. Two Asian urns flanked the fireplace, which boasted the original blue tiles from Italy.

Hilliard had himself reluctantly bowed to the passage of time: the gray from his temples had advanced along with his hairline like a Yankee invading the South. He sported a recently grown moustache, already streaked with silver. His eyes were just as blue, but they now resided behind bifocals. He looked out through these glasses as he studied the room of people before him.

Tulie Barrows sat upright in the same corner of the settee in which she had found refuge the first time he came to the house. No longer curled into a ball, hiding behind unkept hair, the young woman sat with her back ramrod straight, her hair pulled back into a loose, but neat, ponytail. Her once gangly figure had filled out, and the soft sprinkling of freckles across the bridge of her nose added to her fresh natural beauty. The stringy strawberry blond hair had settled into a thick, subdued copper with highlights from summers spent near the lake. Her shyness, however, remained. Her gaze found its home base on a small marble ashtray on the coffee table and stayed there.

Brenn Barrows had claimed the same parlor chair with the red velvet backing she had perched upon seventeen years ago. Hilliard noted with some satisfaction that the woman was not aging well. The teenage baby fat had succumbed to fleshy pulchritude, her chin all but disappearing. At 32, she could pass for ten years older. Her makeup was overdone to appear prettier than her lack of natural assets provided. Her saving feature was a thick head of blonde hair that lay in soft waves about her face, mirroring her father's.

Dawson Kingston was not in the same location he had been on that fateful summer day when Ryder Barrows drowned in the lake. He had distanced himself from Brenn and was seated in one of the Queen Anne chairs closer to Tulie. No longer fidgeting with a coaster, the tanned and buff young man sat with an ease and confidence that Hilliard found admirable. Rachel was missing from the room and had been replaced by two newcomers: Angela and Calvin Peterson.

The front door banged open, and Adelaide Calvo entered the parlor, her demeanor much the same as it had been seventeen years ago. The only difference was her new ranking. She had been promoted to lieutenant. Without apology for her lateness, she claimed an empty chair and extracted a tablet from her leather shoulder pouch. Placing it on her lap, she said, "Ready," as she powered it up and prepared to take notes.

Hilliard sighed and addressed the two people he had not met the first time around.

"You are?" he asked succinctly. The passing years had honed his people skills, although he still preferred the privacy of his desk cubicle. He stared at the rotund woman in an oversized shirt, faded sweat pants, and sturdy shoes. Her hair was a mix of brown and gray, her face weathered with the look of someone who spent a good deal of time outdoors. She gave off an air of steely resolve. *Not one to be messed with*, Hilliard thought.

"Angela...Peterson. First cousin to Rachel and Margo. Was first cousin to Barry before he ploughed into the rocks waterskiing." Hilliard flinched. "This here is my husband, Calvin," she said, hooking her thumb toward the man seated next to her in a wheelchair. "We live in the house over there," she pointed out the window toward the mansion several hundred yards from where they were all gathered. "It was Margo's, but after Barry ploughed..." she paused when she saw the detective's face screw up. "Anyway, we live there now. Both retired."

Her husband suddenly blurted out, "Not me! I'm not retired," he said, his voice a raspy croak. "Workin' on a book about the 'Bayou Slayer'," he said proudly. "Investigatin' it for six years now. Can give you some pointers if you like."

Detective Hilliard smiled. Lieutenant Calvo merely arched an eyebrow at the man. She shifted her leather police belt where a .45 handgun rested in its holster. The leather made a distinct creaking sound. The not-so-subtle gesture caused Calvin to smile.

"Not butting in on your territory," he said amused. "But I got a lot of articles and paperwork on the subject. Fills a whole box. Just sayin'."

Calvo sniffed indifferently. No longer wearing a ball cap and sweatshirt, the officer had donned her full uniform and cap, the same braids protruding.

"Were either of you at the birthday party last evening?" Hilliard asked Calvin. Before the man could answer, Angela piped up. "Both were," she said in her clipped manner of speaking.

"Can you tell me anything about the occurrence at the end of the party when Mrs. Barrows fainted?"

Angela lowered her eyelids and squinted at the man. "Wouldn't think a woman fainting would warrant a police visit," she said accusingly. "What's up?"

Hilliard bristled.

"We're here to see if this has anything to do with the boy's drowning accident in 2006," he said evenly. "I understand there was some commotion about some men seeing a boy on the boat dock last night."

"Drunkin' idiots," she said flatly.

"That may be," Hilliard returned, "but I find it interesting that two men gave me identical descriptions of a small boy standing on the dock at the place where the little Barrows boy had his boat tied up."

"Damn strange happenings on this lake," Calvin blurted out. "Damned strange! I've got articles and files about it," he said dramatically. Tulie was studying her knees and battling tears.

"Calvin don't make an ass of yourself," Angela snapped at him, slapping him painfully in his shoulder. "He collects articles about deaths and stuff," she offered.

"For my research!" Calvin said hotly.

Calvin looked down; his mouth twisted to one side in frustration. Hilliard got the impression the man was used to being cowed by his wife.

"Let's get back to the party," Hilliard said. "Did Miss Rachel faint about the same time the men saw this boy on the dock?"

"Exact same time!" Angela asserted. "I saw her. She was looking down at the lake after she heard that fool Hallace say he saw a boy on the dock. She looked down there and screamed. She folded like a broken lawn chair."

Hilliard was tiring of the woman's affinity for dramatic pronouncements. She seemed to delight in the attention. He shifted gears.

"Miss Brenn," he said, turning to face the same smug expression he remembered. "Did you see anything?"

A quick grin crossed her face.

"I agree with Cousin Angela," she said in even tones. "Some drunk's 'sighting,'" she said, making air quotes with her fingers, "does not warrant a full-on police investigation. Ghost stories are just part of the Broussard heritage, along with the good silver and Civil War remnants. Don't you have more pressing business?"

Just then, Doctor Clarkson walked into the room. He was a stout man with silver hair, glasses, and wearing a pressed black suit. He looked in Tulie's direction and said, "She'll be lying down the rest of the day. I gave her a mild sedative. Nothing too strong. I'm trying to wean her off the stuff."

As the doctor turned on his heel to leave, Hilliard stopped him.

"Doctor Clarkson," he said quickly. "A couple of questions, please…"

The doctor frowned and made a point of looking at his watch. "Two minutes," he said in an agitated tone. "I've got rounds to make."

"Has Miss Rachel been on sedatives this entire time? Since her son drowned, I mean." Hilliard asked.

Clarkson stiffened, a spot of color rising in both cheeks. "What are you inferring, sir?" he asked hotly. Brenn grinned and settled back into her chair to watch the show.

"Not inferring anything," Hilliard replied undaunted. "Several people at the party last night were questioned. All said Miss Rachel looked 'out of it.' They reported they only saw her sipping tea. If it isn't alcohol, I'm guessing it's something else. You just mentioned to Miss Tulie that you were 'trying to wean her off the stuff.' Would that 'stuff' cause her to see things that aren't there?"

The doctor bit down so hard on his lower lip that Hilliard expected to see blood.

"It's a *mild* sedative. Mild! It would not cause hallucinations. She's only supposed to take it at night when she has trouble sleeping or is feeling especially stressed. Her husband is away a lot, and it makes her anxious. It's entirely safe. I would give it to my *own* daughter."

117

Hilliard studied the irate man for a moment. Clarkson pounced on the pause and excused himself, hurrying out of the room before the detective could ask him any more questions.

"Just a bunch of damn drunks," Calvin reiterated.

Hilliard turned to look at the man. "Maybe so," he said, admitting defeat. "Maybe so..." He glanced at Calvo, who shrugged.

"Miss Tulie? You let us know if anything else happens, okay?" Hilliard said kindly as he prepared to leave.

Tulie looked at him, a flush of embarrassment coloring her freckled face. "Do you..." she began awkwardly. "I mean...why would you...do you think something happened to Ryder...I mean...other than an accident? Why are you really here?" she finished, her words disappearing into a whisper.

Calvo looked at the detective and waited for him to answer. It was the same question she had asked him when he summoned her to join him at the Barrows' house.

"Anytime there is a suspicious death, we keep that file open," Hilliard said gently.

"The coroner ruled it an accident," Brenn said abruptly. "Checked the box and everything."

"Wellll," Hilliard began, drawing the word out in his soft Southern cadence, "it's hard for an ole' detective to let go of that bone sometimes," he said, smiling. "Just seems odd that on that poor boy's birthday anniversary, three people we know of saw him standing on the dock."

"Saw a trick of the moonlight on the dock," Angela corrected. "Or them boys from the new subdivision.

Four of 'em keep comin' in my yard and tormentin' my cat."

"You lookin' for suspicious deaths," Calvin piped up. "Plenty of them in this family line, I can tell ya. I've got articles," he repeated proudly. "I research stuff like that," he added unnecessarily.

"Yes," Hilliard said slowly, studying the man. "I may pick your brain one of these days about that."

"Not much to pick," Angela hooted.

Hilliard merely smiled at her. He had no interest in furthering the conversation. As he and the lieutenant made their way to the front foyer, he quietly whispered to Dawson to follow them out.

The threesome stopped at the massive double doors that led out to the front verandah. Hilliard saw Brenn come out into the foyer and look in their direction. The detective opened the door and motioned for Dawson to follow them out. He shut the door firmly behind them.

"Well, young man?" Hilliard asked without preamble. "Whatcha got?"

Dawson didn't feign ignorance. He had caught the detective's eye a few times during the interview.

"Something strange is going on," he said quietly, glancing over his shoulders at the windows to make sure no one was listening in. "You can make fun of me if you want to, but since Ryder's death, some crazy shit is happening."

"Like what?" Hilliard asked, as Calvo powered up her tablet again and braced it on the porch railing.

Dawson looked uncomfortable. Finally, he said, "I live over there behind the pecan grove," he said, motioning in that direction with his head. "I know most of what goes on in the family. I take care of repairs around the houses and tend the pecan grove. I used to take care of both the groves until Mr. Randall sold off Miss Rachel's share to that new subdivision next door."

Hilliard was aware of the fancy new homes that Glasgow Construction had built where Rachel Barrows' parcel of the pecan grove had been. It was aptly named Lake Grove Estates. The small subdivision boasted about fifty houses. Due to the lakefront location, the asking price for the cookie-cutter homes was in the high six figures.

"What about what Miss Angela said?" the detective asked him. "Maybe it was one of the boys from the Estates that Rachel and the men saw standing on the dock last night. Wasn't it dark out?"

"Not that dark," Dawson said. It was the way he said it that made Hilliard pause. He nodded at him, encouraging the young man to continue.

"There are nights," Dawson began, fumbling for the words, "when...well...I hear that damn bell." He paused, studying the detective's face, looking for any sign that the man thought he had rocks loose. When Hilliard's face remained stoic, he finally continued.

"The day Ryder died, the bell on his little boat was clanging. Right after that, I heard Tulie scream. You guys took the boat away the next day, along with the bell. I helped your men load it onto the trailer. But I swear, it's that same bell I hear sometimes." He paused, looking miserable. Hilliard sensed there was more. He waited.

"Ryder's favorite card trick was one he called The Rising Kings. It always ended with the King of Spades card turning up in someone's pocket or under a chair or something, even though the card had been buried in the deck. No matter how many times you shuffle the cards, the King of Spades rises to the top and ends up near the person whose turn it is. It was actually really good. Well…that card has shown up in a couple of places since he died. I've seen it four times in the past 17 years, always someplace different. Just recently it was in the small shed where I keep my tools at home. I was carving a frame for Tulie's birthday present. It was for a picture of her and Ryder the day he died. When I lifted a can of pecan stain, that card was lying under it. There's no way! I just bought the stain. It wasn't there. It's unnerving, I can tell you that!"

Hilliard studied Dawson's face for a few moments. The young man seemed totally convinced about what he was saying.

"I saw the cards on the coffee table the day he died," the detective said. "You, yourself, told us what they were when Miss Rachel reacted to them. Who is to say someone isn't playing a prank on you and using a different King of Spades card?"

This time Dawson squared his shoulders and looked the tall man straight in the eye.

"Ryder had the person who was choosing a card write their name on the face of the card with blue ink. The last time he had his show, it was in the parlor, one day before he died. Brenn wanted it to be her turn that time. She signed her name in blue ink and put the card into the deck and shuffled it. It showed up under her chair. The card that keeps showing up in random places since Ryder died has her name written on it."

"Ok…so Brenn got the card and she's playing a sick joke on you," Calvo interjected. "I noticed that card with the writing on it when we looked down at the cards that day. It was lying on top of the strewn deck. Someone…probably Brenn…has it, and she's having fun scaring you. It would seem to be her style." Calvo's Creole accent softened her words in a singsong quality, but it did nothing to disperse the feeling of tension in the air.

Dramatically, Dawson said, "I burned those cards myself the same day they took the boat away. Rachel told me to. She couldn't bear to look at them. I saw the King of Spades with Brenn's name on it destroyed by the fire."

"What's to keep Brenn from getting another deck of cards and writing her name on the King again?" Calvo asked.

"Because the card from the magic show was special," Dawson said quietly. "When Ryder pulled the card Brenn had signed from under her chair, she freaked out and grabbed it from him, accusing him of cheating. When she yanked it from his hand, it cut his finger. Nothing bleeds like a paper cut. When Ryder grabbed the card back, his blood went all over it. He tried to wipe it off, but the cut kept bleeding on it. There was blood all over the table. It left a dark stain on the cards, including the King with Brenn's name on it. I saw those blood stains burn along with the cards. I watched the King of Spades curl up and burn. It showed up at a séance, too, and it burned there as well on top of a candle."

Calvo eyes narrowed into slits. This all sounded fishy to her. "You had a séance?"

"Never mind," Dawson said dejectedly. He was beginning to feel like a fool in their eyes.

"So, you've seen this same card…that you

burned…show up several times since you burned the deck? And you know it's the same card from Ryder's magic show and the one Brenn signed and he bled on?" Calvo asked.

Dawson nodded.

"Where is it?" the officer asked, eyeing the young man keenly.

"What do you mean, where is it?"

"Didn't you pick it up when you saw it? I mean, that's pretty freaky if you keep seeing a card you swear you burned. What did you do with it?"

Dawson's face reddened. Chewing the inside of his cheek, he finally looked her in the face.

"I didn't pick it up," he said. "It scared me, okay? I left it there and got the hell away from it."

Calvo sighed dramatically and looked at her notes.

"You said you heard the ship bell coming from the lake since the boat was taken away…you heard it clear over at your house behind the pecans?" She glanced to her left toward a massive grove of trees. Dawson's house was obscured from view.

"I didn't say I was at home when I heard it, and I didn't say it was coming from the lake," he said, realizing he was beginning to stumble over his words in his exasperation.

"You just walk around at night, is that it?" Calvo asked.

Dawson regained his composure and glared at the much shorter officer.

"I take care of all this," he said, waving his arm in a wide sweep. "Three huge houses, the properties, and the grove. Yeah, I walk around a lot."

Silence filled the afternoon once again. Only the

incessant sound of cicadas hummed around them.

Dawson finally exploded. "Think what you want! I'm telling you the truth. The card, the ship bell, and people seeing Ryder on the dock. Maybe he's trying to tell you something," Dawson said hotly.

"Like what?" Calvo challenged.

"Like maybe he was murdered!"

10 TEA CAKES

Brenn entered the kitchen and found Tulie surrounded by bowls of flour and sugar. On the island counter was an array of bottles, including vanilla, almond extract, rum, and amaretto. Cubes of butter were softening in a bowl. Several crumbling mounds of wet dough stuck to the counter's marble top.

"What in the world are you doing, Tulie?" Brenn blurted out.

Tulie turned away from the counter where she was studying a stained recipe card. Her face and hair were dusted with flour as was her daisy-covered apron. Wet dough was stuck to her fingers in large clumps. Her face fell, and she looked close to tears.

"I'm trying to copy Mama's recipe for Southern Tea Cakes," she cried miserably. "Mama was supposed to help me, but she...well...she's sleeping," Tulie said dismally.

Several days had passed since Tulie's birthday party, and Rachel had disappeared into a bottle of sedatives.

"Why do you feel the need to make tea cakes so badly?" Brenn asked, picking up the bottle of rum extract to read its expiration date.

"Mama got talked into bringing them to the church fundraiser for the Walker family," Tulie said. "Margaret Ruthers wouldn't leave her alone at my party. Mama finally agreed to bring two dozen of her cakes just to shut her up. I don't want the ladies to think anything's wrong with Mama, so I thought if I make 'em and sneak 'em in with her name on 'em, no one will notice she wasn't there."

Brenn studied her for a moment and looked around at the mess. She looked down at Tulie's matted fingers and snapped, "Tulie! Look what you've done! You take your rings off when you're doing stuff like this. That ring I gave you was expensive, now it's covered in gooey dough!"

Tulie looked down at a mound of dough on her right ring finger. Somewhere buried inside of it was a ruby ring.

Brenn pulled her forcefully to the sink and stuck Tulie's hand under running water, rolling the dough off in small sections. When the ruby finally twinkled into existence, Brenn yanked the ring over Tulie's knuckle and carefully dried it.

"I realize you're not used to wearing fashionable things," Brenn said hotly. "If you can't take care of this, I'll take it back."

Tulie felt ashamed. She had been so surprised when Brenn had entered her room the night of her birthday party after everyone had gone. Brenn rarely came into her room. She sank down on the bed beside Tulie, who was admiring each of her presents, and pulled a small box from behind her back. It wasn't wrapped. It looked like a box a watch had come in.

"Here," Brenn said without ceremony. "Happy Birthday. I didn't want to give it to you at the party. I wanted to give it to you special."

Tulie was surprised and delighted. Maybe Brenn was changing. She lifted the lid to the box and saw an ornate ruby mounted on a gold band resting in toilet paper. She gasped.

"Is that real?" Tulie said, her eyes bulging.

"Of course, it's real," Brenn said. "Take care of it. It cost me half of my inheritance from my mother." With that, she left the room, glancing back to look with satisfaction as Tulie slipped it over her knuckle. She held it up, and it sparkled beneath the overhead tulip bulbs. Brenn grinned, her eyes narrowing, as she crossed out into the hallway, closing the door behind her.

"Can you help me?" Tulie asked her now, surveying the mess in the kitchen. She had carefully pocketed the ruby ring once Brenn dried it and shoved it back at her. She hated giving Brenn any ammunition to make fun of her. To her amazement, Brenn's face softened, and she crossed over to the girl seven years her junior.

"I don't cook," Brenn said gently. "Never learned. Tell you what…we'll go to Orleans (she pronounced it 'Awlins') and pick some up from Maison de Crepe. They make gorgeous tea cakes. No one will know you didn't make them. We can add something on top to make them look unique, like a lemon twill or something."

Tulie brightened. At the same moment, a feeling of dread overtook her. This was not like Brenn. She studied the woman's face. She smiled back at Tulie with what appeared to be genuine sincerity.

"Okay," Tulie finally managed, forcing a smile. "Thank you, Brenn. This means a lot."

Brenn drove her vintage Mustang she had purchased when her mother's inheritance kicked in on her 21st birthday. It was her baby. It was in the original color of Pagoda Green from the 1964 debut. She navigated the tight car-strewn curbs of Bourbon Street and circled twice before grabbing a spot where a minivan was exiting. They walked the two blocks to the bakery past a profusion of off-beat shops sporting bars, oyster restaurants, and Mardi Gras décor. A man dressed like the Grim Reaper walked the sidewalk, posing for pictures with delighted tourists. Tulie gave him a wide berth.

Maison de Crepe was packed with a line waiting at the display counter. Tulie had never seen so many delicacies. The name plates adorning each plate of stacked pastries were all in French. You didn't have to speak the language to point and order something that made your mouth drool. Brenn caught the attention of a beautiful young girl with startling eyeliner and jet-black hair. Tulie hung back, buffeted by the women jockeying for a spot.

"We want three of those," Brenn said assertively, jabbing a finger at the glass toward a plate of tea cakes dripping with vanilla bean frosting. She ignored the snorts of the women she had cut in front of at the counter. "Three of those," she continued, pointing to another plate with orange glaze, "three of those, and three of those," Brenn finished as she rounded out the order. "Double it," she said. "We need two dozen."

The girl looked confused for a moment. "So, *seeks* of each?" she asked in a strong French accent. Brenn paused until she realized the girl had said 'six.'

"Whatever," Brenn shot back.

The cakes were packed carefully into pink boxes with the name Maison de Crepe written in gold embossed lettering.

"Zat vill be $132.75," the young woman said, as she rang up the purchase.

Brenn flinched, but opened her purse and laid down seven $20 bills. The girl looked surprised to get a cash payment. She fished around in the till and finally handed Brenn back her change. "Merci," the young woman said, and moved deftly on to the next customer.

Brenn carefully picked up one box with the receipt taped to its lid and stacked it atop the other. She weaved in and out of customers, stepping on more than one foot. Once they exited the shop, Brenn pushed the two boxes into Tulie's arms, ripping the receipt from the top one. "Well, that's done," she said. "You owe me $133," she proclaimed, rounding it up. "What time are you supposed to be at the church with these things?"

"By 4:30," Tulie said, swaying from side to side to avoid colliding with the people thronging the narrow sidewalks. "$5.50 for one tea cake seems like a lot," she said quietly, not wanting Brenn to think she didn't appreciate her bailing her out of an awkward situation. She never expected it to cost so much. "Is this the only bakery here?"

Brenn kept walking ahead of her, her short heels clicking on the cracked sidewalk. "You want them to look good or not?" Brenn called back over her shoulder. "Those old church bitties would spot tea cakes bought from Piggly Wiggly or Danielle's in a heartbeat. I doubt they shop at Maison."

Tulie realized the wisdom of Brenn's logic and brightened. She would save her Mama's reputation, and that's all she cared about. Rachel Barrows was known throughout Orleans Parish for her tea cakes. If it was a pie you wanted, you called on Dawson's Mama, Helouise, but tea cakes…you went to Rachel.

Brenn seemed in a hurry as she drove the crowded streets of the city. She swerved deftly into Pelican Bank and Trust's drive-through and slammed on her brakes. She leaned back into her seat to allow Tulie to reach across her with her credit card and extract the cash she owed Brenn from the ATM.

"It only does twenties," Tulie said, looking down at the $140 in cash.

"$140 works," Brenn said, snatching the twenties and cramming them into her purse. "Chipping in for gas, you know…"

Once at home, Brenn helped Tulie arrange the cakes on large platters with the name Barrows written on the bottom in black marker. It was necessary to label the plates when so many church functions borrowed your platters. Brenn cut lemon and orange peels into thin slices and curled them around a pencil. She alternated the twists atop the twenty-four delicacies. They weren't trills, but they gave each tea cake a unique touch.

"I thought you didn't cook," Tulie said, admiring how beautiful the simple adornment made the tea cakes look.

"This isn't cooking," Brenn said. "You can add them to martinis, too." She grinned. "Oh, hey…if I'm drivin' ya over to the church, I need more gas money. I'm not a taxi service. Why in the world don't you get a car is beyond me."

Tulie sighed. It was the same recitation she had heard from Brenn and others. She preferred walking to Wings Bend if she needed anything, and she rarely needed much. She reached into her jeans pocket to check for any cash she might have left. Her fingers felt the ruby ring. She pulled it out and placed it back onto her finger. Brenn saw her and said nothing.

Tulie not only paid for the gas with her credit card, but she was also ordered to pump it. The self-serve gas dispenser felt overwhelming. She pushed several buttons, only to be beeped at and watched helplessly as "See the Cashier" was displayed in bold type across the screen. Brenn, who had been busy texting on her phone, finally realized what was going on and jumped from the front seat.

"Tulie, I swearrr!" she yelled, drawing the word 'swear' out in an exaggerated southern drawl. "You may as well be drivin' a horse and buggy! Hand me the card! *Lawd!*" Tulie handed her the card as two men at the pump next to her chuckled. She reddened and climbed back into the car as Brenn pumped the gas, filling her tank to full. Brenn dropped in behind the steering wheel and tossed the credit card to Tulie.

The back parking lot of Bloomington Methodist Church was filled with cars when the two arrived ten minutes later. Ladies lifted containers of food, flowers, and bunting from the trunks of various SUVs.

"I'll wait for ya," Brenn said, as she swung into a parking space and left the car idling. It took Tulie four trips to bring in the four platters. "Oohs and Ahs" escaped the lips of the delighted women in charge of the fundraiser, as they relieved Tulie of her large plates. Margaret Ruthers filled out four name plates in a delicate scrawl with Rachel Barrow's name. She placed them on small stands in front of Tulie's platters.

"Where is your Mama?" Margaret asked, eyeing the cakes with pleasure. They would bring in money for sure.

"She's coming," Tulie lied. "She had to make a stop, and she'll be over. I'm just helpin' out."

Tulie reached over to one of the tea cakes to straighten the lemon twist. The ruby ring on her right hand twinkled in the fluorescent lighting. Margaret glanced down at it and paused. Something about it looked familiar. Before she could say anything, Tulie blurted out, "We'll get the platters tomorrow," and made a beeline for the door and to Brenn's waiting Mustang. She opened the passenger door and sank into the deep bucket seat with a sigh.

"Did they buy it?" Brenn asked, grinning.

"I think so," Tulie said, almost trembling with relief.

As Brenn turned the car toward home, Tulie rolled down the window and rested her arm on the ledge. The morning heat was already climbing. She looked over to see Angie Bringham near her car with her hand down her V-neck, mopping her breasts with a handkerchief. It would be another scorcher. Tulie didn't notice the heat. She had saved her Mama's reputation, and that's all she cared about. She looked over at the ring Brenn gave her on her birthday. The ruby glinted in the sunlight.

"Let me know if the transient on the corner is enjoying my AC," Brenn said bluntly.

"Oh! Sorry!" Tulie exclaimed and rolled up the window.

The fundraiser was a hit. A delighted Margaret Ruthers announced to the ladies retrieving their platters the following day that they had raised $4,700.25 for the Walker family. Thunderous applause broke out. With Gladys Walker's mounting medical bills from her advanced breast cancer treatments, the money would be a welcome relief to her husband, who had been laid off the month before from his job with Hellberg Hydraulics.

Tulie tried to keep a low profile as she searched in the church kitchen for her mother's four platters. Brenn, as usual, waited in her car in the parking lot. Several platters were identical to the white ceramic ones with the raised acanthus leaves. She found two of them and was studying the bottom of another plate near the sink when Adelaine Friggers corralled her.

"Tulie," she said in a saccharin drawl. "Y'all's Mama makes the best tea cakes in the entire wide world. I have a little gathering for my soon-to-be daughter-in-law in two weeks at my place. It would mean the entire wide world if y'all could make me about forty-five of these sweet little ole' cakes. Y'all can make any kind you like! I'll pay whatever! Say your Mama will do it! Pleasssseeee! I don't care if it costs the whole wide world, I'll pay it."

Tulie looked like a deer in headlights. "Ummm...well, I'm not sure what her schedule is...I can ask," she said dismally.

"Perfect!" Adelaine screamed, clasping her hands together with delight. "Y'all have them to my house no later than 11:00 on two Tuesdays from this next one...the 26th! No later than 11:00, ya hear?" She clicked her way out of the kitchen in towering high

heels.

Tulie found the other two platters and carried them out to Brenn's car. It still seemed odd to her that Brenn had been so accommodating lately.

"I'm screwed," Tulie said dejectedly, sinking down into the bucket seat as Brenn pulled out of the church parking lot.

"Why?" Brenn asked, suddenly turning to eye Tulie keenly. "Did somebody say something?" she asked ominously, glancing at Tulie's ring.

"Yeah, somebody said something!" Tulie retorted. "Adelaine Figgers wants 45 tea cakes for some bridal shower for her son's fiancé in less than three weeks!"

There was a pause, and then Brenn suddenly burst into hysterical laughter. Tulie jumped at the outburst and looked at her angrily.

"What's so funny?" she shouted, trying to be heard through Brenn's howling.

"Oh, my gosh!" Brenn cried, hiccupping. "That's rich! You got yourself a regular little business, Tulie!" She broke into fresh peals of laughter that Tulie did not understand.

"I'm not doin' it!" Tulie shouted. "I'm done. I'll just say Mama has too much goin' on to bake the cakes."

She folded her arms and sat back defiantly in the seat.

Two-and-a-half weeks later, Tulie arrived at the Friggers' address in the gated community of Hill Top. Adelaine met her at the door with effusive gushing. She ordered two hapless maids to take four of the platters of tea cakes, while dictating to three other bystanders to each grab "at least two plates." She never invited Tulie inside. Sounds of multiple females laughing and speaking loudly inside echoed throughout the massive foyer Tulie could glimpse from the front doorstep.

When the last plate had been taken from her—after seven trips to Brenn's trunk, Adelaine thrust a stack of crisp $50's into Tulie's hands.

"Tell your Mama 'thanks'!" she said, smiled brightly, and slammed the door.

Tulie counted the money as Brenn steered the car down the winding driveway flanked by expensive bronzes, gold and silver mylar balloons, and perfectly manicured flower beds.

"Well, I came out $52.50 ahead," Tulie said, handing most of the cash to Brenn. "That bakery of yours is ridiculous. Only someone like Adelaine Friggers wouldn't flinch over a $300 tab for tea cakes. Which reminds me. She's rich. Wouldn't she shop for pastries at Maison's?"

Brenn flinched and hurried with an excuse. "Women like Adelaine Friggers have a maid shop for them. I doubt she sends her maid out to walk up and down Bourbon Street. Calm down. If you're lucky, no one else will ask 'your Mama' to bake anymore."

Luck was not in Tulie's corner. Four more Louisiana matrons placed orders within the next three months. Each time she and Brenn frequented Maison's, Brenn insisted on choosing the cakes, and Tulie dutifully reimbursed her in cash. Tulie didn't mind. She hated dealing with stores or cashiers. Let Brenn take control, as she always did. She had backed herself into a corner with the cakes. Her mother continued to live in a haze of confusion: vague most of the day, only to surface to reality on rare occasions. She and Tulie would do a crossword puzzle at the kitchen table on the infrequent days when clarity swam to the surface of Rachel's muddled mind. Then, she was gone again, looking off into the distance with unseeing eyes.

For now, Tulie kept paying for tea cakes, hoping her "new business" would dry up on its own. Her biggest concern, besides her mother's health, was her father's continued absence from home. Maybe if he gave her mother some attention, it would help her.

Tulie had ignored the gossip that followed her to most places she visited. It was the same today as she made her way through the aisles of Humphrey's Market at Wing's Bend. She was used to people finding her odd. But lately, it was not she who kept the gossip mills grinding.

"Poor Reed," she overheard a woman say on the other side of a store aisle. She wasn't convinced it wasn't said loudly enough so that she would overhear the conversation. "He doesn't get to hide inside a pill bottle like Rachel. He has to watch his wife's infidelity in full technicolor!"

"Business trips, my foot," came the gleeful reply. "No man in Louisiana has as many business trips as Randall Barrows! I'd be checking out the folly at their house if I were Reed. Maybe that garden isn't all Margo is tilling."

The other woman gasped at the audacious comment before the two dissolved into giggles. Tulie, her face red, hurried to the counter to pay for her few items. Rosco Humphrey, the store owner, looked at her sympathetically. He had known her since she was a child, buying penny candy from the glass jars on his counter.

"This all for you, Miss Tulie?" he asked kindly. He reached over to the candy jars and lifted the lid to the black licorice, Tulie's favorite. "Y'all better take a few of those," he said, smiling. "I got way too many of 'em and they'll just dry out."

Tulie grinned at him with appreciation. She meekly put her hand into the jar and pulled out three pieces of candy. She paid for her items and gathered up the sack Humprey handed to her.

"Y'all have a nice day," he said. "Tell that pretty Mama of yours I said 'Hey.'"

The last comment was said louder than the rest. It was meant for the two women making their way to the counter, cradling two wine bottles and some gourmet crackers. They eyed the owner smugly.

"This all for you two?" Humphrey asked, his voice lacking the kindness he had shown Tulie.

"Where are the latest magazines?" one woman demanded as she placed the wine bottles on the counter.

"They're on the rack, as always," Humphrey said, scanning the bar codes.

"Not those damned hunting magazines," she shot back. "The women's magazines…fashion, Hollywood…"

"Gossip?" he interjected, leaning forward against the counter with a snide smirk.

She colored, pressed her lips together, and threw two twenty-dollar bills on the counter. Grabbing up the wine bottles, she gripped the other woman's elbow and pulled her from the store.

"Y'all forgot your crackers and your change," he called, smiling. She glanced over her shoulder and shot him a hateful look. She let the screen door slam and continued along the worn front porch until the couple disappeared from Humphrey's view.

His smile disappeared as he took the box of crackers and replaced it on the shelf. He dropped the woman's twenty-three cents' worth of change into a jar near the candy and frowned. The nagging feeling followed him as he loaded the old Coke dispenser out front with cans. Gossip could be deadly in this part of the country. He heard similar whisperings in his store over the years from women gathered in the corner near the beauty products. It was either bashing some newcomer with better looks, a failed party, or a perceived affair between Margo Broussard Tillson and Randall Barrows. It was disturbing. Miss Rachel had gone through a rough time since young Ryder's drowning. Now, all these rumors about her husband and her own sister were circulating. An uneasy feeling came over the store owner. He had seen gossip in Orleans Parish result in disastrous endings. He sighed and walked back around his counter.

11 NEW BEGINNINGS

Brenn's eyes flew open. The room was pitch black. Her heart was racing, and a fine sheen of perspiration pebbled her forehead and upper lip. She lay there in her bed waiting…for what… Something had awakened her, of that, she was sure. A nightmare? She strained to make out anything in the inky darkness. A thin sliver of light finally materialized to her right, where the two heavy draperies were pulled together but for a thin opening allowing in the moonlight. Just as she was rising onto her elbow to reach for the table lamp, the sound of a ship bell clanging sounded from outside her window. She froze.

A faint rustling sounded inside the wall behind her headboard. With trembling fingers, she reached out for the table lamp near her bed and turned the switch. The bright light blinded her for a moment. She blinked repeatedly until the room came into focus. Her watercolor paintings adorned the walls where there had once been posters of teen heartthrobs.

There it was again! A soft flapping sound…what was it? It was a sound she knew, but it felt altered somehow. Suddenly, the memory of something similar she'd heard filled her reluctant mind. It was the sound of playing cards being shuffled together. What she heard now was distorted, but she was sure it was coming from Ryder's old bedroom on the other side of the wall. Then it stopped. Something fell with a soft thud in the hallway outside her door. Agonizing moments passed. Her eyes went to her bedroom door, her breathing coming in quick bursts. A movement caused her to look at the doorknob. It was slowly turning, a shrill *creak* coming from the rusted metal.

Brenn jumped from the bed, preparing to lunge at the door to keep whatever it was from coming in. The noise abruptly stopped. Silence followed. Seconds later, a tortured sigh breathed into the room through the keyhole, like the death rattle of someone's dying breath. The hairs on her neck stood up. She backed away, her eyes fastened on the doorknob. Should she scream? Tulie was two doors away. She would hear her and come running.

A scraping noise came from the base of the door, and suddenly, a playing card was pushed through the crack above the floor. The King of Spades, with her name scrawled across it in faded ink, smiled up at her.

Tulie and Rachel were seated at the small bistro table in the sunroom, sipping coffee, when Brenn stumbled down the steps from the kitchen to join them. She slid into a wrought iron chair and reached for the coffee pot. Tulie smiled at her, handing her a cup and saucer. Rachel merely glanced at her and reached for a scone.

"You look tired," Tulie said kindly. "Long night?"

Brenn spilled the coffee while trying to fill her cup. Her eyes shot a suspicious look in Tulie's direction.

"Why would you say that?" she barked.

Tulie looked at her in surprise as she mopped up the coffee with a wad of napkins. The lace tablecloth refused to release the mocha stain.

"Nothing," Tulie said, confused. She refilled Brenn's cup.

Brenn picked up the cup and looked to her left through the mesh sunroom windows toward the lake. She shuddered as her eyes scanned the dock, shrouded in the early morning mist, the warm lake water released. It rose in ghostlike swirls, hovering in a low-lying fog along the surface and pushing tendrils of wispy smoke onto the shoreline. She swallowed the hot liquid, but it did nothing to warm the chill she was feeling.

"Mama and I are going into the city today," Tulie said, referring to New Orleans. "Aunt Margo's big party is tomorrow, and we're going to look for costumes. We're late going," she said. Brenn didn't need to know why. Rachel was only now able to go outside. She had rallied in the past few days. "Y'all can come if ya want." Tulie turned and beamed across the table at her mother, elated to have these rare moments of lucidity with her.

"I'm not getting anything special," Brenn said moodily. Tulie noticed her stepsister kept glancing out the window toward the lake.

"I'm happy for Landon and Skylar," Tulie said dreamily. "Somethin' happy would be nice. It will be a huge party," she said. "Him bein' Aunt Margo's only child and all. I think engagement parties are so romantic." She sighed and looked over at her mother. "Don't you, Mama?"

Rachel, who was having one of her better mornings, smiled at her daughter. "Romance is for the young," she said simply, a note of sadness in her voice. "I hope it lasts."

Tulie frowned. This wasn't like her Mama, who found magic and romance in everything. Even with Ryder's death, there was sometimes a glimpse of the whimsical, happy woman she had been before that horrible day.

"Yeah, Margo will do it up right," Brenn said, glancing cruelly at Rachel. "She never does anything half-heartedly. Making everybody dress up like *Gone With the Wind* is revolting, even for Margo."

Rachel thrust back her chair and carried her cup and saucer into the kitchen. Tulie looked with disappointment at her stepsister. Brenn shrugged, picked up her own cup, and followed Rachel inside.

Tulie sat watching the mist on the lake for a few minutes. It reminded her of the fog that drifted toward the house on summer evenings when she was little, as the mosquito truck rode by. The hissing sound of the spray shooting out from the side of the utility truck was followed by a pale green miasma that would float eerily through the trees and bushes. Once, she left her window open and watched with fascination as the repellent wafted through the screen into her room. She pretended it was a green, mutated creature from the lake. When Randall found out, he swatted her bottom and told her she could get sick inhaling that stuff. From then on, she watched it through the safety of the glass.

142

The shopping trip to 'Awlins' had been a disaster. It had started out well. Rachel felt a new surge of energy as she drove her Mercedes SUV along the water-flanked thoroughfare. She had not forgotten how to drive, she thought happily. The parallel parking in town had been daunting, but she managed, after several tries and myriad honking horns. It was only when she and Tulie were trying on antebellum-style dresses at Cicily's Costume House and Magdaline's Vintage Apparel that it all went downhill.

Cicily's was crowded. It was the first of October, and the Halloween enthusiasts were in full swing. Rachel and Tulie decided quickly that what they needed would not be found there. Magdaline's, however, had an abundance of antebellum-style dresses. Rachel and Tulie tried on several of the gowns. Sniggering remarks from female shoppers concerning Margo and Randal found their way outside Rachel's dressing room door.

Rachel paid for her and Tulie's dresses and a pair of shoes, and hurried from the store. Tulie insisted they stop for lunch. The gossip continued from nearby café tables, as women bent behind their menus and cast gleeful glances in Rachel's direction. It was impossible for Rachel to ignore it any longer. She had been on so few outings from her self-imposed prison at home since Ryder's death. She now realized these rumors about her husband and her sister had been circulating for some time. They cut the outing short and returned home.

Brenn heard the front door open and slam. She peered around the corner of the parlor to see Rachel, dress bag draped over one arm, hurry up the main staircase to her room. Tulie entered the house behind her, closing the front door. She frowned, shooting

Brenn a look that was easy to interpret—it had not gone well. Tulie carried her own dress bag and shoebox up the stairs. The sound of two doors closing sounded from the second floor. The silence that followed was shattered by Angela screaming from her front porch.

"Y'all get outta my yawd!" Angela Peterson yelled at a group of young boys who were hiding in her bushes out front. She had seen them from the window picking her wild strawberries and tormenting her cat, Beauregard.

The boys scattered, laughing loudly. She watched them cut through her pines and head down to the lake. *That new subdivision has ruined this lake,* she thought heatedly. *It used to be so quiet here.* She glanced with disdain to her right where a stucco wall with terra cotta tiles crowning its top circled rows of new homes, every fourth one looking the same. She could see their rooftops, all in overlapping tiles. It was meant to give off a Tuscan flair.

A small opening was in the middle of the wall, allowing the denizens of Lake Grove Estates access to the lake that once was the private property of the Broussard dynasty. More than once, some stranger would knock on Angela's door and ask to borrow her boat moored to her dock at the bottom of the shallow cliff.

"Like it was *nothing,*" Angela complained to her husband, Calvin, on numerous occasions, as she ruminated on the atrocities of the new neighbors. "Just knock on the door of a total stranger and ask to borrow someone's boat when you've never met them in your life!" She smiled in satisfaction at the memory of giving them an earful before slamming her screen door in their faces. It was their damned offspring causing most of her angst. She wondered how much time one would do in prison for setting bear traps on one's own property.

Angela stood on her porch and looked across the lake to Margo's massive, sweeping lawn. A small army of landscapers had descended upon it in preparation for her upcoming engagement party for her son Landon. Carts laden with colorful flowers sat about the edge of the property as a plethora of men knelt in the plush green grass and planted them around the perimeter. Hammering could be heard as other men atop A-frame ladders pounded long wooden poles into the ground for the string lighting and balloons.

Calvin yelled from inside the house, demanding his breakfast. The large woman sighed and swung the screen door open wide. The day's mind-numbing routine had begun.

Tulie also heard hammering echoing across the lake. She watched from the back porch, amazed at the number of people scurrying about her Aunt Margo's yard. A catering truck had pulled into the back lawn from the front driveway. A woman in a fancy linen suit was walking with her aunt along the rear of the house at the patio. She had a clipboard in one hand and was gesturing in wide sweeping movements with the other. Aunt Margo matched her movements, at which time the caterer would nod and write something down on the clipboard. They moved along, gesturing and nodding. Her aunt paused once and yelled across the yard at a man planting a border of begonias near the boat dock.

"Not there!" she screamed, her voice echoing across the lake. "I told you men, nothing pink over there. Stick to the diagram I gave you!"

Tulie watched in amusement as the worker squatted back on his haunches, hands on his knees, and stared at the harried woman. He looked down at an hour's worth of work, sighed heavily, and began uprooting bunches of flowers.

"Tulie," Rachel said, as she came out onto the porch, handing her daughter a tall glass of tea. "Have you seen Brenn? She was supposed to go into town for me, but I couldn't find her."

"I haven't seen her since coffee," Tulie said. "She's been acting even more strangely than normal lately."

Rachel grinned. Tulie was thrilled to see her Mama having more good days in a row. A light was coming back into her eyes. She had even decided to have the kitchen painted in a color she saw in a home décor magazine. Tired of the old medium brown cabinets, she chose a light sage green with white trim for their new facing. Small wrought iron leaves in forest green would be the door pulls.

Brenn was supposed to be picking up an order of kitchen towels, oven mitts, linen napkins, and placemats that Rachel had placed with Ridgetown Home Furnishings in New Orleans. They matched the new paint colors of the cabinets. New canisters in complementary greens and beiges adorned the countertops, and café curtains in sage green waited on the island counter for the completion of the paint work.

For several days before the painting, Tulie had helped her mother empty the cabinets in preparation for the painters. They tossed out expired boxes and bottles, emptied old tins, and wiped down the shelves. It felt like she had her mother back. Tulie hoped the future

146

would be brighter now.

Brenn surfaced later that morning. Tulie and Rachel were seated at the dinette table in the kitchen, working on a crossword puzzle and laughing. Brenn eyed them contemptuously. She looked disheveled and out of breath. Tulie and Rachel turned to see the girl hurry through the kitchen with a small satchel in her hand. Without a word, she walked by them and made a beeline for the stairs.

"Brenn?" Rachel called after her. "Did you pick up my order from Ridgetown?" Her only answer was Brenn's heavy tread up the stairs to her bedroom.

"What in the world?" Rachel said to Tulie. "She looks like she's been digging in the dirt."

Tulie had also noticed the stains on Brenn's pants. "Maybe Aunt Margo recruited her for lawn duty," Tulie said with a hint of amusement. Rachel laughed. "She would rather *eat* dirt than help Margo," she giggled. "Those two have butted heads from the beginning."

The remainder of the day was spent inhaling latex paint fumes from the kitchen and helping Margo. Rachel and Tulie made several trips through the pecan grove to the mansion. Truckloads of party decorations filled the driveway. The balloons and bunting would be the last thing hung up the next morning, just in case one of Louisiana's impromptu rain showers scudded across the sky that evening. October brought with it temperatures in the mid-80s and sporadic rainstorms. Hurricane season wouldn't end for another month.

Tulie loved the excitement. Rachel was trying hard to be there for her sister, but Tulie could sense the strain between the two. She admired her mother for even helping her Aunt Margo after all the rumors swirling about. It helped that other women of various ages and races thronged the large kitchen, their southern cadence like a lullaby on steroids. Suggestions on how to prepare party favors ahead of time clashed as one matriarch locked horns with another. Margo looked harried as she bounced between stations.

"Tulie!" she yelled. "Go into the parlor and arrange the presents, please. They keep arriving, and they're just stacked everywhere. I was going to put them outside tomorrow, but I don't trust the weather. It's always a crap shoot. Put them on the long buffet near the bay window, okay?"

Before Tulie could answer her, someone called for Margo from the back lawn. She disappeared out the kitchen door, sighing profusely.

Tulie walked into the massive double parlor and stopped. Towers of expensively wrapped presents covered every surface. Most were done up in foil embossed papers in elegant silvers and golds. Rivulets of ribbons streamed from bows everywhere. She started in the corner nearest her and began carrying presents to the long, lace-draped buffet tables. Beginning with the largest presents first, she began arranging them, feeling helplessly inadequate to create a pleasing display around the three large vases of flowers.

She was surprised to see Brenn enter through the French doors from the back lawn. She had cleaned up, put on fresh makeup, and curled her hair.

"Need help?" she asked, surprising Tulie even further.

"Sure," Tulie sputtered. "Some of them are really heavy," she said warningly. "I can't lift that one." She pointed to a massive gift near the fireplace.

"Looks like a TV," Brenn said, her mouth twisted to

one side. "Surprised there's not a Corvette parked outside with a giant bow."

For the next hour, the two arranged and rearranged presents. Tulie was dismayed to see Brenn shake them as if trying to guess what was inside.

"You're going to break something," Tulie finally said.

"I'm sure Mommy will get Landon a new one if something breaks," Brenn said smugly. She picked up several large greeting cards that were placed into a chiffon-draped basket. It was filled with cards that had arrived early. "Wanna guess how much money all these cards have inside?" Brenn asked, fingering her way through them. She looked up to see Tulie watching her with a look of horror.

"I'm going back," Brenn said flatly. "Have fun."

Tulie watched as Brenn paused near the giant present and thumped it. "Yep," she said, "TV!" She walked out into the afternoon sun and disappeared.

The rest of the day was filled with shouting as dozens of helpers filled the house.

"Y'all need more hangers in this closet," one woman shouted.

"No one is going to be wearing coats in this weather!" another barked.

"No, but some may wear shawls. Don't forget, this party is antebellum. Long gowns, gloves, fans, parasols, the whole nine yards. Better safe than sorry!"

Tulie's mood sank as she remembered the long gown she was expected to wear tomorrow. She felt like a sausage being stuffed into a casing when she zipped the dress meant to be worn with a corset. *But it is lovely,* she thought, picturing the soft chiffon in an effusion of shimmering blue layers. Her shoes matched and Rachel had loaned her one of her grandmother's blue sapphire broaches. Tulie wished she felt comfortable in the expensive ensemble. She would have preferred to arrive in jeans and a loose-fitting blouse.

Slamming car doors signaled the end of a long day. Worn-out women bundled themselves into their vehicles and headed home. The landscapers were the last to leave. Margo could be heard complaining to her husband Reed that one of their trucks had left tire marks on the plush lawn near the driveway.

Tulie hugged her aunt goodbye and headed home. It was 6:30, and the sun was sinking. There was a nip to the air, signaling fall had arrived. She walked through the gardens at the side of the house along crushed gravel pathways that wound in and around vignettes exploding with flowers. The large three-tiered fountain at its center gurgled as it spouted water four feet into the air.

The gardens were stunning: a profusion of color, statuary, and strategically placed wrought iron benches. Unlit torches flanked the walkway every few feet. The folly, which stood about twenty feet from the fountain, was hemmed in by manicured beds of Casa Blanca lilies: her Uncle Reed's favorite flower. She stopped a moment to admire them. This was the only place around the lake where they grew. Their orange stamen pollen dusted the white petals—*like freckles*, she thought, and smiled.

Tulie skirted the folly and followed the dirt path leading down the small slope through the pecan grove, hurrying before the dark came. The lake glistened in the fading sunlight, stained with the orange and yellow of the sunset—*like the colors of sherbet,* she said aloud. As the path turned this way and that, Tulie could glimpse the blue of the lake between thick tree trunks. The sound of pecan shells cracking beneath her feet reminded her of the time she stepped on a beetle and recoiled at the sound his broken back made. It was impossible not to step on them as they lay everywhere.

Tulie turned to her right, following the narrow trail, and felt the air change. The incessant noise from the cicadas stopped dead. Silence descended until all she heard was her own breathing. Her heart began to race. The trees seemed to move around her, closing in. The air, thick with twilight's last vestiges of dew, seemed to pause, holding its breath. A bone-numbing chill wafted toward her like an Arctic breath. Shivering, she took a few hesitant steps and screamed! Up ahead on the path, a few feet from her, stood a dark shadow in the shape of a young boy. His head, shoulders, arms, and torso were well formed, although they wavered in and out of clarity. Tulie fell back, covering her mouth to stifle the scream rising in her throat. She looked down to his feet and saw that they were floating a few inches above the hard-packed soil.

The shadow fluttered in the slight evening breeze, threatening to blow away completely. She knew it was staring at her, even though she could not make out the details of the face other than the hint of a nose. Something near the chin opened like a gaping mouth, then closed again. A Daddy Long Legs scurried from a bush onto the dirt path, then turned and scuttled back as it reached the ebony form.

"Ryder?" she squeaked. Her body was quaking, and tears were streaming down her cheeks. It felt as if ice water was running through her veins.

The dark ghost shuddered in the twilight for a few more seconds. Its shoulders and torso then turned a quarter of the way away from her, then another quarter turn until its back was to her. It began floating purposefully down the path, away from her. Tulie stood frozen. Her teeth were chattering with fear, and she worried her legs would give out. She could see the distorted shapes of the tree trunks through the black silhouette as it floated and turned along the path. It paused, and the head turned to look back at her.

"Ryder, please!" Tulie sobbed. No nightmare could compare to the terror she felt. "I'm sorry! I'm so sorry! I didn't know how to save you!"

The head turned back to face the lake, and the shadow continued in slow, fluid movements. Tulie took a shuddering breath and looked around her in hopes someone else was nearby. It was so dark inside the canopy of trees now that twilight had swallowed the sunset. The rising moon sent only a smattering of moonlight through breaks in the leafy ceiling. Finally, she began to place one foot in front of the other, stumbling over tree roots and grabbing limbs for support as she followed the shadow boy ahead of her.

The pecan grove ended abruptly; the lake came into full view. She stumbled gratefully into the moonlight. To the left was the cemetery, its marble vaults shining like bleached bones in the evening light. Beyond, the path branched off toward Tulie's home. She could see the back porch and sunroom from where she stood. The shadow did not turn toward the house. It followed the path down toward the dock. Tulie couldn't move. She could not bring herself to follow it to the water.

As she stood in the light from the rising moon, hugging her trembling body, the black form stopped at the mouth of the dock, and she watched in horror as it turned to face her. A breeze from the water blew through it, and the torso disappeared, only to shimmer back into place moments later.

"Please, Ryder...," Tulie whimpered and sank to the ground; the pebbles from the dirt path biting into her bare knees. She sat there rocking and sobbing as the shadow faced her. Finally, it turned toward the dock and floated along the tired planks, its feet like whisps of smoke softly skimming the boards. When it reached the end of the dock, the head turned once more in Tulie's direction.

By now, Tulie was sobbing hysterically. Small rocks bit into her knees, but she barely felt it.

Moonlight penetrated the black form hovering at the end of the dock. The faint sound of a ship bell rang out, rising to a crescendo as the ghost suddenly dropped over the dock's side and floated slowly across the water; a black stain marking its path. When it got to the spot where Ryder's body had surfaced, it paused and then sank quickly into the dark lake water without leaving a ripple. The shrill ringing of a bell stopped abruptly.

Tulie finally broke, screaming at the top of her lungs. Her cries echoed across the water. Lights came on at her Cousin Angela's front porch, and the lady emerged hurriedly through the door, a hand pressed to her heart. Dawson ran from the pecan grove and was at Tulie's side, his arm around her shuddering shoulders. The sound of pounding feet preceded Tulie's father's arrival, who had run through the sunroom and down to the lawn.

"What in the hell!" he yelled as he raced toward his hysterical daughter. Dawson released Tulie to him. She was still screaming and looking down toward the dock.

Dawson followed her gaze and walked the short distance toward the planks and stopped. He had heard the bell echoing across the water. Something was there, fluttering in the breeze at the end of the pier. He knew exactly what it was, even without the moonlight playing upon it like a spotlight. The King of Spades lifted slightly in the breeze, became caught on the boards, and then finally sailed off across the lake.

12 AN ENGAGEMENT WITH DEATH

Margo sat propped in bed, her back pressed into two overstuffed satin pillowcases. With a huff of exasperation, she slammed the vintage phone receiver into its cradle with a clang. She, Rachel, and Angela still had landlines due to the spotty reception their cell phones received around the lake. She looked across the room at her husband Reed, who was seated in what he called his "Dickens' chair" reading the local newspaper.

"That child should have been drowned at birth!" she said hotly.

He glanced up from the folded pages and waited, sure there was more. There was always more.

"Brenn," Margo clarified without him asking. "She has the manners of a back-alley cat! She sounded like I was bothering her by calling to ask what all the screaming was about. I asked for Rachel, but she said she was outside with Randall, trying to calm Tulie down. When I asked her what happened, she just said—

as smart ass as you please— 'It's Tulie. Do you have to ask? It's just more drama. I gotta get back to my show.' And she hung up on me! Hung up on me!" Margo slammed another pillow behind her back and reached for the martini on the nightstand next to her. After taking a sip, she calmed somewhat and stared defiantly at her husband.

"How can you be so calm with all that's going on?" she demanded. His face had disappeared again behind the raised newspaper. A deep sigh sounded from the chair. He slowly lowered the pages and laid them in his lap. There would be no more reading tonight.

"What do you want me to do?" he asked. He had tried earlier to nuzzle his wife, hoping for some long-removed intimacy. She had pushed him away when the screaming started from across the lake.

"It's that girl!" she shouted, her anger at full boil. "What in hell does Landon see in her?"

"We've moved on to Skylar, I take it," he said ruefully. "I thought we were eviscerating Brenn at the moment."

He regretted saying it as soon as he saw his wife's face go from red to purple.

"Of course, we're talking about Skylar!" she screamed. "I said Landon, didn't I? Do you know what she wants now? Now that everything has been ordered and is being prepared... as we speak... by the caterer. Collard greens! Collard greens at a lavish formal banquet! And why? Because collard greens were served at the barbecue at Twelve Oaks in *Gone with the Wind!* They'll look like soupy tree leaves in this heat! And pie! Now she wants pie!"

"What's wrong with pie?" Reed asked carefully,

feeling landmines all about him. "I like pie. A lot of people prefer pie over cake."

The daggers darted from her eyes. "The whole cake ceremony is about the *cake!* An extremely expensive, very elaborate cake that *Skylar* designed! I can't call Taylor now and ask for pies. Skylar has changed the menu eight times already. You don't do that to the premier caterer in Louisiana!"

"Get Helouise to make them," Reed said simply, eyeing the article he had been reading from the corner of his eye. "She could whip up a couple of pies in the morning in no time. Dawson could help his mom. You don't need many. Most of the guests will want the cake. Nobody makes a pie like Helouise."

"We have 250 guests coming tomorrow!" she shot back at him. "Now I have to worry about pies and collard greens! Something is always going wrong around here! I just know it's going to be a disaster!"

At that, Reed bristled. He shot her a look of defiance and in soft, measured tones—which signaled danger where Reed was concerned—he said, "Are you serious?" Margo felt his antipathy for her across the room. "We've spent...correction...*you've* spent over *$150,000* on this party, and you're going to tell me *now* you expect it to be a *disaster?*"

Margo took another long sip of the gin concoction and reconsidered her approach. When Reed got angry, it took a while to dissipate.

"It was your idea for an orchestra...not a band...an orchestra!" he continued. "We ordered enough crab claws to feed Louisiana for a month! The champagne you picked out is $200 a bottle, the landscaping set me back thousands, and we won't even talk about the catering bill! And...who in hell's idea was it to make a damn cake the size of Texas that looks like a damn swamp?"

"Skylar designed the cake. And it's not a swamp," Margo said defiantly, finally feeling the need to defend all her hard work. "It's a romantic bayou scene. It even has a full moon overlooking the cypress trees. I told her to pick a different theme, but it's not as bad as I thought it was going to be."

"It's a swamp!" Reed said, rising to his feet. "All you need is a damn gator and some water moccasins! Which, frankly, would better suit our son's fiancée's family," he snorted derisively. "If that little tart thinks she's going to move in on our fortune, she's sadly mistaken! You aren't the only one here with a sizeable inheritance that will go to *our* son."

"Why do you do that?" she shot back. "You always say '*our* son' like you're trying to make a point of it. Of course, he's '*our* son.'"

"Really? In what respect, Margo? Can you think of the last time I had a say in raising that boy? Your golden child! I told you he was not cut out for law school, but NO! You had to have a lawyer for a son to impress everyone. And what happened? Huh? He got caught cheating on the bar exam and was kicked out! You think all your diva friends don't know that? I wonder who it was that paid that law student to give Landon the exam answers ahead of time? How much did *that* cost you?"

With that, he snatched up his paper and headed toward the bedroom door. "I'll sleep in the guest room so you can sit here and ruminate about what a *disaster* tomorrow is going to be for your spoiled son and that little tramp!"

"Take that drooling mutt with you," Margo yelled.

"Come on, Hector," Reed said to the large black rottweiler. The dog jumped up from where he had been lying next to his master's chair and trotted over to him. Reed walked out, slamming the door.

Margo slumped back into her pile of expensive bed shams. Her arms were folded in anger; her chest heaving inside her peach-colored negligee.

"Bombastic bottom-feeder," she hissed aloud to the empty room. It was Broussard money that paid for the mansion and grounds, left to her by her Daddy. She'd spend it how she pleased. Reluctantly, she admitted Reed had chipped in for half the expense of the party, but that was when she told him there would be an $80,000 cap on the expenses, which had now doubled. It was bad enough having him paw at her at night; she wasn't about to let him dictate how she spent her money. She wished she had never had to see his bald, wrinkled head again.

Sighing, she grabbed up the phone receiver and carefully rotated the dial on the antique metal plate so as not to chip her expensive manicure. The final turn of the dial slid back into place. She pressed the receiver to her ear and waited for someone to answer the ringing. Finally, the call was picked up. Margo took a deep breath and forced a smile.

"Helouise? How are you?" she cooed with feigned sincerity. "I have an itty-bitty favor to ask of you. I don't suppose you have time in the morning to make a few of your famous pies for our party? The guest of honor has put in a late request for your peach pie. I know it's a terrible imposition, but it wouldn't be a party without your pies! I've been so busy, I totally forgot."

"Oh! Um...how many, Miss Margo?" Helouise asked, surprised to hear her employer's voice. It had been nearly two years since Margo deigned to acknowledge her, and that was to invite her and Dawson to a small Christmas buffet for the servants.

"I'm sure ten will do," Margo said, hurrying on. "We have this monstrous cake for the ceremony, and macarons and other small desserts. I'm so sorry for the late notice. Oh, and I do hope you got your invitation. A few were lost in the mail. I would be mortified if you were one of them."

Silence followed, and Margo hurried to fill it. "Dawson is coming to the party to help out so he could bring them if you have other plans tomorrow evening."

In a curt tone, Helouise promised to make the pies and have Dawson bring them. Before Margo could thank her, she hung up.

Margo shrugged it off. Her thoughts turned to Skylar. She realized her son had succumbed to the cliché blue-eyed blonde with a double-digit cup size. She wasn't proud of it, but no amount of cajoling had changed his mind. She even offered to up his allowance if he moved on to a pedigreed debutante. He was so adamant that Skylar was going to be his bride that Margo briefly entertained the thought that the girl might be pregnant. It took only the sight of Skylar flouncing around by the lake in a string bikini to squash that idea. She sighed. She had to accept it. Her son was going to marry a penniless bimbo, and they would raise wealthy blonde bimbo children, and she would be called Grandma Bimbo. She shuddered and drained the martini glass.

Margo finally gave way to her strung-out nerves. Imitating Skylar's nasal voice, she yelled aloud: "Make sure the invites state that no one is to wear green!" she spat out at the empty room. "I'm the only one to wear that color! I'll be the only Scarlett O'Hara at the party, and I'll be wearin' her famous green gown from the movie barbecue. Don't forget. Y'all put that on the invite!" Margo slumped, looked longingly at her empty martini glass, and thought, *Just get through the day, Margo. Just make it through the day!*

Silence descended, and Margo suddenly realized how quiet it had become. *They must have gotten Tulie under control,* she thought. *That girl is too much like my sister. Rachel has always been high-strung and given to imaginary fears.*

Without Tulie's screams, the Louisiana night closed in around Lake Broussard. One by one, lights were extinguished in the three Broussard mansions surrounding the water. Somewhere, an owl hooted and was answered by a whip-poor-will.

Margo fell asleep going over a checklist of the party preparations in her mind. It wasn't clear how long she had been sleeping when the sound of piano music penetrated through to her subconscious mind. Her eyes fluttered open, and she squinted into the darkness of her bedroom. As the soft waltz continued to echo outside her doorway, she realized she was not imagining it. Her heart faltered. She had heard it before, always at the same time. She turned and looked nervously at her bedside clock. The red digital numbers glowed. It was 2:15. The waltz music continued, lapping up against her door in waves, and then suddenly stopped.

Moments passed, and she waited for what she knew was coming next. It had been months since it happened, and she had hoped the haunting was over. Her heart hammered as she pressed both hands across her mouth. A soft tapping sounded at her door, and she froze, not breathing. Sweat puddled between her breasts and beneath her chin. "Oh God!" she breathed, in barely a whisper. Where was that idiot of a husband when she needed him, sleeping next to her? She waited. She heard a deep, prolonged sigh from the other side of the door, like one rising from a great depth. And then the sound that terrified her the most—the frantic splashing of water and tortured cries. She screamed, and everything became still.

The morning brought with it the sound of cargo trucks parking along the long driveway of the Broussard mansion. Minions from the catering company Confetti Culinary Events spread out in precision toward the backyard. Clusters of dark green and mint green balloons bobbed above the heads of the staff struggling to control the long ribbons that tethered them. Other staff members descended upon the dozens of long conference tables and round table groupings set up around the perimeter of the lawn. They deftly swooped mint-colored linen tablecloths into the air in an arc and lowered them expertly upon the tabletops, smoothing them before moving on to the next one.

The kitchen exploded with enough workers to handle a White House banquet. The noise was deafening as staff clad in starched uniforms shouted over each other while they unpacked expensive delicacies.

Margo teetered into the kitchen on wobbly heels. Her

eyes were puffy and her complexion sallow. Taylor Sinclair, the owner of Confetti Culinary Events, cornered her and began spouting off the details she had on her ubiquitous clipboard. Margo blinked, trying to concentrate. The aspirin had not yet kicked in, and she desperately wanted a cup of coffee.

"Mrs. Tillson?" a young woman with Confetti printed across her polo shirt shouted above the din. "More presents are showing up. Where do they go?"

Before Margo could answer, Reed appeared, looking smart in a pressed striped shirt and khaki slacks. "Follow me," he said, and led the girl into the hallway. Margo was surprised to see him so helpful, especially after last night. He had not even bothered to check on her when she screamed out in the wee morning hours. But then, with his hearing aids out, it didn't surprise her.

The morning continued in a blur of activity. Landon had arrived from his condominium a few hours before the party was to begin. He deposited his antebellum costume in his old bedroom upstairs and strolled around the back lawn, nodding in approval at the arrangements. His golden skin was the result of hours at a tanning salon. It set off his blond hair and blue eyes to perfection. He paid special attention to a pretty redhead wearing a Confetti uniform that showed off her figure and long, tanned legs. She giggled at his comments and blushed at his handsome looks. It was only when Landon saw his father, Reed, staring at him in disapproval that he moved on to inspect the liquor table. He made some suggestions to the bartender, arranging a glittering array of glassware and decanters. When Reed went back into the house, Landon headed for the 'ginger' and whispered something into her ear. She looked around to make sure no one had noticed and nodded, blushing. Minutes later, she disappeared into the garden and headed toward the folly.

At 5 o'clock, the guests began to arrive. The Broussard mansion was transported back two hundred years as long ball gowns with petticoats, short white gloves, fans, and parasols strolled along the manicured lawn. Guests oohed and ahhed over the display of food, strewn lights, and colorful balloons. The flower beds mimicked the different pastel shades of the antebellum gowns. Men wearing top hats and cutaway tails adjusted their collars uncomfortably and fiddled with pearl-studded cravats and ascot ties.

A 20-piece orchestra filled the air with stringed waltzes from their dais set back near the liquor table. A tower of champagne glasses balanced precariously on each other's rims as the amber liquid cascaded down over them. The ladies carefully chose their crystal glasses of Dom Pérignon, beginning at the top while their escorts saddled up to the counter to order the good stuff. Glenfiddich Grand Couronne 26-Year-Old Single Malt, at $699 a bottle, flowed over ice cubes into Waterford scotch glasses. Guests perused the plethora of food offerings, filled their plates, and made their way to round mint-colored linen tables and matching chair covers placed about the lawn. Fresh-cut roses in an assortment of colors were nestled in short vases surrounded by deep green and mint-colored glass beads.

Just as the throng found their name plates and settled into chairs, the orchestra sounded a loud fanfare. All eyes turned toward the stage and then to the French doors. Many of the women gasped as the guest of honor made her way through the open doorway to the patio and onto the lawn. Skylar paused so that all could admire her. She was wearing a replica of the gown worn in *Gone with the Wind* by Scarlett O'Hara to the Twelve Oaks barbecue party.

The flowing gown was of muslin with sprigs of mint green bouquets and ferns adorning it. The bodice was off the shoulders, surrounded in ruffles, ribbons of deep green woven throughout the eyelet. The waist was cinched in by a wide matching sash of brilliant green that tied in the back and hung from a bow down the length of the dress. In her hand, she carried Scarlett's wide-brimmed straw hat with a matching green ribbon.

Skylar only deviated from the movie icon in her choice of jewelry. Spurning Scarlett's choice of a vintage necklace, Skylar chose to wear the gift Landon had given her when he proposed. Small diamonds glittered from her three-tiered necklace with large center pendants. Along with her matching earrings, the jewels caught the sunlight, sending out shards of brilliance each time she moved. Her ample cleavage heaved from the low-cut gown, amplified by a push-up corset. A stiff whalebone crinoline and three petticoats supported the layers of fabric. Her long blonde hair hung in Scarlett O'Hara waves, ribbons of matching green catching it up in a bow. Skylar smiled coyly from behind a fluttering fan as the crowd broke out in applause.

The professional photographer scampered into place and took several photos of the beaming bride-to-be. She turned obligingly as he positioned her against a flowering hydrangea plant. Another playful pose had Skylar holding a cluster of balloons that perfectly matched her gown. Her large diamond engagement ring twinkled in the light. She flashed a smile that belonged on a toothpaste ad, soaking in the adoration of the crowd.

Angela and Calvin Peterson were at the back of the party. Calvin's wheelchair interfered with the milling guests, so he hugged the flowerbeds while Rachel and his wife kept him company. Rachel looked haggard, despite her elegant gold gown. She gazed out at the party in a haze.

Tulie stood nervously by her side, deliberately keeping her back to the lake. Only once did she look nervously toward the dock at her house. Her face was blotchy, and her nerves were strained. When a balloon popped near her, she screamed. Several people turned to look at her in surprise. She backed behind her mother, pretending to adjust Rachel's amber sash. Dawson, who was helping in the background, noticed that something was wrong with her.

"Hey Tulie-O," he said gently, as he brought her a cup of punch before returning to his duties. "You okay? I know last night was really hard. There's got to be a reasonable explanation for it. You're okay. I won't let anything happen to you." He placed a hand on her shoulder and walked back to the bar nearby to pick up more dirty glasses. He carried them into the kitchen and returned to the dessert table with another peach pie. He cut it into slices and positioned it next to a plate of pink macarons.

Landon appeared from the house, tugging on his vest. Embarrassed to be imitating Rhett Butler, he cast furtive glances at his male friends, who gave him a mock thumbs up. He was wearing a white high-notch shirt and collar, a dark blue tailcoat, and slacks. His black and white checked ascot was pinned with a large diamond broach that outshone his fiancée's necklace. He held his top hat in one hand and a diamond-studded cane in the other. The crowd cheered encouragingly. Landon bowed deeply, flashing the dazzling smile that had folded more than one young woman's knees. As if on cue, he glanced at his latest conquest, who had returned from the folly earlier that morning and was busying herself by passing hors d'oeuvres on silver platters amongst the guests. No one noticed the small orange lily stain on the redhead's hem.

The photographer posed the couple, snapping photos and following them around the party as they mingled with guests. Skylar was constantly aware of the camera's presence and posed purposefully for what were to be candid shots.

"If that's what the engagement party is like, can you imagine the wedding?" Angela hissed under her breath to Rachel. "You'd think she was posing for a spread in *Vanity Fair*. Skylar Harris is a tramp. Always was and always will be. She hasn't changed, I'll say that. She dumped our son Dennis when she set her eyes on Landon's wallet. Denny never quite got over it." She took a long swig of her champagne and continued angrily. "Skylar refused to give him back the expensive engagement ring he gave her. It belonged to my mother...his grandmother. The whole thing just devastated him," she said heatedly. "He hasn't dated anyone since. Thousand bucks says that tramp dumps Landon for a richer model within the year. Some people don't deserve to be happy when they've ruined others' chances."

Rachel glanced at her cousin, surprised at her wrath. She had not spent much time with Angela as they grew up. She met Dennis once at a family get-together. He was awkward but nice-looking. This was the first time she heard of Skylar's previous entanglements. *Angela was always bitter about something*, Rachel thought, *and the champagne isn't helping*, yet her cousin, standing next to her, looked homicidal.

Rachel turned her attention to her husband instead of the engaged couple. She watched as Randall made the rounds, often touching the female guests on their shoulder or forearm as he chatted them up. It was a gesture that could be interpreted either way as flirting or merely friendly. Randall worked it like a champ. He only made two stops to talk to Margo, which surprised Rachel. He didn't touch her, nor did he linger. Margo seemed to be watching him as closely as Rachel was, her expression bitter, until someone stopped to congratulate her on the party, at which time she broke out into full southern belle charm.

Margo wasn't the only one fluttering her fan. Skylar stood near the orchestra, surrounded by men. She giggled as she sipped her champagne, touching their arms or playing with their lapels.

"Fiddle-dee-dee," she exclaimed loudly, recreating her Scarlett O'Hara moment as a half dozen men fawned over her. "Why, I haven't even had a morsel of food yet. Who will get me a little ole' piece of peach pie?" she said loudly, fanning herself while fluttering long fake eyelashes.

One of the men dashed to the dessert table where Dawson was placing slices of pie onto dessert plates. "Peach pie!" the suitor ordered, scanning the delicacies.

Dawson slid a serving wedge under a slice of pie from a half-full ceramic pie dish and placed it on a dessert plate. The young man grabbed it and eagerly returned to Skylar's side. Several of the female guests watched Landon's reaction, relishing the drama. His anger flashed as he watched his fiancée flirting with some of the parish's wealthiest bachelors.

"Told you," one of the women whispered with delight to a cluster of middle-aged female friends. "Just look at Galveston Southgate run to get pie for that hussy. I give this marriage a month! She's either flirted with, dated, or bedded half of Orleans Parish. Landon's no angel himself, but he's got to know she picked him for his money."

The gala continued in perfect precision; the unflappable Taylor Sinclair overseeing every detail. She fluttered about, ordering her staff to refill platters or bring more liquor from the house. Margo relaxed as the day wore on without incident. Her lavender gown showed off her curves to perfection. Makeup covered the bags beneath her eyes from her ordeal the night before. Many of the female guests noticed the number of trips she made to the champagne fountain; her increased laughter matched the number of empty glasses she left behind.

It was perhaps the liquid courage alcohol imparts that caused Margo to throw caution to the wind as she draped herself around her sister's husband. Randall looked around in embarrassment and disentangled himself from her grip more than once. The number of women looking in their direction, heads bent toward each other and giggling behind their raised fans, had not escaped him. He finally pried himself away and made his way to a group of men discussing the latest golf course construction over by Lake Pontchartrain.

As the afternoon sun sank behind pines and rock outcroppings, the string lights twinkled overhead. Candles were lit on various food tables, the flickering light bouncing off cut glass platters and drinkware. Couples filled the dance floor near the orchestra, trying to imitate the waltzes of a long-ago era. The moon rose, its reflection streaming across the lake in a ribbon of pale gold.

Margo reached for another glass of champagne. She leaned with her back against the bar counter, surveying with pleasure all that she saw. It was an unbridled success. She turned to see if her son was enjoying the gala she had painstakingly constructed in his honor. She found him standing with a group of young men his age who were to be his groomsmen. Their raucous laughter split the evening—no doubt discussing the upcoming bachelor's party.

She noticed her son look off in Skylar's direction, his face coloring. Even from her spot at the bar, Margo could see the muscle jumping in Landon's jawline. She followed his gaze to where Skylar was standing alone near the entrance to the garden. Margo watched as the young woman looked down at a folded piece of paper, squinted at it, and grinned. After several minutes passed, "Miss Scarlett" suddenly headed for the path leading into the garden, stumbling in her high heels as she disappeared beneath the wrought iron arch. Moments later, Randall set his whiskey glass down, looked surreptitiously around him, and followed her into the garden.

Margo flinched. Her teeth set in anger. She knew

where he was going and what it meant. *Hadn't their clandestine meetings been held more than once in the folly?* She set her half-empty glass down on the bar and headed toward the garden path. She was stopped abruptly by Taylor Sinclair, asking about the remaining crab claws. "Should we put out more, or do you think they've finished for the evening?" she asked, holding her clipboard in readiness. Margo looked at her irritably. "Whatever you think," she said shortly and tried to move past the efficient businesswoman.

"Alright," Taylor said, and made a note. "Now…we have the engagement announcement scheduled for 8:30, so that gives us about 30 minutes to make sure everyone has enough to drink for the toast, etc. We will have the happy couple cut the cake after the announcement. I know we discussed having the guests served at their tables, but some like to choose how big a piece they want…" On and on she went as Margo grew more impatient. Her eyes stayed fixed on the garden arch through which Skylar and Randall had disappeared. She finally dispatched herself from the cloying caterer and headed for the garden. Margaret Ruthers corralled her to compliment her on the party and detained her for another ten minutes.

Rachel, who had remained on the sidelines of the party, was helping Tulie with her blue sash that repeatedly came untied throughout the evening. She felt dizzy. The colors around her swam, and she closed her eyes. When she opened them, she saw Randall walking into the garden. Several men had gone there throughout the night to smoke a cigar, and she thought nothing of it. It wasn't until several minutes later, when she saw Margo enter the garden, that her mind went to a place she had tried to avoid. All the gossip about her sister and her husband sent her stomach plummeting. Tulie thanked her mother for helping her with her sash and walked away toward her friend, Maggie Jo Benton, avoiding the partygoers as much as possible.

"Are you alright?" Angela asked Rachel, who was wobbling on her heels. "Have you eaten anything?"

Rachel stared at her cousin, trying to focus. She glanced to the left of Angela at the lake. Weaving slightly, she stared at the softly moving water. She suddenly started and grabbed Angela's arm.

"Look!" she cried out, sinking her nails painfully into Angela's soft flesh. "There's someone standing on the water, watching us!"

Angela jerked her head in the direction Rachel was pointing, trying to release her cousin's grip from her arm. "Where?" she said, scanning the dark water. Only the moonlight played upon the slowly circulating current.

Rachel squinted and leaned forward, still holding onto Angela for support. "He was right there; a dark shadow standing on the water."

Angela glanced at Calvin, who shook his head in exasperation.

"Let's get you something to eat," Angela said. She waited, reluctant to leave Rachel standing on her own. She looked around for Tulie, who was chatting with a friend near the bar.

"Tulie," Brenn said, suddenly bursting from the garden through the little-used landscaper's entrance near the potting shed. It was a mere three feet from where the bar was set up. She had been noticeably absent most of the evening. Tulie had seen her once earlier, standing near the gift table in the parlor, and again standing alone with a plate of food.

"What is with your sash?" Brenn said sarcastically. Turn around." Brenn pulled the blue satin sash tighter than she needed to. Tulie arched her back uncomfortably. She tied the bow as tightly as she could. "Maybe you should staple it," Brenn said. She walked over to one of the three bartenders and ordered a Riesling.

Dawson, who was collecting used glassware to transport to the kitchen, watched Brenn tying Tulie's sash, seemingly delighted at the distress it was causing the poor young woman. Brenn grinned at him, but he ignored her and walked away with a platter of dirty glasses and an ashtray filled with cigarette and cigar butts. She smirked and raised a glass to his departing back in a mock salute. "Who says you can't find good help?" she yelled after him, laughing.

Angela walked away to get Rachel a plate of food and Calvin another one. He sat moodily watching the party a few feet from the bar. Rachel took Angela's absence as a chance to move away as well. She stumbled across the lawn, looking about her with watchful eyes.

Waltz music filled the night as Rachel stepped into the coolness of the garden, towering elms and myrtle trees blocking the moon. Torches with flickering flames were placed strategically along the garden path. Everything looked surreal, like walking in a watercolor painting. The smell of cigar smoke hung in the air, bringing her back to her mission. Rachel prayed fervently that she would find her husband seated with a group of loud southerners puffing on their Cubans. She paused and listened to their voices, trying to pick out Randall's without venturing farther into the garden. She didn't want him to think she was spying on him.

Stacy Filler and Denise Atkins were coming toward her along the path, their heads bent together in secrecy. Denise laughed, relishing the latest gossip Stacy was imparting. Rachel pushed back into some bushes before they saw her. She stepped on something that made a crinkling sound and looked down, moving her high-heeled shoe to see what it was. A crumpled piece of paper lay there in the shadows. She retrieved it and opened it, her heart sinking as she picked out the word 'folly.' She moved from the bushes and walked to a flickering torch, holding the note up beneath the light. In Randall's unmistakable handwriting, it read:

"Meet me at the folly at 8:00."

Tulie and Maggie Jo Benton wandered into the garden as well, neither wanting to loiter around the party where they knew no one would ask them to dance. Maggie Jo had missed Tulie's birthday party and wanted to hear how it went. They made their way to the fountain and sat on its lowest rim, trailing their fingers in the water, and pushing lilies to one side as they talked. Tulie began to relax.

Two paths split off from the fountain: the folly sitting twenty feet away down the south bend. Tulie did not see her father exit the folly and follow the farthest path back to the party. Maggie Jo's mother called to her from somewhere in the garden, and the girl sighed and hurried away.

Tulie sat running her fingers through the water, the mist from the fountain periodically bathing her in its light, refreshing coolness. Suddenly, Skylar came around the bend from the folly, furiously rubbing at her long, green-colored sash that she was holding in both hands. She looked up and, seeing Tulie, pounced on her.

"Give me your sash!" she said, her southern accent pronounced in her excitement, although her speech was slurred.

"What? Why?" Tulie asked, surprised. She looked down to see a large orange stain on Skylar's sash.

"Never mind! Just give it to me. The announcement is coming up. Hurry!"

Before Tulie could stop her, the girl angrily turned Tulie around and began untying her blue sash.

"Good *lawd*, this is going to clash awfully with my gown," Skylar moaned. "What an ugly color of blue!"

She got the girl's sash untied and demanded that Tulie wrap it around her waist and tie it behind her back. Tulie did as she was told, her hands trembling.

Just as Skylar was beginning to run off, Tulie said, "I need that back! I have to return the dress tomorrow!"

"I'll meet you back here in the folly after the cake," Skylar yelled and hurried off, bumping into a statue as she staggered along the gravel path.

Tulie stood there looking dismally at the green sash. Now, what was she going to wear with her dress? She dipped the stained section of the sash into the fountain and tried rubbing it out. It only made it worse.

Tulie jumped as her Aunt Margo suddenly burst from one of the paths. She accidentally dropped the entire sash into the fountain. It sank halfway into the water before Tulie grabbed it.

"What are you doing, Tulie?" Margo blurted, recognizing Skylar's green-colored sash at once. It was the only one of that color at the party.

Tulie looked at her aunt dismally and told her what had happened. "I need that sash back," she told her aunt. "I have to return the dress tomorrow. Skylar said she'd meet me after the cake and give it back. I was just trying to get this stain out for her, but it didn't work."

Margo stared at the wet sash, her anger building. "You did a nice thing," Margo said through clenched teeth, her eyes fastened on the orange stain. "I'll get the sash back for you and I'll get this stain out for Skylar, don't you worry," she said, forcing a sympathetic tone. "Where are you supposed to meet her...after the cake?"

"In the folly," Tulie said gratefully. "Thank you, Aunt Margo. I'm sorry I got the sash all wet."

"Not to worry. You go on back. No one will notice you aren't wearing a sash."

Tulie realized sadly that her aunt's words were probably true. No one noticed Tulie Barrows.

Margo stood in the flickering torchlight, the orange glow from the flame matching the red rising in her cheeks. She clutched the sash in clenched hands, tears welling up in her eyes. She looked down again at the stained material, and a memory flooded into her mind like a dam breaking.

"You got my dress messy," she whispered to Randall years ago as they disentangled themselves from the small marble table inside the folly. He was buckling his belt and still breathing hard. He smoothed his hair.

"It will come out," he said, no longer interested in being there. "It's just from the lily stamen. You always overthink everything."

The words stung her as she buttoned the bodice of her sundress. The orange stain was a large one from where he had pressed her down onto the tabletop. Lily pollen was sprinkled about the small room like orange confectioners' sugar. She swept at the stain again, but it made it worse.

"I gotta get back," he said dismissively. "Wait ten minutes at least before you come out."

"I know the drill," she said, contempt seeping into her voice.

He kissed her on the cheek as she turned her face away from him. He laughed and crossed the room to the tiled mosaic wall on the east side of the folly. The mural was of a ship at sea, done in brilliant teals, seafoam, and blue tiles. Margo watched as he pushed on a blue tile near the ship's wheel. A small hidden door slid to the side. He disappeared into the old rum runner's tunnel, the door sliding shut behind him.

Margo stood now at the fountain, looking down at Skylar's stained sash. The orchestra music swelled, and she knew the engagement announcement was next. She stashed the stained green sash into a Rhododendron bush near an abstract statue of Zeus. She pushed it down into the leaves and exited the garden, dabbing her eyes and composing herself. Forcing a smile, she joined the guests gathering on the patio where Skylar and Landon were standing. No one seemed to notice Skylar's new blue sash. She held her oversized Scarlett O'Hara straw hat in front of her waist during the picture taking.

Margo and Reed joined the couple on the patio, standing to Landon's right. Skylar's parents also joined them, standing proudly next to their daughter. Mrs. Harris reached to push Skylar's large hat away so that the gown would be on full display for the photos.

Skylar swatted her hand.

"You're drunk," her mother hissed into her ear. "For once, can't you behave in an elegant manner?"

Skylar's face colored. She leaned away from her mother and beamed at the camera. Flashes of light exploded as the hired photographer snapped dozens of pictures, shouting out instructions.

"Look this way!" he shouted. "Good...great. Now, Mrs. Tillson, please turn just a little to your left. Perfect! Mrs. Harris, please turn to your right. There you go! Now freeze!"

After the pictures, a microphone was handed to Margo. She cleared her throat and froze as she saw Randall smiling at her from the crowd. Taking a deep breath, she beamed at the sea of faces and said, "Thank you all soooo much for joining us tonight for this incredibly special occasion. Our dear Landon has chosen..." She paused, and Landon turned to look at her. She cleared her throat again. "...has chosen this lovely young woman to share his life with, and we are too tickled to welcome her to our family."

Landon slid his arm around Skylar's waist, who was weaving. He kissed her on the cheek. His movements were stilted, but the crowd didn't seem to notice. They applauded and whistled.

"And so, to that end," Margo said loudly, "let us all raise a glass to the soon-to-be married couple. Here's to the future, Mr. and Mrs. Landon Tillson!"

"To Mr. and Mrs. Landon Tillson!" the crowd shouted, raising their glasses in the air. Meaningful glances were shot furtively between several southern belles who were not fooled by the fake devotion between the engaged couple. Several inebriated men shouted out, "Kiss her, you damn fool!" Laughter broke out as Landon bowed and pulled Skylar into a deep dip, kissing her long and hard. Hoots of appreciation filled the evening air. Skylar nearly lost her footing. She pushed him away as her straw hat fell to the floor. She grabbed her father's arm and pulled herself up. Recovering quickly, she beamed at the crowd and patted Landon's cheek before retrieving her hat and stepping carefully down from the patio.

The music resumed as the "swamp cake" was cut by the newly engaged couple, portioned into ample pieces, and passed out to the waiting guests. Several other cakes were offered in complementary frosting colors to accommodate 250 people. The older couples made their excuses and departed, longing to get out of their stiff costumes and shoes. Tulie watched Skylar surrounded by well-wishers; her nine bridesmaids gushing over her effusively.

The same male admirer from earlier pushed his way through the ladies and held out a dessert plate to Skylar with another piece of peach pie topped with whipping cream. He beamed with pleasure as the southern belle took it from him and thanked him in true Scarlett profuseness.

"Aren't you just the sweetest little ole' thing to think of me?" She gave him a quick kiss on the cheek and placed a forkful of the pie into her mouth. He walked off smiling, bumping into Brenn for a second time, who seemed to pop up where he was. She stood eating her own piece of pie. She smiled at him and was about to compliment his costume. He looked past her as if she were invisible and moved on.

Skylar downed another glass of champagne, leaning

heavily on Macy Bridgers, her Maid of Honor, as she laughed loudly.

"Be careful, or you'll spill it on that expensive dress," Macy said. She had never seen Skylar this impaired. *What would the wedding reception be like?* she wondered.

Skylar looked down at her skirt and suddenly remembered the sash. She didn't see Tulie standing in the shadows, watching her. Skylar handed her empty dessert plate to Macy and finally broke away from her friends. She made her way to the garden arch, stopping twice to gulp air. She glanced around carefully, gripping the arch for support, her other hand pressed to her forehead. Swallowing several times, Skylar finally released the arch and stumbled into the garden.

Margo saw her and tried to disentangle herself from several women who were asking about the upcoming wedding ceremony. After fifteen minutes of answering questions about the venue and menu, Margo managed to get away and walk quickly to the garden entrance.

Tulie watched her and smiled. Her aunt would fix everything.

Dawson finally had a minute as the guests sat eating their cake.

"Want me to get you some cake?" he asked Tulie, who was standing near the bar. "Where's your sash?" he asked, grinning. "Did you finally lose it?"

Tulie colored and placed her hands protectively across her waist. "No...um...I put it away so I *wouldn't* lose it. It wouldn't stay tied."

Dawson looked at her for a moment. His innocuous question seemed to agitate her. "Ok," he said. "No big deal. By the way, you look really pretty."

Just then, Margaret Ruthers and Daphne Hobart made their way over to Tulie, who stood wringing her hands and nibbling her lips nervously. She was in no mood to talk to anyone.

"Why, Tulie," Margaret oozed, "you look just lovely. Don't y'all feel just so romantic with all this antebellum atmosphere?" She flashed perfect teeth, but her eyes had moved from Tulie's down to the young woman's right hand. "And there's that lovely ring you were wearin' when you brought your teacakes for the fundraiser. Isn't that just a lovely ring, Daphne?"

Daphne Hobart had a startled expression on her face that surprised Tulie, who looked down at the ring Brenn had given her for her birthday.

"Yes," Daphne finally said, her voice strained. "It reminds me of one I used to have." She reached for Tulie's hand and lifted it, studying the ring closely. "Have you had it long?" she asked, her voice tight.

"It was a gift for my birthday a few months ago," Tulie said, feeling uncomfortable under the scrutiny. Something seemed off. Brenn was standing near the bar, watching them intently.

Margaret finally broke the awkward silence. "Well, if you find out where the ring was purchased, you just must tell us. I'm sure Daphne would love to get another one. You see, hers went missing during your Uncle Barry's lawn party that fateful day when he died. I'm sure it's just a coincidence, yours looks just like hers." She flashed her smile again, touched Daphne's elbow, and the two turned to walk back into the crowd. Daphne turned back to look at Tulie with an expression of anger.

Dawson, who had witnessed the strange interaction,

studied Tulie's face. She forced a tight smile and walked away from him. Pushing through groups of people, she looked around for her mother but couldn't see her. *Maybe she's helping in the kitchen*, she thought, and walked across the lawn to the house. She glanced back to see Dawson watching her with a worried expression on his face. She paused for a moment, scanning the crowd for any sign of her mother.

She saw Calvin sitting alone in his wheelchair by the garden bed overlooking the lake, finishing the food from the plate Angela had given him before she blended into the guests lined up for cake. Dawson took Calvin's empty plate from him and walked off toward the bar. Calvin turned his wheelchair and followed him, struggling as he propelled the wheels through the grass. He was ordering a drink from the bar when Tulie turned away.

The garden was now empty of partygoers, the stale scent of cigar smoke lingering. Flames still flickered from tall torches along the winding paths, shrouded in flowers and trees. The orchestra music wafted through the tall oaks, muffled by an occasional breeze. Besides the soft violin strains, only the sound of the fountain splashing over stone tiers could be heard. Long minutes passed.

Suddenly, a woman's muffled cry from within the folly shattered the ethereal atmosphere of the garden. It was absorbed by the fountain's splashing water. The sound of high heels scraping frantically against the flagstone floor echoed from within the tiled structure. A wrought iron chair fell onto its side, the metal clang reverberating in the small room. Moments later, all was quiet. Only the voice of Skylar's father asking over the microphone for Margo and Skylar to return to the patio for the parents' speeches broke the stillness.

As partygoers waited for Margo to join the other parents of the engaged couple, they began looking about for Skylar as well. Tulie came out from the side of the house near the driveway, still looking for Rachel. Calvin motioned Tulie over. She crossed the lawn to him.

"Have you seen Angela?" he asked her irritably. "I'm ready to go home." He mopped his sweating brow and tugged at his shirt collar. Tulie said she had not seen her for a while. She offered to go look for her and walked away.

The members of the orchestra had been accepting requests for antebellum pieces as the guests waited for the final speeches of the night. The celloist and pianist teamed up to perform a requested waltz by Adam Hurst. Melancholic strains of the "Death Waltz" filtered through the canopy of trees that sheltered the garden path. The mournful tune wafted past torch flames and lightly kissed the cold faces of marble statues before ending at the folly where it caressed the locked wooden door.

13 Missing Pieces

The west side of the mansion lay in shadows; moonlight spattered the lawn in infrequent patches. Four dark silhouettes scurried across the grass, hunched over like prowling wolves. They darted behind bushes until they made their way to the side door of the kitchen. Waltz music filled the air along with the incessant chatter of partygoers. They waited beside the door, listening for noises within.

"We're gonna get caught," Frankie Bellamont hissed. "These crazy southerners are always packin.' I ain't gettin' shot just to steal some party food."

"You bailin' now?" Tom Simons sneered. "You knew what we were doin' clear back by the crazy cat lady's house."

"I know, but…"

"Try the doorknob," C.J. Robbins said, looking around him. "Let's get this over with. I'm starvin'!"

Michael Waverly snaked a hand up to the doorknob from his crouched position near the door. The knob turned easily in his hand. He looked to the others for instructions. Tom nodded, and he pushed the door quietly open.

The four boys were looking into a back mud room, packed with empty crates for the catering glasses. Tubs of unused flowers sat along one wall, while tied bundles of trash bags filled another. They tiptoed into the room, pausing to listen for voices as they went. They finally reached the door to the kitchen and turned the handle. Peeking in, they were relieved to see it empty. A loud male voice sounded from outside, amplified by a sound system: something about 'parents' speeches.'

Tom took the lead as the boys, still hunched over, made their way to the island counter, covered with trays of hors d'oeuvres, a section of cake, small finger desserts, and a bowl with some remaining crab claws. Hunger overtook their trepidation; the four snatched handfuls of expensive fare, leaving the cake. It would be too messy to carry away.

Just then, a door opening and closing in the hallway sounded. The boys bolted from the kitchen and hid behind the catering crates in the mudroom, each holding stolen food items. "You didn't close the door," C.J. hissed, but it was too late. Margo Tillson hurried into the kitchen, breathless. In her hand was an expensive gold evening bag. She opened a cabinet door and hurriedly pushed the clutch down behind a row of cookbooks. Smoothing her hair, she scurried from the room.

The boys looked at each other, eyebrows raised. "What was that?" Michael whispered. "She hid that. That's what it looked like." "Maybe it's hers and she didn't want someone from the party taking it," C.J.

said. "Let's see if there's money in it," Tom grinned.

Before the others could stop him, Tom shoved his food into C.J.'s crowded palms and slinked into the kitchen, bent over to avoid someone seeing him from the windows overlooking the gardens. He hurriedly opened the same cabinet door and pushed the cookbooks to one side. Retrieving the purse, he scurried back with it to his friends.

The four hunched over the glittering bag as he unfastened it and looked inside. There was a small wallet, a set of car keys, and a gold necklace with a small heart dangling from it. It was engraved with the name 'Skylar.' Eagerly, Tom opened the wallet. He grinned as he plucked out a twenty-dollar bill and some singles. Beaming at his friends, he pocketed the money. Just as he was about to close the purse, he pulled out the necklace and thrust it inside his jeans pocket. C.J. looked at him with something mirroring panic. "What are you doing?"

Tom ignored him and raced back to the cabinet, burying the purse behind the cookbooks. He turned and ran through the kitchen, the mudroom, and out the side door. The other three followed him out into the darkness, disappearing amidst the tall pines and bushes at the side of the Broussard mansion.

The party was on its last legs. Many guests departed wondering why the engaged couple had not been present to bid them farewell. Not many noticed that the parents' speeches had been omitted. The orchestra music ended around 11:00. Only a few guests remained, seated in rented chairs, eyes blurry and heads lolling as they chattered on, reluctant to end the evening. The catering crew, eager to get home, hurriedly carried the last of the leftover food into the kitchen and began placing it in Margo's airtight containers. They stacked them into the refrigerator, pushing hard to force them into the limited spaces. The rest went into the large secondary refrigerator in the garage. Other members of Taylor's staff were scraping plates and rinsing out glasses, packing them into catering cartons to be taken back to the company and cleaned.

Margo slipped out of the laundry room door at the other end of the house and walked haltingly across the long lawn. She nodded curtly to the orchestra members who were chatting with the last intoxicated couple. She looked about her and disappeared down a side entrance into the garden. It was eerily quiet as she made her way to the back of the winding paths. She passed the fountain and turned to the right. Up ahead, the folly's medieval turrets glinted in the splintered moonlight. She was trembling now, her breath coming in bursts. She reached the closed wooden door where the carving of a wood nymph was centered in its middle. She pulled a bronze key from the slit pocket of her lavender gown and pushed it toward the lock with trembling fingers. She dropped it twice before she managed to find the keyhole.

Margo waited, listening for any sounds coming from the house or lawn. No one seemed to be in the garden. Only fragments of conversation from the orchestra members as they dismantled their music stands and packed away their expensive instruments floated to her on a soft evening breeze. She took a deep breath and slowly pushed the folly door open.

Fragile shards of light from the torches' dancing flames outside followed her into the folly. The overpowering smell of lilies cloaked the room in a funereal assault of the senses. A few feet ahead of her, lying crumpled in the disturbed lily pollen that coated the floor, was the body of Skylar Harris. Margo paused, chest heaving. She turned and locked the door, sinking the room into darkness. Margo pulled the small flashlight from the same pocket that held the key and pressed it on. The horrific scene before her was amplified in the focused beam of light. She feared she should have locked the door sooner, but it didn't look as if anyone had been here.

It seemed like an eternity before Margo could make her legs move toward the still form. She was careful to step only in the places on the flagstone where the pollen wasn't coating the surface to avoid leaving shoe prints. She looked down at the girl splayed out in her antebellum gown, her long blond hair falling across her face. At least she was spared Skylar's last expression. Margo stepped carefully to the mosaic wall and pressed the blue tile near the ship's wheel in the mural, the way she had seen Randall do at least a dozen times before. The small hidden door slid open, and the smell of damp earth wafted in from the dark tunnel on the other side.

She set the flashlight on the small marble table, aiming its beam out into the room. On wobbling knees, Margo bent and slipped her arms beneath Skylar's armpits, slipping her hands around the girl's torso. She noticed Tulie's blue sash was no longer there. She glanced around nervously for it, but it was not in the room. Grunting, she pulled up on the dead weight. Skylar's head fell back, exposing an angry red bruising encircling her neck. Margo shuddered and almost dropped the dead girl. Swallowing repeatedly, she began pulling the body toward the tunnel entrance.

Margo cringed as Skylar's high heels scraped across the hard flagstone floor. Reaching the tunnel, she pulled the body through the secret entrance and leaned it against the hard-packed dirt wall where rum barrels had once stood eons ago. She reentered the folly room and pushed the secret tile. The sound of the small door sliding back into place echoed through the room. Margo picked up the flashlight and walked to the folly door. She fitted the key into the lock, turned it, and extinguished the flashlight. Opening the door slowly, she peered out. She was met with silence. Her body shaking, she stumbled out into the night.

Margo hurried to the statue of Zeus and parted the leaves of the Rhododendron bush next to it. She had to retrieve Skylar's green sash she had stashed there earlier. She couldn't see it. Frantically, she pushed her hands through the branches, sharp twigs cutting into her forearms.

"Shit! Where is it?" she panted. Panic overcame her. The sash was gone.

The following morning found a household in chaos. Helium balloons in two shades of green still bobbed in the breeze in the massive back lawn. The dais was empty of instruments, but the dance floor remained. Myriad tables were still in place throughout the yard, their linens stripped from them.

Detective Hilliard and Lieutenant Adelaide Calvo were seated in gold Chiavari rental chairs near the patio. The Tillson's patio furniture was piled high with boxes of linens and other catering paraphernalia. Hilliard was working a hard caramel, clamping down on it periodically with his teeth as he looked about the stricken group before him. Margo and Reed Tillson, along with Skylar's parents, Clarese and Daniel Harris, sat hunched over in matching party chairs. Mrs. Harris was distraught, continually wiping her eyes with a sodden handkerchief. Landon was seated to one side, his head bowed, studying his shoes.

"When was the last time any of you saw Skylar?" Hilliard asked, still in disbelief that he was once again investigating a mysterious event surrounding this same family. He eyed each of them keenly, looking for any tells as to their truthfulness.

Before anyone could answer, Taylor Sinclair came around the corner from the driveway, her usual efficient manner buried beneath a haggard expression of concern.

"Sorry to interrupt," she blurted, zeroing in on Margo. "We really do need to remove the rental furniture now, and the dance floor, and the champagne fountain, and the platters, and the glassware." She nibbled her lower lip and glanced at the smart watch on her right wrist.

Margo looked at Detective Hilliard in an unspoken query. He looked around him at the remains of the party. He doubted anything of evidentiary value would be found among the folding tables and the dance floor. As he looked over at the portable bartending station, he said, "Leave the bar set, bottles, and glasses."

Taylor's breath caught. "Why?" she said, her voice an octave higher. "We have another party this evening and we need that."

"Skylar Harris is missing," he said succinctly. His blunt remark was met with sobbing from Skylar's mother. Mr. Harris shifted in his seat and shot the detective a look of contempt. "I need to have the bottles of open alcohol and all the used glasses tested. That goes for the ones brought into the kitchen last night. Nothing is to be cleaned. We don't know if she was drugged." Mrs. Harris let out a small cry and buried her face on her husband's shoulder. He placed a protective arm around her, his face red.

Taylor squared her shoulders and pressed her clipboard to her chest. "The glasses and plates were rinsed last night after the party. It's how we do things. They are in their crates in the kitchen if you want to look at them, but my people always rinse off the rental ware before it's taken back to the store and run through our commercial washer."

Hilliard sighed. Too much of the party had already been cleared away and compromised, precious evidence possibly destroyed.

"Can I take the bar setup?" Taylor pressed. "The alcohol belongs to the Tillson's. They paid for it. It was going to remain here anyway. Surely, you don't need the bar. I have enough glassware for the parties I have booked for now, but I would appreciate some cooperation on your part for the bar."

Hilliard rose and crossed the lawn to the portable bar. He studied the open spaces behind it, the small sink, the water tank with an unfastened hose, myriad containers of cherries, lime slices, peanuts, and green olives, all covered with lids.

"Take the bar," he said, "*after* my men collect the open bottles." He raised his hand toward two police officers who were searching among the bushes along the perimeter of the lawn and motioned them over. "Bag these," he said, making a sweeping gesture toward open bottles. "I need them dusted and tested when you get them back to the station. We'll be taking DNA and prints from everyone at the party, so the prints and bottle contents matter. The lab will test it all for drugs. Check the trash for the corks if any are missing. Clear?" The two officers bobbed their heads. "And I want the bar outlined on the lawn with spray paint, exactly where it is standing. Tell the photographer to get pictures of everything before they take it. Basically, get pictures of the whole damn yard!" They hurried off to retrieve their evidence gear from the back of their patrol car. One of them grabbed the sleeve of the police photographer and spoke to him, motioning toward the bar area.

"Speaking of pictures," Hilliard said, turning to face the irate caterer. "I need the name of the photographer from last night. We'll need to see the photos from the party."

Taylor sighed in exasperation. She lifted the metal clip from her board and pulled a small file folder from the back. Opening it, she plucked out a business card and stiff-armed it toward the detective. He nodded his thanks. She waited impatiently as the pictures were taken of the bar area, tables, stage, and lawn. Finally, she motioned for her own minions to begin breaking down the dance floor and tables.

"Ms. Sinclair," Hilliard said, "one question, please. You were here for the duration of the party?"

She nodded curtly and glanced at her watch.

"Did you notice anything in particular about the bride-to-be...Miss Harris? Anybody bothering her? Did she look distressed at all?"

"She looked drunk," she answered pointedly. "I had more on my mind than watching Skylar Harris."

192

"When did you last notice her?" Hilliard asked, undaunted."

Taylor paused and thought for a moment. "Well, I know she was at the cake cutting because I oversaw that. After that, I can't say. Mrs. Tillson scrubbed the parents' speeches at the last minute. Why? I don't know. We had everything orchestrated. As it was planned as the last event of the evening, it didn't derail my itinerary too much."

"How lucky you weren't inconvenienced," Hilliard said and walked back to the group of parents seated at the patio. Before he could resume his interview, the caterer thrust a final invoice into Margo's hands and walked away.

Hilliard took a moment to study the faces before him. Only Reed Tillson seemed in control. Obviously, the Harris' were worried, and the groom-to-be looked close to a breakdown, his head still bowed and bobbing.

"Ok…back to this," Hilliard said. "Before they take the chairs we're sitting on away." Calvo opened her tablet and sat ready to take notes. "Who saw Skylar last?"

"We posed for pictures after the engagement announcement," Skylar's father finally answered, after a prolonged silence from the group. "They, uh, cut the first piece of cake. I saw her talking to a few guests and then I was overwhelmed by people talking to me at the cake table. That was the last time I saw her." He pressed his lips together and looked down.

Margo felt the detective's eyes on her. Her face was flushed as she said deftly, "The same for me. I was busy all throughout the party, as you can imagine. The only time I noticed her, other than when posing for pictures, was at the cake table. What she was doing the rest of the party, I have no idea. There were a lot of people cornering me all night. It was hard to keep track."

The soft tapping sound from Calvo's fingertips as she entered the statements into the tablet was heard as silence once again descended.

"Did she seem okay?" Hilliard asked, his eyes still on Margo, but it was meant for all of them.

"Fine," Reed said. "Eating up all of the attention."

Mr. Harris shot him a hateful look. Reed Tillson seemed unfazed by the absence of his son's fiancée. Margo Tillson appeared distracted and nervous, her hands gripping each other in her lap.

"Did she look worried?" the detective asked. "Anyone bothering her at the party?"

Five people shook their heads in unison.

"I'm told her car is still here," Hilliard said. The tapping continued from Calvo's direction. "How about her keys, purse…?"

Margo shifted in her chair. It was a slight movement, but Calvo noticed it.

"We can't find her purse," Skylar's father said. "We've looked everywhere. Her keys and wallet were in it."

"If the purse is gone," Calvo interjected for the first time, "could that mean she left under her own volition? Maybe left in someone else's car?"

Mrs. Harris's head jerked in her direction. She stammered as she blurted out, "Are you saying my…my daughter ran out on her own engagement party? That's ridiculous! She was so excited for this! She s-s-pent months on dress fittings, and…and…" She broke down again, burying her face in her hands.

"I'm sorry," the lieutenant said quietly. "We must explore all the possibilities. We'll be checking her credit cards and bank statements for any new transactions to show if she is using them."

Margo shifted again. This time, Calvo faced her directly. "Is there something you'd like to add?" she asked, her tone resolute.

"The money is missing," Margo said in frustration.

"What money?" Calvo asked.

"The engagement presents money," Margo said, her voice coming stronger. "The basket for the gift cards is empty. It was full the last time I passed through the parlor. It was sitting next to the presents. A lot of relatives and close friends gave Landon...and Skylar...some pretty hefty gifts in the form of cash."

Calvo studied the woman, her eyes narrowed in concentration. "Is it usual for people to tell you what they plan on giving as gifts?" she asked evenly. "And why cash? Wouldn't gift cards or checks be a better option?"

Margo blushed. Landon shifted in his chair. "It's a tradition in the Broussard family to start newlyweds off with enough money for a down payment on a house, some nice furnishings, etc. Our family has always given cash. Checks with six digits can take time to clear a bank. The substantial amounts were from family members. Of course, we were going to help Landon with the honeymoon expenses." Landon shot her an embarrassed look. Calvo sensed there was more to the need for cash.

"Landon?" the lieutenant said, finally directing a question to the groom-to-be. "Where would the gifts of cash be deposited?" She kept the question short and waited patiently. The young man shot his mother a look of contempt. Sniffing loudly, he set his jaw and turned to face the officer defiantly, "Into my *mother's* bank account...for now. I was cut off from *my* bank account some time ago. I'm irresponsible with money, it seems," he said angrily. Margo blanched uncomfortably.

"Ah," Calvo said, finally satisfied. "That explains the cash. You couldn't hardly ask the guests to write checks out to your mother. Your secret is safe with us," she said to Landon, who flashed her a look of appreciation. He looked to his soon-to-be in-laws, however, flushed with embarrassment.

"Well," Hilliard interjected hurriedly to quell the awkward silence, "If the gifts that *were* in the form of checks are cashed, we'll know it."

Margo caught the lieutenant's bemused look that she gave the detective. She bristled and said, "It may not have escaped your notice that women in the south pride themselves on bragging about their largesse. It's not unusual at all to—shall we say—let it slip on what you spent on something."

Hilliard couldn't help but grin. He picked up the thread. "How much would you guess 'the largesse' came to, all told?" he asked pleasantly, "In cash, that is?"

"Close to $400,00," Margo said succinctly. Hilliard's look of shock seemed to please her.

"Anything else missing...besides the gift basket cards and Skylar's purse?" Calvo asked.

"Yes," came the strangled sobs from Skylar's mother. "My daughter!"

Once again, Detective Hilliard and his trusty sidekick, Lieutenant Calvo, found themselves in Rachel Barrows' parlor. The same faces looked at the twosome in various emotions ranging from contempt to weariness. Hilliard felt he was trapped in an endless Clue game where the suspects remained the same, only the weapons and motives changed.

"We'll keep this short," he said, wanting to be anywhere but here. "When was the last time y'all saw Skylar at the party last night?"

Brenn, in her usual haughty manner, said, "I saw her go into the garden sometime during the party. That's the last time I saw her."

"During what part of the party?" Hilliard asked her.

"Let me think," she said, placing a finger to her chin in mock concentration. "Hmm…it must have been just after they cut the cake. She was laughing with some bridesmaids and then headed into the garden. She looked a little…how should I say?...blitzed."

"Where were you standing when you saw her?" Hilliard asked. Calvo's ubiquitous tapping filled the air.

There was a pause before she answered. "I was…well…I was tying Tulie's sash when I saw Skylar go through the arch into the garden. And before you ask me what time, I don't know."

Hilliard noticed Tulie glance at her stepsister and look away. "Miss Tulie?" Hilliard asked kindly. "How about you? When did you last see Skylar?"

"At the cake ceremony," she said, her eyes down.

Tulie shifted uncomfortably in her chair, her face flushing. Calvo looked over at her curiously.

"Is there something else?" Calvo asked her gently.

"Did you see her after that?"

"No...not after...but before...in the garden," she said haltingly. "She...uh...came over to me at the fountain and wanted to borrow my sash."

"Your sash?" Calvo asked. "The sash to your dress? Why?"

"Hers got dirty," Tulie said. "They were going to make the engagement announcement and take more pictures, so she asked to borrow mine."

"So that was before the cake ceremony. Did you give it to her?" Calvo asked.

"Yes. She was pretty upset, and I didn't know how to say no. I told her I needed it back cuz my dress is due back today. She said she would meet me at the folly after they cut the cake and give it back." She lowered her eyes.

"Did she meet you at the folly as planned?"

"Not me. I saw Skylar go into the garden after they cut the cake, just like she said. But Aunt Margo offered to get my sash back, so *she* followed Skylar, not me."

Hilliard shot a meaningful glance at Calvo, who stopped her typing.

"Your Aunt Margo offered to get your sash back?" Hilliard asked, trying to keep his tone even. "When did she offer to do that?"

"At the fountain, right after Skylar took my sash. I showed her Skylar's sash that had some orange stain on it. I tried to wash it out in the fountain, but I made it worse. I was upset about getting my sash back, so Aunt Margo took Skylar's wet sash and said she would meet Skylar and get my sash back. She was going to try to get the stain out of Skylar's green one."

"And that was just before the engagement

announcement and cake cutting?"

Tulie nodded. "I heard them over the microphone saying the announcement was next and for everyone to fill their glasses for the toasts, so I went back to the party to watch."

Hilliard turned to Calvo. "What time was the engagement announcement?" he asked her. She flipped to a file on the tablet and said, "8:30."

"8:30," Hilliard muttered under his breath. "After the announcement, what happened?" Hilliard asked Tulie, who sat dejectedly next to her mother. Rachel had not met the detective's eyes since he arrived.

"They posed for more pictures, and then they walked over to the cake table and cut the first piece. I didn't see Skylar eat any. She was talking with other people and eating pie. She then hurried over toward the garden and went in. She looked a little drunk. Aunt Margo followed her a little while later. I was happy because Aunt Margo was helping me get my sash back."

Hilliard paused, digesting the information. He noticed Dawson shoot a furtive glance in Tulie's direction. He filed it away for now. He finally turned to Rachel.

"Did you see Skylar after the cake cutting?" he asked. It seemed to be the last time people saw the guest of honor.

Rachel pressed her lips together, her eyes darting along the patterned area rug. After several moments, she said, "I don't remember seeing her after the cake." She kept her eyes down.

Dawson was of little help. "I was kept hopping, cleaning up after people and serving food," he said ruefully. "Just the hired help. Didn't notice her. Some guy grabbed a piece of pie for her, that's all I know."

Calvo glanced over the notes she had just taken. She looked up quickly, her eyes darting to Brenn.

"Brenn," she said. "We seem to have a discrepancy here. You just said that the last time you saw Skylar was after the cake cutting when she went into the garden. When we asked you where you were when you saw her, you said you were behind Tulie, tying her sash. But that can't be right. Miss Tulie wasn't wearing her sash then. Skylar had it and was wearing it during the cake ceremony. She wore it into the garden. So, I'll ask you again. Where were you when Skylar entered the garden after the cake ceremony? The last time anyone seems to have seen her alive."

All eyes turned to Brenn, who sat rigidly in her chair, her eyes darting along the floor for an answer.

"Oh…yes…that was the other time I saw her go into the garden…I forgot. She, uh, went in just before the engagement announcements, I think. It's not like I was keeping tabs on her! It's no big deal."

"So, you saw her in the garden at the time Tulie said Skylar got her sash dirty?' Did you see or hear anything suspicious?"

Calvo could see the wheels turning in the young woman's brain as she scrambled for a lie.

"I didn't say I was in the garden," she practically snarled. "I said I saw her go *into* the garden." She pressed her lips closed and stared defiantly at the officer. Calvo noted it in her tablet and put an asterisk next to it.

After a few more perfunctory questions, such as, did any of them see Skylar with her purse that night, and receiving negative answers, Hilliard wrapped it up.

"We may have questions later," he said. He noticed Rachel breathe a sigh of relief that the interview had concluded. "Please, if you remember anything at all, even though you think it's not important, give us a call. You'd be surprised how many cases are solved on the tiniest detail. And," he added, "with this town's propensity for gossip, if you hear that anyone has seen or heard from Skylar, I'd appreciate knowing. We can keep your name out of it."

Dawson rose abruptly from his chair and walked out of the room. The sound of the screen door slamming in the sunroom heralded his departure.

Hilliard and Calvo walked out to their car. The two took their seats, Hilliard behind the wheel. He reached into his sports jacket pocket and pulled out a hard caramel and popped it into his mouth. He started the engine and then turned to the lieutenant. Her green eyes were glittering in the manner he had come to recognize.

"Yep," she said, smiling, "Margo lied."

Margo walked brusquely across her backyard. Skylar's parents had finally gone home after the police interrogation that morning. She glanced down at Rachel's house across the lake and noted the detective's car was still parked out back. Now was the perfect time for what she had to do. Party balloons still festooned the wooden poles placed about her property. *Taylor missed those*, she thought hotly, her nerves frayed. Her pulse was pounding in her ears as she looked down irately to see the yellow spray paint staining her grass in a rectangular shape where the police had marked off the bar station's position from the night before.

She turned down the short dirt pathway a few feet

from where the bar station had sat. The gardener's tool shed sat up ahead, cloistered in a stand of pine trees. She entered the small cottage-like structure, the air moist with the smell of potting soil and insecticides. A shovel hung from a pegboard against the back wall.

The gardener's path from the shed led to the far side of the folly. Her short-heeled shoes made no sound as she walked along the hard-packed dirt, following the parallel tracks she assumed were made from the gardener's cart. Forster Boreman was the only one who used this trail. Only rows of indifferent bushes flanked the little-used dirt path as she hurried toward the folly, shovel in hand.

Filtered sunlight glinted off the quartz in the stone façade as she reached the wooden door. She stopped abruptly, heart pounding. She once again fumbled with the key, unlocking it and swinging the door open. Nervously, she peered inside. It was as she had left it. Heart pounding, she walked quickly to the mosaic wall, once again stepping on the flagstone flooring where there was no pollen to receive a shoe imprint. She leaned the shovel against the wall.

Margo paused and steadied herself, her heart pounding. Finally, she pushed on the small blue tile. The door slid open, and she held her breath, lips pressed tightly together. She just wanted to get this part over with. The meager sunlight shining in from outside the folly door played a few feet inside the earthen tunnel. Margo gasped in horror. Skylar Harris' body was gone.

14 FALLING FOR EVIL

Flashlights illuminated the mosaic-tiled walls of the folly as several police officers peered in from the open doorway. Evening had fallen by the time Detective Hilliard arrived. He strolled to the doorway and looked inside at the small room about the size of a one-car garage. The air here was moist and smelled of lilies, which were everywhere in standing planters and garden beds just outside the door. The sweet fragrance was cloying in the early evening humidity. He studied the mosaic mural across the room of a three-masted schooner tossed about in seafoam and blue ocean waves. A small marble table was sitting off to the left, flanked by four wrought iron chairs, one lying on its side. There were no light fixtures, only a few large pillar candles residing in weathered bronze wall sconces, their wicks blackened.

The detective asked the officer nearest him if they had found anything. The young man looked around the room and considered his answer. Officer Palmer had made the mistake before of giving an opinion on a possible crime scene too early. It made its way into a report, and he was challenged on it later when it turned out he was dead wrong.

"Well, sir, we were instructed not to enter until you got here. I have been studying it from here, sir. There are some signs that something may have happened at the table and over there," he said, pointing toward the center of the room, "but I'll leave that to you to decipher. There on the tabletop, you'll notice what appears to be disruptions in the orange lily pollen."

"Disruptions?" Hilliard asked, suppressing a grin. It was obvious the young officer was trying to impress him.

"Yes, sir. Smears, if you like. The pollen is everywhere, and it coats most of the table, but here, in the middle, it has been disturbed. To my eye...and again, I bow to your expertise...it doesn't look like someone wiped it deliberately to clean the table. If they were doing that, they would have cleaned the entire table, not just swiped this one area."

Hilliard played his flashlight over the tabletop from his vantage point inside the doorway. It sat only four feet away. He stooped to look beneath it at the heavy wrought iron legs supporting the marble top.

"That's a good observation," he told the young man, who looked pleased at the recognition. "It does seem to coat the table except in this one spot."

Officer Palmer nodded sagely. "My thoughts exactly," he said. "And the floor beneath that same section of the table also shows signs of the pollen being disturbed. Think someone was standing there?"

"Possibly, but not in a stationary way. There's no one

shoe print. Someone was moving about." The detective stooped again but saw nothing else that was helpful concerning the table.

"There's more," Officer Palmer said proudly, emboldened by the detective's approval of his first discovery. "There are scrape marks on the floor over there, and again, the pollen is all messed up. In fact, this whole area looks like a scuffle went on."

Stepping carefully to avoid the pollen dust, the detective made his way to the center of the room. Hilliard's eyebrows lifted in anticipation as he bent to study the floor near the wall with the mosaic mural.

"Yesss...," he muttered. "It certainly does. These scrapes are interesting." He followed one set of the deep scratches with his eyes until he saw them stop at the wall just beneath the image of the sailing ship. "That's odd," he said. "The marks are side by side, like..."

"Someone was dragged," Palmer interjected excitedly. "Someone in heels!"

Hilliard turned to eye him, a thin grin tugging at his moustache. "Oh?" he asked, "Do tell."

Officer Plamer missed the sarcasm in the detective's voice. "Regular shoes wouldn't leave marks like that," he said excitedly, playing his flashlight over the trail of gouges. "Plus, these marks are fresh. The stone looks newly scratched: it hasn't weathered yet, and there's no pollen in the grooves. My guess is these flowers are constantly shedding all this orange stuff, and if the door is open and a breeze comes through here, it's probably worse." He paused and looked at Hilliard for approval.

The detective focused his flashlight on the marks on the uneven flagstone floor. They did appear fresh and could be made by sharp shoe heels, or some other explanation might present itself.

Jonas Polk, the police photographer, arrived, and Hilliard stepped back to the left of the doorway to let him do his job. Bright explosions of light lit up the room in stark relief as the photographer began from the doorway and then slowly stepped inside in protective footwear, trying to avoid stepping in the places where the pollen showed signs of being disturbed. Hilliard watched with interest. Something caught his attention.

"Polk," he said, "don't step there! What is that?" he asked, pointing his flashlight at the large section of flagstone where most of the pollen was missing. Polk squatted, placed a scale next to the spot, and shot several photos of the area Hilliard was interested in. "Hard to say," he said. "Could be a small portion of a rubber sole imprint. It's pretty narrow, though, and there's not much of it."

Once the photographer had thoroughly covered the room, Hilliard walked to the wall and ran a hand over the tiled artwork there. He looked down again at the parallel markings on the floor. Had someone dragged someone to the wall and propped them up there? *That doesn't work*, he thought. *The marks go all the way to the wall and stop. They would have stopped a few feet away from the wall if someone were dragged here and then propped up on their butt. He looked back toward the open door. It was clear that multiple people had been in and out of the folly. Most of the pollen near the door and in the middle of the room was gone.*

Palmer watched the detective working things out in his mind. Hilliard looked at the markings on the floor and ran a hand over the tiled wall again. "It looked like this when you first got here?" he asked the young officer.

"Yessir," Palmer said, nodding. "The minute I saw how easy it was to disturb this pollen, I made sure no one went in till you got here."

"Polk!" Hilliard yelled to the photographer who was exiting the room. "Get some of that wall," Hilliard said, gesturing to the ship mural. "And of the fountain area outside, all the pathways, etc."

The detective walked out into the evening as clouds scudded across the moon. The garden took on a menacing feeling without the lunar glow. Bobbing orbs of light from myriad flashlights looked like ghosts playing among the shrubbery as half a dozen police officers pushed their way through manicured bushes. Only the gurgling, splashing sound of the fountain broke the stillness. Hilliard played his own flashlight along the gravel path leading to the folly. It had been disturbed by too many shoes. There was no way to know how many partygoers had gone into the folly.

Lieutenant Adelaide Calvo arrived, a telltale spot of white fettuccine sauce on her lapel, telegraphing her reason for being late.

"Lobster or shrimp?" Hilliard asked, grinning.

Calvo looked surprised and said, "Excuse me?"

"Fettuccine," he smirked. "I'm a lobster guy, myself." He pointed to the glob of white sauce on her lapel. She self-consciously wiped it away with her hand, leaving a small white stain on her dark blue uniform.

"Anything?" she asked, looking down at the shirt stain dismally.

"Some marks on the floor in the folly," he answered.

"Possible scuffle there. One of the chairs is knocked over. There is this orange lily pollen everywhere in there, and some of that looks like something disturbed it...disrupted it," he said, smiling. Calvo missed the joke. "Could be important, don't know yet. Question is, where is Skylar Harris?"

Rachel watched the orbs of light play about Margo's property from her bedroom window. Her heart was hammering as she thought about the events of the previous evening. The note with Randall's handwriting was hidden inside a harlequin doll's right vest pocket where it sat grinning out into the room from its place on the dresser. She pulled it from its hiding place and looked at it, tears streaming down her face.

"Meet me at the folly at 8:00."

The words were burned into her brain. How could her sister do this to her? And the stained sash, she watched Margo shove into the bushes not far from where she had been hiding when she followed Randall into the garden.

Rachel had known about his other dalliances after Ryder's death. She had tried to rationalize them away. After all, she had disappeared into a dark abyss fueled by sedatives and alcohol. For months at a time, she would barely leave her room, the heavy draperies drawn, and the phone removed from its cradle. Randall had finally abandoned their bed in resignation, taking over the guest room.

Tulie had taken on the responsibility for her care: bringing her meals on a tray that she forced fed to her. Rachel's biggest guilt was knowing Tulie's own pain and grief at losing her twin brother had been pushed to one side as she battled to save her mother from destroying herself.

It was almost 9:30 p.m. when the police officers wrapped up their investigation at the gardens and folly across the lake from where Rachel watched. Their car lights disappeared through the pines lining Margo's driveway. Rachel's breathing escalated as she contemplated her next move. She couldn't bear not knowing. She'd had enough pain to last her a lifetime. She would confront her sister.

Tulie sat on the edge of her bed, rocking softly, her anxiety finally abating. The bus ride to New Orleans earlier took longer than she thought. By the time the detectives left, she had only two hours before the store would close. The bus picked her up at Wing's Bend. The driver took the two large dress bags from her and placed them into the bus's luggage compartment. She sat in the musty-smelling seat and watched with agitation as the bus squealed to a stop to take on new passengers every few minutes.

Finally arriving at the bustling city, Tulie retrieved the dress bags and carried them into the costume store with the name Magdaline's Vintage Apparel emblazoned across the bay window outside. She waited as the haughty woman behind the counter took her time checking Tulie and Rachel's dresses for any stains or defects. Tulie held her breath as the woman held up the blue sash that was neatly folded atop Tulie's dress. It was creased in several areas, but it was expected from a sash that was made to tie into a bow at the back of the gown. The clerk studied it, replaced it, and nodded.

"Fine," she said succinctly. "We'll all settled here.

Your deposit went toward the rental charge. The balance will be charged to the card on file. Have a nice day." With that, she scooped up the two dresses and disappeared through a door into the back of the store.

The bus ride home went a little faster. Fewer people boarded as they headed away from the city. Tulie had spent the time watching store windows filled with Halloween décor. A smattering of houses they passed showed toothless jack-o-lanterns grinning eerily from doorsteps. A sheet fluttered from a tree branch near her window, its eyes drawn on with marker.

By the time Tulie walked the short distance home from Wing's Bend, she was feeling better. It was over. She sat now in her room filled with the familiar darkness, bringing with it a sense of peace. No one would bother her now.

Brenn was seated in the dark sunroom, watching the police officers scurry about Margo's property like rats trying to find their way out of a maze. She sipped her iced tea languidly as she maneuvered the pieces of the puzzle together in her mind.

She knew several things about what happened at the party, including her Aunt Margo taking Skylar's purse from the closet during the confusion over the parents' speeches. Brenn had seen her reach up and take it down from the top shelf of the coat closet, where several other ladies' purses were deposited for the evening. Brenn had barely had time to hide behind a towering fern in the hallway. One minute sooner, and her dear Auntie would have seen her. It gave Brenn time to rethink her mission. As tempting as it was to have all those rich ladies' purses sitting there for the taking, Brenn decided she couldn't risk it.

So why did Margo take Skylar's purse? She pushed the question around in her mind, waiting for it to land into a recognizable slot. *Did that mean Margo knew Skylar wouldn't be needing it any longer?* The thought sent a delightful shiver down her spine. *Did Margo know Skylar wasn't coming back?*

Something moved near the cemetery, and Brenn froze, her heart racing. A shadow moved among the tombstones. Brenn held her breath, the tall glass of tea poised in mid-air. The figure moved off onto the path that headed through the pecan grove toward Margo's house. When it stepped into a swath of moonlight, Brenn felt relieved. It was Rachel. *What was she doing? She was usually asleep by 10:00.* Brenn set the glass down quietly and slipped noiselessly out the screen door.

Only a few lights were on at Margo's mansion when Brenn exited the garden. She had followed Rachel through the pecans, trying desperately not to step on the noisy shells. Rachel went up the narrow trail along the cliff that came out near the folly. Keeping to the shadows, Brenn walked several feet behind the darting form of her stepmother as Rachel picked her way along the dark garden path. She waited and watched as Rachel walked across the sweeping lawn and onto the patio. She looked around her and then let herself in through the unlocked French doors.

Brenn crept to the patio and tiptoed across the flagstone, keeping in the shadows beneath the overhang. Pressing her back into the wall of the house, she peered slowly around the edge of the French doors and looked inside. The parlor was dark. She could make out the table of engagement presents sitting in the shadows, still waiting for Skylar's return or some decision to be made about what to do with them.

Voices came from the back of the house, but she couldn't make out the words. She recognized them as belonging to Rachel and Margo. They sounded angry. Brenn moved from the patio to the side of the house where the voices were coming from. She crept to the bushes outside the large window of the music room and peered inside. She just caught the backs of Rachel and Margo exiting the room. Sighing, she squatted in the bushes and tried to imagine where they might be going. Minutes passed, and a pool of light suddenly fell in a square upon the lawn in front of her. She looked up to see Margo's bedroom light through the open curtains.

Within minutes of the light coming on, the raised voices of the two women made their way down to her. She could make out only a few of the words, but it was a heated argument, of that, she was sure.

Rachel stood quivering with rage as she faced her older sister. Their argument had moved upstairs to avoid the prying ears and eyes of the small wait staff Margo employed. Only a few maids remained cleaning up what was left of the engagement party the day before. They were still finding catering glasses and cigarette butts throughout the first floor.

"Are you seriously going to deny that you are having an affair with Randall?" Rachel spat, swaying slightly. She grabbed the upright poster of Margo's massive canopy bed to steady herself. "This is his handwriting!" Rachel continued as she reached into her pocket and retrieved the crumpled note she had picked up in the garden bed the night before. "The whole town knows about you two. Only I was stupid enough to ignore it!" Tears were streaming down her face as she shook with rage. The room tilted on its side, and she clutched the bedpost.

Margo took the note from her sister and read it. Her face crumpled in anger. Rachel misunderstood her reaction.

"You have no right to be angry with *me*," Rachel screamed. "I saw you follow him into the garden. I found that note. I also found this!" With that, she dramatically pulled the stained green sash from her side pocket. It was creased and dirty, and the water damage from the fountain was clear. The lily stain was the size of a fist now and had faded to a dull sienna brown.

Margo's face went ashen. "Where did you get that?"

A look of satisfaction flashed across Rachel's face. She had finally gotten the reaction from her sister she was hoping for.

"Where you stashed it in the garden!" she spat. "Couldn't get dressed fast enough after my husband got through with you?" She was crying again, near hysterics

"You idiot!" Margo cried; her eyes fixed on the green sash. "That isn't mine! If you weren't so hopped up on booze and pills, you would know I was wearing lavender last night! And! I never saw this note!" Her hand was trembling as she held the creased piece of paper before her sister's face.

Rachel paused for a moment, her blunted mind trying to retrieve an image of her sister's dress the previous night.

"I hate to burst this hate bubble you have for me, dear sister," Margo said angrily, "but that sash belongs to Skylar's dress, not mine. *She* was wearing green and was in the folly with your *loyal* husband, not me. That stain on it is from the lilies in there. And now, she's missing!" She paused, watching Rachel's face.

Taking advantage of Rachel's momentary distractedness, Margo lunged at her and grabbed the sash from her hands. The sudden movement caused Rachel to fall forward, grabbing onto a tea cart to break her fall.

"How about I just give this to the police?" Margo said, her face almost feral. "It probably has Randall's DNA all over it. And yours! What happened? Did he kill that girl? Or maybe you both did."

Rachel lunged at her, screaming, "*You* had it! Your DNA is on it as well! You came out of the folly and hid it! What did *you* do to her?"

Rachel grabbed one end of the long sash. The two women wrestled over it. Rachel wrapped it around her right wrist as she tried to gain an advantage. In a burst of anger, Rachel shoved her sister. Margo screamed as she fell against the tea cart, toppling it. The vintage Victorian rotary phone and an expensive statuette of a shepherdess crashed to the floor. The statue shattered.

In a burst of rage, Margo lunged at her sister. She shoved her with both hands, her face suffused with hatred. Rachel cried out and fell backward, still holding onto one end of the sash. It was pulled tightly between the two women as each struggled to take it. Margo suddenly released her hold on the sash, causing Rachel to plummet backwards. She hit the window behind her, followed by a loud cracking noise. She snatched frantically at the drapery nearest her as the sound of breaking glass filled the room. The window shattered, and the steamy night air rushed in.

"Help me!" she screamed as she felt the heavy velvet drapery tear away from the curtain rings. She was halfway out the window, shards of broken glass cutting into the backs of her thighs. The sound of the final threads of the drapery tearing filled the momentary silence as Rachel clung to it, her eyes wide with terror. The final curtain ring suddenly broke loose. Margo watched in horror as her sister fell out into the darkness, one hand still clutching the heavy drapery.

Rachel's body crashed through a large impatiens plant and landed partially on the lawn. Her lower torso lay atop the flowering bush, which buckled and broke beneath her weight. The burgundy drapery fluttered down over her.

Brenn covered her mouth to suppress a scream as she squatted inside the bush mere inches from where Rachel's body landed. She heard the sickening crack as her stepmother's neck broke. The cicada's hissing stopped abruptly. Everything seemed to freeze.

The block of light on the grass from the window above suddenly filled with the silhouette of Margo's head as she appeared, looking down at the broken form of her sister. Small glass shards fell into the bushes; one just missed Brenn's head. She held her breath, hoping her aunt could not see her in the shadows. When Margo pulled back inside, Brenn made a run for it. She darted across the dark lawn and hid behind a row of foxgloves, waiting to see what would happen next.

15 A WATERY GRAVE

Moonlight lay in patches about the side yard, like a giant distorted chessboard. Towering pines, live oaks, and elm trees impeded its path. Brenn crawled crablike to a hydrangea bush, the sickly-sweet smell of a honeysuckle vine overhead making her dizzy. She could see Rachel's twisted form across the lawn. She had not moved.

Margo suddenly appeared at the corner of the house. She paused, gripping the siding as she peered into the moonlight-speckled side yard. Stepping slowly, she approached her sister, looking continually about her for any signs of prying eyes. Brenn sat still, her knees burning from maintaining the same squatted position.

Margo halted as she reached her sister's body. Rachel's lifeless eyes stared up at her. Her head was tilted to one side, lying at an unnatural angle, her long black hair pooling around her like a dark bloodstain. Margo's body was shaking uncontrollably. She bent over and reached trembling arms toward her sister, only to recoil and pull back. Brenn could hear her sobbing, and for a brief moment, felt pity for her.

Someone laughed from within the house, and Margo pulled back into the shadows of the eaves. Two of the maids passed by the parlor window, only inches from where Margo was flattened against the house. Her heart was pounding. She looked down at Rachel's broken body, the burgundy bedroom curtain still tangled about her. *If the women looked out the window…*

The whir of a vacuum coming to life caused both Brenn and Margo to jump. The sound was at the back of the parlor. Margo knew she had to move now. Glancing continually at the parlor window, she knelt beside the still form and lifted Rachel's shoulders. Her head fell back in such a way that Brenn knew her neck was broken. Margo gasped and dropped her back onto the lawn. She wrung her hands and bent over in anguish. Brenn could hear her heavy breathing and muffled "Oh my God, oh my God," in choked bursts.

The sound of the vacuum from inside the parlor stopped. Moments later, it resumed farther away, coming from the vicinity of the main foyer. Margo breathed a sigh of relief. Something glinted in the moonlight to her right. A long metal landscaper's cart sat at the end of the house, still laden with leftover potted flowers from the party's plantings. Margo stared at it for a moment and looked down at Rachel. With sudden resolution, she walked quickly to the cart and began removing the small containers of flowering plants, placing them on the lawn. Yanking on the long handle of the flatbed cart, she pulled it over to her sister. The curtain from her bedroom window lay half-covering Rachel's torso. She rolled her sister up into it. Her body was quaking as she pushed her damp hair from her face.

A sharp crack came from within the trees bordering the lawn. Margo froze, as did Brenn. Chest heaving, Margo waited. The sound was not repeated. It spurred her into a flurry of activity. *Someone could come along at any time,* she worried. Grabbing the end of the thick velvet curtain that encased Rachel's head, she lifted it onto the cart. Panting from the exertion, she then swung the rest of the bundle up onto the flatbed.

Brenn's knees were on fire. She could no longer stay in the same position. As slowly as she could, she shifted to the left and stretched out first one leg and then the other, keeping behind the thick row of flowering bushes. Margo glanced suddenly in her direction, eyes darting frantically along the foliage. Brenn held her breath. After several uneventful seconds, Margo took a deep breath and turned back hurriedly to her task. She began placing a few of the potted plants back onto the cart surrounding Rachel's body.

Margo took hold of the cart handle and began to pull it across the grass toward the back patio area and the lawn overlooking the lake. She cringed as the metal wheels emitted a sharp creaking sound beneath the weight of the grizzly cargo. The grass made it hard going. The thick, sodden air bore down upon her, and she struggled to breathe. Despite the calendar showing October, the air was still sticky with humidity.

Light was coming from the kitchen windows near the garden. She laid the handle down and tiptoed to the window closest to her. Slowly, she rose up on her toes and peered in. The room was empty.

Margo grabbed up the handle and strained to pull it along toward the garden path, just a few more feet away. Once, she thought she heard someone behind her and whirled to face an empty yard. Brenn ducked just in time behind a thick tree trunk at the edge of the lawn.

Moments passed. Margo's eyes darted about the yard. Brenn pressed herself against the biting bark and held her breath. Something rubbed up against her bare legs, and she jumped. She looked down to see Reed's dog Hector sniffing her shoes. Heart pounding, Brenn reached down slowly to pet the large rottweiler's head. The dog licked her hand. Margo turned back to the cart and continued on toward the garden arch. The dog spotted her and growled. He sprang from behind the tree, leaping toward the woman, barking furiously.

Margo dropped the handle of the cart. Her eyes flew to the kitchen windows closest to her. Hector reached her, hackles raised. "Shut up, you dumb mutt!" she hissed, stooping to allow the dog to smell her hand. Hector stopped barking and began licking the proffered fingers, his tail wagging. The dog then moved to the bundle on the cart and began sniffing the curtain wrapping Rachel's body. Margo panicked and grabbed the big dog's collar, pulling him away. Hector growled at her, straining to return to the cart. Suddenly, Reed's voice sounded from around the corner of the house, coming from the driveway.

"Come here, Hector!" he yelled. Margo darted into the shadows of the nearby trees and waited, praying her husband would not come around the house. "Hector!" Reed called, his voice sounding closer. The dog hesitated and then bounded off toward his master's voice as Margo felt her knees buckling. She bent over, catching her breath. She waited, and after making sure Reed and the dog were gone, grabbed the handle of the cart with a burst of determination. Groaning from the exertion, Margo continued, pulling the cart until she and her load disappeared beneath the arch at the mouth of the garden.

Brenn waited a few minutes and then followed. She could hear the squeaking of the cart's wheels up ahead and an occasional expletive from Margo as she tried to navigate the heavy load along the curving gravel paths of the garden. Finally, the squeaking stopped. Brenn waited and listened. An echo came from the folly, and she realized Margo had taken the cart inside. A grin crossed Brenn's face. She knew exactly what Margo had planned.

Rather than go to the folly, Brenn turned to a short path that took one to the cliffside overlooking the lake and the shoreline below. It was a short drop—maybe 40 feet. It was jagged rock, however, and no one ever tried to get down to the water from here. They always followed the path past the folly and down the trail through the pecan grove. Unless…

Fifteen minutes passed, and Brenn wondered what Margo was doing. She kept her eyes fixed on a cluster of bramble bushes near the shoreline below. The moonlight bathed the water like a searchlight. The sloshing sound of small waves lapping the shoreline was hypnotic, making time seem like it had slowed. Brenn fidgeted with impatience. One of the bushes below suddenly moved, pushed aside by unseen hands. Margo emerged from the opening, looked carefully around her, and then turned her back to the lake. Heaving, she pulled the cart toward the water, using both hands as she walked backward.

Brenn knelt behind an outcropping of rocks near the cliffside and watched her. Margo's fancy shoes sank into the mud as she struggled with the cart through the wet ground. She stopped twice to catch her breath, looking over toward Rachel's and Angela's houses. There were no lights on at Angela's, and only Tulie's bedroom lamp showed through her window.

Gathering all her strength, Margo grabbed the handle and yanked it hard. The wheels squealed beneath the weight. With one final tug, the front wheels of the cart sank into the lapping water of the lake. Quickly, she grabbed the potted plants and set them in the mud. She grabbed one end of the drapery and pulled it toward her. It slid a few feet until one end dropped over the edge of the cart, the burgundy velvet material dipping into the small waves.

Margo hurried around to the other end, encasing Rachel's shoulders and head. For the second time—and with two different women—she put her arms beneath a dead body and lifted. She stood Rachel's body upright as it slumped over her left shoulder. With an audible grunt, Margo shoved the bundle over. It went headfirst into the lake and lay there in the shallow water, rolling slightly with the waves' motion. With her breathing coming in jagged spurts, Margo grabbed one end of the drapery where it was wrapped around her sister's body and pulled.

Brenn watched in horror as her aunt tugged on the curtain, and Rachel's body began rolling out of it into the water. With a final hard yank, the curtain came free, and Rachel began to sink into the lake. Margo pulled the drapery toward her to keep it from sinking as well, bundling it together, its wet, soggy fabric impeding her progress.

Suddenly, she cried out. Rachel had all but

disappeared beneath the soft waves, now several feet away from shore. Her right arm bobbed momentarily above the surface as her body rolled over beneath her weight. Still wrapped around her wrist was Skylar's green sash, trailing along the water like seaweed. Rachel's arm finally sank beneath the surface. Margo watched in horror as the last piece of green fabric sank from view.

She stood panting, her body frozen in a surreal time warp. Nothing felt real. Then, from the corner of her eye, she saw movement from Rachel's dock. Heart pounding, she whipped her head in that direction. Margo screamed and immediately clapped a hand to her mouth. She stumbled back, almost falling as her shoes sank into the thick mud. She stared in disbelief at the dock. Floating a few inches above the pier was the wavering black shadow of a small boy.

She felt him staring at her, sure that the two black hollows were eyes. Margo's eyes bulged with horror as she watched the black ghost in front of her. *It had to be a ghost*, her fractured mind screamed. *She could see through it.* It faced her for a few moments, then turned, and glided silently a few feet toward the dock's entrance. She felt bile rising in her throat as she fought the urge to scream again. It was coming ashore!

Suddenly, Angela's dog Chester appeared at the side of the lake near the dock. He let out a long growl, his hackles raised as he stood frozen, watching the black form.

"Chester! Get your butt over here!" Angela screamed from her porch, somewhere behind the stand of pine trees. Chester paused, let out another guttural sound, turned, and sprinted back home.

The dark silhouette stopped its movement. It wavered for a moment before turning to stare over to where Margo stood, frozen with fear. It looked out at the spot where Rachel's body had disappeared beneath the surface. Long minutes passed. Finally, it grew dimmer, splintered into wisps, and disappeared. Margo collapsed onto the cart.

Brenn saw it all from her hiding place atop the cliff. The horror of watching Rachel sink into the lake was eclipsed by the shadow of the boy she had just seen on the dock. She shivered in the moonlight, panic pounding inside her ribcage. *This isn't happening*, she thought wildly. *None of this is happening! Ghosts weren't real. Her stepmother hadn't just sunk into the lake!*

But she had seen the ghost. It was Ryder. She was positive. Who else could it be? The séance with the ship bell ringing...the writing on the blackboard. The playing card passed beneath her door. He had come back! If it was Ryder, he had just watched his mother's dead body sink from view, just as he had.

The night fractured into several realms of impossibilities as Brenn grappled with the panic. Rachel was dead and now buried in the depths of the lake. She had seen the sash wrapped around her stepmother's wrist, slowly sinking into the water. She knew what it was and who had worn it last night at the engagement party.

Brenn's mind shattered into myriad nightmares, her body quaking. *Why did Rachel have Skylar's sash? Rachel had gone to Margo's tonight to confront her about something. And rather than call emergency when her sister fell from the window, which appeared to be*

*an accident from where Brenn was watching, Margo
had just buried her beneath the water. Why?*

Brenn finally broke and ran from the rocks, hunched
over in the shadows. Once, she heard the creaking
cartwheels from the lake below and assumed Margo
was pulling the cart back towards home through the old
rum runners' tunnel. She passed the folly and picked her
way along the path through the pecan grove, jumping at
every noise. A screech owl screamed, and she cried out.
It burst from a tree overhead and flew off into the
darkness.

Tulie heard a scream coming from the direction of the
lake. She gripped the bedspread of her tester bed, heart
pounding, and looked toward her bedroom window and
the darkness beyond. Her small table light only made
the night outside harder to see. She shivered and
waited. After a few minutes, the cicadas picked up their
interrupted song, filling the southern night with their
incessant buzzing. Still, she sat there, paralyzed with
fear. Tulie tried to swallow, but no saliva came.

She finally lifted herself from the bed and walked
trancelike toward the window overlooking the lake,
pecan grove, cemetery, and her Aunt Margo's house on
the cliffside. *From which of those did the scream come
from?* Ryder's old tire swing swayed in the wind that
was picking up outside. Its knotted rope creaked against
the rough bark of the giant elm it was tied to outside her
window. She couldn't see the dock from her window,
for which she was grateful.

Nothing seemed out of place as she peered cautiously
out, seeing her own frightened reflection in the
lamplight striking the dark glass. The moonlight lit up

the area around the lake, bathing it in a golden glow. The pecan grove sat in darkness, pushed farther back from the water's edge, and sheltered by the cliffside to its right. Tulie noticed movement above the cliff and raised her eyes to her aunt's back lawn. The helium balloons were still bouncing in the breeze, tethered to ribbons.

Gusts of wind suddenly scudded across the water and whipped the balloons into a frenzy. They pulled on their bright green ribbons and pressed against pine trees. The sound of popping latex could be heard. A few that were still inflated escaped and rose into the air, the wind sending them off over the treetops.

Tulie watched in fascination as one of the balloons dropped over the cliffside and toward the lake. It rose and fell in the gusts, its long ribbon catching on the water. It would rise again, but a shorter distance as the ribbon became saturated and submerged a little more each time, pulling the mint-colored balloon down. Finally, it succumbed and lay on the surface where it floated, a captive of the waves being pushed toward the shore. Tulie shivered as she watched the balloon, its wet surface glistening in the moonlight, come ever closer to their dock below. It moved as if it had a life of its own, determined to make it to shore. The green ribbon trailed behind it, and Tulie recoiled as Skylar's sash flashed into her mind. A sash she held in her hands, belonging to a woman who disappeared from her own engagement party. She let out a muffled cry and yanked the curtains closed.

The following morning, Forster Boreman dropped down from his 1988 Ford truck, crumpled his

Styrofoam coffee cup, and tossed it onto the floorboard. He slammed the truck's creaking door and walked from the Broussard driveway to the side yard. He had been the mansion's landscaper and gardener for two decades. He refused to call it the Tillsons' house after poor Mr. Barry died in the waterskiing accident. To him, it would always be the Broussard mansion. He butted heads with Margo Tillson almost daily. He'd lost track of how many times the woman asked for plantings where they had no business being. He rounded the corner of the house to the side yard.

Forster paused and looked at his cart sitting near the window, steps away from him. He had left it near the patio. The small pots of plants resting upon it were a mess, some with broken heads, and there was mud all over the containers. He scratched his head. Forster reached for the handle and found it caked with mud, as were the wheels. "What in the world?" he said aloud. "That damn party planner," he groused. *She had been moving his things around for several days as she micromanaged the arrangements for the engagement party,* he thought angrily.

Shaking his head, he sighed and walked over to the hose curled onto its holder attached to the house near the patio. He turned on a hard spray and began cleaning the handle and wheels. He gave the damaged flowers a drink of water and turned off the hose. Just as he was about to take the cart to the garden, he paused. There were small pieces of glass lying in the grass and flowerbed. He looked up and saw a few shards still embedded in an empty window frame above him in a room upstairs.

Forster stooped to pick up the glass pieces before

someone could step on them. He laid them on the cart and stopped, mouth gaping. "What in tarnation?" he said, placing both hands on his hips. There, beneath the window with the broken glass, was a celosia bush nestled in freshly dug up dirt mounds. The tall, orange, magenta, and gold flowered plant had not been there before.

"What happened to the impatiens I had here?" he said aloud. He leaned over the plant and lifted its bottom leaves to study the ground beneath it. It was clear someone had recently planted the bush.

"This is all wrong!" he said hotly. "This doesn't belong here! It needs full sun!"

He stood looking at the new plant in bewilderment. *Wait a minute*, he thought. *I know this plant.* With grim determination, the gardener strode around the corner of the house, past the patio, and into the garden. As he did so, he noticed what looked like parallel tracks in the grass and along the gravel garden path. He walked around three turns and came to an area where the sun fell in full strength. There, where the celosia had been, was a large hole, filled partially with small rocks.

16 AN ANCIENT CURSE

The investigation into Skylar Harris's disappearance continued. Hilliard ordered Skylar's credit card and bank records. There was no activity on either statement after the engagement party. It was in stark contrast to the flurry of spending debt the young woman accrued leading up to the celebration. A payment to the fancy costume company Magdaline's in New Orleans came to $658 alone. Other retail purchases went into triple digits. The detective shook his head. She was maxed out on two of the cards. The Master Card had a credit balance of only $34.78.

"She ain't livin' off her cards," Hilliard said to Lieutenant Calvo as they poured over the statements. "Her bank account is no better--$188.54. If she ran off, she's livin' off her looks cuz this lady is broke!"

"Unless she took the money from the gift basket," Calvo said. She studied the statements before her, shaking her head and sighing. "How does one woman need this much stuff?" she asked. "Damn!" She paused, running a finger down a list of shoe stores. "That's enough shoes to make Imelda Marcos salivate!"

She glanced up, grinning at Hilliard, only to see the vapid expression he gave her. "Marcos owned 3,000 pairs of shoes," Calvo said, dipping her chin as she looked up at him for signs of life. "Her husband was Ferdinand Marcos...president of the Philippines."

"What has that got to do with Skylar Harris?" Hilliard asked.

Calvo stared at him, sighed elaborately, and changed the subject. "We need to interview the key people again," she said. "That girl did not run off, unless some millionaire who owns a shoe franchise picked her up in a private jet behind the pecan grove."

At Hilliard's blank expression, she decided to save the sarcasm for someone who caught what she was pitching. "I'm just not buyin' she ran off with the money, left her car, left her party, and left the clothes she wore before changing into her costume. You don't think someone is gonna notice a girl in a hoop skirt looking like she's just walked out of a party at Tara? Let's start with the cousin," she said. "I got the feeling Angela and Calvin Peterson were holding back. We'll save Margo for last," she said, her green eyes twinkling again.

"How exactly does Angela fit into the Broussard legacy?" Hilliard asked, hoping to reclaim his footing. He popped a hard caramel into his mouth, crunching on it loudly.

"From what I know, Angela is Rachel Broussard Barrows' mother's stepsister's daughter. She's fourth in line for Rachel's money should something happen to Randall. With Ryder gone, she's third in line if both Rachel and Randall are deceased. If something happens to Tulie or Brenn...you get the picture."

Hilliard's forehead furrowed as he tried to follow along. "So, Rachel's aunt's...or step-aunt's daughter?"

Calvo nodded as she flipped through her notes on her tablet. The noise the detective was making with the candy irritated her. She opened the file labeled Broussard Wills. Running a finger down the text there, she came to Rachel's will.

"If Rachel dies, Randall gets it all. There's a notation that appears to be something Rachel added that says, 'In the event of my death, my husband Randall Barrows inherits all my financial assets, portfolio, and properties. A trust is set aside for the children. I trust that he will fairly disperse those assets in equal shares among my two children, Ryder and Tulie Barrows, once they reach 21 years of age. In the event of the passing of one of them, that share will pass to Brendyl "Brenn" Barrows, my stepdaughter. In the unlikely event that all of the above-listed names should be deceased and have no living heirs, the money will pass to my cousin Angela Peterson."

"Interesting," Hilliard said quietly. "So, now with Ryder's passing, Brenn inherited his share. Tulie already turned twenty-one, so she has her share, correct?"

"Yeah, but Randall gets the lion's share. Rachel made the will after the twins were born and Brenn moved in with them, and it looks like she never changed it. Rachel and Randall made a boatload of money when they sold that pecan grove to the developers. There's also the Broussard fortune that was split between Tucker's three kids: Margo, Barry, and Rachel. When Barry died in the waterskiing accident, his share was split between Margo and Rachel. He had no wife or kids. Margo is still sitting pretty with her cut, the house, and her parcel of land. I've heard through the grapevine that the same developers are hounding her to sell her pecan grove so they can build Phase 2 of Lake Grove Estates. She's sittin' pretty."

"You certainly seem to know a lot about this family," Hilliard said, grinning. "Late night reading?"

She grinned back at him. "My cat has few needs. My time is my own," she said, arching her eyebrow at him playfully.

"Ok, Cousin Angela's house it is," he said, rising from his creaking desk chair.

"Aren't we going to call first?" Calvo said, rising as well.

"Nope."

Forster Boreman knelt in the stifling heat, replanting the celosia bush back where it belonged in the garden between a small statue of a fawn from a Shakespearean play and a black wrought iron bench. He hoped the back-to-back transplanting wouldn't kill the flowering plant, now missing several of its blooms. He wiped his brow and sat back on his heels.

The crunch of gravel sounded behind him, and he turned his head to see one of Margo's maids coming toward him. He smiled at her. *Brixi Carter was a breath of fresh air in a house of vipers*, he thought. He could see the tall glass of lemonade in her hand as she walked toward him, smiling. She reminded him of his oldest daughter, who was about to go off to college. Both had thick brown hair, usually pulled back into a ponytail. Both had brown eyes and dimples.

"You are an angel from above!" Forster said, beaming. He reached eagerly for the glass, condensation running down its beveled edges. Brixi usually brought him something cold to drink on her workdays at the mansion. She came five times a week.

"I don't know how you stand workin' in this heat," she said, her southern drawl pronounced. "I'd *die* without the house AC!"

"You get used to it, but my wife is constantly harping on me about skin cancer." He took a long swallow of the cold beverage, ice cubes sliding up against his lips. Wiping his mouth with the back of his hand, he took a breath and asked, "How's the drama goin'? I hear the bride-to-be booked it from her own engagement party. When the mail carrier already knows, you know all of Orleans Parish is a twitter!"

Brixi smiled broadly and dropped onto the wrought iron bench. She leaned forward eagerly as she imparted the latest gossip from inside the house.

"Well...Miss Skylar *is* missin'," she said breathlessly. "Just up and disappeared after they made the big announcement. No one has heard from her. All the presents are still in there," she said, jerking her head in the direction of the house. "All hell is breakin' loose with Miss Margo." She rolled her eyes. "She was hollerin' at someone last night, probably that poor husband of hers again. Anyway...there's broken glass everywhere this mornin.' The glass in her window in her bedroom is completely shattered. She claims she tripped over the tea cart and that tall bronze floor lamp fell and smashed the glass. You know what I think?" she asked, grinning. She made the gesture of tipping an invisible bottle up to her lips with her fingers. They both laughed.

"I saw glass in the grass this mornin'," Forster said, handing the empty glass back to the maid. "The weird thing is, someone took this plant out and put it under the broken window. What for? The impatiens I had there were doing great, and they are nowhere to be found. It's just odd."

"Something else that's odd," Brixi said, lowering her voice to a whisper. "The curtain to her bedroom window is gone. I looked in the garbage can in the garage and everywhere. I thought if it was just torn, it could be mended. That fabric was not cheap, I can tell you that! Anyway…I can't find it."

Forster looked at her, his mouth twisted to one side as he took it all in. "Something really strange is going on here," he said, looking again at the plant he had returned to its rightful place. "You be careful, okay?" he said, turning to look at her. When she smiled at him, he added quickly, "Who's gonna bring me lemonade if you go missin?"

Brixi rose and sighed as she looked around the garden. "It's so gorgeous here," she said. "Hard to believe anything bad could happen in a family that has it all."

"I've worked here a long time," Forster said. "Plenty of bad things have happened to this family. You've been here what? Five months? Sometimes, I think there's a curse on the Broussard's. That's all I'm goin' to say."

"There's a curse on the Broussard land," Calvin Peterson said dramatically. He was seated in his wheelchair on his front porch, a laptop propped up on a small table attachment. On a patio side table next to him was a tower of magazines, newspaper articles, and random papers, threatening to spill onto the floor. Detective Hilliard and Lieutenant Calvo were seated on weathered rattan chairs. Beauregard had taken a liking to Hilliard, who was allergic to cats. He surreptitiously moved the cat away with his foot from his pant leg where the animal was winding around and around it, its long, fluffy tail erect and twitching. He looked down dejectedly to see cat hairs coating his lower leg.

Before Hilliard or Calvo could respond to the man's sudden outburst, Angela came out through the screen door with a platter of glasses and a pitcher of tea. The door slammed behind her, its rusty spring vibrating, as she set the drinks down on a small patio table covered in dust and watermarks.

"Calvin! Do you realize how idiotic you appear sometimes with all the things that come pourin' outta your mouth?" she said disgustedly, as she poured four glasses. "There's no such thing as cursed land!"

Hilliard sighed. He had seen their contentious banter before. He hoped to head it off.

"Mr. Peterson," he began quickly, "what…" That's as far as he got.

"Cursed land goes back eons!" Calvin shouted at his wife, scaring the cat, who jumped nimbly down the three stone steps near the handicap ramp to the weed-infested sidewalk and disappeared into some bushes. Hilliard felt relieved and swept the hairs coating his pants with a napkin. It did nothing but make them float about before they settled upon him again.

"This here was Choctaw territory," Calvin continued, snatching the glass of tea and a napkin his wife handed him, with a look of disdain in his eyes. "They were here long before the Broussard's owned this." He made a sweeping gesture with his left arm toward the lake and shoreline. Hilliard noticed for the first time the size of the disabled man's biceps filling his short sleeves. He had seen that before with people who propelled themselves in wheelchairs; their upper body strength was pronounced.

"Mississippi flowed over there," Calvin said, pointing to the back of the lake away from the three mansions. "It started changing its course over the years; still is. 'Nother hundred years it won't look the same as it does now. It's a force of nature, no matter how much man has tried to maneuver it for his own purposes."

His voice became raspy, and he paused to drink his tea. "The Broussard's come along after the Choctaw were all gone, built that monstrosity of a house over there, planted sugar, and made a fortune off the backs of slaves and illegal liquor. Story goes, Brett Tucker Broussard, helped 'Ole Miss' change its course so that the river would run up closer to his shoreline. That's where they brought the rum in and left it at the dock over there. Course the dock's been rebuilt a few times since then, but it's in the same place now as it always was."

Angela sighed, rocking back and forth in a white Adirondack chair, fanning herself with a newspaper.

"How much of this are y'all goin' to listen to?" she asked. "I'm pretty sure that isn't what you came for."

Ignoring her, Calvin pressed on. Hilliard sighed deeply, but Lieutenant Calvo was soaking it up like a sponge.

Calvin continued. "So, when the river forced its way

back into its original course, it left behind what you call this here 'blind lake.' You can find 'em in lots of places where a river was and then wasn't."

"So, Brett Broussard diverted its course in the early 1900's," Calvo clarified. "I'm not sure how that relates to the land being cursed."

Calvin's eyes narrowed; a sign Angela knew well. He was about to lower the boom. He leaned forward in his wheelchair, his forefinger tapping the top of the closed laptop for emphasis, "That lake out there," he said, his voice oozing suspense, "that lake is covering sacred land. It was the burial ground for the Choctaw Indians. Brett knew that. He didn't bother to relocate the graves. He just let the water flood in. Those bodies are buried in mud and silt under thirty to forty feet of water. We're talkin' men, women, *and* children."

Calvin nodded, looking vastly pleased at the looks of astonishment on Hilliard's and Calvo's faces. He let it sink in for a moment as both surprised officers looked at the lake innocently shimmering through the cropping of pines along the cliffside. A cliffside that led down to a small white cross bearing the names of three Broussard descendants who had tragically died in that same water.

"And little Ryder," Calvo said in hushed tones, turning her gaze to the dock protruding into the water from the shoreline at Rachel Barrow's home across the way. Silence followed her statement as her words hung thick in the air. Even Angela appeared cowed by the thoughts going through each of their minds.

Just then, a scream shot from the pines and the group jumped; Hilliard spilling his tea down his shirt. It was not a human cry, but that of a wounded animal.

"Damn it!" Angela screamed, jumping from her rocking chair, tea from her glass splashing everywhere. She ran to the steps and looked off across the short expanse of lawn to the cliffside. Beauregard came charging from the bushes and up onto the porch, where he sank down on his haunches and began licking a bloody wound on his back leg. Four boys burst through the pines and ran like the devil was after them toward the new subdivision. One was carrying a slingshot.

"Your parents are gonna to hear about this!" she screamed after them. "You hurt my cat, you damn delinquents!" The boys disappeared through the opening in the stucco wall surrounding the new homes. Angela, still panting in anger, wetted her napkin with her spit and knelt beside her wounded pet. She tried to press it to the cat's wound, but it hissed at her and loped off down the steps again, limping painfully.

"You saw that!" Angela shouted to the detective. "That's gotta be against the law! They shot my cat with a slingshot!"

Calvo tried to calm the woman. "We will certainly find out who the boys are and take care of this," she said kindly, her Creole accent soft and assuring. It had no effect on Angela, who rose angrily to her feet and stormed off down the stone steps in search of her wounded pet.

The two officers rose, feeling the time had passed to get any meaningful testimony about the party or the participants from the Petersons. Hilliard was mopping his stained shirt with a wad of napkins. As they crossed the porch, Calvin stopped them, gripping Hilliard's forearm. His eyes shone. "Check your local history," he said, grinning. Calvo found his face repulsive. "Don't think it's over," he said, relishing his moment. "The Choctaw have a sayin." He leaned forward. "When shadows walk, somethin' evil is about to happen."

17 Rachel

Margo's voice on the phone was frantic. Randall had never heard her like that before.

"You have to meet me now!" she screamed into the phone after Randall repeatedly told her to calm down. "Drive to McCallister's and park in the dirt parking lot. I'll be there in 10 minutes."

"What the hell is the matter?" Randall asked her again.

"Just meet me!" She hung up.

Ten minutes later, Randall pulled into the deserted parking lot of McCallister's. The small produce stand was a local favorite, offering everything from boiled peanuts to farm-fresh fruits and vegetables. It opened at 11:00 am each day throughout the year, transitioning to pumpkin sales in the fall and handmade Christmas wreaths in the winter months. A few minutes later, Margo's black BMW pulled in next to him. She bolted from the car and jerked open Randall's passenger side door.

"What is the damn emergency?" he asked hotly

before she had barely settled into the seat next to him. He quickly calmed down when he saw the state she was in. Her face was ashen, and for once, she had foregone the makeup and perfectly coiffed hair. Her hands were shaking, and it was evident she had been crying for a prolonged period.

Margo swallowed several times, her hands clutching her leather purse that sat in her lap. Her chest was heaving, and she repeatedly put her head down, bobbing anxiously.

"Margo!" he begged.

"Why did you do it?" she finally said, her voice choked.

"Do what?" he suddenly felt trapped. This was going to be about him. He was sick of hearing her allegations of his alleged womanizing.

"Skylar," she said and began to sob.

Randall was shocked. He didn't realize anyone knew about Skylar meeting him in the folly at the party. The next thought was one of fear. If Margo knew, did Rachel?

"Skylar is a flirt," he began lamely. "It was nothing. She followed me into the folly and I…"

"I don't want to hear it!" Margo shouted. "It's all your fault! If you had kept your pants on, none of this would have happened."

"Margo, take a breath. Nothing happened. Nothing is worth this outburst of yours. For Pete's sake…this is the emergency you had to see me about…some stupid hookup at the party that was nothing."

"A hookup with my son's fiancé!" she screamed. "Is no female off limits to you? Don't sit there pretending that was the only time you were with her! A friend of mine saw you two at a bar in Baton Rouge, kissing! I was a fool to think I was the only one you were having an affair with. I knew all the rumors about you! I realize the only reason you came after me was to hedge your bets in case Rachel divorced you. You married her for her money. You only wanted me for mine. You did all this! You killed my sister!"

Randall recoiled, pressing himself against his car door, wondering if she had finally lost her mind. As she burst into hysterical sobs, he worried that she might have a gun packed inside her purse. The way she was holding it so tightly concerned him.

"Margo," he said finally, his voice lowered, forcing a calm demeanor he absolutely did not feel. "Margo," he repeated as he hesitantly placed his hand on her forearm. If she opened her purse, he at least had a grip on her. "I would not harm Rachel. I'm an asshole who has cheated on her, but to say our affair is killing her is unfair. All she's heard are rumors. We can end this right here if it's upsetting you so much."

She turned on him with hate blazing in her eyes. She flung her arm up violently, tossing his hand away from her. "She's dead!" she screamed, her face suffused with pain and horror. "She's dead!" Her body was trembling so badly that Randall felt genuine panic.

"What do you mean, she's dead?" he said, his own body beginning to shake. "I saw her go into her room last night after the party. She was upset about something, but she was okay."

Margo took a shuddering breath and turned haunted eyes to him. "She came to see me late last night. She was really upset. She thought *I* met you in the folly at the party. She didn't realize it was Skylar until I told her."

Randall flinched, "So, she knows that Skylar..."

"Shut up and listen to me!" Margo screamed. She jerked her purse open, and Randall reached to grab it. Margo jerked it farther away and yanked out a piece of creased paper. He leaned away from her in confusion. "Does this look familiar?" she croaked, thrusting the note Rachel had shown her the night before.

Randall took the worn paper and felt his stomach roil.

"Meet me in the folly at 8:00."

He could feel her hatred. Before he could say anything, Margo cleared her throat. She took a deep breath and continued.

"She came over. We went into my bedroom. There were maids still cleaning up downstairs. She was so upset. She said she found that note in the bushes in the garden. She thought it was for me, and I had tossed it there. She also had Skylar's green sash that got orange pollen on it in the folly." Her anger rose again, and Randall flinched as she broke into violent sobs. "I told her it wasn't my sash!" she screamed. "I told her it was Skylar's, and you were fooling around with *her*, not *me*. But she wouldn't listen!"

Margo put her hands over her face, crying hysterically. Randall began to say something, and she cut him off, screaming her next words:

"I grabbed the sash from her, but she wouldn't let go! It got tangled around her wrist as we wrestled for it. She shoved me, and I shoved her back. It was an accident! It just happened so fast! She fell against the window, and it broke. I was trying to reach her when the curtain she grabbed broke loose and she...she..."

"Oh God!" Randall's face went pale. He put his head down, trying to stop the sudden dizziness that overtook him. His heart was racing so badly that he feared he was having a heart attack. He fought the urge to reach across the car and strangle the woman who had just turned his world on its ear. Anything to stop her incessant crying!

"Is she really dead?" he finally gasped.

Margo nodded, her arms wrapped about her to control her violent trembling. "She's in the lake," she cried.

Randall's head jerked back, and he grabbed the steering wheel of the car with his left hand, his knuckles white. "She's what?" he screamed. "What the hell are you talking about? You said she fell out of your window!"

Margo bent over, emitting sounds in an octave he'd never heard. The horrible reality finally hit him. The colors around him blurred, and a roaring sound like a train filled his head. "You...you put her in the lake?" he finally choked out. "Holy Mother of God, you didn't really put her in the lake?" Vomit rose in his mouth, and he gagged.

Margo looked at the man over whom she had obsessed for three years and felt repulsed. He was weak. She was the strong one. Anger flared up in her.

"Don't even think of putting this on me!" she hissed. "You don't think I know about Skylar and what happened to her?"

Randall turned his pain-ravaged face to her. His look of shock turned to panic.

Tulie was seated at the small kitchen table when Brenn entered the room. A plate of toast and two cups of steaming tea were set out. Tulie was blowing on hers. She turned to Brenn and said, "Mama's not up yet. You can have her tea if you want."

Brenn swallowed. The images of the previous night played before her like a flickering horror movie. Rachel wasn't coming back...ever. *Tulie would never survive the news,* she thought, and looked anxiously at the innocent face looking up at her. *I'm sure as hell not going to be the one to tell her,* Brenn thought.

Just then, Randall entered the kitchen. His face was the color of a bleached seashell. He had something in his hand that looked like an envelope. His eyes were on Tulie. Brenn had the feeling he hadn't even seen her standing there.

"Are you okay, Daddy?" Tulie asked, helping him as he struggled to sit down in the chair next to her. "Do you want some coffee?"

"No...I..." he began. His eyes were mere slits, and his head lolled. Brenn wondered if he was nursing a hangover.

"Tulie," he said, his words a mere whisper. "You've got to be brave for me, okay? You can do that, right?"

Brenn watched as Tulie's face took on the pained look she had worn since Ryder's death. She saw her steel herself for whatever it was her father was about to tell her.

"Your Mama is..." he paused again, rocking slightly in his chair. "She, uh...well, she hasn't been doing too good since your brother drowned," he said. Tulie gripped the table, her heart stopping. "She needed some time to think. We haven't been doing too good, ya know. So, she went away for a while to...uh...figure out what she wants to do." He looked down at the envelope in his hand. "She left you this note." He pushed the envelope across the table to his daughter with a trembling hand.

Brenn leaned back against the kitchen counter in shock, knocking over a pitcher of sweet tea that was steeping in the sun coming in through the sink window. She ignored the tea pouring across the counter and dripping into the sink.

Tulie took the envelope in trembling hands, not wanting to open it. Tears were streaming down her face as she finally pulled the pale blue stationery from the flap. The paper shook in her hands as she read it aloud, choking on the words:

"Dearest Tulie,

You are my heart. You will always be my heart. I want to be the mother you deserve, and I haven't been myself for a very long time. I need to go away for a bit and find a way to get myself straightened out so I can be there for you. Ryder's death was hard for all of us. I will get in touch later when I'm ready to come back. Please don't tell anyone. This town gossips so much, and I've had enough gossip about my life. So, please, just go about your days. If people ask where I am, tell them I'm visiting your Cousin Jenny in Alabama for the rest of the summer. I love you! Never forget that.

Mama"

Tulie threw the letter on the table and ran from the room to the back stairway. She bolted up the stairs, screaming, "Mama! Mama!" Brenn could hear her footsteps pounding along the upstairs hallway and into Rachel's bedroom, which was directly above the parlor.

Tulie's scream echoed throughout the upstairs. Her mother's room was empty.

Brenn lunged across the room and snatched up the letter before Randall could stop her. He watched her face as his daughter quickly scanned the words. Brenn's forehead furrowed in confusion, her mouth hanging open. She looked at Randall with an expression that was hard to read.

"This is her handwriting," she said in shock. "How can this be her handwriting?"

Randall stood up quickly, gripping the back of his chair. "Why wouldn't it be her handwriting?" he asked shakily. He snatched the letter from her hand and walked toward the door to the hallway. "It's been a hard morning, Brenn," he said tiredly, his shoulders hunched. "I need to worry about Tulie now."

He walked out as Brenn sank into a chair that had been meant for Rachel. She looked down at the teacup Tulie had set out for her mother. The brew was no longer steaming. She reached over to the pale blue envelope and pulled it to her. Randall had forgotten it. She stared in total disbelief at the dainty handwriting scrawled across its face: "Tulie." It hadn't occurred to her father that Rachel's absence would affect her too. Rachel had raised her from a teenager when her mother died. True, they had never been close, but it only cemented Brenn's belief that she was never a part of this family, not after the twins were born. She was a footnote in her father's life story.

The painful realization moved once again to her carefully constructed vault that she had created in her mind long ago. She would not look at it now. Now, she had something more urgent to deal with. How could this letter be? Rachel was dead! She saw her fall. Saw Margo throw her body in the lake. Saw the green sash go down with her.

The kitchen clock clicked out a steady, monotonous ticking as she sat there, still staring at the envelope in her hand. Tulie's sobs could be heard coming from above. She was still in Rachel's room.

Pieces of the previous night kept playing out in her mind. *A fierce argument between Rachel and Margo. About what? Rachel's neck broke when she landed next to her after falling from Margo's window. Margo, wrapping the body in the drapery. Margo, pulling the cart through the mud to the lake. Margo yanked the burgundy curtain until her sister rolled out of it into the water. Rachel's body sinking, rolling slowly over, her arm bobbing on the surface for just a moment, the green sash... The green sash... Margo. Rachel's murder...it was murder! The argument... Margo had to have done something for Rachel to crash through a window. Skylar's sash...Skylar missing...*

Brenn rose to her feet, her mind whirring. A plan formed, tentative at first, then filled in with practiced precision. A cruel smile played across her lips. She jumped as a knock came at the back kitchen door. She looked to see Dawson's mother standing there, smiling through the screen. "I brought Rachel a pecan pie," she said. "Is she up yet?"

18 SECRETS

Brenn tiptoed into Rachel's bedroom and closed the door behind her. Her father had moved out of the conjugal bed years ago when Rachel's depression over Ryder's death took a toll on him. It was then that the rumors of Randall's dalliances began to circulate. The room was decidedly feminine: reams of peach chiffon draped over the canopy of the bed, with a deeper shade of coral found in the thick draperies that were tied back at the windows. Randall had taken off again, and Tulie could be heard sobbing from her own room; her door closed.

Rachel's room housed a large array of perfume bottles on the vanity table, a jewelry box, an ornate antique hairbrush and hand mirror, a figurine of a white dog nestled in peach-colored poppies, and a jewel-encrusted hair comb that belonged to Rachel's great-grandmother. Brenn perused the items, noticing more than one perfume bottle bearing a Tea Rose label. It was Rachel's favorite fragrance, and many had gifted her the scent on special occasions.

It was clear Tulie had spent time here earlier in the

day. The impression of her body was still evident in the expensive satin bedspread. Brenn pictured her lying there, curled into a ball, weeping over her mother's sudden departure. The thought of Tulie caused her to cut short her leisurely perusal of the room. She could come back at any moment.

She crossed to the large wardrobe and opened the double doors wide. Pushing aside a few dresses, Brenn looked at the bottom of the closet. The suitcases were gone. Her face puckered in confusion. She next shifted through the dozen or so dresses hanging there. She knew Rachel's clothing as well as anyone, having seen her every day of her life since she was fifteen years old. Several of the dresses were missing, along with three pairs of shoes.

Brenn turned to the mahogany dresser and opened the top drawer. It had been rifled through, not Rachel's usual organization of underwear. The second drawer was missing several tops, and it too was in disarray. Some slacks were absent from the bottom drawer.

The heat in the room closed in around her as she stood pondering the situation. The windows had been closed, and it was becoming claustrophobic in the stagnant air. Brenn wiped the sweat from her brow and turned to look again at the open wardrobe. She thought again of the blue envelope she had hidden in her room with Rachel's recognizable handwriting. *What in the world was happening,* she thought.

Tulie lay on her bed, her eyes swollen from weeping. She was cried out. Rachel's shawl was wrapped about her. She had taken it from her mother's room along with a bottle of her Tea Rose perfume. Tulie had dabbed some on her wrists and now lay curled in a ball; her mother's fragrance and vintage shawl encasing her like loving arms. It was all she had left until her Mama returned. But a dark dread sat like a weight on her heart. She couldn't shake the feeling that her mother was never coming back. They had always had the same connection that Tulie shared with her twin brother Ryder. They knew intuitively when the other was hurt. Tulie believed strongly that her mother *was* hurt. That's as far as her mind would let her go for now.

The lively chatter of young women assaulted Brenn's ears as she entered her Aunt Margo's kitchen through the back door. The tower of catering crates was gone from the mud room, and only Margo's four maids in crisply starched uniforms were busily sorting leftover food in the containers from the refrigerator to make more room. Several were wiping down surfaces and sweeping up the floor. They turned as Brenn walked in.

"Remains of the Day?" Brenn asked snidely, her grin twisted in mock irony. The young women seemed to miss the inference to the famous quote and shrugged.

"Some of the remains are on the second floor," one giggled, and the others joined in.

As if on cue, Brixi walked in from the back hallway, hefting a filled garbage bag. She dropped it to the tiled floor with a sigh. The sound of broken glass could be heard coming from inside the bag. Brenn eyed it keenly.

Maude Gleason, one of the housekeepers at the sink, turned to look at Brixi. "Is she still in a mood?"

"She says she tripped over the brass floor lamp in her bedroom," Brixi whispered, glancing toward the back staircase. "Says that's what went through the window and made the tea cart fall over. I think she was drunk. That lovely figurine of the shepherdess is broken into pieces," Brixi said, nodding toward the garbage bag. "Probably cost more than my car. She says to tell you that when the window glass man shows up, to take him up to her room."

Brixi lugged the garbage bag to the back door and pulled two others over to it from the kitchen counter area.

"Let me help," Brenn said suddenly. Brixi looked shocked. Brenn Barrows never helped anyone but herself. "They go out into the garage, right?" Brenn asked, moving toward the three heavy trash bags. Brixi nodded, happy to be relieved of the duty. She went back into the kitchen.

Brenn pulled each of the bags along the flagstone sidewalk to the back of the house near the driveway. She opened the side garage door and stepped into the cool darkness, feeling for a light switch. The air smelled of stale gasoline and grass clippings. Her fingers finally hit the switch, and she flipped on the lights. Four large garbage cans sat lined up against the wall. Two were filled to overflowing with trash from the party.

Brenn hurled two of the bags into the third can that was half full. She then turned her attention to the final bag of trash she had pulled from the kitchen; the one Brixi had brought down from Margo's room. She untied the plastic opening and looked inside. There were small boxes filled with broken glass from Margo's bedroom window. She lifted each of these out carefully. Beneath them was a scattering of cigar butts, some empty champagne bottles, and used tissues. Wrinkling her nose, she pushed the tissues to one side and saw the shattered remains of a white statuette, its head and body broken in multiple places.

Brixi sighed and placed a hand to her back. She spent two hours helping Skylar's parents load up the engagement presents. A few friends came along to help. They filled the seats and the back of several expensive SUVs. Brixi's heart went out to Mr. and Mrs. Harris, who looked as if they had been through a war zone. They were dazed and haggard. Obviously, there had been no word from their missing daughter.

Mrs. Harris asked Brixi to "please get rid of the flowers" that still sat in centerpieces along the gift table. "I can't bear to see them," she said, her voice hollow. Mr. Harris got into Skylar's car and waved to his wife to head out. With that, they pulled away from the house and disappeared through the pines.

Brixi brought each of the three giant vases into the kitchen and placed them near the sink. The other maids had gone for the day, except for Stephanie, who was always on call for Miss Margo. She had her own quarters at the back of the house. Brixi lifted clusters of wilted hydrangeas and roses and placed them heads down into a garbage bag. The fetid smell of stagnant water rose from the vase openings. The sprigs of baby's breath came last, and she snapped them in half to fit them better into the bag.

Sighing with exhaustion, the maid pulled the soggy bag out of the mudroom door and along to the garage. The hired men would set the large cans out on the driveway early the next morning. As she flipped on the garage light, she could picture the joy of going home in just a few more minutes. It was the last of her duties for the day. In her mind, she was planning dinner in her small apartment when she noticed another garbage bag leaning against the trash can closest to her.

Brixi flipped the light bag of flower remains into a near-full container and reached for the other bag resting on the floor. As she lifted it, the ties came undone, and she dropped it. She bent over to re-tie them and saw several magazines nestled inside. They were the expensive kind she could never afford; spotlighting women's fashions that were equally out of her reach. She eagerly lifted out one after another, salivating over the covers of *Elle, Vogue, Harper's, Southern Lady,* and *Vanity Fair.*

"Margo won't care," she whispered happily to herself. "She threw them away." As she lifted the last magazine from the bag, she stopped and stared with astonishment at what was hidden beneath the glossy pages. An expensive pair of baby blue leather pumps lay there, caked in mud. One of the short heels was chipped. She had seen Margo wearing those shoes just one day before. *How odd*, Brixi thought. *But, if you have her kind of money, I guess you throw expensive shoes away when you mess them up gardening.* She eyed them for a minute and then snatched them from the bag. If they were a size 7, she was in luck.

The following morning, Angela Peterson knocked on the back screen door to Rachel's sunroom as the early morning sun sent streaks of light through the low-lying lake mist. She was surprised to find the door latched. She rapped a second time, and Brenn's head finally peered around the corner of the kitchen door. Looking decidedly displeased, she stepped down into the sunroom and unlatched the door. Angela swung it open without waiting for an invitation.

"No word?" she asked abruptly.

Brenn didn't pretend to misunderstand her question. "No. I'm sure Rachel will let us know where she is when she feels like it," Brenn said evenly.

"Let me talk to Tulie," Angela demanded. "I'm makin' groceries, and I want to see if she needs anything from the store." Brenn had not moved from her spot inside the doorway, effectively blocking the large woman's entrance into the sunroom. She smiled smugly.

"I always hated that southern expression," she said. "Why can't you just say you're going to *get* groceries? Besides, Tulie already talked to you this morning," she said pointedly. "She is too upset to see anyone. Police keep coming here asking questions about Skylar, like we're supposed to know something. Now Rachel has taken it into her head to pull a vanishing act just because my Dad can't quit eyeballin' every woman that goes by."

Angela set her jaw and stared at the girl through lowered eyelids. "Oh, I think we both know your Daddy does more than just 'eyeball' women." Brenn's nostrils flared, and she tried to reach behind her stepcousin to close the door. Angela refused to budge. "Tell Tulie I'll check on her later."

Angela slammed the screen door before Brenn could catch it and backed down the steps to the lawn. She looked behind her to see Brenn returning to the kitchen, where she slammed the door. Sighing, Angela walked along the worn dirt path that lay hard against the shoreline. The lake mists crawled in spider-like wisps among the tall reeds and grasses bordering the water. She passed the stucco wall bearing the engraved name Lake Grove Estates to her left and glowered at the terra cotta-colored tiled rooftops. Why in the world Rachel let Randall badger her into selling her share of the pecan grove was beyond her. The new subdivision was an eyesore. Instead of the relaxing sounds of whippoorwills and owls at night, she was now privy to the sound of backyard radios blasting and the laughter of intoxicated party guests. It seemed like there was always a barbecue going on.

Scowling, she walked through a stand of pine trees and called out for Beauregard, who had not shown up for breakfast.

"Kitty, kitty, kitty," she called in shrill tones. "Come on, kitty!" She bent to look beneath the pine tree that was Beauregard's usual hiding spot. The cat was nowhere to be found. She walked on, peering into bushes, and then stopped abruptly. Up ahead, she saw the same four boys at the side of her house, plucking flowers from her trellis.

"Get outta there!" she screamed, breaking into a run. Her arthritic knees kept her from a full sprint, but she cleared the ground as fast as she could go. The boys turned to see her charging toward them. Laughing, they tore off into the woods bordering the cliff. Calvin looked up in surprise at her outburst. He was sitting in his usual spot on the front porch; the laptop was open where it sat on the table attached to his wheelchair. He was unprepared for the wrath about to rain down on him.

"Why in hell didn't you stop those heathens from destroying my flowers?" she screamed, as she ran up to the porch. "You just sit there, immune to anything that doesn't interest you! You didn't hear those boys just right there around the corner from you?"

Calvin sighed. Another day, another diatribe.

"A—I didn't hear them. B—I'm working on my book, which is a bit more important than some flowers. C—I thought you were going to talk to their parents."

Angela's face was flushed in anger. "I have to know which ones *are* their parents, don't I? How do I know which houses are theirs? And they aren't just 'some flowers!' Those are Angel's Trumpets, and I've nurtured them along to get them to the gorgeous display they are. Margo let them run to seed. Gardens take a lot of care."

"Glad something is getting care," Calvin said smugly. "Breakfast would be nice."

He had returned to his laptop, missing the missile of hate Angela's eyes shot at him. She walked to the side of the house to her garden and cried out. The boys had stepped on her heirloom roses, snapping their stems. They lay like broken popsicle sticks, their pink and coral heads already withering. In the front of the bed, a begonia plant was completely decimated, its pale pink blooms scattered around it. A few empty places on the Angel's Trumpet vine showed where the boys had ripped off several of the largest trumpet-shaped flowers.

"They have destroyed my Louise Clements roses and torn up my Angel's Trumpet plant! They took some of the biggest blooms! I'll kill them!" she screamed; her voice choked with sobs.

"You may not have to," Calvin said loudly, so she

could hear him from the porch. "I research poisons for my books. If I'm not mistaken, Angel's Trumpet is also called the Devil's Trumpet. It's deadly nightshade."

The sound of laughter and voices near the lake beneath her window reached Tulie's ears as she lay on her bed in her darkened bedroom. She had pulled the heavy curtains closed the morning her mother left, not wanting to see another day's light enter her room. Half-eaten plates of food sat on a hand-carved hope chest of her great-grandmother's that her mother had given her. Rachel's wedding dress was inside, and mementos from her wedding to Tulie's Daddy.

The voices grew louder until they were right beneath Tulie's window. She lifted herself from her bed and walked to the curtains, gently pulling one aside just enough to look out. Walking near the family cemetery were four young boys, around ten or eleven.

"Blow the trumpet again," one yelled out laughing. "Sound the charge! We'll storm the castle on the hill," he said, pointing a long stick he carried at Margo's mansion above them on the cliffside.

The tallest boy placed a large white flower in the shape of a long trumpet-shaped bell to his lips and made a tooting sound. He laughed, and then did it again, taking in a breath with the flower pressed to his lips and blowing into it. "Doot do dooooo!" he yelled, mimicking a bugle.

The boys walked off along the path through the pecan grove, whacking at bushes and tree trunks with long branches they had picked up along the way. They began pelting each other with fallen pecans until it became too painful. They resorted instead to throwing them at the thick tree trunks; the monotonous *thunk* sound repeating over and over until they were finally too far away.

Tears streamed down Tulie's face as she released the curtain, once again encasing the room in shadows. The boys had reminded her of Ryder. He was close to their age when he drowned. The loneliness and feeling of loss settled into her chest, and she fell back onto the bed, her quiet sobs filling the room.

Margo stood in her bedroom, checking the new window glass installation for flaws. She looked hesitantly down to the lawn below where her sister had fallen. Even in broad daylight, it felt surreal. Margo flinched as she saw the brightly colored red flowers of a new bush that had been planted there. *The gardener knew then! What was his name? Finster? Fowler? It was an odd name. Would he mention it to other people that someone switched the plant under her window?*

The sun went behind a cloud, and Margo shivered. Each time the doorbell rang it was that damned detective. Skylar had been missing for three days now. There was nothing else they could possibly ask them that they hadn't already. She had not heard anything about Rachel, so she and Randall's plan to show Tulie and Brenn a fake note had worked.

Margo and Rachel had always had similar handwriting. All through school, Rachel had written essays for Margo's classes to keep her sister from failing. Margo had, in turn, copied Rachel's handwriting over the years for various jokes. Once, she sent out invitations to Rachel's 18th birthday party—in Rachel's handwriting—to four different boys her sister had dated at various times, telling each of them she wanted to rekindle their romance. All four showed up at the party, two with floral bouquets, leaving Rachel to handle the fallout. The only difference in their handwriting was Rachel's slanted a little more to the right—an easy thing to replicate.

Margo backed away from the window. She glanced up at the naked curtain rod with only a few rings remaining. She had removed the matching curtain to the left of the window that had shattered. Live oak tree boughs swayed in the breeze across the lawn, their gray moss dancing like spirited ghosts. She felt suddenly vulnerable to prying eyes. She would have to order new curtains today.

Backing away from the window, Margo looked down at the tea cart that had toppled the night of the fight. The statuette was gone, but the vintage phone was once more in place. The room seemed to be mocking her with memories of two nights ago and Rachel's fall through the glass. Her nerves frayed. She walked to her master bathroom for a glass of water and flipped on the light; instantly surrounded by marble and glistening fixtures.

The sound of water filling the sink basin brought back the sound of sloshing lake water. She trembled as she filled a small tumbler and raised it to her lips, shutting off the faucet with her other hand. Her head pounded, and she pulled open a drawer in the sink cabinet next to her, looking for an aspirin bottle. Not finding one, she slammed the drawer and hunched over the counter, her hands gripping the marble edge.

The room echoed with the sound of water dripping. She reached automatically for the sink faucet and tightened it harder. The sound continued in a rhythmic beat...*drip, drip, drip*. It was coming from behind her. She lifted her eyes to the mirror before her and stared, petrified. In the reflection was the massive shower, its black and gold curtain pulled to one side. Draped over the curtain rod was a long green satin sash. It was wet with a large orange stain dominating its center. The fabric was wrinkled and frayed. Water ran along it and dripped onto the marble floor, forming a small dirty puddle of lake water. She screamed and ran from the room.

19 LOOSE THREADS

"Where are we?" Detective Hilliard asked. He was seated at his desk in a small room with dirty windows. It was Day 5 of the Skylar Harris investigation. Across from him was Lieutenant Calvo, her chair pulled up to the other side of his desk, leaning over her tablet. Next to her elbow was a notebook and a stack of well-thumbed index cards.

"You mean where *aren't* we?" she said, her mouth twisted to one side. "We've interviewed almost all of the guests from the engagement party. A few people were off on cruises or other vacations, but they were older couples with nothing to gain from Skylar's disappearance. The only thing of note was the following comments." She picked up the stack of index cards and cleared her throat.

"Several of the female guests were eager to share the rumors that Randall Barrows and Margo Tillson are having an affair." She looked over at the detective to gauge his reaction.

"An affair or a fling?" he asked, clamping down with his teeth on a toothpick that had pierced his club sandwich during lunch.

"Not sure what the difference is, but according to at least a dozen guests, it had been going on for some years," Calvo said. She waited for him to answer.

"Ok, they're having an affair. Rachel Barrows is out of it since their son's drowning in the lake, he's feeling the need for companionship... What does that have to do with Skylar Harris going AWOL?"

"Nothing," Calvo said, fighting the urge to confront him on his casual dismissal of a marital affair. She flipped to another card. "I have twenty-nine reports from the guests saying Skylar looked intoxicated later in the party. Not unusual at a gathering like that. She seemed unsteady and was slurring her words, according to these interviews. The last time she was seen was entering the garden under the big arch after the cake-cutting ceremony. She ate a piece of pie, chatted with her bridesmaids, and went into the garden."

Hilliard rolled the toothpick back and forth along his bottom lip with his tongue. He leaned back in his chair, the springs creaking loudly, and sighed.

"Tox reports on the drinking glasses yet?" he asked.

"Preliminary tests show nothing. If someone slipped something into her drink, like Rohypnol or some other date rape drug to incapacitate her, it didn't show up. You only have about 28-48 hours before those drugs are no longer detectable on glassware, etc. You can test urine and hair samples for them, but we have no body. No body, no tests."

Hilliard placed his hands behind his neck and

stretched his chin toward the ceiling.

"Oh," Calvo said suddenly, flipping to a file on her tablet. "This may be nothing, but I did check on those boys bothering Angela Peterson's cat. It took knocking on a few doors. Here's the thing: one of the boys is in the hospital. They are saying it looks like he's been poisoned."

The detective bolted upright in his chair and stared at her in disbelief. "Poisoned? Which kid?"

"His name is Tom Simons. His mother took him into the ER yesterday. I talked to her. She said the boy was slurring his words, hallucinating, having trouble breathing, etc. The tests are still ongoing, and he's being monitored, but the symptoms point to some kind of poisoning. He seems to be improving."

"Any idea where he got hold of poison? You're sure he's one of the four boys tormenting Angela and her cat?"

"Yep. Same boy. Parents have no idea where he may have gotten hold of poison. They don't even use insecticide. I talked to the other boys. They say Tom is like the ring leader and he instigates most of the vandalism around the lake," Calvo said, glancing down at her notes. "I don't think Angela will be bothered anymore. I talked to their parents and put the fear of God into the boys. If you're asked, there's a new police violation called 'Pet Pestering' that results in six weeks in jail."

Hilliard's eyebrows rose in shock. When he saw the smile spread across her face, he laughed. "Duly noted," he said. "The dreaded 'Pet Pestering' infraction is now on the books." Then his expression took on a more serious tone.

"We have a missing young woman," he said tiredly, "a garden folly that looks like a struggle may have ensued inside—although a lot of party guests could have been in there—a turned-over chair, scrape marks on the floor... Did we get the photos back from Polk?"

"Yes," Calvo said, and pulled a brown manilla folder from beneath the spiral notepad. She handed it to Hilliard.

The detective opened the folder and began laying the glossy photographs of the folly, garden, and back lawn across the desk. He spread them apart with his fingers and hunched over them. He plucked one from a group showing pictures of the garden paths and held it up. Peering through his bifocals, he said, "This is interesting."

Calvo took the photo from him and studied it. It was the hard-packed dirt path used by the landscaper that led from the tool shed to the folly. In the close-up of the path were parallel markings that ran the length of the trail.

"Probably the gardener's cart," Calvo said.

Hilliard pulled the photo taken of the side of the Broussard mansion where a gardener's cart laden with potted flowers sat and slid it over to her.

"Look closely at the two photos," Hilliard said, his eyes suddenly bright. "Those tracks are too narrow for a cart wheel, and the tracks have tread, like a bicycle tire."

"You think someone on a bike went up the trail?" she asked incredulously. She looked back and forth between the photo of the cart and the one showing tracks in the dirt.

"No!" Hilliard said, sounding exasperated. "The

markings are parallel...two wheels side by side. The landscaper's cart has four metal wheels, and they are broader than that, and... the cart wheels have no tread. What do we know that would make those marks?" He waited, leaning forward eagerly.

Calvo studied the picture. Her head jerked up, eyes bulging. "You don't mean...?" she said, suddenly coming to life. "A wheelchair?"

Hilliard leaned back in the creaking chair and smiled. "Could be," he said. "Look at this one." He leaned forward and selected another picture from the lineup. "I had Polk take a close-up of this inside the folly. It's an impression in the pollen. Polk said it had tread marks like maybe a rubber shoe sole. What if it's a portion of the same tire mark? And...no one was wearing tennis shoes at that party! It was all fancy tuxes and gowns."

Calvo stared at the picture and then lifted her eyes to meet his. "Holy crap!" she said.

Margo clutched Rachel's cell phone that Randall had provided in one hand, pressing it hard against her ear. She licked her lips nervously as it began to ring. After several seconds, an apprehensive voice answered.

"Yes?" It was the tone of one expecting a solicitor.

"Hi Jenny! It's Rachel! Rachel Barrows, your cousin," Margo said nervously.

There was a long pause on the other end of the line. Margo worried that perhaps she had not emulated her dead sister's voice as well as she thought she had.

"Wow," Jenny said, finally. "It's been a while." Another awkward pause followed.

"Yes, it has," Margo twittered, trying to calm her

voice into a more conversational tone. "Life just seems to go along, doesn't it?"

"Yes, it does," Jenny said, a hard edge coating her words. "I think the last time I saw you was Ryder's funeral…like…17 or 18 years ago. Did you get my invitations to Dulaney's wedding and Patrick's retirement party?"

Margo floundered. This was news to her. It was also obvious that while Rachel had received invitations to their cousin's family's special occasions, she had not.

"I..I..well, you know. Ryder's death was hard…still is. I pretty much shut down. I'm terribly sorry I missed your events." Margo waited, biting her lip.

"Well, it's water under the bridge now," Jenny said, sounding like she was eager to end the call.

"Actually, that's why I'm calling," Margo said, her voice dripping with affection. "It's been too long. I was wondering if you would be okay with me paying you a visit? I need to get away for a while, and it would be lovely to see you and catch up."

Another prolonged silence filled the line. Finally, Jenny answered, her voice bordering on contempt.

"Lovely? I see. Well, I'm afraid this wouldn't be a 'lovely' time for me right now. We have a big vacation to Europe coming up and Dulaney's baby shower. You probably didn't know that my daughter is expecting, either. This is just not a good time for us, Rachel. Sorry."

Margo paused, picking her final words carefully.

"Of course! I understand. How thrilling. A new baby! Please tell Daphney I said 'Congratulations!'"

"It's *Dulaney!* Not Daphney! Thanks for calling, Rachel. Take care." The call ended abruptly.

Margo sat back with a sigh of relief. She had done it. It was all she needed to do for now. The call would be traced to Rachel's cell phone. It would look like she was still alive. She took a deep breath.

A tap came at the bedroom door. "Come in," Margo called, pushing the small phone into her pocket. Brixi peeped her head around the partially open door and said softly, "You wanted your dress from the party taken back to the rental store, Miss Margo?"

"Oh, yes. It's probably late. Argue with them if they want to add late charges to my card on file. They also owe me the deposit back. Make sure you tell them to refund it to my card. The dress is in the closet in the gray clothes bag. I've got to go and meet Skylar's parents at their place. We have to decide what to do about the gifts. What a mess!"

Margo rose from the bed and then paused. She was uncertain how to ask the maid a question that was haunting her. Brixi waited, anticipating further instructions.

"Brixi," Margo began haltingly. "You don't clean my bathroom, is that correct?"

"No, Ma'am, Stephanie handles your room." The maid looked inquiringly at the woman, who seemed distressed.

"Yes, of course," Margo said vaguely. "Did Stephanie mention anything out of place in my bathroom?" Margo cringed, realizing the question sounded inane. An image of the dripping green sash hanging over the shower curtain rod flashed through her mind, and her breath caught. When she had gone back later to take it down, it was gone.

Brixi blinked and then said, "Uh, no, Miss Margo.

Why? Is something wrong? Is something missing?"

Margo shot her a quick look, her eyes wide.

"Why did you say that? Why would you automatically think something was missing?" she asked, her voice rising an octave.

Brixi stepped back, prepared to flee if she had to.

"Nothing, Miss Margo! Honest! You just asked if she said anything was out of place. My mind naturally jumped to something missing. I can assure you that Stephanie is not the kind to take things."

"And you?" Margo asked, "Are you the kind to take things? I believe I saw you with one of my magazines when I entered the kitchen yesterday. I don't suppose you typically buy *Vogue?*"

Brixi colored and gripped her hands together. She knew Margo had fired maids for less.

"They were in the trash," Brixi muttered, her eyes on her shoes. "I didn't think you wanted it anymore."

"Is that all you took?" Margo asked, panic suddenly knocking on her ribs. The muddy shoes she had discarded had been hidden just beneath the magazines.

Brixi looked up at her employer. If she admitted to taking an expensive pair of shoes, she would be sacked for sure, even if they were in the trash.

"That's all...just one or two magazines! I'm sorry, Miss Margo. I didn't think you would care since you threw them away. It won't happen again."

Margo relaxed. It didn't appear the girl had seen the shoes. She needed to calm down.

"It's fine, Brixi," she said, forcing an even tone, "just ask next time. I'm not comfortable with you digging through my trash to start with."

"No, ma'am," Brixi said hurriedly. "The tie came

undone, and I dropped the bag. I wasn't snooping, I promise."

Margo stood and ran her hands along her slacks, smoothing them. She picked up her purse from a table near the door. "Make sure you get that dress back to the store," she said and left the room.

Brixi stood near the closet door and took a few calming breaths. *That was close! And what was all the fuss about the bathroom?* She waited a minute until she could hear Margo's voice in the kitchen below talking to Stephanie. Brixi couldn't make out the words. Then the back door slammed.

Tiptoeing, Brixi entered the large master bathroom, flipped on the light, and peered around. Everything seemed to be in perfect order. The fixtures were glistening, and the marble tile floor shone in the overhead light. A few discarded towels lay about, but that was Stephanie's job. Margo didn't leave many items out on the countertops, preferring a clean, clutter-free feeling. Shrugging, she backed out of the room, clicking off the light.

Brixi opened the door to the massive walk-in closet to the right. Reed's closet sat next to it, its door open. His clothes hung neatly from hangers. Margo's closet was larger and housed an array of expensive clothes hanging from the rods, some with price tags still attached. A revolving shoe rack dominated the back wall, filled with high-heeled shoes and brand-name pumps. At the front of the closet nearest to her hung a large dress bag with the name Magdaline's Vintage Apparel emblazoned upon it in gold lettering. Brixi lifted the heavy bag from the rod and carried it to the bed, where she draped it across the satin duvet. She unzipped it carefully to avoid snagging the lavender chiffon fabric. Confident it was the right dress, she zipped it up again.

Brixi turned toward the large bedroom window, naked without its usual window coverings. The blazing sun filled the room; the temperature rose by the minute. She looked up at the curtain rod to where a few rings still hung, one of them bent and dangling as if some force had pulled the drapery from it.

"Missing curtains, missing fiancé...a fiancé Margo didn't want her son to marry...muddy shoes hidden in the trash..." Brixi whispered her thoughts aloud to the empty room. Her mind suddenly went into overdrive.

Detective Hilliard and Lieutenant Calvo went in search for the costume shop on their list. The sidewalks of New Orleans' tourist section were brimming with people of all ages. Hilliard's eyes bulged as a lady in a string bikini hung from an open doorway a few feet ahead, beckoning to the male pedestrians.

"Anything goes," Calvo said, noticing Hilliard's surprise. "You don't get out much, do you?"

The detective ignored her comment and averted his eyes as they passed the doorway with a neon sign atop it blinking the word, "Ladies." Calvo grinned. There was an awkward innocence to the lumbering giant that raised him in her estimation, despite his shrug at Randall Barrows' infidelity.

The two paused outside the bay window of an expensive-looking shop with the name Magdaline's Vintage Apparel scrawled across the middle window in gold gilt lettering. In the display window was a variety of antebellum clothing bespeaking the elegance of a bygone era. Mannequins draped in exquisite gowns held dainty parasols, gloves, and fans. The only nod to Halloween was two plastic pumpkins with LED glowing eyes.

"So, we know by the photos that Taylor Sinclair's photographer handed over to us" Hilliard said, "that Skylar is wearing a green sash at the beginning of the party and a blue sash in the pictures during the announcement and cake cutting. Tulie said in our interview that Skylar borrowed her blue sash because Skylar's green one got 'dirty.' Tulie said her Aunt Margo followed Skylar into the garden after the cake cutting to get Tulie's sash back for her. What we don't know is, *did* Margo get the sash and return it to Tulie. Tulie didn't say, and I forgot to ask."

"Let's go see," Calvo said and pushed open the glass door.

A shop bell tinkled as the two officers entered. Several women moving dresses on hangers turned to look at the uniformed lieutenant and the towering male in slacks and a sports coat with her.

"May I help you?" an older woman asked, approaching the couple with some trepidation.

"Yes, ma'am," Hilliard said politely. "We would be appreciative if y'all could help us with a question about some party dresses we're trying to pin down."

The woman's eyebrows rose, but she maintained her composure.

"I'm not sure I understand," she said. "I'm the manager here, what can I help you with?'

"Did you rent a gown to a Miss Tulie Barrows, a Miss Skylar Harris, or a Miss Rachel Barrows about five days or so ago?"

The manager looked surprised. "I can check my records," she said. "Is there anything wrong?" she asked, eyeing the gun in Calvo's holster.

"No, just looking into a few discrepancies in some reports we're dealing with. No big deal," Hilliard said, flashing an awkward smile. Shmoozing people was not an art he had acquired.

She paused and then said, "Follow me, please." She led them through standing floor racks and mannequins in all manner of costumes. Lieutenant Calvo nodded to the customers' surprised faces as they filed past them to a counter at the back of the store. The manager went behind it and brought up a sales ledger on her computer.

As she clicked on different dates, Hilliard noticed a young boy staring up at him, who was standing next to a woman looking through vintage dresses on a display rack nearby. Hilliard grinned at the boy.

"How come you're so tall and she's so short, but she's got the gun?" the little boy asked, his neck bent all the way back as he looked up at the detective. Calvo looked at the boy in amusement.

"Well," Hilliard said, "it's for convenience. She holds my gun for me, and I can set my soda can on top of her head if I need both of my hands for something. It's like having a portable side table following me around."

A few women nearby burst into laughter. The mother of the boy looked embarrassed and pulled him over to her. Calvo glared up at her partner, her mouth twisted to one side.

Hilliard turned back to the woman at the computer and noticed a young woman standing next to him at the counter. She was sighing impatiently. Her white starched uniform interested him. Finally, a store clerk came out from the back of the store and stood across the counter from the young lady. She spoke to her in crisp tones.

"I'm afraid we have a problem with the dress," she said. "There's some kind of orange stain around the hemline. I can't refund your deposit until we see if it can be restored to the condition in which you rented it."

"It's not my dress," the young woman said nervously. "It's my boss's. I'm just returning it. She won't be happy with me if I tell her you're keeping her money."

The young store clerk looked at the manager, who paused her computer search for the officers. She had overheard the conversation between her clerk and the young customer.

"What is it, Theresa?" she asked impatiently.

"It's a damaged dress, Miss Hyland. We don't return deposits if they are damaged."

"No, indeed, we do not," the manager said curtly, eyeing the young woman who was now chewing on her lips. "What's the name?" Miss Hyland asked bluntly.

"My name? I'm Brixi Carter. But the dress was rented by my boss...Margo Tillson."

Hilliard jerked his head in the young girl's direction. He couldn't believe his luck. Margo Tillson had turned in a dress with orange stains. She had also lied about the times she saw Skylar at the party.

"We'll have to get back to Miss Tillson after we see if the dress can be cleaned," Miss Hyland told the hapless Brixi. "Until then, we cannot release the deposit, and there will also be a cleaning charge." She turned away and returned to the computer as Brixi made her way miserably from the store.

"Ah, here it is," Miss Hyland said with relief, her cursor poised above an entry. "We did rent two dresses to Miss Rachel Barrows and Miss Tulie Barrows. Miss Rachel's card was used for the payment and security deposit on the two dresses. They were both returned in good condition; the deposit put toward the final balance. Miss Tulie Barrows signed the receipt of their return. Miss Skylar Harris did rent a dress from us, but it has not been returned. She ran up quite a bill with special fittings for the dress, which were paid in advance."

"No chance it was returned and missed being recorded?" Calvo asked politely.

Miss Hyland shot the lieutenant a look of contempt.

"As I clearly stated, the dress has not been returned yet!"

"The other two outfits were complete?" Hilliard asked carefully. "I believe the dresses had sashes…"

She cut him off. "Yes, all accounted for. Miss Tulie's blue dress and sash, blue satin shoes. Miss Rachel's gold dress and sash, no shoes."

"Bear with me," Hilliard said, feeling her impatience. "Are you sure the sash belonged to the blue dress? It's the one that came with the dress when it was rented?"

Miss Hyland eyeballed him contemptuously. "Of course it's the same sash. We're very careful about people substituting articles. We've had problems in the past with customers wanting to keep an expensive artifact they rented and tried to return an imitation. That sash is the one that goes with that dress! Is that all you need? I have people waiting."

"There *is* something else," Hilliard said, undaunted by the manager's abrupt dismissal. "I need a copy of that ledger entry, and….and you won't like this…I'm taking Miss Margo Tillson's dress with me."

20 Blackmail

Randall Barrows stood nervously inside his open front door, one hand holding onto it firmly. Detective Hilliard and Lieutenant Calvo stood in the afternoon heat without an invitation to enter the Barrows' mansion.

"It's just a few questions," Detective Hilliard repeated. "It will only take a moment."

Randall stood where he was, still holding tightly onto the door. He pressed his lips together into a firm line and finally stepped back to admit the two officers.

"Thank you," Hilliard said, stepping into the foyer that had a faint smell of mildew about it. The air was stale and brought no respite from the fall humidity.

"In here," Randall said curtly, and led them into the same parlor they had by now memorized. He remained standing, telegraphing his desire for a short visit.

"We have tried to speak with your wife a few times since the engagement party to go over a few things,"

Hilliard said without preamble. "I understand from your daughter, Brenn, that Mrs. Barrows is away on vacation, is that correct?" He noticed Randall Barrows' rigid stance and strained facial muscles.

"Yes...yes, she is," he stammered. "She hasn't been well. Our son's death has been a lingering problem for her. I'm not sure how good the pills Clarkson gives her are. Sometimes, I think it makes things worse. At any rate, she needed some time to herself...away from the lake, and the uh...ghost stuff that fool Hallace was talking about."

"Where did she go?" Calvo asked.

Randall paused as his eyes darted down to the right. "She, uh, she left a note saying she was going to see a cousin for a while."

"Name, please?" Calvo asked, her ubiquitous tablet poised.

Again, Randall paused. This is what he feared might happen.

"I believe the note said her Cousin Jenny...in Alabama."

"Do you have a phone number for Cousin Jenny?" Calvin asked pleasantly. Again, a nervous pause before Randall crossed to a small secretary desk and opened a drawer. He pulled out a pink address book. As he thumbed through it, Calvo noticed his hand was shaking.

"It's 555-230-8990," he said, his voice thick.

"Thank you," Calvo said, entering the number on her tablet. "When do you expect her back?"

This time, the man's body language was unmistakable. He rocked from side to side, pushing his blonde wavy hair from his forehead. A thin vein appeared running down between his eyebrows.

"She was, uh, vague on that point," he said, running his tongue over his dry lips. "It isn't something you can plan, you know? I mean, when you're going to feel like coming back."

"I'm sure," Calvo said soothingly. "But she is remarkably close to Tulie. I shouldn't think she would stay away very long." Silence followed. "Oh well, we can ask her that ourselves. We'll give Cousin Jenny a shout." She smiled.

"We need to speak with Tulie for a minute," Hilliard said abruptly. Mr. Barrows was making him nervous with his obvious distress.

"She doesn't know anything more about her mother's plans than what I've told you," Randall said hurriedly. "This whole thing has been stressful for her."

"It's about another matter I need to speak with her," Hilliard said evenly. "Only take a minute."

Randall paused. Finally, he turned on his heel and walked to the base of the main staircase visible through the open double parlor doors. "Tulie," he yelled up the stairs. "Come down here, please."

"Brenn too, please," Hilliard called to him.

"Brenn isn't here," Randall said. "She's in the city."

The bottom of Tulie's legs appeared on the stairs below the ceiling level of the hallway. She bent to peer into the parlor and stopped when she saw the officers. Calvo smiled encouragingly at her, and the young woman finally descended the remainder of the stairs. She shot an enquiring look at her father, and then walked slowly into the parlor. Clasping her hands together tightly, she waited.

"Miss Tulie," Calvo began. It had been determined

in the car on their way over that the lieutenant would manage Tulie. "We have a couple of quick questions for you. When we were here a few days ago…the day after the engagement party…you said your Aunt Margo was kind enough to meet Skylar in the garden after the cake ceremony to get your blue sash back. Do you remember telling us that?"

Tulie's eyes were wide with fear. She tried unsuccessfully to control her breathing. She glanced at her father, who was standing off to the side, his own demeanor one of trepidation.

"Yes," she answered simply and waited.

"Did your aunt get the sash from Skylar and return it to you?" Calvin pushed.

Tulie looked again at her father, her hands twisting in knots.

"No. Aunt Margo came out of the garden without it when they announced the parents were supposed to give a speech. So, I…I got it back without her." She looked at the floor, her sleeveless blouse rising and falling with her deep breaths.

"How? How did you get it back?" Calvo asked gently. The air was filled with tension, and she was afraid the girl was going to bolt at any moment.

"I don't remember," Tulie said, slumping into herself as if hoping to disappear.

"Tulie, that's a child's answer," Calvo said, a hint of exasperation entering her voice. "Of course you remember. We've been to the dress store. You returned your dress and your mother's. The blue sash was with your dress. You got it back somehow. How?"

"I just found it!" she blurted, her eyes rimming with tears. "It, it was on the ground. I was looking for my

Mama, and I saw it lying on the ground."

Calvo paused and looked at Hilliard. His eyes were mere slits behind his glasses as he studied the quaking girl in front of him.

"Tulie," Calvo said in the coaxing tones of one dealing with a child. "Think hard. Where did you find the sash on the ground?"

"I don't remember," Tulie yelled.

"Tulie, are you covering for someone? This is serious. Please. We need to know what you know," Calvo pleaded.

Tulie stared at her for a moment, and Calvo saw pure fear in the young woman's eyes.

"I don't know," Tulie cried out and ran from the room. Her feet pounded up the stairs. The sound of a door slamming followed her.

Two pairs of eyes shifted over to Randall, who looked frozen in place. The chirring sound of insects through the screen window filled the room.

"I really must ask you to leave my daughter alone now," he said, anger replacing the nervousness he had been portraying. "She's been through a lot. She doesn't have anything to offer about this missing girl. Skylar Harris is bad news. She's run off! That's all there is to it. Somebody with more money than Landon came along, maybe even encouraged her at the party, and she took off. She was flirting with everybody!"

"I can't promise you that we won't have more questions," Hilliard said evenly. "But that's all for now. We'll get in touch with your wife and see if she has any helpful information. I'm sorry for bothering you."

Randall flinched, but regained his composure. He led them to the front door and held it open wide. A blast of humid heat rushed into the foyer. The two officers stepped outside and turned to tell him 'Goodbye,' but he had already closed the door.

Jennifer Hutchins answered the phone on its third ring. She wiped her hands on a kitchen towel as she cradled her cell phone on her shoulder.

"Yes?" she asked, in the same frustrated tone with which she had answered Margo's call.

"Miss Hutchins?" Lieutenant Calvo asked pleasantly.

"I don't want any," Jenny said, preparing to hang up.

"I'm not selling anything," Calvo said hurriedly. "This is Lieutenant Adelaide Calvo with the Orleans Police Department. I just need a moment of your time."

Jenny placed the towel on the kitchen counter and leaned against it. A few seconds of silence ensued.

"Miss Hutchins?"

"Yes."

"I'm calling to talk to Rachel…Rachel Barrows, is she there, please?"

Jenny's face turned red. "No, she is not. I don't know where she is, but she is not here. Why? What did she do?"

"She hasn't done anything," Calvo said, surprised. "We just need to speak to her, and we were told she was visiting with you for a while."

"She called, inviting herself to come see me, but I told her this is a bad time," Jenny said shortly.

"When did she call you?" Calvo asked.

"This morning, early. I was quite surprised. I haven't heard from her in a long time. We aren't close cousins if you get my drift. If that's all…"

"How did she sound?" Calvo pressed.

"Sound? I don't know. Fine, I guess. A little nervous, maybe. Like I said, we aren't close. We don't see each other much. I saw her at her son's funeral… a long time ago."

"17 years," Calvo said. She was disliking Jenny Hutchins more by the minute. "And no hint at all as to where she was going after you turned her down?"

Calvo could sense the heat coming through the phone.

"I have *no* idea! And if she's in some kind of trouble, I'd be the last to know anything. Have a nice day."

Angela Peterson let out a wail. Calvin looked up in alarm from a crossword puzzle he was filling in.

"What is it?" he shouted, even though his wife was standing less than ten feet away from him in the coolness of the shadowed parlor. Angela was clutching the phone receiver in both hands, shaking violently.

"They found Beauregard!" she cried. "He's in Margo's garden. He's dead!" She dropped the phone and ran sobbing to the kitchen.

Reed Tillson stood in his air-conditioned kitchen facing the attentive faces of six of his staff. His tone was conspiratorial as he gave his instructions.

"I cannot stress enough the importance of this party," he said, placing steely eyes on each of the four maids and two male stewards in turn. "You have done magnificently in keeping it a secret for the past two weeks; not an easy feat where my wife is concerned. Plus, y'all had the added machinations of the engagement party to deal with." Reed noticed the sudden air of embarrassment among his staff as he brought up the unfortunate party.

He glanced at the kitchen wall clock and continued, "I have to handle a situation that came up," he said. "Something concerning an injured cat. I need y'all to help with this. We will welcome the guests in an hour. Stephanie, lead them into the parlor and remind them to keep quiet. Jefferson, you will wheel the cake in, candles lit, ten minutes after you hear the guests yelling, 'Surprise!' He glanced about him at the island counter laden with dainty finger sandwiches, chocolate-covered strawberries, freshly cut crudities, dips, and baskets of home-baked cookies.

"Brixi?" he continued. "You and Melanie pour the mimosas. We'll have Margo open her birthday presents after everyone has eaten. Questions?"

"Who is cutting the cake and serving it?" Brixi asked.

"Maude, you oversee that," he said. "Stephanie, you will hand Mrs. Tillson her presents when it comes time to open them. Now, remember, when you hear Mrs. Tillson's car pull up, stay quiet. I'll head her off with an excuse about needing her upstairs until the guests arrive. They've been told to come through the patio doors without knocking.

"Alright! Well done, all," he continued. "Let's make this birthday party a happy one. Mrs. Tillson has been through a lot. I don't need to tell you that. I appreciate y'all more than I can say. Oh, one last thing—let's not bring up that she is turning 60. The candles on the cake are tastefully organized to look like part of the motif. I warned her friends to forego the usual birthday cards with tasteless jokes about age." He smiled amicably, knowing the stress his wife put the servants through daily.

At 10:30 am, Margo pulled into her driveway. She turned off the motor and reached for a large shopping bag holding custom-made bedroom curtains in the seat next to her. Reed came from around the corner of the house and intercepted her as she exited the car.

"Emergency!" he said, smiling at her. "I need your help. Gary Masters has invited me last minute to a gentleman's fundraiser tonight, and it's black tie. Would you please come upstairs and help me pick out what to wear?"

Margo eyed him keenly. "Since when do you ask my opinion about your attire?" she asked, walking up the sidewalk toward the side door that led into the mudroom and kitchen. Reed caught her arm and steered her in the opposite direction. "You have a package in the foyer," he said lamely. "Let's go in the front door."

"You are acting even stranger than usual," she said, annoyed at being herded like cattle. They walked into the foyer, where there was indeed a package waiting for her. "At least someone remembered my birthday," she said smugly, looking at the Miami address. "At least my Florida friends haven't forsaken me."

"You can open it after lunch today when I take you out to celebrate," Reed said hurriedly. "Right now, I need your fashion sense."

They walked along the long hallway, past the closed parlor doors, and ascended the staircase to the master bedroom.

At 11:00, guests began tiptoeing into the parlor through the French patio doors. The fifteen women quietly took their seats, each relinquishing their gifts to a maid in a starched white uniform. The presents were placed with care on a white lace-covered table near the fireplace.

A hush fell over the room as Reed's voice came booming from outside the closed parlor doors. It was their signal. "Of course, I'm going to spoil you for your birthday!" he yelled. "I have made plans for more than just lunch today, and you'll love it." With that, he pushed open the double parlor pocket doors with a flourish.

"Surprise!" the women yelled in unison, jumping to their feet. They clapped with delight as Margo stumbled backward, her eyes bulging. Within seconds, a massive smile spread across her face, and her eyes twinkled with excitement.

"Oh my!" she yelled happily. "Oh, my heavenly goodness! Look at this!"

She waltzed into the room, forgetting Reed, who remained just inside the open doorway. He watched as his wife worked the room, hugging each woman with delight. Despite being ignored, he was content. He had pulled off a surprise party that many thought impossible. He shook his head, grinning, and walked off toward the kitchen.

The morning turned into early afternoon as the house echoed with the excited twittering of over a dozen females. Maids collected used plates and napkins, refilling the champagne flutes with mimosas until tongues were thick with the orange juice and champagne concoction. Finally, the presents were passed to the birthday girl, who was moved to a large Queen Anne chair at the head of the room to open her gifts. Brixi handed each gift to Stephanie, who in turn, placed it in the eager hands of her employer.

Margo looked about, beaming upon them all, like a queen bestowing her attention on grateful subjects. She cooed over each elaborate bow and wrapping. She thanked each guest in turn as she held up her treasures of porcelain, costume jewelry, and coupons to fancy New Orleans spas.

"You are spoiling me!" she cooed happily.

"Well, Reed really did all the hard work to have this party for you," Melanie Wentworth said. "By the way, where is Rachel?"

Margo paused, surprised at the sudden question. She and Randall had kept Rachel's "visit" to her Cousin Jenny's a secret as much as possible.

"Oh...well, she's on vacation," Margo said, forcing a tight smile. "Reed probably waited too long to inform her of my party, and she couldn't switch dates. She and I will catch up when she gets back."

The explanation seemed to satisfy the nosy guests. Finally, her personal maid Stephanie handed her the last present, a look of confusion on her face. She did not remember the red foil-wrapped present being there earlier.

Margo deftly untied the red satin ribbon and slid a long-manicured nail under the tape securing the foil wrapping paper. It fell away, revealing an ordinary-looking brown cardboard box. Puzzled, she lifted the lid to find crumpled white toilet tissue paper stuffed in piles. She looked around her with an air of embarrassment as she began picking up each wad of paper. Suddenly, the color drained from her face. Her hands were shaking as she leaned back away from the box in her lap.

Looks of surprise swept the room as several women

nearest her tried to peer into the box. Stephanie stepped over to her distraught employer and looked inside the tissue wadding. Nestled there were several pieces of broken statuary. She immediately recognized the white shepherdess that had broken in Margo's room the night after the engagement party. Stephanie hesitated, not knowing what to do with the strange present.

"What in the world, Margo?" Margaret Ruthers said. "You look like you've seen a ghost!" She picked up a wad of the toilet tissue near her shoe and said sarcastically, "But I get that one-ply paper would horrify anyone." The guests erupted in laughter.

Margo recoiled from the present, gasping. The box fell to the floor, the broken statuette pieces spilling out onto the Aubusson rug. A white index card lay among the bone China shards with lettering written across it in black marker. Margaret, who was nearest to it, picked it up and tried to pass it to Margo, who looked at it as if it were a snake coiled to strike. When she refused to touch it, Margaret read it aloud:

"Sorry this **BROKE**. Thought you might want it back.
I stuck my **NECK** out to get it for you.
I looked till I was **GREEN** in the face but couldn't find one just like it.
Didn't want to leave you in the **DARK**.

Talk to you soon."

Margo snatched the card from Margaret's hand and shoved it into her dress pocket. She looked anxiously about at the startled expressions of her guests and struggled for words. She finally forced a strained smile and thanked them all for the wonderful gifts, "Including the prank gift," she said, hoping to save the situation. "Reed never forgave me for breaking this little statue he gave me on our anniversary one year. He's just messing with me," she said jovially, but the guests' faces remained puzzled.

The women departed after several minutes of forced small talk. Margo retreated to her room. The box with the broken statue had been taken away by Stephanie to the kitchen and placed in the cabinet beneath the sink until further instructions. The maids whispered amongst themselves as they cleared up after the party. Brixi cornered Maude, her closest friend in the Tillson's wait staff, and her new roommate. She looked about her carefully to ensure they were alone in the mudroom.

"Something odd is going on," Brixi said in a whisper, her hand clutching the other maid's arm. "The broken window and missing curtains, for one." All the staff knew about the window in the master bedroom, so there was no need to elaborate.

"I found muddy shoes in the garbage the day after Miss Skylar went missing," Brixi continued in hushed tones. "They were Miss Margo's. They were chipped up and caked in mud. She was acting like something was missing from her bathroom —what, I don't know. But she seemed stressed out about it. Now, this present with a broken statue in it. I picked up the pieces of that statue myself in her bedroom and threw them out with the garbage. What's it doing back here in a present? And that note! Did you see the words in bold black? BROKE NECK GREEN DARK! Miss Skylar's dress was green. Did someone break her neck?"

Maude stared at her, her brown eyes the size of golf balls. She was audibly panting, fear rising from her stomach. "You don't think…" she began, clutching Brixi's arm.

"All I know is, Miss Margo hated Skylar Harris! *Hated* her! Now she's gone, and whoever wrote that note knows what happened," Brixi said ominously.

A sound came from the kitchen, and the two broke apart, exiting the mudroom to see Brenn Barrows standing there.

"And that's where we put the extra trash bags," Brixi said loudly, creating a cover story for why she and Maude were huddled in the mudroom.

Upstairs, Margo collapsed on her bed; a migraine threatening to take hold. Pinpricks of light flashed at the corners of her eyes as a freight train roared through her head. Reed's voice could be heard outside the window, ordering the removal of a dead elm tree. She pressed her hands to her ears, which only amplified the thunder inside her skull. With great difficulty, she rolled onto her side and sat up. A bowling ball rolled to the front of her face, and she gripped the duvet.

After several pain-filled minutes, she rose unsteadily to her feet and made her way to the master bathroom. Reaching behind her, she unzipped her dress and let it puddle to the floor. Stepping out of it, she slid her slip straps off over her shoulders and let them fall in a heap. She opened several bathroom drawers before finding one with the prescription bottle with the medication for her frequent headaches. She popped the top and tipped the bottle up to her lips, letting two pills fall into her mouth.

Margo reached for the tumbler and turned on the tap over the sink. She filled it and let it run as she splashed her face with the cold water, feeling a momentary sense of relief from the heat and the pain. A memory surfaced, and she whirled around to face the shower curtain, her head screaming in protest at the sudden movement. There was nothing there. The curtain rod sat innocently in the overhead light.

Holding onto the doorframe for support, Margo teetered back to her bed and sank gratefully onto the cool comforter, finally lying back onto the pillows. She threw one arm over her eyes to block out the light. The other arm she pushed beneath the pillow next to her and waited for the pills to kick in.

Something pricked her finger, and she yanked her hand away. Rising slightly onto her elbow, she flipped the pillow over, fearing some bug was beneath it. Instead, a white index card lay there, the block handwriting in black marker read:

"Leave $50,000 in cash in an envelope inside the tire swing at Rachel's house tomorrow night at 11:00. For starters…"

21 FLOWERS

Earlier, while Margo's birthday party was in full swing inside, Reed walked over to the driveway as Angela pulled her car up to the house. He waited with trepidation as the large woman climbed from the driver's seat, her face swollen with tears. Forster, the Tillson's gardener, waited at the end of the sidewalk that led into the sprawling back yard.

"Angela," Reed said gently. "I'm so sorry. Even now, I'm praying it isn't your cat. Forster here found it this morning, just before Margo's party was starting, and said he had seen it at your house before when he helped you with some plantings. I called you as soon as he told me," he stumbled on, not sure how to handle the situation. "Margo is at her party inside. She's been dealing with some…"

"Where is he?" Angela said curtly, cutting him off. She refrained from mentioning she had not been invited to her cousin's surprise party…only the fancy ladies.

Reed looked at Forster, who started off toward the garden arch at the end of the sidewalk. Reed and Angela followed. No one spoke as the hefty landscaper led them along the gravel garden path toward the fountain. He paused and turned to face the woman who had a handkerchief pressed to her mouth. She was trembling.

"He's...um...over there, in that batch of lilies," he said gently, pointing off to his right and up the path a few feet.

Reed hung back. He had already seen the cat, and it wasn't an image he wanted to see again. Angela sobbed as she stumbled the short distance to where a stand of Casa Blanca lilies lay bent and broken. A few feet away was Beauregard. He was lying on his side, his stomach sunken as if the air had been syphoned from him. His eyes were open, and his tongue, now a dull black, lolled between pointed teeth. It was clear he was dead.

Angela let out a piercing scream, confirming in Reed's mind that it was indeed her missing cat. She bent toward her beloved pet but could not bring herself to touch him.

"I can't!" she wailed. "I can't!" She turned and ran blindly up the path. Minutes later, her car roared to life, and she tore off down the driveway, narrowly hitting Margaret Ruther's Mercedes and a small red sports car belonging to another of the party guests.

Forster walked over to look at the cat, and Reed reluctantly followed him. A dusting of lily pollen coated Beauregard's fur. Nearby was a puddle of vomit.

"Well, it's obvious," Reed said sadly, forcing himself to study the scene. "The cat got into the lilies and probably licked the pollen that got onto him. When he

292

licked his fur, it poisoned him. These flowers are deadly to cats. Strange thing is, they're not toxic to humans or dogs, or I never would have planted them. But they are to cats. You can see where he threw up before he died. I guess I never thought about a cat getting in here."

Forster was quiet as he surveyed the broken lilies. At least half a dozen were bent completely over and snapped.

"I may be wrong," he began, "but cats don't usually pounce on flowers like that. They kinda weave in and out of stuff. Me and the Mrs. have had cats all our married life. This here looks like maybe the cat was thrown into those lilies. See how the whole patch is broken over? I've never seen that cat come farther than Miss Rachel's. Not with your dog around."

Reed stared at the snapped flower stalks and then over to the cat coated in orange pollen.

"Who would do a thing like that?" he asked quietly.

"Someone cruel who knows lilies are deadly to cats," Forster said, a chill running along his forearms.

Lieutenant Calvo knocked softly on Angela's front screen door. She took a deep breath in preparation for the upcoming conversation. After several moments, Angela appeared on the other side of the screen, her eyes barely visible through swollen eyelids. Her complexion was blotchy, and she had aged overnight.

"Mrs. Peterson," Calvo began quietly. "I am so deeply sorry to bother you. May I speak to you for a minute, please?"

Angela paused and finally pushed the door open, stepping aside to admit the officer. It took Calvo's eyes a minute to adjust to the darkened room after coming in from the dazzling sunlight. As the parlor came into focus, she realized all the curtains were pulled shut. Angela waited. She didn't offer the lieutenant a chair.

"First of all," Calvo began in her soft drawl, "I'm so deeply sorry about Beauregard. I know your affection for him." She waited, but Angela didn't respond. The only sound coming from the woman was a series of sniffles.

"We are waiting on the report, but all indications are that it does look like he died from ingesting the lily pollen. It causes kidney failure..."

Angela abruptly raised her hand to halt the rest of the sentence. "I know what he died from!" she said hotly. "Those boys killed him!"

"No, ma'am," Calvo said, fearing an onslaught was coming her way. "Lilies are highly toxic to cats. They lick their fur to get the pollen off and..."

"I didn't say it wasn't the pollen that killed him, but those boys threw my cat into those flowers! I saw it for myself. They were all broken. I've never seen Beauregard break a flower in my life, and I raise tons of them in my garden. Frankly, he isn't interested in them! He never once set foot on Reed's property because of that vicious dog he has. Not once! So, how did he end up in Reed's flowerbed?" She ran the edge of her hand under her nose, sniffing loudly.

The lieutenant paused for a moment, choosing her words carefully. "Are you aware that one of those boys is in the hospital?" she asked slowly. "He, uh, well, he shows signs of poisoning as well." She waited, watching the large woman's face.

"Poisoned?" Angela blurted out, seeming genuinely

shocked.

Calvin suddenly appeared and wheeled himself into the room. The lieutenant had the impression he had been listening from the hallway. Her eyes went impulsively to the wheels of his wheelchair, noting the thin bicycle-like tires and tread.

"Told you," he said, looking at his wife with an air of satisfaction. "Devil's Trumpet. Deadly Nightshade."

Calvo looked at him in shock. "What are you saying?" she asked, her heart rate escalating.

"Those boys," Calvin said eagerly. "They were in Angela's garden a while back. Stepped all over her flowers. She said several of her trumpet flowers were torn off the vines. Those are deadly. All you have to do is inhale them or eat them...hell...you can absorb it through your skin. I told her at the time that if they took off with those flowers, they were messing with Deadly Nightshade."

The lieutenant looked from Calvin to his wife, who was standing stiffly in the dim light of the room.

"Was this before your cat went missing," Calvo asked, "or after?"

Angela's head jerked in her direction, and her body convulsed. "What are you implying?" she shouted. "That I had something to do with that boy being sick? They picked my flowers. I didn't hand them to him!"

"No," Calvo said, taking a firmer tone, "but did you try to find his parents and warn them? Surely, you didn't just let a group of young boys walk off with poisonous flowers and not do anything?"

"Get out of my house," Angela spat. "How dare you? They killed my cat, and you stand here accusing me of willfully harming one of those delinquents? That's like feeling sorry for a burglar who got shot while robbing my house! Get out!"

The screen door slammed behind the lieutenant after Angela herded the officer from her house. Calvo could hear her screaming at her husband all the way down the sidewalk to the squad car. She sighed, climbed into the driver's seat, started the engine, and cranked the AC. She picked up her cell phone and punched in Hilliard's number.

"Did you survive?" he asked, forgoing a formal greeting.

"I know how a fileted fish feels," Calvo sighed. "She is certain those boys killed her cat, and she denies any knowledge of what happened to Tom Simons. Calvin thinks Tom may have been poisoned by playing with some of Angela's trumpet flowers…Devil's Trumpet or something like that. He says it's a member of the Deadly Nightshade group. I suppose it's possible. Any news from the hospital?"

"Yeah. Calvin may be dead on, pardon the pun. They pumped Tommy's stomach… took a urine sample." The phone call crackled, Hilliard's words coming in spurts as the service was interrupted. "His symptoms… indicative…same poison found in belladonna… …nightshade and other poisons of that genus. He's going to be ok. They have him hooked up to an IV. He's…temporary blindness from touching his eyes with the sap or part of the flower. The doctor says he will…fully recover. The other boys confirm he was blowing on one of the big flowers…Angela's garden, pretending it was a bugle…enough if he was inhaling that stuff. The doctor said he would have felt the effects within a few hours."

"You're breaking up," Calvo said, "but I think I got most of it. The cell service by the lake is awful." She drove up Angela's driveway and out onto Broussard Lane. The cell service improved. "So, what about the cat?" Calvo asked. "It's too much of a coincidence. Both Tom and the cat are poisoned by flowers. Do you think Tom could have thrown the cat into the lilies *before* he stole Angela's flowers? I suppose he could have run across the cat while the boys were playing with the flower and thrown it into the lilies before Tom started feeling sick. Maybe it's all just some sort of sick karma."

"I don't believe in karma," Hilliard said. "And I don't believe in ghosts or curses. But I swear, I have never seen so many deaths surrounding one group of people! Speaking of which, did you look into those family deaths I asked you to?"

"Yes. I started with the brother…Margo and Rachel's brother, Barry. He died in a waterskiing accident one year before Ryder died. Sounds like just one of those tragic things. I tracked down one of Barry's friends who was in the boat the day of the accident. He picked up Barry's waterski from the water while the paramedics dealt with the body on the rocks. He says he took the boat back to the dock and put it and the ski away in the boat house. I guess it was an expensive ski, and he felt he didn't have the right to dispense of it."

"What's his name?" Hilliard asked.

"Roger Hendersen."

The following morning, Brixi tapped lightly on Margo's bedroom door and waited. There was no answer, so she gently turned the doorknob and peered in.

"Miss Margo?" she called out quietly. "You have some mail that looks like birthday cards that arrived in the mail this morning."

The room was empty. She noticed her employer's purse was gone from the small table near the door, signaling that Margo had gone somewhere. Brixi walked over to the neatly made bed and placed a stack of mail on the duvet. She peered about the room curiously. Piles of opened presents were stacked against one wall, the expensive gifts still residing in pastel tissue papers. Brixi stepped over to them and bent to take a closer look. The cardboard box with the broken statuette was not among them. A large bag with what looked like new velvet window curtains sat near the closet door.

She turned to leave just as her cell phone pinged in her pocket. Brixi pulled it out and read the text from Stephanie, Margo's personal maid.

"If you're still talking to Miss Margo, would you bring down the dirty towels from the bathroom for me? I'll bring up some fresh ones in a minute."

"She's not here," Brixi typed. "I just left the mail on her bed. I'll bring them."

Brixi walked into the bathroom and turned on the light. The three towels hanging on the hooks by the shower were still fresh and untouched. She picked up a damp towel draped over the bathtub, another wet towel dropped on the floor, and picked up a lid to a prescription bottle that had fallen beneath the cabinet overhang. She looked about for the bottle it belonged to but didn't see one. As she picked up a wet hand towel next to the sink, a brown prescription bottle rolled out from beneath it and fell onto the floor with a clinking sound. It was missing its lid.

Brixi bent and picked it up. Something inside thudded to the bottom of the bottle. She tipped the bottle up and was surprised to see an expensive diamond ring fall out into her palm. *What a strange place to hide jewelry,* she thought. She held the ring up and studied it. The platinum band housed the largest diamond she had ever seen. Two emeralds rested against it on either side. Her breath caught as it twinkled from the overhead light.

A door sounded from downstairs and Brixi hurriedly replaced the ring in the bottle and screwed its lid back on, standing it on the counter where it had been hidden beneath the towel. She grabbed the three soiled towels in both arms and hurried from the room.

Margo climbed the front staircase just as Brixi was hurrying down the back servant's stairs. Margo entered her room and set her purse down on the table. The mail on her bed caught her eye, and she walked over to it. She sighed loudly as she flipped through the letters in various pastel envelopes. They were clearly birthday cards. She sat down heavily onto the edge of the bed and placed her head in her hands, tears seeping between her fingers.

A tap came on the door, and Margo hurriedly wiped her cheeks with the back of her hand. She straightened and patted her hair into place. "Come in," she called.

Stephanie entered the room with an armful of folded towels. "Sorry to disturb," she said, smiling. "I have your clean towels." Without waiting for Margo to respond, she walked quickly into the bathroom and placed the towels in their proper places. She hurried back into the bedroom.

"Do you need anything?" she asked her employer when she exited the bathroom. "Have you had any lunch?"

"I'm not hungry," Margo said. "Was this all the mail? I'm expecting some legal papers," she said tiredly.

"Brixi brought it up, but I would think that's all of it," Stephanie said. "I can ask her, if you like."

"Why did Brixi bring it up?" Margo asked sharply. "You're supposed to handle my things."

Stephanie hesitated, surprised at the woman's tone.

"I was working on the Thank You notes for your gifts in the parlor downstairs, like you asked me to, Ma'am, so I asked Brixi to bring the mail up to you. I didn't think you'd mind. You seemed anxious to get the Thank You's out. I hope I didn't do wrong. She came straight back down. I did ask her to bring down your wet towels. It won't happen again."

The maid waited, her hands clasped tightly in front of her. Working around Miss Margo lately had been akin to walking a tight rope without a safety net. Miss Skylar's disappearance was weighing on her employer more than the maid realized.

"I'm just tired," Margo said after a moment's pause. "But I prefer you be the only one in my rooms, are we clear on that?"

"Of course, Miss Margo," Stephanie said gratefully. "If I can bring you a tray, please let me know."

With that, she eased out of the room and closed the door quietly behind her.

Margo rose and pressed a hand to the back of her neck. She rolled her head tiredly and walked into the bathroom. Flicking on the light, she unzipped her slacks and pushed them down until she could heel out of them. She kicked them to one side and began unbuttoning her silk blouse. She looked at her reflection in the mirror and cringed. Overnight, crows' feet had appeared at the edges of her eyes, and there were brown shadows in the hollows on each side of her nose.

A flashback from a few hours prior ran through her mind. She had been hurriedly dressing to meet Randall at their usual spot in the parking lot by McCallister's produce stand. Randall's phone call ordering her to meet him had rattled her; his voice sounded panicked. *It has to be bad news*, she thought, and so she hurriedly changed out of her robe. A migraine was threatening, and she had pulled one of the many medicine bottles from the cabinet drawer and flipped open its lid. The lid had fallen to the floor and rolled to where she couldn't see it. She looked down into the bottle to see Skylar's engagement ring there. She had grabbed the wrong bottle.

Randall called again, and Margo set the bottle down near the sink. He was yelling about Rachel's Cousin Jenny calling him. He wanted to know if Jenny had called her, too. Margo answered in the negative, and he yelled at her again to hurry and meet him. He abruptly hung up. Margo's head was pounding as she bent to look for the missing bottle lid. The room spun, and a wave of dizziness overtook her.

"This has to end," she cried to the empty room, as she gripped the marble counter. Grabbing a hand towel, she wetted it beneath the faucet and pressed it to her forehead; the cold water reviving her temporarily. She flung it aside as her mind raced. *Had they found*

Rachel's body? Is that why Randall demanded to see her? Feeling nauseous, she hurried from the room to keep her meeting with a man who was losing control.

Now back at home, Margo pulled her arms through the silk sleeves of her blouse and tossed the garment to the floor. *Randall was coming unglued,* she thought, exhaustion overtaking her. He was yelling at her in the car that the police now knew Rachel never went to Jenny's house in Alabama. Margo had spent almost an hour this morning reassuring him that they were still okay. So what if Rachel didn't go there? As far as the police knew, she simply went somewhere else after Jenny turned her down. If Randall wasn't careful, he was going to blow everything!

Her eyes went to the prescription bottle sitting on the other side of her sink, and her heart skipped. The lid she had dropped earlier was now screwed back into place. She reached for the bottle and, holding her breath, opened the lid to peer inside. With a sigh of relief, she saw the diamond engagement ring still there. The sensation soon passed as she realized someone had to have replaced the lid back onto the bottle after she left. It was still missing when she hurried out the door to meet Randall. There was only one person she knew of who had been in her bathroom while she was gone: Brixi.

22 The Past Has Long Shadows

Stephanie sat anxiously waiting for Margo to enter the parlor. She had received a text from her a few minutes earlier demanding that she meet with her. *What had she done wrong now?* the maid wondered.

Margo entered the room, the sound of her flapping sandals preceding her. Stephanie was shocked at her haggard expression. She seemed even more stressed than she was a few minutes ago in her room. Stephanie remembered Brixi telling her the shower towels had not been used when she asked Brixi where the rest of the dirty towels were. That meant Reed must be sleeping elsewhere, and Margo was foregoing using the shower.

Margo sat on the edge of a high-backed chair and faced the maid who waited nervously across from her. Stephanie shifted in her chair and prepared to be fired.

"Stephanie," Margo began with a preamble. "It has not escaped your notice that odd things have been going on. The fact that Skylar Harris decided to up and abandon my son during his engagement party is out of my control. The embarrassment it has caused me is enough. But it appears that someone has been in my room, and I believe you may have some information for me on that account."

Stephanie looked surprised.

"I did tell you that Brixi brought down some wet towels for me this morning," she began feebly. "She left some mail for you, but other than that, I'm usually the only one in your room."

"Who all helped with the...the cleanup after the window broke?" Margo asked. It was a subject she would rather avoid, but she had to have some answers.

"Um...," Stephanie paused, casting her memory back five days to the morning after the engagement party. "Brad and Wes picked up the broken glass and put the pieces in some boxes," she said. "Brixi and I cleaned and vacuumed."

"Did Brad and Wes pick up the statuette pieces?" Margo asked, eyeing the girl keenly.

Realization dawned on Stephanie. This was the reason for the meeting. The birthday present with a broken statue inside, and the strange note accompanying it.

"No, ma'am. Brixi and I picked up the pieces. It didn't look like it could ever be repaired, so I put it in the garbage bag with the broken glass from the window."

"And you took the garbage bag to the garage?" Margo asked, her face taut.

"No, ma'am. Brixi brought the garbage bag down. She was collecting all the trash bags from the party and taking them to the garage," Stephanie said, fearing it was Brixi about to get the sack, not her.

"Has Brixi said anything to you lately?" Margo asked, careful in her wording.

"Well, Brixi can be a little immature," Stephanie said, feeling a renewed confidence that her job was secure. "She gossips, but then most of the girls do. It's harmless, really." Inwardly, she cringed, remembering Brixi mimicking Margo drinking as the reason the floor lamp fell over and smashed the bedroom window. "She has a good heart, but she can be a little scatterbrained. Maude is closest to her of all of us here. They went in together on an apartment a few weeks ago."

Margo pressed her lips together. "Tell Maude to come in here, please," she said finally.

Stephanie rose quickly from her chair, eager to be finished with the interrogation. She hurried out into the hallway. A few minutes later, a young maid with mousy brown hair and a profusion of cheap rings adorning each finger entered and waited for instruction.

"Sit down, Maude," Margo said, watching the girl's face closely. "You're not in trouble," she added hurriedly as the maid looked close to tears.

Maude sniffed and nodded but looked unconvinced.

"I understand you are good friends with Brixi," Margo said. "I just want to ask you a couple of questions, and your job here is dependent on your veracity, do you understand?"

Maude paused, a look of confusion on her face, before she slowly shook her head no.

"What don't you understand?" Margo asked, her temper rising.

"What veracity means," the maid said, embarrassed.

Margo sighed. "It means you must answer me

truthfully. Now…has Brixi been telling you anything in the way of gossip about me?"

Maude's eyes widened, and she nibbled her lower lip anxiously. A million lies flew through her mind, but her paycheck won out in the end.

"Yes, ma'am, a few things," she said, clutching her apron with clenched fingers.

"What?" Margo demanded.

"Well, she did mention looking in the garbage and keeping some old magazines. She said she thought you were acting strange since the party…the engagement party. She said she thought it was odd that your bedroom curtains are missing…that they weren't in the garbage. Um…I guess that's it…oh! The note from your birthday party. She's been talking about that."

Maude waited, her anxiety at fever pitch. Margo could fire her for being part of Brixi's gossip and not reporting it to her.

Margo's eyes narrowed.

"Did Brixi pull that broken statue out of the garbage as well as my… magazines?"

"I don't know that, Miss Margo," she said quickly, hoping to undo the damage. "I saw her bring the bag down from your room and I heard broken glass when she dropped it on the kitchen floor. She did drag all the garbage bags out of the kitchen but that's all I know."

Margo wanted desperately to ask about the green sash she had found hanging in her bathroom and the note beneath her pillow, but it was too risky to mention. The wet sash from the shower rod had disappeared. She also wanted to know if Brixi had seen her muddy shoes in the trash, but again, it was too risky to mention, as was who had replaced the lid to the prescription bottle in her bathroom.

Maude waited as Margo searched for other questions to ask her. She suddenly hit on one.

"Maude," she said in a gentler tone. "I'm glad I got this chance to talk with you. I need to do better about getting a feel for my employees…their needs, etc." She forced a smile devoid of warmth. "Your salary here, for instance. Do you find it adequate?"

Maude blinked, confused at the sudden turn in the conversation. She had gone from fear of being fired to being asked if more money would be useful.

"I…I…I'm grateful for the job," the maid countered, not sure what response would be appropriate.

"Not what I meant," Margo said, the hard edge returning. "You and Brixi share an apartment, correct? You have money for the bills, food, etc?"

"It's tight, but we are doing okay," Maude said. "It will be a bit better now."

"How so?" Margo asked, immediately alert.

"Well, Brixi came into some money," Maude said, brightening a little. "Brixi told me her grandmother died and left her a little money. We treated ourselves to a nice dinner out." Maude smiled at her employer with a look of total innocence.

Margo's stomach clinched.

"When did she come into 'some money?'" Margo said, trying unsuccessfully to hide her anger.

"She…she told me this morning before we came into work, when she was paying the rent," Maude said, gripping the chair arms. "May I be excused, please?" Maude asked, half-rising from her chair. Margo's face was scaring her. She was afraid her next question might be about the ring Brixi told her she saw in a medicine bottle in Margo's bathroom.

Moments passed as Margo tried desperately to process the added information. Finally, she said, "You can go." Maude hurried from the room.

Margo sat staring out the French doors toward the patio and back yard, with the lake beyond that. The memory from the night before flooded back. A nightmarish event that would be forever with her. She saw herself walking through the pecan grove toward Rachel's house, the moon lying on its side in a slim crescent of light. Mosquitos buzzed relentlessly near her ears, several biting her face and hands. She swatted at them angrily, using the envelope in her hand to wave them away.

She recalled reaching Rachel's side yard and glancing nervously at the cemetery next to her, its vaults sitting in huddled masses, the decayed bodies of her ancestors cloistered inside. She swallowed and looked about her for anyone living who was waiting in the darkness. Finally, she stepped to the weathered tire swing and placed the envelope inside. She pushed it down until none of its white paper showed.

Margo remembered pausing in the shadows of the giant tree. She could see Angela's house from there, which meant Angela could also see the tire swing from her windows. Was the broken statue present, and a note from Angela? Had she picked the blackmail money location? Margo glanced up at Tulie's window above her, half expecting her niece to be watching her. The window was dark. She shook her head at the momentary thought of madness. *Tulie? A blackmailer?* It was no use. It could be anyone. She suspected Brixi.

Margo turned and headed back toward her house, her

head pivoting to watch the trees for prying eyes. Once she reached the cliffside, her thoughts moved to more pragmatic prodding: how to replace the $50,000 cash that now lay hidden in a child's tire swing.

Margo's memory of the prior evening faltered at this point. She trembled as she remembered entering the dark gardens near the folly, averting her eyes as she passed the medieval structure. She wished they had not removed the tiki torches after the engagement party was over. The darkness in places where the moonlight was blotted out by the trees was frightening.

Up ahead sat the fountain, sitting in a welcoming halo of moonlight. The sound of splashing water, however, only intensified her nervousness. She walked around it, feeling its light mist caressing her face. As she passed, she felt something fall from an oak branch above her head. She felt a rivulet of water run down her forehead. Something was dangling from her hair, sending fetid streams of water past her nose and mouth. Margo jumped and reached up quickly to her hairline. Her fingers wrapped around something slippery and wet. Panicking, she hurriedly pulled it away from her hair, a thin cry escaping her lips. In the pale remnants of moonlight, she looked at the green-stained sash wrapped about her fingers. Water dripped from it and ran along her arm. She screamed and flung it from her.

Roger Henderson reached into the barrel filled with boat oars, retrieved a key hidden there, and unlocked the padlock to the Broussard boat house. He slid the garage-style door open on squeaking wheels. Detective Hilliard and Lieutenant Calvo followed him inside the dark enclosure that smelled of lake water and decaying tackle. Roger reached up and pulled a string toward him. An overhead bulb illuminated the room where a large waterski boat sat bobbing in the current. A smattering of life jackets littered its floor, the smell of mildew rising from their faded fabric.

"It's over here," Roger said, leading the officers to the back of the room. A long wooden table took up most of the back wall. It was covered with fishing paraphernalia, jars of rotten salmon eggs and cheese, a pair of rusty pliers, a dusty screwdriver, and some stacks of nylon ski rope. Cans of motor oil were strewn about, along with a battered metal gasoline container. A discolored cooler was pushed beneath the table. To its left was a stand of waterskis, leaning against the wooden planks.

As Roger took each ski and set it aside, Hilliard asked, "Surely, someone has used the boat in the past 17 or so years?"

"I don't know," Roger offered. "Looking at these skis, no one has used them in a long time. I doubt this family is eager to get back out on *that* water."

Calvo glanced at him, noticing his emphasis on the word "that." A small shiver ran along her spine.

"I'll be damned," Roger said suddenly. "It's still here. I hid Barry's ski he used that day in the back. I didn't want his family to see it and feel sad," He carefully pulled a large slalom ski from the back of the dozens of skis. He stood it up against the table and backed away so the officers could look at it.

Hilliard immediately noticed the top rubber binding. It was where Barry's front foot would have been. It was hanging loose, unattached to the ski on the left-hand side. He looked to the right side of the same binding where three black metal screws anchored it tightly to the ski. Contrarily, the left side showed two empty holes where screws used to be and were now somewhere at the bottom of the lake. Only the top screw hung stubbornly to the loose binding.

Hilliard lifted the rubber binding onto its side, like opening a can with a can opener and lifting the lid still anchored by a piece of metal to the can. He studied the bottom of the remaining screw. He looked again at the three still holding the other side firmly in place. Glancing at the cluttered table top he picked up a Phillips-head screwdriver and began unscrewing one of the screws from the right side.

"What are you doing?" Calvo asked him.

"Just curious," he said. The screw finally came free, and he pulled it from the rubber. He plucked the only remaining screw from the left side where the binding had given way and laid the two screws side by side in his open palm.

Calvo's eyebrows shot up in surprise as she bent to look closer at the hardware. Roger let out a long whistle.

"Would you look at that?" he said. "The left one is shorter. That would hardly bite into the ski."

"And if all three screws on the left side let go…" Hilliard didn't need to finish the sentence. He looked at Calvo with a look of resolve. "This was no accident," he said. "Roger? You were there that day. Did you see anyone around this ski? Anyone who could have had the opportunity to tamper with it? I realize it could have been done anytime before the party that day."

Roger thought back. "That's a long time ago," he said. "I really don't know. I do know Barry was skiing on it a week before he fell. As for the day he died, I wasn't paying attention. To be honest, I was nervous about the competition Barry set up. I'm not as good as the other guys. He teased me about it on the boat. Barry could be mean when he wanted to."

"Did anyone have a reason to wish him harm?" Calvo asked.

"He liked to get in your face," Roger said uncomfortably, feeling like a traitor as he stood there in his dead friend's boathouse. "There may have been a few guys that wouldn't mind seeing him fall on his ass, but not kill him."

"It's possible that's all this was meant to be," Hilliard said. "The screws let loose during the competition, and he falls. No one could have predicted when they would let go, if at all. The impact of him hitting the water from the ski ramp would probably be enough. I'd appreciate it if you don't say anything about this," Hilliard said. "Especially to the sisters or other members of the family. They are dealing with enough right now."

Roger assured them he would keep it to himself. Hilliard took the ski and screws as Roger walked them out. He was about to slide the large door shut when Hilliard said, "Hold on! I want the screwdriver," he said. "Probably shouldn't have picked it up. We may still get a print off it besides mine. No guarantee whoever switched the screws used it, but you never know." He looked sheepishly at Calvo, who twisted her mouth to one side.

"I'll throw you a bone," she said, grinning, as the two walked back into the boathouse for the screwdriver while Roger waited outside. "That was pretty smart of you to think of the screws."

312

"The screw was too short," Hilliard said. "I want to see if it was filed down or if someone just bought shorter screws. Since Barry was the only one to use that ski, it's pretty clear someone wanted to hurt him."

"You have to give whoever it is props," she said. "It's pretty diabolical. Who would have thought it was anything but an accident?"

The sound of the water sloshing up against the boat filled the neglected room. Calvo looked down into the green water and shuddered.

Margo slid into her car seat and tossed her purse into the passenger side. She adjusted her sunglasses and started the engine. Just as she was about to put it into reverse, Reed appeared through the open garage door.

"Where are you off to?" he asked, leaning into the window she lowered.

"I've got a manicure appointment," she said shortly, annoyed at his interference.

He glanced at her polished nails and cocked his head. He leaned away from the window and looked down into her anxious face.

"I'd get a new salon if you need them done again so soon," he said, acrimoniously. "You just went for your birthday three days ago."

He walked away before Margo could retort. Angrily, she backed up, shoved the gear shift into drive, and peeled off down the driveway. Still fuming, she almost missed the stop sign that appeared suddenly to her right. She slammed on her brakes, and her purse flew forward, spilling its contents out onto the floorboard.

"Shit!" she screamed and leaned over to pick up her purse. She scooped up the scattered array of lipsticks, breath mints, a compact, and her wallet. Her hand froze in mid-air as she looked at the final item that had spilled from her purse. It was a white index card like the one from the birthday present with the broken statuette and the one she found beneath her pillow. In the same black garish letters, it read:

"$50,000 was a nice start. I think $150,000 has a nice **RING** to it, don't you think? Same tree swing. Same time. Tonight!"

23 WHAT THE NEIGHBOR SAW

Reed sat perched on the edge of his massive mahogany desk that dominated the Tillson library. He pulled a crystal ashtray over to him and carefully balanced his cigar on its edge. Margo glared at its smoke curling languidly up into the air, detesting the overpowering smell that permeated the room. She sat in a high-backed leather chair across from her husband, her body rigid and teeth clamped tightly shut.

"Your nails look nice," he said sarcastically, glancing down at his wife's hands clasped in her lap. The nail color and its condition seemed unchanged. She had returned to the house a few minutes prior when he stopped her in the hallway and led her into his library. When Margo didn't respond, he changed the subject. "You still haven't explained why you have now decided to sell off the pecan grove," Reed said, his voice determined.

Margo's face reddened. "I don't owe you an explanation," she said tersely. "It's my land, my house,

315

my pecan grove. I can do what I want with it."

"True," Reed said, "but we discussed leaving it alone. Its value goes up every year with all the development going on around here. That was to be Landon's future for he and his family." He halted awkwardly.

"You mean the family he was going to have before his fiancée ran away?" Margo shot back. "You just made my point. The land has gone up, and the developers have increased their offer. They want to build the second phase of the Lake Grove Estates. Rachel sold her acreage. You didn't seem surprised about *that*."

"Randall bullied her into selling her pecan grove," Reed said mildly. "We have money. What's the hurry?"

Margo's face flushed, and her jaw muscles jumped. She clutched her hands together until veins were surfacing like purple vines.

"What's going on?" Reed asked. "You look like you're about to implode. Is there something you're not telling me? Why the sudden need for cash?"

"What's wrong?" she screamed. "Other than Angela screaming about a dead cat, our son's bride-to-be disappearing into oblivion, the relentless questions from those two detectives, gossip everywhere....take your pick!"

"You left out our son being one of the persons of interest in her disappearance," Reed said smoothly. "Seems a few of the party guests informed the police that Landon was furious at Skylar for flirting all night and ruining their engagement celebration. Besides, none of that has to do with a hasty decision to sell off millions of dollars of prime real estate," he said,

316

reaching for his cigar. He ignored Margo's look of pure hatred as he sucked on the end and blew smoke toward the ceiling.

"You've been listening to my phone calls," she yelled.

"No," Reed said calmly. "I've been listening to your conversations at the front door. $2.5 million, I believe, is their current offer to tear down the trees and build houses. *And*, giving the newcomers access to our lake. Why would we want a noisy subdivision right next to our garden, and strangers paddling around and screaming? I repeat, we don't need the money."

He looked at his wife he had been married to for three decades. He no longer recognized the fun and feisty woman he had cherished. A sudden feeling of nostalgia overcame him.

"I keep trying, Margo," he said, his voice filled with sadness. "I thought the surprise birthday party might earn me some props, or, heaven forbid, a hug and a heartfelt 'Thank You.' I got neither. I realize you see me as an old, boring, stupid man. I'm not stupid," he said, his words pregnant with meaning. He looked at her with pain-filled eyes. In that moment, Margo realized he knew about her affair.

She bolted from the chair and headed for the library door. "It's my grove and I'll sell any damn thing I feel like," she said, her voice lowered to a guttural growl. She jerked open the door and exited, slamming it loudly behind her.

Detective Hilliard popped another hard caramel into his mouth, raking it loudly back and forth along his teeth until Lieutenant Calvo threatened to shoot him.

"We're at a dead end," she said, reaching over and moving the bag of caramels from the detective's reach. She held up her hand, fingers splayed, and began ticking them off with her other hand.

"One, no Skylar, no body. Without a body, we have nothing to test. We've interviewed everyone until we are down to asking for their favorite color. Two, the results came back that the screw from the waterski was not filed down. You could buy those screws in any hardware store or ski shop. They're stainless steel that go with a traditional aluminum plate. But it was almost twenty years ago! Who's going to still have credit card receipts or remember somebody buying screws, *if* they even worked there after all this time? They also could have paid in cash.

"Three, Ryder's death seems to be a tragic accident. We don't have anything else to go on. Four, Angela's cat does look like someone deliberately killed it, but we have no proof of who. Five, Tom Simons is home from the hospital. He was lucky. Maybe he learned a lesson about stealing flowers from other people's gardens. Do you know how many flowering plants grown in the South are poisonous?"

"That's quite a speech," Hilliard said dejectedly, knowing she was right. They were nowhere. Rachel Barrows was still on vacation, although no one knew where. The thought prompted his next question:

"So, you think Skylar Harris going missing and Miss Rachel taking off at the same time is nothing more than a coincidence? Pretty strange to me."

"You think Rachel killed Skylar?" Calvo asked incredulously. "Why? For what?"

Hilliard shrugged and swallowed the last fragment

of his candy. "Who knows what is going on behind these mansion walls?" he said ominously. "Maybe Rachel found out about his cheating on her and thought his eye had wandered to Skylar. Maybe we have two missing persons. Possible we could have a double murder." He eyed the lieutenant and was pleased to see her surprise.

"Rachel left a note, and we know she called her Cousin Jenny, stating she needed to get away. You sound like someone is just running around killing people in Orleans Parish?" she said, her tone intentionally sarcastic. "You sound like Calvin Peterson with his Bayou Slayer obsession."

"No. I think someone is running around Lake Broussard, not the whole parish. In fact, I'm deeply afraid someone else is going to die before this is all over," he said, stretching across his desk until his fingers closed in on his bag of caramels.

Brixi Carter sat on her tattered, overstuffed couch and wiped her eyes. Her roommate, Maude was reading the letter Brixi handed her.

"I'm so sorry," Maude said, laying the letter on the coffee table. "I know you were really close to your grandmother."

"She raised me," Brixi said, blowing her nose on a paper towel. "Going to her funeral is going to make it so final. I still can't believe she left me some money and a few of her favorite things. That letter was lying inside the box over there that Uncle George mailed me from her house."

Brixi looked at the keepsakes on the coffee table she had unpacked from the package her uncle had set aside for her. She picked up the antique pill box and ran trembling fingers over its dainty porcelain top. Next to it was a photo album that she could not bring herself to look at yet. Some postcards from the few places Brixi had traveled with her grandmother were scattered across the scarred tabletop. Finally, there was a large cut glass crystal vase with a geometric diamond motif.

"That was Granny's favorite thing," Brixi said, staring at the empty vase. "Grandpa gave it to her on their wedding day. He said it was for all the flowers he would fill it with for the rest of their lives."

She began crying again, and Maude brought her a glass of cold sweet tea.

"Do you want me to go with you to the funeral?" she asked softly. "I don't mind."

"Thank you, but no. Margo wouldn't like losing two maids at the same time. You go to work and let me know what gossip I miss," she said, forcing a wan smile.

"I hope there is nothing more to report!" Maude said. "I was sweeping the patio when that woman police officer walked by carrying a white garbage bag with that dead cat inside. This place is giving me the creeps!"

"I know," Brixi said, wiping her nose. She looked at Maude with worried eyes. "Please be careful. Something is not right over there. What if...what if Margo has something to do with Skylar going missing?"

Maude's face tensed. She wished Brixi would stop talking about her suspicions.

"Just listen to me," Brixi said, tired of holding her secret. "Why would she throw away perfectly good shoes? She could have paid to have them cleaned. When was the last time you saw Margo Tillson walking in mud up to her ankles?"

"Why would Skylar's missing have anything to do with muddy shoes?" Maude asked, her breathing shallow.

"I don't know…maybe Margo hit her over the head with that broken statue," Brixi said. "You saw her face when that woman read that note that came with the statue at her party. I told you this already. Why were those words in caps? GREEN, NECK, DARK, BROKE… Skylar was the only one wearing green at the party. I think Margo may have done something to her. Maybe she's buried her out in that big garden and that's why Margo's shoes are muddy! And that big ring in a pill bottle in Margo's bathroom! What if it's Skylar's? I'm tellin' you, I think she did something to her."

"I told you to leave it alone," Maude said nervously. "She already knows you went through her garbage. You should get rid of those shoes," Maude implored her. "You'd be fired for sure if she ever found out. Just mind your business and stay out of her room. You're skating on thin ice. I'd hate it if she fired you."

Maude did not repeat her conversation with Margo that morning. She'd wait until after Brixi got back from her grandmother's funeral. She was having a hard enough time without knowing Margo was asking a lot of questions about her.

The next morning, Margo entered her home, slamming the front door. Her hair was damp from the humidity, and it clung to her neck. She walked past the open door to the library and looked in. Reed looked up from his desk, where he was going over the household ledgers.

"It's done," she announced dramatically, without entering the room. "Signed, sealed, and delivered. They start tearing down the pecan trees soon." She flashed him a smile of pure evil and walked away, her high heels clicking along the black and white marble hallway.

Margo entered the kitchen and paused in the doorway. "Pour me a tall glass of tea," she said to Maude, lifting her hair away from her clammy neck.

The maid hurried to a cabinet and pulled down a glass. She opened the refrigerator and carried a large pitcher of tea to the counter, where she filled a tall tumbler.

"Do you want ice?" she asked nervously. She didn't usually wait on Miss Margo. Her duties were housecleaning and doing some laundry.

"What do you think?" Margo asked, shaking her head. "Of course, I want ice. Where's Brixi?"

"Oh, I'm supposed to tell you that," Maude said, pressing the refrigerator's ice dispenser until several square cubes sloshed into the glass of tea. She turned and handed it to Margo, wiping the edge of the glass with a kitchen towel. "She, uh, her, her grandmother died."

"So, you said the other morning," Margo snapped unsympathetically.

"The funeral is tomorrow," Maude hurried on. "She left for that. It's in Charleston…South Carolina."

"She left without clearing it with me?" Margo asked, surprised.

"She was pretty upset. I think she thought you would

know she would be going to it. Her Granny raised her."

Margo looked at the hapless maid for a moment, and a new thought struck her. Her demeanor suddenly changed.

"Well, of course, she must go," she said in saccharin tones. "I'll have to send her some flowers when she returns."

She turned and left the room, tea in hand. A feeling of relief swept over her. *If Brixi were away, the blackmail notes would stop. The maid's absence would give her time to produce a solution. She couldn't fire her. She knew too much. Brixi must have seen something the night Rachel fell, and saw her put her in the lake*, she thought. *Hadn't she felt someone was in the yard that night, watching as she put Rachel's body on the cart? It all pointed to Brixi. The green sash that had been around Rachel's arm, the broken statuette, the magazines that had covered her shoes in the trash. Now, the appearance of the green sash would stop! Brixi must have bought one like Skylar's and was using it to blackmail her. She wished she hadn't run away the night she left the ransom money when the sash dropped from a tree in the garden into her hair. When she looked for it near the fountain the next morning, it was gone.*

Stephanie said Brixi was in her bathroom, and someone had put the pill bottle cap back on. If Brixi did see Skylar's ring in the pill bottle, what of it? It was highly unlikely the maid knew whose ring it was. But what if she did recognize it? The latest blackmail note had the word RING in caps. It had to be Brixi. Had she seen something at the folly the night of the engagement party, too? The various thoughts played out in her mind until she felt the beginning of a headache tapping on the door to her temporal lobe.

Brenn walked into the kitchen, and Maude turned in surprise to see her there. She hadn't heard her enter the house. She wondered how long she had been standing in the mudroom.

"Calm down," Brenn said haughtily. She opened the refrigerator and helped herself to a cold plum.

"Miss Margo just left. I think she is going upstairs," Maude said, assuming that was the reason for Brenn's sudden visit, although she was around a lot lately.

"Good to know," Brenn said smugly. She grinned at Maude and walked into the adjoining mudroom and out the side door into the sunlight.

The weekend passed in a miasma of swirling insects and record-breaking heat. October pulled an Indian Summer from its hat. The temperatures were in the mid-ninety's and the humidity still wrapped around one's face like a hot, wet washcloth.

Monday morning, Gladys Pritchard tapped lightly on apartment 14, one door down from her own in the dilapidated Wing's Bend Apartments. The hallway reeked of various cooking odors and tired carpet. Dime store pictures of Paris and the Hawaiian islands hung on the walls of the long corridor in cheap frames to brighten the yellowing paint. It only reminded the inhabitants of places they could not afford to visit.

Gladys tapped again, a little louder this time, and Brixi Carter cracked the door and peered out.

"Mrs. Pritchard," she said, sounding none too pleased to find her busybody neighbor standing there.

"Hello, Brixi, dear," Gladys twittered. "I got some of

your mail by mistake again," she said, holding up several envelopes as evidence.

Brixi opened the door and took the mail from the woman. "I have a couple of yours, too," she said and walked the few steps to the small kitchen. Mrs. Pritchard followed her in.

"Oh!" Brixi said as she turned and almost collided with the elderly woman. "I didn't know you came in."

If the comment was meant as a reprimand, it completely missed its mark with Gladys Pritchard. She stood in the small room that served as a kitchen and living room and took it all in, her bleary eyes darting about. Brixi handed her three pieces of junk mail.

"How was your poor Granny's funeral?" Gladys asked, her eyes looking past Brixi to a small statue of a blue cat.

"It was sad," Brixi said, not wishing to encourage the conversation. She took a step toward the open door to hurry the woman out.

"Yes," Gladys said, still perusing the room. "They so often are, aren't they?"

Her eyes fell on the large glass vase sitting atop a small dinette table tucked into a corner under the only window in the room.

"Oh my!" Gladys exclaimed, pressing her veined hands together in delight. "Isn't that the most lovely thing you've ever seen?"

Before Brixi could stop her, the old woman hurried over to the vase and touched it gingerly.

"My grandmother left it to me," Brixi said tiredly. She wanted to unpack and find something to eat. It had been a long bus ride from the airport.

"Lead crystal," Gladys breathed. "They just don't

make vases like this anymore. My mother had one. Heavy things, aren't they?"

Brixi moved protectively to the vase and put herself between it and her neighbor.

"Thank you for bringing over my mail," she said, and placed a hand on Glady's thin forearm, leading her to the door.

"Maude has a letter in there, too," Gladys said, her head on a swivel as she looked about her on the way to the door.

"I'll give it to her when she gets off work," Brixi said, almost pushing the woman into the hallway. "Thank you so much."

Brixi shut the door. Gladys stood staring at it for a moment, wondering if the girl was peering at her through the peephole to see if she had gone. Sighing, she took the six steps to her own door, opened it, and went inside.

"Oh no!" Gladys cried out suddenly. She grabbed a towel and waved it over her head, trying frantically to herd her escaped parakeet back into its cage.

"Penelope, you naughty bird," the eighty-two-year-old widow shouted. "That's the third time this month."

The bird flew from the shabby living room into a short hallway that led to a small bathroom and the only bedroom. Gladys shuffled hurriedly after it.

"Don't you dare poop on my bedspread!" she yelled.

Several minutes later, the bird was back in its cage, and Gladys collapsed into a sagging armchair, trying to catch her breath. A loud thud sounded against the outside of her door, and she jumped.

"My lands!" she said, rising painfully to her feet. She hobbled to the door and pressed an eye to the peephole. The hallway appeared empty, but she could hear muffled voices nearby. She opened the door and poked her head around the frame, looking toward Brixi's apartment next door.

Gladys could hear the sound of two female voices coming from Brixi's open doorway. She strained to make out the words with her limited hearing. One voice said something she could not understand and then the voice she recognized as Brixi's exclaimed, "Margo? Flowers for *me?*"

The old woman backed into her apartment and closed the door with a smile. *How nice*, she thought. *People still remember to bring flowers when there's a death in a family.*

Maude Gleason inserted her key into the lock of apartment 14 and shoved the door open with her shoulder. She was carrying two bags of groceries and a purse. The room was dark, the curtains drawn, which was unusual. The roommates usually had the curtains open and a small, battered window air conditioner running. The room was stifling and stuffy. She felt her way to the kitchen counter and dropped the two bags.

"Brixi?" she yelled, thinking her friend might be lying down after her long ordeal with her grandmother's funeral.

Maude reached across the counter and flipped the light switch in the kitchen. It illuminated the small living area as well. As she turned to step over to the window, her foot kicked something sticking out by the dinette table. She looked down and screamed.

Officer Clairborne tapped on the partition to the small

detective's cubicle. Hilliard, who was filling out some reports, looked up from his desk, his face a question mark.

"Good thing you're sitting down," Clairborne said. Lieutenant Calvo stepped away from a battered gray filing cabinet to listen in; her curiosity piqued.

"I won the Powerball?" Hilliard asked, grinning.

"Pretty sure this would be the opposite," Gleason said smugly. "I just got a call from a very hysterical young woman. She came home to find her roommate with the back of her head caved in."

"Why aren't you giving it to Benton?" Hilliard asked.

"I think it's something you might be interested in," the officer said, enjoying the suspense he was creating.

"Spit it out, Clairborne," Hilliard said, tiring of the game.

"Like I said, this young woman just got home from work and finds her roommate dead…"

Hilliard's nostrils flared, and the officer hurried on, "She came home from work where she *and* her dead friend are maids. They work for Margo Tillson!"

24 FORTUNES

Wind whipped the lake, sending small waves sloshing against the shoreline. Beneath the surface, particles of broken reeds and other lake debris danced inside the dark green water. The moonlight fought its way through the murky depths until it was swallowed completely by the darkness below. Something was floating there, lodged between two upright poles anchored in the mud. Fragments of kelp moved with the current and wrapped around two decomposing arms. They threaded their way through strands of undulating black hair like macabre ribbons. A face, bloated and green like its watery grave, was tilted up, its mouth open in a silent scream. A small bluegill swam out from between the parted teeth. Suddenly, the eyes opened.

Tulie sat up in bed and cried out. Her sheets and pillowcase were drenched in sweat, as was her nightgown that clung to her like wet tissue paper. She covered her face with her hands and sobbed in the darkness of the early morning hour.

Hurricane warnings flashed across television screens throughout the lower southern states. It was that time of year again. While Bernice didn't threaten to make landfall for another three days, the usual warnings for preparedness made the evening news. Plywood sales went up, and empty shelves where bulk packages of bottled water once stood were all signs of the impending storm.

The wind pushed Tulie about as she walked up the cracked banquette of Hutchins Street, clutching her purse to her stomach. She had never seen this side of New Orleans before. The faubourg sat not far from the French Quarter, or Vieux Carré, where Tulie had been forced to wait while a brass band led a funeral procession toward the St. Louis Cemetery No. 1. The traditional parade of secondline mourners waving handkerchiefs and walking in a shuffle step took their time as pedestrians looked on.

Tulie finally found her way to the narrow shotgun houses sitting in weed-infested lots; some leaning as if the Louisiana hurricanes had pushed them into permanent submission. Neglected flower pots sat on broken steps; dead flowers dangling over their sides in their final death throes.

Tulie glanced down again at the small piece of paper in her hand and looked up at the house number nearest her. 3482. She looked two houses farther down and walked slowly toward its faded periwinkle blue door. In the dirty front window was a cardboard sign, bowed by the heat. It read:

FORTUNES
$10

A sudden gust of wind blew down the narrow street, knocking Tulie nearly off her feet. She pushed her hair from her face. It was only the gale that forced her to take those final steps to the sagging front porch and knock. Several clusters of peeling paint fell from the impact and fluttered to the cement step. A voice sounded from somewhere inside and Tulie jumped.

"Come in. The spirits await!"

A small bell tinkled overhead as Tulie slowly pushed open the door. It was dark inside with only a few flickering candles lighting the surroundings. The sickening sweet smell of sage incense clung to the still air. She shut the door against the wind and waited near it, afraid to venture farther inside.

"Come through, come through," the same voice intoned.

As Tulie's eyes adjusted to the dim lighting, she made out parted red curtains up ahead in a doorway. Beads hung from the opening in assorted colors. As she stepped nervously toward them, she became aware of the muffled sound of chanting set to music.

"Don't be afraid," the voice said, closer now. "Come in. Don't keep the spirits waiting."

Tulie stepped through the beads. They cascaded over her shoulders, bouncing in jingling tones, as she walked through the opening and saw a woman seated with her back to her. Her hair was piled atop her head in abandon, stray pins struggling to contain it. Before her, there was a round table, draped in purple. Lit candles surrounded the room in diverse sizes, most burning down to small nubs of wax.

"Sit!" the woman said. Tulie stepped nervously to the chair opposite the mysterious figure and sat down gingerly, still clutching her purse. She looked at the face across from her and inhaled sharply.

Madame Sangers had changed dramatically with the years. The theatrical makeup she had worn to Tulie's mother's séance many years ago--once highlighting her catlike eyes and sculpted cheekbones--had the reverse effect now. The deep purple eyeshadow only managed to sink her drooping eyelids into folds of caked color. The cheekbones now sagged, melting into folds around her mouth and jawline. The hair was more gray than the vivid black Tulie remembered.

The woman, in turn, studied Tulie without recognition. Her hooded eyes lowered to Tulie's purse.

"The spirits demand payment first," she said.

Tulie sat still, not comprehending the short directive.

"Put the ten dollars on the table and we will begin," Madame Sangers said tiredly.

"Oh!" Tulie said, embarrassed. "Yes."

She opened her purse and pulled out the ten-dollar bill she had put there for her visit to the medium. She gently placed it unfolded on the table and waited. Madame Sangers reached with long, veined fingers and pulled the money toward her. She placed it in a black wooden box with a crescent moon carved on its top near her elbow.

"You don't remember me," Tulie said quietly, afraid she might be disrupting the flow of things.

Madam Sangers paused, a flash of nervousness playing across her face.

"Should I?" she asked.

"You gave a séance for my mother," Tulie said, "a long time ago, in our house. We were trying to reach my brother, Ryder, who drowned in our lake…"

332

She stopped. Madame Sangers fell back against her chair, her face suddenly ashen beneath the makeup. Tulie was surprised at the look of horror on the woman's face.

"That was you?" Madame Sangers gasped. "I...I...had no control over what happened that night. No matter what you came here to accuse me of, things did not go as planned."

Tulie sat in shock as the medium's words tumbled out of her. Madame Sangers moved to the front of her chair as if preparing to rise.

"No!" Tulie said quickly. "I'm here to ask about something else. I need your help. Please!"

Madam Sangers paused and finally sat back, her body on alert. Her hands remained firmly on the table.

"My mother," Tulie began, the tears already forming. "She's been gone for almost two weeks. She's the one who hired you to do the séance for Ryder. She left a note saying she was going to see our cousin for a while. You see, all this strange stuff has been going on, and she hasn't been well. She's never gotten over Ryder's death, and...there are these horrible rumors about my Daddy and...anyway...I don't think she really *did* go away. She wouldn't leave me! I think something happened to her. Can you help me?"

Madame Sangers sat in silence for several long minutes, studying the young woman across from her. She remembered her now. She had been a small girl, not yet a teenager, when she gave the séance at Rachel Barrows' home. She chose her next words carefully.

"What 'strange stuff'?" she asked, repeating Tulie's words, a knot forming in her stomach.

"I think your séance brought my brother back," Tulie

said, willing to risk whatever happened next. She had to know. "Several people have seen him, including my mother and me. He's always just a shadow figure but I know it's him. If something did happen to my mother, I need to know," Tulie said, choking back tears. "I'm having these horrible nightmares. You spoke to Ryder after he died. Can you see if you get anything from my mother?"

The medium looked down at her hands and realized they were trembling. She had tried to forget the séance over the years. It had never happened to her before. The bell, the words on the chalkboard... Finally, she reached for a worn deck of cards that set next to the black box and pressed them between her palms. She closed her eyes and waited. The chanting music from an old phonograph player swirled hauntingly through the room.

"Answer my questions with one word only," she said. "Do not give me more information than I request."

She shuffled the cards smoothly, a motion she had done a thousand times before over the years, relieving desperate clients of their $10 and their skepticism. The cards, worn and bent, melded into each other like warm butter. She took her left hand and divided it into three piles. Taking up the deck again, she laid out a series of seven cards in a row before her.

Tulie looked at the strange markings of constellations and odd symbols on the back of the cards. They were larger than normal playing cards and gave off a musty smell when the medium shuffled them. Her heart was racing as she waited for Madame Sangers to begin. Would she find out where her mother was?

The medium tipped her head back dramatically and

waved her hands over the cards in three sweeping movements. The chanting music continued in the background. Sighing deeply, she opened her eyes and placed a weathered hand on the first card to the left.

"Rachel Barrows, we summon you here. If you are among the spirits, we ask that you reach out to us. Your daughter Tulie is here and wishes to know you are safe." She inhaled deeply and began.

"This first card is your mother's recent past," she said. She flipped it over and revealed the Two of Cups. A thin smile creased her face. "An engagement or marriage," she said. "Is your mother divorced now? Perhaps a second marriage is forthcoming."

"No," Tulie said, "she's still married to my father..." She stopped abruptly when she caught the warning look from the medium. "Oh, sorry...I mean, no."

"Well, the card definitely is pointing out an engagement or nuptials..."

"There was an engagement party for my aunt's son, but his fiancée is missing..." Tulie clapped a hand over her mouth as the medium arched an eyebrow in her direction.

"Do not elaborate!" Madam Sangers threatened. "You are blocking the frequency with your blabbering! This card is for your mother's past. It shows she was married, that's enough!"

Tulie nodded and folded her hands in her lap.

Madam Sangers hand moved to the next card to the right and lingered there.

"This card is for money," she intoned. She flipped it over. The Four of Pentacles was revealed. "Ah!" she said. "The rounding out of a venture. Did your mother enter into a lucrative venture?"

"Yes, she sold her pecan...sorry. Yes." Tulie slumped over in embarrassment.

Madame Sangers sighed loudly as an admonition. "Was the money great?" she asked, suddenly interested in the card's meaning.

"Yes," Tulie said and pressed her lips together to ensure she didn't prattle on.

Madame Sangers looked disappointed that this was the first time the young woman had followed the rules. More information about the family money would have been beneficial to her.

"This card is your mother's current state of mind," she said, moving her hand to the third card. Tulie bit her lip and waited. Madame Sangers flipped over the card to reveal the Moon. "Interesting," she said, sounding genuinely intrigued. "This is a card of secrecy. 'Things look different beneath the light of the moon,'" she said, quoting something referring to the Tarot card's definition. She stared at it for a moment, a heightened tension showing in her shoulders and breathing. "Something pertaining to your mother is cloaked in secrecy," she murmured. "Does this mean anything to you?"

"Only that I don't know where she is," Tulie said, forgetting the 'one word only' rule again.

The medium studied the girl for a moment and continued. She reached for the next card and said, "The fourth card is your mother's hidden fears." She turned this card over a little more slowly than the others and drew in a deep breath. "The Tower!" she said ominously. Tulie looked fearfully at the card showing a tall medieval tower in flames; a woman falling head down from its parapet. "Was your mother afraid of someone?" Madame Sangers asked pointedly. "Did she feel there was danger around her? The card shows someone falling...has she had an accident where she fell? It could mean many things," the medium said, before Tulie could answer. "But it definitely means danger. I ask you again...is your mother afraid of someone?"

Tulie paused. She had seen her mother as someone sad and depressed due to Ryder's death and the rumors about her father and Aunt Margo. Plus, he was always away from home. But she had not thought of her as afraid.

"I'm not sure," Tulie said, her brow furrowed.

Madame Sangers allowed the three-word answer. The card had surprised her, and she cast her thoughts back all those years. Tulie watched the medium's face tighten. Aware that the girl was staring at her, Madame Sangers gathered herself together and reached for the next card.

"Card five is the situation surrounding your mother now," she said, her voice shaking slightly. Her hand trembled as she held her breath and quickly turned over the card.

Both the medium and Tulie gasped at the same time. A face of pure evil looked out at them from the Tarot card.

"The Devil!" Madame Sangers whispered.

"What?" Tulie screamed. "What does that mean?" She no longer cared about the rules.

"Clearly, there is malevolence surrounding your mother," the medium said, this time her voice quaking. "I see evil."

She bent her head, trying to steady her nerves. "Are

you sure you want to see the last two cards?" she asked, raising her head to look Tulie squarely in the eyes.

Tulie was wiping the tears streaming down her face. Small hiccupping sobs exploded from her open mouth. She sat frozen.

Madame Sangers moved her hand to the sixth card and let it linger there. Her fingertips were trembling. She finally grabbed the edge of the card and said, "This card is your mother's current state." She couldn't bring herself to turn it over. Tulie suddenly reached across the table and flipped it over. The Death card lay face up on the table.

Tulie screamed and bolted from her chair, accidentally banging her hip against the phonograph player. The chanting music skipped; the needle caught on the new scratch. Tulie pushed through the hanging beads at the open doorway and ran to the front door. She battled with the old-fashioned latch until she finally lifted it, flung the door open wide, and raced blindly out into the wind.

Madame Sangers sat staring at the card with the image of the Grim Reaper standing next to a river of black water. He was draped in dark robes, his skeletal face sunk in shadows. The medium's heart was pounding. After several strained moments, she reached for the last card Tulie had not yet seen. Pausing, she whispered to herself, "The final outcome." She flipped it over hurriedly, sitting back as if to distance herself from what it might be. The image of a gold statue, wearing a blindfold and holding up an unbalanced scale, adorned the worn card.

"Justice!" Madam Sangers said loudly. "Yes," she said. "I've waited too long. It is time for justice!"

She rose from her chair and lifted the needle from the phonograph record. As she exited the room, she blew out each candle, streamers of wispy smoke curling until they faded into the darkness.

Brixi Carter's body was removed from her small apartment at 8:48 am. She had lain throughout the night in her small apartment as her body and apartment were looked over for anything of evidentiary value. The coroner checked the appropriate boxes on his form and scribbled in the jargon that tattooed his reports: Blunt force trauma to the back of the head, frontal lividity (body was not moved from its final resting position), no other signs of trauma, no defensive wounds.

Brixi's roommate, Maude, and their neighbor Gladys Pritchard were allowed to enter the apartment briefly. They were the last two people to see Brixi alive. Detective Hilliard was talking to other neighbors in the hallway, but no one had heard anything or seen anything unusual. Lieutenant Calvo waited with the two women inside the sparse living room. Hilliard walked inside, running a hand through his hair. *The rabbit hole surrounding the Broussard family was a warren of death*, he thought.

"Maude…may I call you Maude?" Calvo asked the grieving roommate who had phoned in the murder of her friend and co-worker. "This is never easy, but I know you've probably watched enough TV shows to know we have to ask these questions as early on as possible if we are to find who did this."

Maude lowered a wad of tissues from her red and swollen eyes. She looked down at the short officer with an incoherent expression.

"I don't know what I can tell you," she said, her voice thick with emotion. "She'd been gone to her grandmother's funeral in South Carolina. I haven't seen her since Friday. I came home last night after work, opened the door and..." She sank into a chair before Calvo could warn her not to touch anything.

"Do you know of anyone who would hurt her?" Calvo asked.

Maude shook her head no and sobbed into her tissues.

"Does anyone else have a key to your apartment?" Calvo asked. "The door doesn't appear to have been broken into, and your window is five floors up with no balcony or fire escape."

"No," she said.

"Then it's possible she opened the door to her killer," the lieutenant said. She turned to the elderly woman who was staring at the bare floor where a section of carpet and padding had been removed next to the dinette table.

Calvo glanced down at her tablet and her notes.

"Miss Pritchard," she said kindly, trying to get the woman's attention.

"Mrs..," Gladys said. "I'm a widow. I haven't been a Miss for a long time."

Calvo smiled. "Mrs. Pritchard," she corrected. "You said you witnessed someone inside this apartment door yesterday afternoon. Tell me about that."

Gladys licked her lips eagerly, feeling the importance of the moment. She was their star witness.

"Something hit my door," she said, her eyes twinkling. She was the same height as the lieutenant and looked her squarely in the eye. "I had just managed

340

to corral my wayward Penelope and was sitting down. It was a *loud* thud on my door. When I looked out, I saw Brixi and Maude's door was open." She turned to indicate the apartment door behind her.

"I heard two women talking," she hurried on. "I couldn't hear what the one was saying, but I did hear Brixi. I recognized her voice, you see. She has a somewhat nasal quality to her voice."

Maude burst into fresh sobs. Gladys looked at her, not comprehending that her use of the present tense concerning Brixi was causing the young woman distress.

"What did you hear Brixi say?" Calvo asked, leading Gladys into the kitchen. It didn't offer much distance from the living room, but they were still searching the back rooms, and there was nowhere else to take her.

"Let me think," Gladys said, her eyes wandering back to the spot where the body had been. Her ghoulish delight in staring at the spot was wearing on the lieutenant.

"Mrs. Pritchard?"

"Huh? Oh yes! Um, Brixi said, 'Margo. Flowers for me?' I believe that was it."

Hilliard stopped flipping through the coroner's first impressions and looked over at the old woman in shock.

"She said *what?*" he barked.

Gladys was taken aback and took a moment to recover her composure.

"I heard her say, 'Margo.' I think it was said like a question….like 'Margo?'" Gladys raised her voice in a question mark. "Then she said, 'Flowers for me?' also in a question. She sounded surprised and happy."

"Anything else?" Hilliard asked, commandeering the

interview. Calvo didn't mind. It gave her a chance to type out the interrogation on her tablet. She had forgotten her small voice recorder.

Gladys thought hard. "No. That's all I heard. I felt happy for her that someone gave her some flowers. I went back inside and closed my door."

"Did you see who the person was inside her door?" Hilliard asked. "This is very important."

"No. They were too far inside. I assume whoever it was is named Margo."

At that, Maude's head jerked up and she went white. "Oh my God!" she cried. "Margo told me she was going to bring Brixi flowers! I'd forgotten. Brixi said she thought Margo had done something bad! She warned me to be careful. I didn't take her seriously! She had been snooping in Margo's things. But I can't believe she would kill her!"

Hilliard turned and looked at Lieutenant Calvo, who stood looking as if lightning had struck her. *Was the whole case they'd been working on about to break open?*

"You didn't hear anything when you went back into your apartment, Mrs. Pritchard?" Calvo pressed her. "A struggle, a noise, anything?"

"No, just the thud on my door before I opened it. I turned on my game show when I got back, so I wouldn't have heard much. I always watch *Grab the Goods* every weekday at that time."

"And what time is that?" Calvo asked.

"It starts at 4:30," Gladys said. "It has lots of lovely prizes. I like lovely things."

"Thank you, Mrs. Pritchard, for your cooperation," Calvo said, sounding somewhat disappointed that the woman couldn't offer more. She placed a hand on Gladys's elbow to escort her out. "We may be back if we need to trouble you further."

Gladys didn't move. She was staring at the dinette table, her forehead furrowed.

"What has happened to that lovely vase?" she asked. She turned to Maude, pressing her hands together in supplication. "If you don't want the vase, I would love to have it," Gladys said hungrily.

Maude looked surprised at the woman's audacity. She looked over at the table and sniffed. "She's right. Brixi's vase is gone. Her Granny gave it to her. It was there when I left for work this morning."

"You're sure?" Hilliard asked. He bent to look beneath the table for signs of broken glass. When he saw none, he walked into the kitchen and opened the cabinet beneath the sink with gloved hands. He pulled out a full trash can and pushed its contents aside. There were empty cans of chili, a pizza box folded in half, some soda cans, used paper towels, and sections of watermelon rind, but no glass. He opened the few kitchen cabinets and looked inside. Only a smattering of canned goods, mismatched plates and glasses, and some paper goods were on the shelves.

"Did you see any glass?" he asked Maude. "Anything out of place when you got home tonight?"

"No," she cried. "Brixi's suitcases were in the bedroom. She hadn't even unpacked yet. If Gladys said someone brought Brixi flowers, where are the flowers?"

"And where is that lovely vase?" Gladys said sadly, clasping her hands and sighing.

Just then, one of the police officers entered the small living room from the back bedroom area. He held up a pair of shoes covered in dried mud in his latex-gloved hands. "Just found these hidden behind a shoebox of photographs in the bedroom closet," he said.

Maude's head dropped to her chest, her body trembling. "Oh my God!" she sobbed. "I told Brixi to get rid of them. She found them in the garbage under some magazines. Those shoes belong to Margo Tillson."

25 "A HURRICANE HITTIN'"

Detective Hilliard steered the car through the crowded streets of New Orleans. Above the eclectic mix of old and new buildings, storm clouds hung low and threatening. No stranger to hurricane watches, the detective paid scant attention to the change in the barometric fluctuations.

"I'm not happy about this," Lieutenant Calvo said, for the third time since they left a squalid apartment complex where Maude Gleason had just moved in with her Aunt Beverly. The apartment she shared with Brixi was still a crime scene. She told the officers she couldn't have stayed another minute there anyway and made arrangements to stay with her aunt until she found another place.

"The hurricane?" Hilliard asked innocently, clamping down on a hard caramel.

Calvo shot him an insolent look, knowing he was being sarcastic.

"You know damned well what I mean," she said. "We are literally sending that poor girl into the lion's den! If we believe Margo killed Brixi, why in hell are we asking Maude to go over there and scout things out for us?"

Hilliard rolled the hard candy across his teeth. The Lieutenant fought the urge to unholster her weapon.

"Can't you become addicted to soft caramels?" she asked indignantly. "I'll buy you a year's supply."

"Nope," Hilliard said, and rolled the candy back the other way. "Can't you bring a voice recorder to interrogations instead of that annoying tablet? Maude is all we have," he said, hurrying on. "We talked about this. She knows what the vase looks like. I asked the investigators to keep Brixi's death under wraps for another 24 hours so we can shake the tree a little. We're only ten minutes behind Maude. Nothing is going to happen to her in ten minutes."

Calvo turned to look out the window at the gray sky. The grumpy clouds matched her mood. She prayed they had not made a mistake.

Maude entered the sprawling plantation estate through the mudroom door with her key. It was oddly quiet. No sounds came from overhead or from the first floor. Only Forster, the landscaper, had greeted her as she walked along the flagstone sidewalk from the driveway.

The maid opened two of the bottom cabinets in the mudroom where the vases were kept. Margo had received so many flowers from the local florists for her birthday that the cabinet space was bursting with glassware in assorted colors and shapes. Maude gently moved them around to make sure she checked each one.

Brixi's large lead crystal vase was not one of them. She felt relieved. That was her only mission: to look for the vase. She didn't want anything else to do with cornering Margo. She was now frightened to death of her employer.

A new thought struck her, sending her heart into palpitations again. *What about the garbage cans in the garage?* Knowing the detective would be showing up at any minute, Maude pushed herself one more time. *Just do this and you're done,* she told herself. She exited through the mudroom door and followed the flagstone path to the side door of the garage. Forster had moved on and was nowhere to be seen. Entering, she flipped on the overhead light and faced the row of trash cans. Sighing, she lifted the lid to the one closest to her and peered inside. The trash had been collected that morning at the curb, and the cans had been replaced inside the garage. Only one kitchen bag of ruined fruit sat at the bottom of the first can. The next three cans were empty.

Nibbling her lips, she glanced about the massive 4-car garage. Plenty of places to hide something. There wasn't enough time. Maude turned to leave when her eyes fell on Margo's BMW. The shiny black exterior glinted beneath the fluorescent lighting. She stared at it and debated. The car meant Margo was home and could catch her at any minute, but...*One last time*, she said again.

Maude walked to the passenger side door and pressed her face to the tinted glass. It was hard to see clearly inside. The overhead light through the windshield reflected off a metal travel mug resting in the cup holder of the console. Next to it were a pair of sunglasses. Something sitting on the floorboard on the passenger side glinted, sending off a small shard of light. She pressed her face harder against the glass. She couldn't make it out. Holding her breath, Maude gently lifted the door handle. A loud alarm erupted from the car, echoing throughout the garage. It came in short screaming blasts. The maid covered her ears and ran for the door.

Maude darted into the house and grabbed her purse from the mudroom hall tree. Chest heaving, she turned to race back out the door.

"What in the hell is going on?"

Maude whirled to see Margo standing there, cringing with each blast of the car alarm.

"I was just going to go see," Maude said, her knees knocking. She pushed her purse behind her and waited.

"I'll do it," Margo said heatedly, pushing the girl to one side. She stormed out the door with her car keys clenched in her fist.

Maude made a dash through the kitchen. She would head out the front door and get to her car while Margo was in the garage. She unlocked the door and opened it, rushing out only to bump full force into Detective Hilliard, who was about to knock.

"Whoa!" he said, steadying the terrified girl.

The car alarm suddenly stopped, the ensuing silence seeming louder than before.

"I can't stay here," Maude cried. "I'm scared to death."

"Ok, it's ok," Lieutenant Calvo said, taking her arm. "We shouldn't have sent you here." She shot a meaningful glance at Hilliard. "What's wrong? What's with the car alarm?"

348

"I was trying to find the vase," Maude said, her voice a small quiver. "I looked in Margo's car through the window and thought I saw something on the floorboard that might have been glass. When I tried to open the door…"

"Oopsy," Hilliard said, grimacing. "Where's Margo now?"

"In the garage. I guess she turned off the alarm. I want to leave now!" Maude said, pushing back from the detective. "You can look for it. It's not where the vases are kept, and it wasn't in the garbage cans in the garage, but garbage day was today, so it may be gone…"

Before Maude could move, Margo suddenly appeared behind her in the open front doorway. Her face was flushed with anger.

"What the hell do you want *now?*" she barked, incensed that the two officers were back again. "There can't be anything else you need from us!"

Detective Hilliard smiled, which only served to make the woman in the doorway angrier. "It's interesting that your first thought wasn't one of hope— that maybe we had good news concerning Skylar Harris." He gave her his most innocent look.

Margo's face transitioned from anger to surprise. She stuttered something incoherent while glancing at Lieutenant Calvo, whose own face was one of resolution rather than innocence.

"Won't take but a minute," Hilliard said, and pressed past the irate woman into the hallway. The lieutenant followed him inside, just as the wind outside began picking up steam. Maude had no choice but to follow them inside.

Margo pushed hard against the door to close it

against the gale and stood facing the two officers, her face red and throbbing.

"This is not a good time," she said through clenched teeth. "Does it ever occur to you that people might be busy?"

"No," Hilliard said, looking around. "Pretty quiet today," he added. "Servants' day off?" He watched her closely. Her face continued to show the same contempt.

Once inside the foyer, Hilliard dropped the pretense and faced his opponent.

"I'm afraid we *do* come with some bad news," he said, taking a step forward.

Margo braced herself. Images of Rachel's body sinking into the lake flooded her mind. Had they found her? Or Skylar?

"Your maid, Brixi Carter, was found dead last evening," Hilliard said, his eyes zeroing in on Margo's like lasers. The reaction the detective had expected was not the one that hit the room like a cannonball.

"*What?*" Margo screamed, grabbing the edge of the hall table. She looked between the detective and the lieutenant with eyes bulging with surprise and terror. "You can't be serious! What happened to her?"

Hilliard's first thought was one of admiration. *The woman can act*, he thought. She looked totally taken aback by the news.

"She was murdered," Calvo said calmly, but she, too, was unnerved by Margo's response. She had dealt with plenty of guilty suspects and knew all the signs. This was not one of the usual reactions.

Margo turned a frightened face to her maid, as if pleading for some sign that this was all a prank.

"Maude, I thought she just got back from the funeral

yesterday. How can she be dead?" Margo begged.

Maude was frozen in place, standing slightly behind the towering detective for protection. Margo stared at the girl as if she were an alien life form. Several seconds passed.

"Mrs. Tillson," Hilliard said, stepping closer to the woman who looked like she was about to collapse. "We have a witness who said you were heard in Brixi's apartment yesterday afternoon. Something about flowers. What can you tell us about that?"

Margo turned her head to face the man with a look of shock. "I was *not* at her apartment!" she screamed. "I don't even know where she lives! I've *never* been there!"

Again, Hilliard had to admit, the lady was good. Her raw emotions seemed authentic.

"It will be beneficial to you if you just talk to us," he said. "Where were you yesterday afternoon?"

Reality dawned. They were here to question her about a dead body. A dead body that was in her employ. A dead body she suspected of blackmailing her.

"You're going to have to be more specific," Margo said, getting her second wind. "What time yesterday?"

Hilliard thought back to Maude telling the officers that she arrived home around 5:15 pm. after leaving Margo's at 4:00 and picking up some groceries. She said Margo was talking on the phone in the parlor just before she left.

"Let's say 4:00 to 5:30," Hilliard said.

"I was here," she said, running the prior afternoon through her mind.

"Alone?"

"No," she said. "Stephanie was here."

Maude shifted, her face tensing. Calvo noticed it.

"Maude?" the lieutenant asked gently, afraid the girl was going to collapse at any minute. "Did you see Stephanie as you were leaving yesterday?"

Maude could feel Margo watching her. She kept her eyes on Detective Hilliard's shoes.

"Well, yes. She and I walked out at the same time," she said, feeling her stomach flip. "Miss Margo sent her out for a restaurant pick-up."

The heat emanating from Margo was tangible. Her blouse rose and fell with her ragged breathing.

"That was *before* you left," Margo said firmly. "She was just getting back when you saw her, not *leaving!*"

The image of Brixi lying with her skull cracked open flashed before Maude's eyes. Her tears accompanied a new feeling now: anger.

"No ma'am," she said, lifting her face to stare Margo in the eyes. "She and I left together. I saw her get into her car. We were talking about Tilliard's naming a menu after you because of how often you order dinner from there."

"That's something we can follow up on," Calvo said, entering the restaurant name into her tablet. "That will show us when the order was placed and when Stephanie picked up the food." She gave Margo a look of satisfaction.

"We are done here," Margo hissed. "You have nothing to arrest me for."

"Not yet," Hilliard said. "We *can* get a warrant to search your property, however."

"Search for what?" she demanded, but Calvo noticed a look of fear in the woman's face.

Margo faltered, her mind racing. *Brixi had taken magazines from her garbage can. Did she take the muddy shoes she wore the night she rolled Rachel into the lake? Had she told Maude about them, and now the detectives knew? Is that why they suspected her of killing her own maid? Because Brixi knew things?* She became lightheaded and reached for the wall.

Calvo grabbed her arm before she could go down. Taking several deep breaths, Margo rallied and straightened, weaving slightly.

"May we have your permission to search your house, or do we come back with a warrant?" Hilliard asked succinctly.

A train wreck was going on inside Margo's mind. She ran a laundry list of the things that might incriminate her concerning Rachel's death and Skylar's disappearance. She had disposed of the curtains, and the broken statue had been thrown into a back-alley dumpster days ago. Skylar's ring was the only thing, but no one would find it where she had hidden it now.

"Go ahead," she said finally, a defiant look on her face. "I want it noted that I cooperated."

"I'll take that as a 'Yes,'" Hilliard said, slipping on blue latex gloves he had pulled from his jacket pocket. When he was met with silence, he turned to Calvo and said, "Get Mrs. Tillson to sign a release form. I'll need keys to any locked cabinets or closets," he said, looking at Margo, as he slipped into the routine he knew by rote. "And I'll need your car keys," he said.

Margo's surprise showed through her anger. "Just what are you looking for? I know enough to know that a legal search warrant has to list specific items. You can't just go through my house carte blanche."

"Up on your CSI, I see," Hilliard said. "However, under section 165 CrPC, we can search without restriction. You just consented by saying 'Go Ahead,' which gives us the Legal Right of Entry. You can remain here with Calvo, filling out the form. Your keys, please."

Margo flashed a look of hatred at the detective as she fished for her car keys from her pants pocket. She walked to the library and returned with a ring of keys for the house.

"You can figure out which key is which for yourself," she said heatedly. "And, if you set my car alarm off again, you're on your own. It's touchy." Her lips curled in anger, but inside, her heart was skipping in spasms.

"Thank you," Hilliard said. He shot Maude a meaningful look. She led the way to the kitchen, and he followed her out the side door.

Calvo couldn't shake the feeling that Margo's actions were way off. She didn't seem nervous if they searched her house and car for what was probably the murder weapon that bashed in Brixi Carter's head. She just appeared angry. *Maybe we're wrong,* she thought as she led Margo to the kitchen dinette table. *Or she has already gotten rid of the vase.*

Hilliard unlocked the BMW as Maude waited anxiously inside the garage door. He whistled and bent into the passenger side door. With gloved hands, he carefully lifted a large cut glass vase from the car floor and turned to Maude, who was staring at it in horror.

"Is this the vase?" Hilliard asked her. As he took a step toward her, she backed away, a hand to her mouth and tears brimming. "Yes," she said in muffled sobs.

"Yes. I'm positive."

Carrying it carefully, Hilliard took the vase outside and around the back of the garage to his car. Opening the hatchback, he placed it carefully into a large brown evidence bag and sealed it. He laid it carefully on its side and buffered it with a toolbox and an emergency road kit so it wouldn't roll around. He turned to Maude, who had followed him, not wanting to let him out of her sight.

"What do I do now?" she cried. "I just helped you. Now, Margo knows I think she killed Brixi. I'm scared! And I'm out of a job."

"We'll make sure you're okay," Hilliard said, placing a hand on the frightened girl's shoulder. "Does Margo know anything about the aunt you're staying with? Did you use her as a reference or anything?"

"No. I haven't spent much time with Aunt Beverly. I felt bad asking her to help me. I won't stay there long. I don't think I want to live here anymore."

"Well, don't head out yet," Hilliard warned. "Not till this is over. We'll keep an eye on you. If this vase has any evidence on it, Margo will be safely locked up soon. You did good in there," he said. "Your friend would be proud of you."

The thought of Brixi sent her into fresh tears and she turned and walked over to her car. Hilliard locked his door and walked back around to the front door. Without knocking, he entered and found Calvo talking to Margo at the dinette table.

"We're done here," he said, giving the lieutenant a meaningful look. "For now..." he amended. He laid Margo's keys on the table in front of her. "Same old words," he said, addressing the woman who was glaring at him. "Don't leave town."

"You're finished...already?" Margo asked in surprise. "Did you find anything?" Calvo noticed the woman was holding her breath.

"We'll be in touch," Hilliard said, ignoring the question.

Calvo rose and powered off her tablet. Margo remained seated, seething with anger.

"Tell Maude to come in here!" Margo blurted out.

"Pretty sure you need to get a new maid," Hilliard said, his blue eyes boring into hers. "Make that *two* new maids. If I hear of you bothering Maude, you'll be dealing with one very agitated, tall detective who has reached his limit with one very narcissistic, rich socialite. Am I clear? We'll let ourselves out," Hilliard said. He and Calvo exited through the front door and closed it, pulling it hard against the wind.

They hurried to the car and tried a few times to open the doors against the force of the wind, which was escalating. Once inside, the car doors slammed on their own.

"Good grief!" Calvo said, rubbing her elbow that had been smacked by the slamming door. "You going to tell me?"

"It was there," he said, his voice filled with disbelief.

"You're kidding!" Calvo said excitedly, sitting upright. "Right there in her car?"

"I don't get it," Hilliard said. "She didn't even hesitate to hand me the car keys. Mad, yes, but... She could have sent us off for a search warrant and removed it while we were gone. She could have lawyered up. I am honestly baffled."

"Me too," Calvo said. "But I feel something is about to break wide open. Maybe it's the storm coming. It reminds me of that song by Sheena Easton," Calvo said, her voice husky. 'I know it's gonna come like a hurricane hittin'.'"

Hilliard felt a shiver run through him and said, "And that hurricane is heading straight for Lake Broussard."

Tulie lay in her bed, watching the shadows from the swaying leaves outside dance across her ceiling. The tree limbs thrashed about in the oncoming storm, one of them striking her window repeatedly. *Tap. Tap. Tap.* It's monotonous rhythm sounded like skeletal fingers rapping to get in. She rose and walked over to the window. *Tap. Tap. Tap.* The limb scratched across the glass. Something was perched along its long branch, only a few feet from where she stood looking out. As her eyes adjusted to the darkness within the canopy of leaves, she screamed and fell back. The shadow of a boy was balanced on the branch, holding onto it with both hands. He was facing her, his eyes like two dark holes. Suddenly, he leaned out toward her as his mouth dropped open and the sound of a clanging bell rang out from it in a tortured scream.

26 RISING TIDES

The following morning, the shrill ringing of a telephone landline echoed through the long front hallway of the Barrow's home. Brenn picked it up on the fourth ring.

"Hello?" she said.

"Put Randall on," Margo said bluntly.

Brenn bristled but remained standing where she was.

"He's sick," she said without emotion.

"What do you mean he's sick?" Margo asked, her anger rising. "I just spoke to him yesterday."

"Well, Margo, that was yesterday. Today, he's sick. Anything else?"

"What's wrong with him?" Margo asked, sounding frantic. "It's important I speak to him."

"He got sick and started throwing up last night," Brenn said. "Maybe something he ate."

The way she said it sent a chill down Margo's spine.

"Surely, he can talk on the phone for a moment. I said it's important."

"And I said he's sick," Brenn said. "Tulie hasn't been herself either. Must be goin' around. You take care that nothing happens to *you*," Brenn said with mock sincerity and hung up.

Margo sat at the library desk, her right hand still gripping the receiver. She slammed it down and sat with her head bowed, breathing hard. She had to speak to Randall. There may be a way to get this whole thing back on track. Brixi was dead. There would be no more blackmail notes, no hemorrhaging of money. She hadn't realized when she signed the developer's contract that it included a 120-day due diligence period on their behalf. She was yet to see a red dime of the pecan grove sale. Landon's engagement party had put a dent in her bank account, and she had shelled out $200 thousand in blackmail money.

She leaned forward on her forearms until the stale odor of Reed's ashtray overpowered her. Angrily, she stood up, shoving his tooled leather chair back with so much force it hit the credenza behind it, knocking over framed photos and an equestrian trophy from his glory days in the arena. Looking at the fallen pictures of a once-perfect family, she clenched her fists in rage. *How could it all be such an unmitigated mess?* The stuffy smell of the cigar butt assaulted her nostrils. She grabbed up the ashtray and hurled it across the room, a trail of ashes following it.

Stephanie suddenly appeared at the doorway to the library and looked in with surprise.

"Are you alright, Miss Margo?" she asked, looking about the room for the source of the crash she had just heard from the hallway.

"Where were you yesterday?" was Margo's heated response. "I didn't see you all morning."

The maid took a moment to answer.

"Mr. Reed gave me the day off when I asked a couple of days ago," she said sheepishly. "He said Brixi and Maude could handle things."

Margo cringed at Brixi's name. "Since when do you ask Reed for a day off and not me?" she said heatedly. "You are my personal maid…not his."

Stephanie didn't want to say that Margo's husband was much kinder to the staff when they needed time off. She covered by saying that he didn't want to bother Margo with all that was going on. Just then, the phone rang.

"I'll talk to you later," Margo said, waving her away dismissively. "I'm expecting a call. Close the door."

Stephanie closed the door but waited on the other side, listening, curious as to what was happening. She had seen neither of the maids when she came in, and Margo was in a white hot temper.

"Hello?" Margo said, hoping beyond hope she would hear Randall's voice on the other end of the line. Instead, there was only silence.

"Hello?" Margo repeated. A high-pitched static noise filled the airwaves, and she cringed, pulling the receiver farther from her ear. "Who is this?" she barked.

The static stopped, and a deep robotic voice assaulted her ear:

"Flowers for the dead. Flowers for the tomb. Now your rival is gone, baby dead in the womb. Tonight. $200,000. The storm's comin'."

Stephanie jumped as her employer let out a scream from inside the closed room. The clang of a receiver slamming into its cradle followed.

Tulie sat in her room, the draperies once again closed

against the outside world. The wind battered the house, its ancient boards creaking in protest. A branch from the elm tree outside her bedroom window attacked the glass until it threatened to shatter. She covered her ears and pressed herself farther into the pillows she had stacked against her headboard. The room spun around her. She pulled a pillow closer to her chest, her arms folded tightly around it; her knees pulled up in a protective cocoon. She reached for the tea Brenn had brought her to help with her nausea; its steam curled into the dimly lit room. The hot liquid filling her mouth was the only thing that felt real. Everything else was in a haze.

Tulie leaned her head back and closed her eyes, forcing the tears that had been balancing there to cascade down her cheeks. *Her mother was dead. She was sure of it now. She had felt it without the psychic's card reading. But what had happened to her? Why were her nightmares of her mother always pertaining to water?*

The hinge on her bedroom door squeaked. It barely registered. Sounds seemed so far away. But as the door creaked open, Tulie turned her head gently to look in that direction. For a moment, only the feeble light from the hall table lamp shone in. The house was cast in darkness from the turbulent skies outside. Expecting Brenn to walk in to collect the teacup, she waited.

A chill ran along Tulie's arm as the small hairs there stood on end. An overwhelming smell of Tea Rose perfume filled the room. Tulie sat up and clutched the pillow tighter, her hands shaking violently. The room became glacial, as if a freezer door had opened. A current of air sent the chill air swirling in eddies as something moved past her bed. Tulie shivered, hugging the pillow tighter. A movement across from her caught her attention, and she jerked her head in that direction. A dark form stepped from the shadows near her closet and floated toward her bed, its feet several inches above the floor. Her chest heaving, Tulie strove for breath. The fog in her head thinned as terror overtook her. The thing lifted its arms, releasing long black tendrils. They moved fluidly in the air. Tangled strands of hair circled its head like Medusa's snakes, as its long dress swept back and forth on an invisible current. The last thing Tulie saw before her world went dark was what appeared to be a long ribbon, dragging along the floor.

Hurricane Beatrice hit the Louisiana coastline in the wee morning hours. It had been downgraded to a Tropical Storm by the time it made landfall, but it was no less destructive. The power went out throughout New Orleans, sending emergency utility vehicles scampering. They knew the drill. 911 was bombarded with phone calls as frightened denizens lamented over downed trees, mutilated rooftops, and flooded roadways. It was the same thing every hurricane season. No matter how far in advance storm warnings went out, the locals did little to prepare for it. "We'll just ride it out," was the mantra. But once roads were cut off and food supplies diminished, they panicked.

Reed ran about the house with a flashlight, checking windows and reassuring Margo, who was having a meltdown. Stephanie was kept busy mopping up rainwater that was pouring in through a broken kitchen window where a large tree limb protruded into the room. Lightning flashed relentlessly as thunder rolled in waves, loud bursts shaking the rafters until the china and wine glasses rattled in their cabinets.

An explosion split the air, and Margo screamed.

"That lightning hit something close by," Reed said knowingly. "Stay away from the windows," he told Margo. "Drink something!" He was tired of hearing her wailing. Her constant pacing up and down the marble hallway in her bedroom flip-flops was on his last nerve. "Sit down!" he yelled.

Margo was in no mood to argue. She grabbed up a whiskey decanter in the parlor and poured a full glass, its amber liquid sloshing over the side as she tried to get her trembling hands under control. She took a long swallow from the glass, almost emptying it. The room tilted as a stream of warmth flowed through her body. With a sigh of relief, she sank into a high-backed chair away from the French doors and windows overlooking the back and side yards. She stuffed the decanter between her thighs where it was within easy reach. She polished off the glass and poured another one, downing several swallows. The room began spinning.

"Shit!" she heard Reed yell through her haze of alcohol. "There went the dock!" He was in the kitchen looking out toward the lake.

Margo leaned her head back against the tufted chair cover and giggled. "Which dick are you referring to?" she shouted, ending in a peel of laughter.

"Dock!" Reed shouted angrily. "The lake water has flooded most of the shoreline. Our dock just split apart."

Margo refilled her glass and cradled the near-empty decanter in her lap.

"Hickory dickory dock," she slurred. "The mouse ran

up the clock. The dock broke down, there goes the town, hickory dickory dock." She laughed hysterically at her revised rhyme. A few minutes later, her head fell forward onto her chest; her sonorous snoring matched the thunder outside.

At Angela's house, the storm raging inside matched that of the thunder outside and hurricane-force winds.

"Dammit, Calvin," she screamed. "You could at least double-check the windows! Help me!"

Brenn looked out through the Barrows' kitchen door at the nightmare outside. Tree limbs were flying across the lawn. The cemetery was coated in fallen leaves and debris. Lake water thrashed about as if the Kraken was rising from its depths. She would have to ride it out. Randall and Tulie were useless to her now.

Frail streaks of sunlight pierced the sodden sky as morning dawned on a scene of pure destruction. Margo was curled up on the parlor couch, slumbering without care or any idea how she got there. Reed was outside, surveying the damage. He stepped over broken branches and shards of flower pots. Bushes along the perimeter of the backyard were in shreds, their foliage scattered everywhere. The wrought iron arch leading into the formal gardens was leaning precariously to the left, propped up only by a broken oak tree. He picked his way to the landscaper's trail instead.

Water dripped from the tattered canopy of leaves overhead as Reed made his way along the muddy garden path. By the time he reached the folly, he looked as if he had stepped fully clothed from a shower. The air was thick with the smell of earth and flowers that now lay beheaded and dying all around him. As he turned the bend, he breathed a sigh of relief. Only a few terra cotta tiles lay broken on the ground from the folly rooftop. It was lucky there were never windows installed. The heavy stonework had saved the decades-old structure that had been in the Broussard family long before he was born. His stewardship over it and the other plantation buildings was something he felt keenly since marrying Margo. She had only seen them in terms of monetary value. His was a desire to preserve a legacy.

After unlocking the door and peeking quickly inside the ancient structure, Reed continued around it, following the path that led to the pecan grove and down along the cliffside to the lake below. He stopped and stared in dismay at the decimated trees before him. Pecans lay in mud everywhere, intertwined with pine needles and leaves. Dozens of pecan trees were uprooted and lying in mangled heaps, their branches intertwined as if they had been trying to hold each other up against the battering of the storm winds. Gnarled roots protruded from the ground; their nakedness was uncovered in the sunlight.

It was as Reed feared. The trees were old, still bearing, but close to their expiration date. Years of coastal storms had eroded the grove's flooring. To his left was a massive trunk lying on its side, split in half. Impossibly large roots had pulled a section of land up with them; sinews of dirt dangling in the air. It left a gaping hole filled now with mud and rainwater. He reasoned that this was the lightning strike they heard.

He headed back to finish surveying the damage to the main house. The roof was damaged, of that he was sure, having listened to tree branches striking it throughout the storm. As he crossed the back lawn, he glanced down at the lake and shook his head. Only half of the dock remained, tethered tenuously to a broken piling. *The insurance companies will be inundated with calls*, he thought. It would take some time to begin the clean-up and repair.

Reed entered through the French doors into the parlor, picking up shards of glass as he went. He found Stephanie there applying cold compresses to Margo's forehead.

"Let her sleep it off," he said unkindly. "I need your help cleaning up all this mess. I'm happy to pay you extra for helping me."

Stephanie smiled at him gratefully. He was the only reason she stayed. He was a decent man who cared about the estate. He treated the staff well and tried hard to keep his wife happy.

"I'd be glad to help, Mr. Reed," she said. "How about I make you some breakfast first? It's going to be a long day."

"Are the phone lines up?" he asked, hoping against hope.

"Yes, sir," she said. "About ten minutes ago. Is it bad out there?"

Reed looked down at his wife, who was sleeping with her mouth open, drool puddling on her shoulder.

"Not as bad as it is in here," he said ruefully. "Breakfast would be nice," he said, and the two left the matron of the house to her whiskey-induced coma.

The rest of the day was filled with the sound of trucks; their loud engines as invasive as the thunder had been the night before. Reed had flashed his wallet, guaranteeing him a position of priority for a clean-up crew. His gardener, Forster, was already at work carrying smaller limbs to the driveway and raking up foliage. At 2:00, a massive truck with the name Hamilton's Tree Service pulled into the driveway. A large man of African American descent jumped from the driver's side just as Forster was coming around the corner with another load of branches.

"We're here for the downed trees," the driver, Marshall Jamison, said without preamble. "What's the best way to pull the truck closest to them?"

Forster thought about it and finally said, "It's the pecan grove he called you about. You need to go back out on the road there, go east to the first turnoff, and you'll be goin' down a dirt road. About half a mile in, there's a small house. That's the Kingston place. They work for Mr. Reed. Pull into their driveway and around to the back. That's the closest. You'll see the busted trees from there."

"How many we talkin'?" the man asked, glancing at his watch. "We're on call for half the parish."

"Don't doubt it," Forster said. "You should make bank off all this mess. I looked at it earlier. It's a bunch, I ain't gonna lie. At least 20-30 trees. A really big one that is gonna require some major cuttin' up!"

A young man leaned from the passenger side of the truck and yelled down at the two men.

"How long?" he asked.

"20-30 trees," the driver repeated. " Radio in. Let's get Franklin and Beau out here to help." He jumped back up into the cab and backed the truck out onto Broussard Lane, where it roared out of sight; chainsaws rattling from the back as it went.

The humidity returned later in the afternoon. The

short respite that followed heavy winds was over. The four crewmen made their way through the grove as the roar of chainsaws marked their progress. They started with the thinner trees, clearing a path for the larger ones. The grating sound of wood chippers kept time with the saws as they ground limbs into chips of mulch.

Marshall Jamison and Franklin Danvers ran an eye over the hulking trunk of the biggest fallen tree.

"Damn!" Marshall said. "Bet that thing is a hundred years old or more! Shame!" He walked to where the roots were lying on their side, their gnarled fingers reaching for the air they had been denied for so long. "Let's start here," Marshall said. "Get the rest of this root system out so we can cut it all up."

Franklin took the hoe and shovel he had been carrying and began striking the ground near the hole the uprooted tree had left. The ground gave way easily in its sodden condition. After several minutes of swinging the metal head into the ground, he struck something hard. Figuring it to be a rock, he stopped to clear it. He brushed the caked mud away and froze. The scream that rose from his throat was like that of a wounded animal. He fell back onto his bottom, scurrying backward on his heels and elbows crablike away from the hole.

Marshall came running, afraid his workman had injured himself. When he saw the look on his co-worker's face, his stomach lurched. Franklin's face was frozen in horror. The terrified man lifted a trembling arm and pointed toward the exposed roots.

Marshall stepped cautiously toward the hole and stopped. His heart skipped. Before he was even up over it, he could see blond hair and part of a decomposing hand sticking up from the mud.

27 BURIED SECRETS

Tulie watched the myriad flashing lights as each emergency vehicle arrived at her Aunt Margo's house. The colors blended and rotated like a psychedelic dream. Tulie took another sip of tea and smiled as the sunroom spun slowly around her.

"There's fireworks at Aunt Margo's, Mama," Tulie slurred, smiling across the bistro table at the chair across from her. "It's just for us," she said dreamily. "You haven't touched your tea. Here, I'll warm it up for you." Tulie topped off the cup across from her, nearly dropping the heavy silver teapot.

The invasive sound of barking shattered Tulie's moment of bliss. She turned her head slowly to see her Cousin Angela walking briskly toward the back porch with Chester in hot pursuit behind her. The monotonous sound of sirens suddenly stopped, as did the dog's howling.

Angela stomped up the steps to the porch and swung

the screen door open wide.

"What is going on up at Margo's?" she demanded, looking up at the chaos erupting throughout her cousin's backyard.

Tulie looked up at her from her chair with a dazed expression. She blinked several times and smiled.

"They're putting on a fireworks show for me and Mama," she said, thickly. "You can watch with us. I'll get you a cup." Tulie slid her chair back as if to rise, but found the effort too much to handle. She slumped against the wrought iron chair back and stared at the red and blue lights through the mesh windows of the sunroom.

Angela stood as though hit by a bolt of lightning, her face in shock. She looked at the steaming cup of tea across from Tulie's own, and her heart sank. She became aware of the soft scent of perfume wafting through the room.

"Tulie," she began, her voice unsteady. "Those aren't fireworks, honey. Something bad has obviously happened at Margo's. Are you alright? You don't look well." She glanced again at the cup sitting before an empty chair across from Tulie, whose head was barely managing to stay upright.

Tulie looked up at her and a thin smile slipped slowly across her face. She then looked across the table and addressed the chair.

"Mama? Is something bad happening at Aunt Margo's? No more bad, okay? No more bad."

Angela grabbed the young woman's shoulders and shook her until Tulie nearly passed out from the dizziness. "Stop it, Tulie," she screamed. "Your mother is not there! You need to stop this right now!"

Brenn appeared in the doorway from the kitchen. Her expression was wooden as she gazed down at the sunken sunroom and the scene playing out. Angela stepped toward her, her face filled with hate.

"This is your doing!" she cried. "You encourage her to believe her mother is here when you know she's not. Ever since you moved in with this family, things have gone wrong. This was a happy family!"

Brenn's face twitched with anger as she stepped down into the room and confronted her cousin.

"*This* family? This *is* my family! I had every right to be here with *my* father. Where was I supposed to go after my mother died?" She was struggling to hold back the tears rimming her eyelids. "You're just some leech that moved into a house that was meant only for *our* family. You and that cripple you bully!"

Angela lunged at the girl, stopping just before she slapped her. She stood pulling in great gulps of air to calm herself.

Tulie sat looking straight ahead as if none of the drama was going on behind her. She tilted her head to get a better view of the swirling lights on the cliffside. Brenn glanced at her and smiled. "I think your Mama wants some more tea," Brenn said. "Oh, and Mrs. Collins wants to talk to you about making tea cakes for her charity event coming up."

Brenn glowered at Angela as she turned to walk back to the kitchen. She stopped and looked out through the window screen to the flashing lights across the lake. "I wonder what happened now," Brenn said innocently and climbed the two steps to the open kitchen doorway. She turned and said, "I'd love to stay and chat it up with you, Angela, but Randall is very sick. Since Tulie is useless and Rachel is…well, you know… it leaves it to me to take care of *my* family." She turned and disappeared inside the house.

The next morning, the news of a body being discovered buried in the Broussard pecan grove spread like wildfire through Orleans Parish. To the small community, it would always be considered the Broussard pecan grove, the Broussard mansion, the Broussard lake… No one ever referred to the properties as the Tillsons' or Barrows' despite Margo and Rachel inhabiting the houses. It belonged to the Broussard legacy, and that's how it would always remain.

By nightfall, the area news channels were touting their "exclusive" footage of the crime scene. Various angles of the uprooted pecan tree were shown with close-ups of the hole that was once a young woman's grave. Interviews with the workman who found her were not to be had. His other crew members had little to offer, other than hearing Franklin scream and watching as the body bag was carried past them later that day to the coroner's vehicle.

The local coffee house was brimming with ladies all a-twitter as they bent forward eagerly over beignets and lattes, their eyes glistening and their breathless words at fever pitch.

"It has to be Skylar Harris!" they panted, their ghoulish enthusiasm as thick as the air outside the air-conditioned coffee house. "Who else could it be?"

Dr. Dylan Douglas, the new forensic pathologist and medical examiner for Orleans Parish and outlying areas, took on the grisly job of autopsying the young blonde woman who lay on his operating table at the New Orleans Morgue. Detective Hilliard and Lieutenant Calvo overlooked the procedure, as did two of the officers first on the scene. It didn't take fingerprints or DNA to assure the detective that the partially decomposing body lying naked on the cold metal slab was Skylar Harris. Her body had been in the ground for two weeks. He recognized her blond hair from the party photos, still holding the waves she had so carefully created to resemble her idol, Scarlett O'Hara.

The soiled and bug-eaten green dress was lying on a table across the room; the smell of earth still clinging to it. The matching shoes were resting next to it, waiting to be placed into evidence bags. Hilliard had already taken a close look at the high heels. He had to admit, they could very well have made the scratch marks they saw in the folly after Skylar disappeared from her own party. Part of the green leather was peeled away near the bottom of the heel and the hard tip was scratched and bent on the edge.

Hilliard took a deep breath as the coroner announced they were ready to begin. He started with an exterior examination of the young woman's head and torso. Hilliard had only been to two other autopsies. Lieutenant Calvo, however, seemed unfazed as she leaned forward to watch the procedure with fascination.

"She has some signs around her neck that could be from manual strangulation," the coroner said, beginning with the head area. "But, I am not seeing petechiae in the whites of her eyes or other places you would typically see if she had died due to asphyxiation."

After examining the rest of her body, he found only a few dull bruises on her forearms. "These are consistent with someone possibly grabbing her arms," he said. He found no other trauma to the outside of her body. Dr. Douglas picked up a scalpel and Hilliard braced himself. The ME made the ubiquitous Y-incision in the body's chest that opened her from her pubic area up to her collarbone. Pinning back the opening, the medical examiner studied the organs inside, which were intact enough to disclose pertinent information. Hilliard swallowed as the heart was removed, along with the stomach and other organs, and placed into sterilized metal pans. A small recorder whirled, capturing Dr. Douglas' detailed analysis of the body's condition. Suddenly, he stopped and looked up at the detective meaningfully.

"This woman is pregnant," he said.

It was Lieutenant Calvo who lost her professional demeanor and blurted out, "What? Are you sure?"

Hilliard looked at the area the coroner was indicating inside the deteriorating uterus. "How far along was she?" he asked solemnly.

Tom Simons moved his scrambled eggs around his plate without interest. His parents sat next to him at the breakfast table in their home in Lake Grove Estates.

"You need to eat something, Tommy," his mother said worriedly. "The doctor said you need to get your strength back. Here, at least eat some toast to start."

Mrs. Simons placed a slice of buttered toast in front of her son. Tom stared at it. His eyes moved to the open newspaper across from him, to the headline his parents had been discussing for the past ten minutes. In bold print, it read:

SKYLAR HARRIS'S BODY IDENTIFIED AS WOMAN FOUND IN BROUSSARD PECAN GROVE!

Tom took a drink of orange juice, his hand shaking. The tremors were nothing new, not since he arrived home from the hospital the day before. The doctors had assured him the poison was no longer a threat. His vision had finally cleared, although his eyes still burned. The drops they gave him settled into crusty pools at the corners of his eyelids. The headline swam in front of him.

"That lady they found," he said, his voice small and scared. "I think I know something about her."

His mother and father looked at him in surprise. Mr. Simons set down his coffee cup and turned to his son.

"What do you mean, you know something about her?"

Mrs. Simons held her breath, setting her fork down slowly onto her plate.

"Don't get mad at me," Tom said, suddenly sounding like a toddler instead of a boy soon to turn thirteen. "We were just messing around."

Mrs. Simons' stomach dropped, and she grabbed the table. "Oh my God!" she gasped. Tom hurried to control the conversation.

"No! We didn't do anything to her," Tom said frantically. "Me and the other guys were just fooling around. We snuck into the kitchen during her party and stole some food. That's all! But…" he paused, trying to gauge the fallout of his next words. "We saw something. And now…it might be important."

Detective Hilliard and Lieutenant Calvo sat across from the frightened young boy in the Simons' living room. Calvo took the lead. She had proven when Tulie was little that she was better at handling children during painful interrogations than the socially awkward detective.

"Tom? First of all, we're so glad you're okay. You had a close call," she said, smiling encouragingly at the boy. "No more fooling around with plants, okay?"

Tom managed a feeble smile and nodded. He had confessed in the hospital to taking Angela Peterson's trumpet flower and playing with it as if it were a bugle. He waited for the tough questions he knew were coming next.

"What happened at the Tillson's kitchen the night of the engagement party?" Calvo asked, a small tape recorder placed on the coffee table between them. She made a point of showing it to Hilliard, who grinned feebly.

"Are we going to get in trouble for taking the food?" Tom asked first.

"No. Just don't do it again," Calvo said. "Now, what happened?"

Tom looked at his mother for reassurance and took a deep breath. "We were taking some food from the kitchen counter when Mrs. Tillson came in," he said.

"Margo Tillson?" Calvo asked to make sure. "How do you know Mrs. Tillson?"

"She's yelled at us to get out of her pecan grove a few times," Tom said, looking guilty. "We weren't hurting nothin,' but she said stealin' nuts lyin' on the ground is still stealin'."

"Ok. What did Mrs. Tillson do when she entered the

kitchen that you think we should know about?"

"Well, when we saw her come in, we ran back into the room behind the kitchen and hid behind a bunch of crates and garbage bags. She didn't see us. She went to one of the cabinets and shoved some books around and crammed a gold purse down behind the books, and left. She was hurrying and looked upset. We just all thought it was a strange thing to do."

"Do you know what time this happened?" Calvo asked.

"No, Ma'am. Somebody was talking with a mic out back about 'parents' speeches' coming up. That's all I know."

"Did anything else happen?" Calvo asked, glancing down at the recorder to make sure it was recording.

"I was curious, so I sneaked over to the cabinet and pulled the purse out from behind the books and took it back to my friends." He stopped and looked at his father's face. It held the look he expected. He was in trouble.

"Go on," Calvo said.

"There was a wallet in it, and some car keys," Tom said, pausing again.

"Did you take anything from the purse?" Calvo asked, sensing there was more.

Once again, Tom shot his father a furtive look. "Yeah...I mean, we shouldn't have, but there was a little money, like around $20 or so, and I did take that. I'm really sorry. I'll give it back!" He looked pleadingly at the officer, fearing he was about to be put into handcuffs and hauled off to jail.

"Did you see whose purse it was?" Calvo asked, her voice sounding more urgent than angry. "Did you look in the wallet other than for the money?"

"I saw credit cards, but I didn't take em'," Tom said, hoping that small moment of restraint might help his cause. "So, I don't know. I didn't pull them out and look at them. But..." He reached behind him and pulled something from his jeans pocket. "This was in there. It's why I needed to tell my parents this morning, after I heard them talking about who the dead lady is. I didn't know," he began to cry as he held out a dangling gold chain with an engraved heart upon it. Calvo took it from him and drew in her breath. The name on the heart said Skylar.

There was a moment's silence as the gravity of the situation set in.

"Am I going to jail?" Tom bawled, looking to his mother to save him.

"No, Tom," Hilliard said, finally speaking. "Who else knows you have this?" He suddenly felt worried for the boy.

"Just the guys. They didn't tell anyone cuz they didn't want to get in trouble either."

"Did you see anything else?" Calvo asked, laying the necklace down gently on the table.

"No. I put the purse back where I found it," Tom said, "and we split."

"Which cabinet do you remember?" Calvo asked.

Tom thought for a minute and said, "It was right across from us, next to the refrigerator. It was all books...cookbooks, I guess."

"Tell me exactly what the purse looked like," Calvo said.

"Um...I don't know...small. Fancy gold bead stuff. There was a little pocket inside, but it just had a tube of lipstick in it. It just opened by pushing two metal knobs apart. That's all."

"Did it have a strap or chain?"

"No, ma'am.'

Calvo considered her next question carefully.

"Tom? You've been very brave in coming clean on what you and your friends have been up to. I have one more question for you, okay? Did you hurt Mrs. Peterson's cat?"

"We, uh, we did shoot it with a slingshot, but I didn't mean to hit it, I swear! I just wanted to scare it. She yelled at us really good!"

"After that," Calvo said. "I was there the day you shot the cat with the slingshot. Did you kill the cat or do something to it in Margo Tillson's garden?"

The look of surprise on Tom Simons' face was so genuine that the lieutenant was sure he was innocent of causing Beauregard's death.

"No, Ma'am!" he said. "The cat is dead?" he asked, looking scared.

"Yes. It looks like someone threw it in some lilies, hoping the poor thing would get sick and die. Lily pollen is poisonous to cats."

Tom looked at her, his face saddened. "I promise, we didn't do anything to her cat, nothing like that. I'm really sorry it's dead."

"Thank you for your honesty," Calvo said.

"So, I'm not going to jail?" Tom asked hopefully.

Calvo smiled. "No. I have a feeling your father has some form of punishment coming, which I hope is not too harsh considering all you've been through." She looked meaningfully at Mr. Simons, who managed a wan smile. "What I do want is your promise, Tom, not to mention this to anyone! Do you understand? Not your friends, not anyone! Don't go near any of the Broussard houses. Stay away from the lake. I need you to become a monk!"

"A what?" Tom asked, surprised.

"Just stay around your house," Calvo smiled. "You should be resting up anyway."

The two officers left. Once inside the car, they turned to each other.

"I think we have who killed Skylar Harris," Calvo said. "We're almost there. A few more people to question, but it looks like we have motive, opportunity, and means. We also have evidence," she said, holding up the necklace. It swayed from her fingertips as the sunlight glinted off the gold. "What was Margo Tillson doing with Skylar's purse...and hiding it?"

Angela Peterson opened her front screen door and sighed.

"I figured you'd be showing up," she said flatly, stepping back to allow Hilliard and Calvo to enter her foyer. Lieutenant Calvo looked at her in surprise, wondering what the cryptic statement meant. "Calvin!" Angela screamed down the hallway into the shadows. "Come on out! We have company."

The soft sound of rubber wheels coming along the hardwood floor sounded as Calvin Peterson rolled his wheelchair into view from somewhere in the back. Angela gestured to the parlor, and the officers followed her in. Calvin wheeled his chair next to a window by the fireplace and waited. On his tray was the local newspaper and a pair of scissors.

"I see you've read the headlines," Calvo said, noting

the paper and the bold type. A small headshot of Skylar Harris was centered in the article accompanying the banner. The coroner had agreed to leave out the information that Skylar was pregnant at the time of her death.

"Hard to miss!" Calvin said bluntly. "Y'all still don't believe this whole area is cursed? How high is the body count now?"

Hilliard had tired of the man's obsession with the curse of the Broussard's. In an uncharacteristic retort, he said, "I'm surprised you are leaning toward a curse and not the Bayou Slayer." He arched an eyebrow as he fixed the man with steely eyes, amplified by the detective's bifocals.

"They caught him," Calvin said dejectedly, "or don't you read the papers? He was in jail in Arkansas when Skylar went missing."

"They allegedly caught him," Hilliard said, unable to contain a sardonic grin. "DNA results aren't in. I do read the papers. You seem disappointed. Would you rather his killings continued, or was a book deal more important? Fresh bodies keep his name in the spotlight."

Calvin leaned forward in his chair with his eyes blazing.. Calvo headed off the rapidly building exchange. She opened the folder she carried in her left hand and fished through some photographs.

"Mr. Peterson," she said, walking over to his wheelchair. "Were you at the folly the night of the engagement party?"

Her question seemed to shock both Angela and Calvin. It quelled the hateful look on his face immediately. Before he could answer, Angela chimed in.

"Of course, he wasn't at the folly! I was with him all night. He sat at the back by the cliff, next to the bar."

"We have statements saying you left him twice: once to get him a plate of food, and another to go to the cake table. I believe you were seen heading to the cake table just before Skylar went into the garden, after the announcement and cake cutting."

Angela bristled.

"The man is in a wheelchair, in case you hadn't noticed. He didn't race around the party like he was in the Indianapolis 500!"

"It's interesting you should say that," Calvo said. She stepped to Calvin's wheelchair and laid two photographs atop the newspaper. She watched his face as he looked down at them. His flushed color and jumping jaw muscles told her all she needed to know.

Angela stepped toward her husband and snatched up the photos. She studied them for a few moments before clarity dawned. She looked down at him with a look of shock on her face.

"What is this?" she asked, her voice hoarse. When he didn't answer, Calvo jumped in.

"It appears something making tracks very much like the tread on these tires here," she said, pointing down at the wheels of Calvin's chair, "went up the dirt path the gardener uses to the folly that night. That second photo is a piece of the same tread mark found *inside* the folly near where it appeared a scuffle went on."

Angela stared again at the pictures and then down at the wheels. Her face paled.

"Calvin?" she breathed, "What is this?" she repeated.

His face contorted with anger as he faced each of the

officers, ignoring his wife's question.

"Alright, I went to confront Skylar. I saw her going into the garden and figured that I could catch her there and get my son's ring back. I was going to point out to her that she had another man's ring now and was getting married. There was no need to keep a family heirloom. But when I got to the folly, she was lying on the floor. I wheeled my chair a little way in to see if she had passed out. She was drunk most of the party. But then I saw a reddened area at her throat, and she looked dead. I looked down and realized I was leaving prints in the pollen, so I backed out and hurried back to the party just before Tulie found me. I told her to tell Angela I wanted to go home."

Angela's face remained frozen in disbelief.

"You *saw* her? Why didn't you tell someone? Why didn't you tell *me*?" she yelled accusingly.

Calvin's anger flashed, and he turned his chair a fraction to face his wife squarely.

"Because I thought just maybe *you* killed her!" he yelled. "You disappeared when you went for cake and didn't come back. You were ready to kill her over what she did to Dennis! I'm sorry, but yes, I wondered if you had a fight with her over the ring, and you did something before you could stop yourself. Your damn temper is famous around here!"

Angela stared at him, her eyes bulging. "You thought I...?" She suddenly whirled to face the two officers who were watching her closely. "I didn't kill that little...!" She caught herself and stopped. Her breathing was coming in bursts. She fought to calm the frantic sound in her voice. "I didn't kill her," she said, an octave lower. "And I know Calvin would never do such a thing."

Calvo walked over to Angela and took the two photos from her shaking hands.

"Mr. Peterson," Hilliard said evenly, stepping closer to tower over the man who looked up at him with fear in his eyes. Gone was the cocky attitude. "I need you to think. When you saw Skylar lying there, as you say, was she wearing a blue sash?"

Calvin looked surprised at the question. He thought back, cringing at the thought that he had been so close to being caught with a dead body and a motive to kill her. He saw her lying there, blonde hair splayed out and falling across her face. One arm was thrown out onto the floor, the other across her chest. He remembered the dress because she had flaunted it all night, but he could not remember something as detailed as a sash.

"I don't remember," he said, hoping his answer did not sound evasive. "I was not studying her frock when I saw her. Once I realized she was dead, I just wanted out of there. I did notice one thing, however. I thought it odd. Her engagement ring was gone. I looked at her fingers, hoping that maybe she was still wearing Dennis's ring. She used to wear it like it was costume jewelry all the time. It was like rubbing it in his face. But neither ring was there." His voice took on a hardened tone. Angela shot him a warning look. "That's all, I swear. I didn't touch her."

Hilliard faced Angela, who finally made eye contact with him as silence suddenly descended over the group.

"That leaves *your* whereabouts," he said. "Your own husband just said you left for cake and didn't come back. Where were you?"

Her face flushed crimson as she kneaded her kitchen

apron in her clenched fists. Choosing the lesser of two outcomes, she let go of the fabric and faced him.

"I was in Margo's parlor," she said defiantly. "I took envelopes from the gift basket that I knew had money in them. I knew which relatives were giving cash. They had been bragging for weeks about how much each was giving. Every damned family gathering I went to! It was rubbing my face in it! *'Angela! The poor relation! How lucky Angela scraped together enough to buy Margo's house from her.'* Lucky? She didn't even lower the asking price, even though I was a blood relative! I'm not sorry I stole it. I felt it was karma just waiting for me to cash in! Take the money that was going into Skylar Harris's pocket so I could replace what my mother's ring cost. She ruined my son's life!" She thrust her chin out stubbornly and waited for the fallout.

"I'll be damned," Hilliard said, his eyes blinking behind his glasses. "I was not expecting that!"

Angela turned toward a towering antique bookcase and reached up to the second shelf. She pulled a thick book from the middle and opened it, her face red with anger. The book's interior had been hollowed out. Inside was a large lavender potpourri pouch. She pulled it from its hiding place and shoved it toward the detective.

"Here! Take it. It's all there. Every penny." She slammed the book shut for emphasis. Calvo took the pouch and was about to open it when the sound of sirens wailing suddenly sounded outside. The high-pitched scream of emergency vehicles grew closer until it was obvious they had pulled onto Broussard Lane.

"Now what?" Angela cried, racing for the window.

28 REVENGE FROM THE GRAVE

Detective Hilliard and Lieutenant Calvo raced down the handicap ramp at Angela and Calvin Peterson's home. They jumped over fallen limbs and strewn foliage from the storm. An ambulance and two police cars were pulling up to the back of Rachel and Randall Barrow's home, which sat a few hundred yards along the lake. Foregoing their car, the two officers ran along the dirt path connecting the two mansions, arriving just as a gurney was being pulled from the back of the ambulance.

"Morris!" Hilliard yelled, recognizing one of the uniformed policemen who was heading to the back porch. "What's going on?"

"Got a call from a young woman here that her father was unresponsive this morning. He's been sick, according to her. After finding the Harris girl's body over there," he nodded toward the pecan grove, "I thought it best to check it out."

Lieutenant Calvo shot a worried look at the detective

as they followed Officer Morris into the sunroom. An EMT and others flooded in from outside. They found Brenn standing at the top of the two steps that led into the kitchen. She looked harried, but her voice was in control.

"He's in his bedroom," she said, before anyone could ask her a question. "When I took him up some lunch, he was unconscious. I couldn't get him to wake up."

"Is he breathing?" an EMT asked as they pushed past her. Two men holding each end of a gurney followed close behind.

"I think so." Calvo noticed her answer was strangely flat.

"Did you touch anything?" Hilliard asked, stepping past her into the kitchen. She turned to face the detective and Calvo. The small recorder was already churning inside the lieutenant's front pocket.

Brenn eyed him with the cool look of contempt he felt she reserved solely for him. How many times had he questioned this arrogant young woman concerning death, a disappearance, and now an emergency phone call concerning her father?

"No," she said shortly. "Other than the tray of food I took up. It's still there in his room. Tulie has been fading in and out since Rachel's self-imposed exile, so I've been taking care of him. She's not been feeling well, either. Before she got too sick, she helped with meals for our father once in a while. Mainly making him her tea cakes. It's his favorite."

"How long has he been sick?" Hilliard asked. Brenn's unemotional responses cemented his dislike for the girl.

"Oh, about five days," she said. "I figured it was the

flu. He had a fever and kept throwing up. When he lapsed into some kind of delirium this morning, I called Dr. Clarkson. In the meantime, I took him up some lunch. That's when I found him passed out."

The heavy sound of two men struggling to bring a heavy gurney down the main staircase sounded from the foyer. Their voices were elevated and urgent.

"Call it in," one of the ambulance crew said, breathing raggedly beneath Randall Barrow's weight. "Get a room open! Tell them we have a pulse, but it's weak."

Hilliard and Calvo stepped into the hallway opening and watched as the men made the final descent down the stairs. Randall's body was covered in a white sheet up to his chin with heavy straps pinning him to the gurney. His face was a sickly gray, and perspiration peppered his forehead. His thick head of strawberry blonde hair was matted to his face with sweat.

The officers stepped aside to allow the EMTs to carry the gurney through the kitchen and down the steps into the sunroom. Hilliard noticed Brenn's detached manner as her father was carried past her.

Officer Morris appeared and asked the detective if he was taking over the situation. Hilliard shot Brenn a sardonic smile, and answered, "Yes, indeed I am!"

A frightening thought occurred to Calvo.

"Where's Tulie?" she asked, her voice urgent.

"In her room. Where else?" Brenn said unfeelingly. "She spends most of her time holed up in there."

"You check on Tulie," Hilliard said, "I'll take Randall's room. You…," he said, pointing a finger into Brenn's smug face, "You stay here! Morris, will you please babysit this young woman while we're upstairs?"

Morris looked surprised at the detective's choice of words, but nodded and pulled out a chair from the dinette table for Brenn. She plopped into it and folded her arms defiantly. She showed no emotion at the sound of the sirens wailing outside as the ambulance carrying her father departed.

Hilliard and Calvo took the stairs in tandem. At the landing, she went left as he went right. The detective entered Randall's room through the open doorway. A policeman was taking photos of the room.

"Get pics of the food tray, too, Baldwin," Hilliard said. He had worked on several cases with the efficient young officer and liked him. The detective stepped over to a vintage tea tray with wooden handles sitting atop a nightstand near the bed. A plate with a sandwich sliced in half at an angle sat atop a napkin. Next to it was a dollop of potato salad and a plastic cup of chocolate pudding; a congealed film already covering it. On a separate dessert plate sat two small cakes with white frosting dripping over their sides. A tall glass of what looked like iced tea sat next to it, the ice cubes all but dissolved as condensation puddled beneath it.

Hilliard studied the bed. The covers were thrown back. He noticed the pillow case and a substantial portion of the sheet were damp. He assumed it was from perspiration.

"We need to bag the bedding," Hilliard said aloud. He stooped and peered beneath the bed. There was nothing there. He looked through wardrobes and dresser drawers, only to find the usual array of clothes for a man with Randall Barrows' money. Two fancy watches sat atop a dresser, along with the man's wallet and car keys. Oddly, what looked like his wedding ring was also there, sitting in a blue porcelain dish.

The room gave up no other secrets. It was well taken care of. The drapes were open, and sunlight shone in through parted, ecru-colored sheers. The sound of an air conditioner purred from a window unit nearest the bed. What Hilliard found concerning was that Randall Barrows no longer shared a room with his wife. He wondered how long that had been going on...and why?

"Do me a favor," Hilliard said to the young man who was still snapping photos. "Can you take that tray of food just as it is? Do you have something in the form of an evidence bag or carton that you can lift it into? Dust it for prints...all of it, please. I'm requesting the food be tested."

Hilliard didn't wait for a response. Taking one last look around, he exited the room and left Officer Baldwin to gather up the evidence. As he reached the staircase and started down, he heard Calvo's soft cadence coming from behind the closed door to Tulie's room.

"Tulie, sweetheart, I'm worried about you," Lieutenant Calvo said, alarmed at the dazed and confused condition in which she found the young woman. "We need to get you in for some tests, okay?"

Tulie stared at the uniformed officer seated beside her on her bed. A look of faint recognition registered in her eyes, but she remained silent. Her head was weaving from side to side as though watching an invisible tennis match.

Calvo rose and opened the heavy velvet draperies to allow more light into the room. She noticed the air conditioner in the window was unplugged. Tulie's table lamp did little to dispel the gloom in the small bedroom. The air was stale from a lack of circulation. She opened a window, a stream of warmth entering the room.

Tulie blinked in the sunlight. Her face puckered in an obvious objection to the intrusion of light. She crawled to the back of her bed and propped up against the headboard. She pulled a large pillow up against her chest. The lieutenant sat again on the edge of the bed and placed a hand on Tulie's arm.

"Tulie? Do you know anything about your Daddy being sick? Do you know what might be wrong with him?" Calvo asked gently.

The room swam around them as Tulie tried to pull focus on the face near her. It felt like struggling up from a dark well. A few words pierced a part of her brain still operating.

"Daddy is sick," she said, sounding like a small child.

"Yes," Calvo said. "What is wrong with him?"

"Daddy is sick. Mama will take care of him. Mama always takes care of us," Tulie said, and a sad smile crossed her face. "Mama checks on me. She was here the other night," she said, sounding far away. "She came back for me."

The lieutenant paused. Tulie was clearly in need of medical attention. The rest could wait. She seemed to be hallucinating. She was having trouble breathing, and she seemed close to losing consciousness. Calvo punched in the 911 number into her cell phone and requested an ambulance. It took several tries to get the address out as her phone kept dropping the call in the spotty cell phone service around the lake.

"Let me help you up," Tulie," Calvo said, standing and bending toward the girl to put an arm around her. As she lifted Tulie's limp body, she stumbled against the nightstand and sent a photo crashing to the floor. Stooping, Calvo picked it up. It was a framed photo of Tulie and Ryder, standing at the mouth of the dock outside. Ryder was wearing a pirate patch over one eye. Calvo studied it. The tragic happenings to this family weighed on her. As she scanned Ryder's image, she stopped and pulled the photo closer to her. There was something in the boy's left hand, barely in view at the bottom of the picture.

Tulie looked over at the photo in the lieutenant's hand. "That's me and my twin brother," she slurred. Her eyes glistened with tears. "Dawson took that, just before I went to paint the rocks gold. I wish we could start that day over," she said, her head falling forward onto her chest.

"Come on, Tulie," Calvo said, and helped the girl to stand. She wobbled and almost fell back onto the bed. Calvo tightened her arm about Tulie's waist, and they began the slow walk from the room. In the lieutenant's other hand was the photo from Tulie's nightstand.

For the second time, an ambulance pulled up outside the Barrow's back porch. Angela, who was fuming a few feet away, lunged forward when Lieutenant Calvo appeared at the sunroom door with a dazed Tulie on one arm.

"Dammit!" she yelled. "Someone tell me what's going on! That policeman won't let me in."

Two medics took Tulie by both arms and loaded her onto a stretcher. They placed her in the back of the ambulance. Angela peered in at them as they began checking her young cousin's vital signs.

Calvo walked over to the woman who was about to burst wide open.

"They took Randall in," Calvo said, knowing Angela watched the ambulance depart earlier. "He's really sick. We don't know why, yet. Tulie is showing signs of possibly being drugged. I'm asking you now, not accusing, just asking, do you know anything about this?"

Angela didn't hesitate. "Yes!" she blurted out so forcefully that Calvo took a step back. "Something *is* going on here. Tulie thinks her mother is back. I've seen her talking to an empty chair like her Mama is sitting right there. She's seeing things! I agree with you. I think someone is drugging her."

Calvo thought back to Tulie's last remarks to her in her bedroom upstairs a few minutes ago. She said her mother had come back for her.

"To your knowledge, is there any way Rachel is back and hiding out somewhere?" Calvo asked.

"What part of me seeing Tulie talking to an empty chair did you miss?" Angela spat. "No, Rachel is not back! Why would she hide out at her own house? It's that Brenn! Nothing has been right since that little brat moved here. Everybody she hates either dies or disappears."

"That's quite an accusation," Calvo said, but she found herself curious. "Was Brenn at Barry's party when he had his accident?" Calvo asked.

"Hell yes, she was there," Angela said. "She wouldn't help me set up for it. I heard Barry yelling at her somewhere upstairs about her stealing his watch from the boathouse. A few minutes later, she came flying down the stairs and headed outside. Still…y'all can't blame her for my cousin falling on some rocks waterskiing."

Calvo tucked the information away.

Waiting until the ambulance carrying Tulie had pulled safely away, the lieutenant excused herself and walked away from Angela, who resignedly returned home. Calvo entered the kitchen to find Hilliard seated across from Brenn at the dinette table. Morris had gone upstairs to help Baldwin with bagging the bedding. Calvo chose to lean against the kitchen countertop and watch. Hilliard had his own small recorder running in front of Brenn, whose look of defiance read like a neon sign.

"Other than the lunch you took up," Hilliard continued, where he left off before Calvo entered the room, "what else had your father had to eat today?"

"He likes a cup of coffee in the morning," she said, her tone softening somewhat. "And he always has one of Tulie's tea cakes."

"When did he slide downhill?" Hilliard asked.

"I told you already," her guard was up again. "He didn't look good this morning, worse just before lunch, so I called Dr. Clarkson, who never showed up. When I took him up his lunch, he was like you saw him— passed out and sweating."

"You said he was acting like someone in a state of delirium," Hilliard reminded her. "What exactly was he doing?"

She paused, weighing her response. "You know, mumbling gibberish, breathing hard, sweating a lot. He reached out and grabbed my arm and it scared me. That's when I called the doctor."

"Did you recognize anything he said?" Hilliard asked, watching her face.

Brenn cocked the eyebrow he had learned to despise.

"The meaning of the word 'gibberish' is to speak incoherently," she said in a monotone. "Are we done here? I suppose I ought to go to the hospital and check on him."

"You *suppose?*" Calvo interjected for the first time. "Yes, I suppose you should. A family member will have to fill out the forms. I hope you're up on your family's insurance policies." Unable to stomach the girl for another minute, Calvo walked to the refrigerator and opened it. It was crammed with food. She moaned. At least a dozen plastic cartons sat with sealed lids, bottles of soda, a pitcher of tea, vegetable bins exploding with produce, bags of bread and rolls, a large bowl of potato salad, various jars and bottles of condiments, olives, and pickles filled the shelves.

She turned to look back at Hilliard, who shot her a question mark face. She stepped back to allow him to see inside the refrigerator. He caught her meaning and sighed as well. "Tell them to take it all," he said. "Make sure they are dated." He paused and said, "Are there pudding cups in there?"

The lieutenant pushed around some containers and bottles and replied, "No. No pudding."

"That was the last one," Brenn said, knowing the significance of the question. "Look for yourself in the garbage under the sink. I took him up the last one."

Calvo shut the refrigerator door and turned her attention to the small kitchen garbage can beneath the sink. There was indeed a discarded cardboard container that had once held six pudding cups. Brenn watched her with interest, a puzzled look on her face. The lieutenant moved on to the other cabinets, filled with canned goods, tins, cannisters, and glassware. This would have to be tested as well.

Hilliard noticed Brenn stiffen when the lieutenant opened the cabinet with the canned goods. She relaxed when Calvo shut the doors and washed her hands at the kitchen sink.

"Looks like a pretty well-stocked pantry and fridge," Hilliard said evenly. "Who'd have guessed you as the little woman of the house?"

Brenn shot him a look of pure hatred.

"We have a woman who shops for us," she said acidly. "Nice, huh?" She cocked the ubiquitous eyebrow and grinned.

"I'll let the guys upstairs know to process all this," Calvo said, ignoring the girl. "They will be *so* happy!" She managed a grin as she walked from the room toward the stairs.

Hilliard turned in his chair and winked at Brenn, who had risen from the table. "Looks like take-out for a while," he said to her, and pushed his chair aside. He looked down at the defiant young woman and said firmly, "I'll allow you to check on your father, but I need you to come to the station for some questions," he said. "Tomorrow morning is fine. You are not to leave Orleans Parish."

Brenn recoiled as if slapped. "You don't have any right to tell me what to do!" she screamed. "My father and sister are sick! They need me. I don't have time to come talk to you about anything!"

"Yeah, you kinda do," Hilliard said forcefully, his eyes hooded.

"Why?" Brenn demanded, her hatred for him rising like the waves of heat outside.

"Because I told you to," he said. "We'll be right behind you if you're heading out to the hospital," he added. "I'm worried about your father and sister as well. Shall we?" He motioned to the kitchen door as if waving her into a waiting carriage. Calvo entered the room and nodded that things here were going smoothly. Brenn snatched her purse from the back of her chair and marched out the door.

Detective Hilliard and Lieutenant Calvo drove behind Brenn toward the hospital, where Randall and Tulie had been taken. Hilliard was in a foul mood. He thought of all the loose ends still needing to be tied up. Skylar Harris had been found, but who had killed her? Where was Rachel Barrows? There was no way she would have left Tulie this long. No one had heard from her since her phone call to her Cousin Jenny. No activity on her credit cards or bank statements. The call to Jenny was the last one recorded on Rachel's cell phone records. Attempts to ping her phone's location had garnered nothing. It was either dead or destroyed. Skylar's body was starting to give up some evidence, and he hoped it was enough to put all the pieces together. Angela admitted to stealing the engagement money, so that mystery was cleared up. They still had a dead cat and Ryder's death. He had never been satisfied it was an accident. And then there was poor Brixi Carter's murder.

The two cars pulled up to a railroad crossing and waited for a passing train. Hilliard kept his eye on Brenn's car ahead of them. Calvo took the opportunity to reach into her satchel and pull the framed photo she had taken from Tulie's room. She passed it over to him.

"Notice anything?" she asked, her eyes glistening.

"You'd make a lousy poker player," Hilliard said, grinning as he picked up the photo. "Your eyes light up like a foodie at a smorgasbord when you're on to something."

She smirked at him and waited.

Hilliard studied the hand-carved frame, admiring the craftsmanship, and then turned his attention to the photo of Tulie and Ryder at the dock.

"Dawson took it just before Tulie started painting her rocks," Calvo said. "Which means, it was only minutes later that Ryder was in the water." She studied the detective's face, looking for any sign of excitement. Finally, he blinked and leaned forward, peering out through the bottom of his bifocals at the picture. Calvo smiled.

"What is it?" he asked, peering at it as closely as he could. "A roll of papers?"

He opened his glove compartment, took out a small tool kit he kept there, and selected a screwdriver. Turning the photo over, he unscrewed the back of the frame from the section holding the picture in place. The car vibrated from the passing train. Prying it open, he gently lifted the glossy picture out and turned it over. Calvo leaned over eagerly.

"It looks like he's holding a map," Calvo said. "It must be the one Brenn made."

Hilliard stared at the rolled paper, clearly showing brightly colored images and markings in paints and colored markers. His eyebrows knitted in concentration. Something was nagging him. Something important. It waved tantalizingly from the edge of his memory. Suddenly, his eyes lit up, and he grabbed the lieutenant's arm next to him. Calvo leaned back in shock. He had never touched her before.

"She had it with her!" he shouted. Calvo had never seen him so excited.

"Who?"

"Brenn! Remember when we questioned all of them after Ryder's death? Rachel said Brenn came through the kitchen while she was making lunch before the pirate hunt started. Brenn held up her map she was making, and Rachel saw it. The next time Rachel saw her, she was all the way up on the cliff at Margo's, yelling down when Tulie was screaming on the dock that Ryder was in the water. Dawson said Brenn was carrying the map when he saw her up on the cliff just before he started digging the hole. Brenn admitted she had it then! She said she was double-checking the distances on her map, remember? If Dawson took this photo just before Tulie went to spray rocks, when did Brenn get the map back from Ryder, and still make it all the way up to the cliffside?"

29 BREWING STORMS

Detective Hilliard and Lieutenant Calvo spoke in whispers to the doctor overseeing Randall Barrows' emergency treatment. Brenn sat nearby at the Admitting window, chafing under the deluge of forms to be filled out pertaining to her father. Tulie had been taken to the Emergency.

"Mr. Barrows is a very sick man," Doctor Hammerhill said solemnly. "We have done a gastric lavage, obviously, and he's been given quinidine to control the cardiac rhythm, but his symptoms are far advanced. He can speak, but I wouldn't get my hopes up. Between the high fever and delirium, it's pretty spotty."

"Do you know what's wrong with him?" Hilliard asked, fearing the answer. Whatever was affecting Randall Barrows might be the same thing happening to Tulie.

"The bloodwork was only just done," the doctor said, looking somewhat annoyed that the detective expected answers when the patient had only been brought in an hour earlier. "Based on his symptoms, it could be some kind of viral infection…it's hard to say right now."

"Can you rule out poisoning?" the detective asked, his heart racing.

"I can't rule out much, right now," the doctor said, glancing at the clock on the wall over Hilliard's left shoulder. "Except the common cold."

"It's imperative we talk to him," Hilliard said, annoyed at the doctor's dismissive nature.

Doctor Hammerhill frowned but finally nodded his consent and asked an orderly to show the officers to the ICU. Hilliard glanced at Brenn, who was sighing elaborately as she handed over an insurance card. She seemed anxious, the heel of her foot bouncing up and down on the linoleum floor. Turning to Calvo, he said, "I think you should stay with her. Also, see what you can find out about Tulie."

The lieutenant didn't look pleased at missing out on the interview with Randall, or being designated Brenn's keeper, but she understood the necessity of not letting the girl out of her sight. She nodded, and Hilliard hurried off after the orderly.

Detective Hilliard was not prepared for what lay waiting in the ICU private room. Randall Barrows was unrecognizable. Gone were the chiseled good looks. His face was bloated and bloodless. An IV tube was taped to the back of his left hand. The right hand, which was resting across his chest, jerked in random movements. His eyes were closed; the lids swollen into two balls of puffed flesh. He was hooked up to a monitor that beeped repetitively at his bedside. A nurse stood scribbling something onto his chart. She glanced up as the orderly and the detective walked in.

"This is a detective," the orderly told her. "Dr. Hammerhill gave him permission to talk to the patient." With that, the young man turned and exited the room, closing the door behind him, which emitted a soft hydraulic hiss.

Hilliard stepped closer to the bed and stood to the left of Randall, wondering what to do next. A small voice recorder was humming inside his shirt pocket.

"Can he hear me?" the detective asked the nurse, who was eyeing him curiously.

"He was talking earlier," she said. "He was able to tell me his name, but he seems unaware of where he is or how he got here. He slips in and out quickly. Please don't press him too hard. I just gave him a Valium for the convulsions. I'm not sure if you'll get much."

She left the detective and stepped out into the hallway where a nurse's station sat only a few feet away. The door closed slowly behind her.

Hilliard leaned over the prostrate man and spoke softly near his right ear.

"Mr. Barrows? Can you hear me? Please. If you can hear me, I need to talk to you. Your daughter Tulie is sick too, and she needs your help."

Several minutes passed without response. Hilliard did notice more movement in Randall's hands and his breathing seemed deeper. Finally, Randall's swollen lids blinked, and he peered out at the detective through the small slits of flesh.

Hilliard leaned closer, taking hold of Randall's forearm.

"Mr. Barrows, do you know why you're here? Do you know why you're sick? You and your daughter are in bad shape. Please. Can you think who would want to hurt you both?"

Randall's eyelids slid closed again. A trickle of sweat ran down from the corner of his right eye. Hilliard squeezed his arm again.

"Please!" he said, speaking louder. "Randall? Randall!"

Randall began choking, and the alarm went off. Hilliard backed away quickly, looking toward the door for help. The same nurse hurried into the room. She adjusted the drip on his IV and reached for the cup of water on a bed tray nearby. Placing a hand behind his neck, she leaned him forward and pressed the cup to his lips. A small amount of water found its way into his parted lips; the rest ran down his chin and puddled into the folds of his neck.

"I think it best if you leave," she said in the efficient cadence that was part and parcel of a trained nurse's persona.

Randall's spasm calmed. He squinted out at the room until his focus took in the detective next to his bed. A faint sign of recognition played across his face.

"Mr. Barrows," Hilliard said quickly before he lost him again. "Can you tell me anything about why you and your daughter are so sick? Anything about what's going on?"

To the detective's surprise, tears began flowing from the corners of Randall's eyes. His lips trembled. In a sudden rush of words, his voice sounding as if he had swallowed razor blades, he whispered, "She's dead."

Hilliard blinked and glanced at the nurse, who looked uncomfortable with the conversation.

"I need to speak to him in private," the detective said,

his voice adamant and filled with authority. "You can wait just outside the door, and I promise to call if I need you."

She pulled the chart to her chest, her arms folded around it, and stared at him in defiance.

"Dr. Hammerhill gave me permission, and this is police business. I need to hurry here." He pulled himself up to his full height and fixed his eyes on her until she jerked her head angrily and departed.

The moment the door closed, Hilliard leaned over the patient, happy to see Randall's eyes following him.

"Who's dead?" Hilliard asked, his hand once again on Randall's forearm.

"Rachel," Randall wept. "Rachel is dead. Margo...fight... fell out window...accident. But..." his chest heaved, and the detective worried he was about to have a heart attack. Hilliard waited breathlessly, not daring to push the man. Each word seemed to take a toll on the patient, his breathing labored. He pushed each word out in a gasp. Randall's rapid breathing spiked on the monitor, and the detective knew the nurse would be barging back in at any minute.

"What happened, Randall? Please..."

Randall's face dissolved into spasms of pain. "We... having an affair," he sobbed. "Me... Margo. Rachel broke neck. Margo...panicked...so...she...she...put her in the lake!" He stopped, his chest heaving.

Randall's breathing became more obstructed. The detective hurried to calm him as he jerked his head to look over his shoulder at the closed door. Randall's confession had him reeling, but he had to maintain control before he lost the chance to talk to the man before him. But was this delirium? He sounded coherent, but Hilliard found the story so outlandish that it couldn't possibly be true.

Randall's head rolled back and forth on the pillow, sweat running down his face to mix with his tears.

"Randall…Skylar Harris's body was found," Hilliard said hurriedly. "What happened to her?"

Just then, Randall arched his back in a massive convulsion. His head bent back, and his neck muscles protruded in tight bands. He began choking and gasping for air. Alarms rang out from the cardiac monitor, showing the ECG's rhythm and rate escalating. His oxygen saturation was tanking. Hilliard released Randall's forearm as the nurse and Dr. Hammerhill hurried into the room. The nurse moved quickly to the patient's side and placed her fingers on his wrist. She glared at Hilliard as she gauged Randall's pulse. The doctor glanced at the monitor and pressed a button.

Almost immediately, two male nurses arrived and began hooking the patient up to a ventilator, placing the mask over his mouth and nose. Doctor Hammerhill ordered a second IV bag of phenytoin to control the seizures.

"I'm afraid I need you to leave," the doctor barked, in a voice that brooked no discussion.

Hilliard backed away slowly, hesitating by the door. Randall's body arched again, almost bending him in half, and then collapsed onto the bed. The monitor flatlined. As the detective watched in horror, the medical team applied the paddle electrode, sending jolts of electricity into Randall's heart. He lurched with each shock, but dropped unresponsive. After what seemed like a lifetime of applying the paddles, the team stepped back dejectedly. The heartbeat failed to register as the monitor's monotonous tone filled the room. Randall Barrows was dead.

Detective Hilliard left the ICU room and leaned against the wall a few feet away. Not in his wildest dreams did he expect Randall to die. In slow motion, he texted a few short words into his phone and leaned back against the wall. A flurry of activity was going on around Randall as hospital staff in white coats ran to and from his room. Hilliard prayed he would hear that the patient had somehow recovered, but it was not to be. He turned to look as the sound of running feet reached him. Lieutenant Calvo hurried up to him, out of breath and flushed.

"It can't be true," she said. "It just can't be true."

All Hilliard could manage was a feeble nod. He would tell the lieutenant about Randall's deathbed confession later. Now, he needed to sit down. Calvo followed him to a row of blue-gray fabric-covered chairs in a small waiting area. They both collapsed onto them. Hilliard turned dull eyes to her, and then, as if suddenly remembering, he sat upright and asked, "Where's Brenn?"

Brenn raced home from the hospital. The lieutenant had suddenly run off after looking at a message on her phone. Unbeknownst to Brenn, the text message was from Hilliard saying, "Barrows just died." Brenn was signing the last form when Calvo ordered her to "wait there," as she turned and ran for the elevator. Scribbling her name, Brenn pushed the form toward the admitting clerk and bolted from her chair. The woman called after her, but she was already pushing through the revolving door to the outside parking lot.

Brenn arrived home and found two police cars still parked in the back. She pulled off into a stand of live oaks and bushes along the driveway, burying the car in the thick foliage. She jumped from the seat, pushing the car door shut quietly. Walking softly across the packed gravel driveway, she went around to the front door and entered the house. She stopped in the foyer and listened. Voices were coming from the kitchen. Panic knocked against her rib cage. She tiptoed quietly along the marble floor and peered around the door frame into the kitchen.

The refrigerator door was open, obscuring the policemen's view of her as she pulled back into the hallway. Boxes of food were covering the island counter; some in plastic containers from the refrigerator, and others filled with canned goods from the cabinets.

"Why are we taking cans that have clearly not been opened?" Officer Baldwin asked.

"Good question," Officer Morris said, surveying all the boxes they would have to load into the two patrol cars. "We just follow orders," he said ruefully. "At least the refrigerator is done," he said, shutting the double doors. "How much do you have left? I'm starving."

"About two more shelves, but we're out of boxes," Baldwin said, looking about him. "What if we take in what we have and grab a quick sandwich. We can get more boxes and come back."

"That's a plan I can live with," Morris said, smiling. "We need to take the refrigerated stuff to the lab, though. It's already boxed. Let's do that first and then grab a bite and come back. I think I can fit the cold stuff in my car if you can load your boxes in yours."

The two officers grabbed a box each and headed out of the kitchen, into the sunroom, and out to their cars. Brenn made a dash into the kitchen and ran to the canned goods cabinet, which was standing open. In horror, she saw that the top shelf that held the canisters of extra sugar, flour, and cinnamon was empty. The square tin can with the red geraniums imprinted on it was gone.

The sound of the two men returning up the stone steps into the sunroom alerted her. She whirled to run and saw the top of the sugar canister sticking out of a box on the counter. Glancing quickly at the kitchen door, she raced to the box and lifted out the canister.

"I pulled an extra shift for you last month," Officer Baldwin said, as the two men crossed the sunroom.

"Yeah, and I got you Saints tickets for your birthday. Good seats!" Morris said, his voice inches from the open kitchen door.

Brenn moved the flour canister to the side and saw the red geraniums peering out. She grabbed the tin and ran, hunched over, out into the hallway just as Morris and Baldwin entered the kitchen. Morris grabbed up another box of cold containers as Baldwin replaced a cannister from the counter into his box and followed the other officer out. After several more trips, the two men left, closing the kitchen door behind them.

Brenn stood in the coat closet near the front door, trying to slow her pounding heart. She listened as the two cars pulled away, the sound of gravel crunching beneath their wheels. She prayed they hadn't spotted her car concealed in the stand of trees.

Silence descended on the house as she exited the closet and stood in the hallway, the tin can cradled in one arm. A distant sound of rolling thunder reverberated against the ancient walls. Brenn felt the weight of the huge home pressing in around her. She had never known it to be this quiet. She felt she could hear the ancient cypress wood floorboards breathing beneath her feet. She was alone. No sounds came from the upstairs bedrooms where once Rachel, Randall, Tulie, and Ryder had spent their days and evenings. She was the last one standing.

She would have to hurry. They would know by now that she was not at the hospital. If she could get back there and come in a different entrance, she might be able to pull it off that she had only gone to the hospital cafeteria or something, and had been there all along, waiting for news of her father. She smiled. How clever she had been through all of it.

Something moved on the staircase across from her, and she jumped. *There must be another policeman here*, she thought wildly, and began backing along the hallway toward the front door. She watched the stairs from the side, waiting for a pair of legs to appear from beneath the ceiling overhang. She paused. Nothing happened. Perhaps she had imagined it. It was dark at the base of the stairs with the storm outside pushing its grayness through the sheers of the windows and feeling its way through cracks in the doors.

A soft sigh came from the bottom stair rung. It floated and hung in the air, becoming at once a part of the faded wallpaper and antique furnishings. It carried with it a numbing coldness that Brenn could feel through her clothing. It ran along her arms and pebbled her neck with goose flesh. The hallway seemed to shorten around her, pulling itself together in scattered rugs, forcing her toward the inky darkness near the stairs.

Then it moved. The black compression of shadows took shape, slid past the newel post at the base of the stairs, and floated toward the hallway. It turned toward Brenn, who was flattened against the wall near the hall table. Her hand was pressed to her mouth, her eyes wide in a crazed look of panic and fear. She gripped the large tin with her other hand, her fingernails biting into the metal sides.

Impossibly, a body formed from the tangled mass of shadows, beginning with a small torso. Arms sprang from its sides and hung like sinews. The short legs wavered and undulated as they struggled for definition, hemmed in by the outline of what appeared to be shorts. A jawline formed, indistinct at first, then quickly surrounded by soft mounds of cheeks and an outline of a nose. The eyes were sunken hollows, darker than the ebony mass in which they sat. Tiny fragments of wavy hair floated about the head as if pushed by a current of air.

Brenn was sobbing now as she finally found the strength to move her legs. She stumbled and nearly fell as she backed away toward the front door. Her body was trembling so badly that she had to clutch the tin with both hands so as not to drop it. She could feel the waves of cold emanating from the thing as it moved toward her, its feet never touching the floor.

"Please!" she breathed, her teeth chattering from the cold and fear. "Leave me alone!" It continued moving toward her, its black reflection staining the large urn it passed. "Leave me alone!" she screamed, her hand reaching behind her for the doorknob that would let her escape.

The jarring sound of the front doorbell shot through the hallway, and she screamed. She whirled to face the massive wooden door. *The detectives,* she thought wildly. *They found out she wasn't at the hospital.* She turned back to the hallway, her heart pounding. It was empty. She looked hurriedly around her, fearing the thing would come flying at her from the open library door next to her. The stairway at the end of the hall sat in shadows, but she could not see the small figure among them.

The doorbell rang again, propelling her into action. She ran for the kitchen doorway and tore through it, racing down the steps into the sunroom as she gripped the can tightly. The air pressing in through the mesh windows smelled of rain, and she could feel the wet warmth heading in from the lake. The sky grumbled as she opened the sunroom screen door and stepped down to the porch.

Brenn crossed the porch and reached a foot out for the step leading down to the lawn. Dawson suddenly appeared from nowhere, careening around the porch from the side, and slammed into her. The tin can fell from her hands and hit the floor. The lid popped off and its contents spewed out onto the weathered boards.

"Brenn!" Dawson cried in surprise. "Man, I'm so sorry! I didn't see you until I turned the corner. Are y'all okay?" He reached out to steady her, as she grabbed for the railing to keep from falling.

"You idiot!" she screamed, looking in dismay at the scattered contents of the can. She bent and hurriedly tried to corral the tiny fragments of crushed leaves and seeds before the breeze coming off the lake could dispel them. She used the can lid to group them together and sweep them back inside the tin. Dawson stepped forward and bent to help her. He scooped up a handful and placed it inside the tin.

"Don't help me!" she yelled, frantically scooping the tiny brown and green pieces into the can with its lid. After she had gathered as much as she could, she stood and kicked the rest off the porch and into the bushes. "What are you doing here anyway?" she said angrily, clamping the lid back onto the tin.

"I heard Tulie and Randall were taken in ambulances this morning," he said. "I noticed there were still some police cars here, so I came over to ask how they are. I called the hospital, but they said only family could see them. They wouldn't tell me anything." He looked at the girl, shaking with anger and panic. "Are you okay? You look like a bomb went off!"

"Well, as you can clearly see, the police are gone now," she yelled, ignoring his last comment. "I'm in a hurry. I need to go check on them because I actually *am* family."

With that, she hurried off down the steps and ran around the corner of the house to where her car was hidden. Dawson waited until he heard her back up and drive off down the driveway at a high rate of speed. He looked down and carefully moved his foot that had remained in place after he stepped forward to help Brenn gather up the spilled contents of her tin. There, beneath his shoe, was a small heap of crushed bits of dried leaf and flower fragments. He pulled a pack of gum from his jeans pocket and lifted a stick from it. He opened the wrapper and chucked the gum aside. Taking the foil wrapper, he gently pushed the mound of broken leaves, seeds, and flower fragments into it and meticulously sealed it. He placed it in is denim shirt pocket and dropped down the stone steps to the lawn. Glancing up at the gathering clusters of black clouds, he headed off past the cemetery to the path through the battered pecan grove.

30 IF PICTURES COULD TALK

Detective Hilliard sighed. An array of reports and photographs lay strewn across his desk like a roadmap to murder. Two days had passed since Randall Barrows' death. Reporters camped out in the parking lot at the police station and assaulted him each time he appeared as he dashed madly to or from his car.

"You guys know the drill," he yelled, pushing a photographer who was blocking him from getting to the steps to the building where his small cubicle resided. "We just received the toxicology reports for Skylar Harris and Randall Barrows. We are going over those now. When I know, you'll know, unless it will impede the case."

"You always say that!" Valerie Bordeaux complained, her microphone crammed into his face. The call letters of her television station were emblazoned on its handle in a block clip-on. Hilliard shot her a look of defiance, repulsed by her overdone make-up and perfectly coiffed hair, stiff with hairspray.

"Yeah, we detectives are funny that way," he said,

414

repulsed by all the media attention that fed ghoulishly off the tragedy of people dying. "You'd think we'd put you guys first over the misery this is causing the families so that you can have a prime-time headline that will put you ahead in the ratings. I can be a selfish prick," he said hotly, and shoved a man holding a boom mic out of his way.

Hilliard found the lieutenant waiting for him at his desk. She appeared haggard and dejected. He dropped into his chair.

"This family!" she said, summing up both their thoughts in two words. "If I weren't investigating it, I would never believe all these deaths could surround just *one* family! At least Tulie pulled through."

"That is a blessing,' Hilliard nodded, pushing a pile of photos around on his desk with his forefinger. "No one is going to get past Angela Peterson," he said, allowing a small smile. "The woman is a dragon. She'll make sure Tulie is safe. I just hope the poor girl survives staying with her and Calvin."

"You realize we have not ruled them out for Skylar's death," Calvo said, eyeing him closely. "Is Tulie going to be alright there?"

"I don't see them as killers," he said, although he felt the same niggling doubt Calvo did. "Angela admitted to taking the money. She couldn't be in two places at the same time—stealing the cash pot and murdering Skylar. I think the money was good enough for her to exact her pound of flesh. Calvin, on the other hand… we do have physical evidence from his wheelchair tracks that he was there, and he admitted to being near Skylar's body. Still, how do you strangle a healthy, albeit intoxicated, young woman from a sitting position? Angela loves

Tulie. She won't let anything happen to her."

"Even if she inherits if the rest of the family is dead?" Calvo asked, cocking her head to one side.

Hilliard chewed on that for a moment.

"You have a point," he said, "although it would be a really dumb thing to pull off with all the attention on this family and Tulie living right under her roof. Let's find another place for Tulie if we can. With what she just went through with losing her dad, and her mom still gone, the girl needs some family around her. If what Randall said is true, Rachel is dead. I don't know if Tulie is going to survive getting that information," he said worriedly. "Search and Rescue are continuing to put divers in the lake as we speak. I will be shocked if they actually find Rachel in that water."

Lieutenant Calvo nodded sadly and took a brown manilla folder from her satchel. She settled into her chair, flipped it open, and began reading off the latest reports handed in.

"The tox report for Randall shows he was clearly poisoned. Elevated levels of atropine, scopolamine, hyoscyamine, and hyoscine were found. These are alkaloids that work by paralyzing the parasympathetic nervous system. It can lead to coma or death. Here's the kicker. Tom Simons showed the same alkaloids in his system. We know he was poisoned by placing the Angel's Trumpet flower in his mouth, inhaling it, and sucking on the flower itself. What are the odds he and Randall show similar tox reports?"

"Similar symptoms, too," Hilliard said. "Both were hallucinating, vomiting, fevers, eye issues." He shook his head. "So, how did Randall get hold of Angel's Trumpet?"

"You didn't let me finish," Calvo said, arching an eyebrow at him. "Tox report number 2: The food tested from the Barrows' house is back. Nothing was found in any of the refrigerated goods or stuff from the cabinets. Nothing from the sandwich, potato salad, or chocolate pudding from his lunch tray. But! Are you ready? The frosting on the tea cakes from Randall's tray came back positive for poisonous alkaloids. You guessed it…atropine, hyoscyamine—that's the one that causes hallucinations and delirium—and scopolamine. The parts of the plant were probably boiled, turned into a liquid, and added to the frosting in high concentrations. In smaller doses, you could slowly poison someone, while inducing hallucinations."

Calvo paused and looked at the detective, waiting for his reaction. He sat stunned. And then her meaning finally hit him.

"Tulie's hallucinations!" he said. "Angela said she was seeing Rachel when Rachel wasn't there. Do we have Tulie's findings from ER?"

Calvo flipped through some pages and pulled out a report.

"Tox number 3," she said importantly. "Tulie Barrows' blood work…care to guess?"

"The deadly threesome?" Hilliard asked, referring to the alkaloids he could not pronounce without reading them.

Calvo nodded.

"Good Lord," he said. "It's diabolical!" He sat shaking his head. He stared at the scattered photos swimming in front of him. "How do you go about setting up the deaths of so many people?" He steepled his fingers and elbows on the desk and looked across at the mocha-colored face before him. "Randall said Margo put Rachel in the lake," he said. "I'm not sure if he was hallucinating when he told me. Except, he did say he and Margo were having an affair, which confirms all the rumors. If that part is true, then maybe the rest of what he said is, too. He said it was an accident and mentioned a window. We know Margo had a broken window in her bedroom the day after Skylar disappeared. Was it true that it was an accident that Rachel fell? He has only Margo's word for it. I mean, who puts their own sister's body in a lake, accident or not?

"And Skylar?" he continued. "Did Margo kill Skylar? We know she lied about the last time she saw Skylar that night and that she was by the folly when Tulie handed her Skylar's stained sash. We know she told Tulie she would get Tulie's sash back from Skylar and that she was seen going into the garden at about the time Skylar disappeared from her party. Maybe Randall was fooling around with Skylar, and Margo killed her."

Calvo plucked another report from the folder and paused for emphasis.

"No, maybe about it," she said ominously. She looked down at the report and, punctuating each word, she read aloud: "'The DNA of Skylar Harris' fetus and that of Randall Barrows match.' Skylar was pregnant with Randall's baby."

The shock on Hilliard's face was the most pronounced Calvo had seen yet. He stared at her through the top part of his bifocals, his eyes wide and darting from side to side as he rearranged the puzzle pieces.

"There's more to Skylar's report," Calvo said, taking

a deep breath. "Her blood showed elevated levels of flunitrazepam: a central nervous system depressant. It belongs to a class of drugs known as benzodiazepines. Her stomach contents showed remnants of peach pie and some liquidized substances."

"So not the same stuff as we're seeing in Randall, Tom, and Tulie?" Hilliard asked, confused.

"No, totally different but just as deadly in high doses. The street name for it is Rohypnol—the date rape drug."

Hilliard opened his desk drawer and grabbed a caramel. He unwrapped the hard candy and popped it into his mouth, his cheeks sinking in as he sucked furiously on it. Calvo had never seen him this rattled.

"Continuing on," the lieutenant said, looking down again at Skylar's report, "According to this report, the absence of petechiae in the whites of her eyes and face, along with little trachea damage, shows she did not die from strangulation. Her hyoid bone in her neck was intact, which typically would not be if she had been manually strangled. Her cause of death was the elevated levels of flunitrazepam. It is sometimes prescribed for insomnia. It affects balance and speech, causes confusion, etc. Alcohol drastically increases its toxicity."

"Everyone said Sklar looked drunk and out of it at the party," Hilliard mused. "She was downing a lot of champagne, but if she had been taking something because she wasn't sleeping, maybe she overdid it."

"Or, someone doctored her food or drink," Calvo said. "It is common for people to crush the white pills into a powder and snort it to hallucinate, or slip it into someone's drink, making them easy to manage. Hence, a date rape drug. In high doses, it's lethal."

Calvo allowed him time to percolate over the avalanche of information she had just thrown at him. Hilliard finally looked at her and began to unravel his thoughts aloud:

"So, the strangulation marks on Skylar's neck...why? Did someone try to strangle her, not knowing the drugs in her system were going to kill her anyway? This makes no sense. If you're the one who put this stuff in Skylar's food or drink, knowing it was enough to kill her, you wouldn't then risk being seen strangling her. You'd have just waited for her to die. My head hurts," he said, placing a hand to his forehead."

"Let's work this out," Calvo said, hoping by talking about it, something would emerge to unravel the confusing turn of events. "Let's say Margo covers up Rachel's death by burying her in the lake—we think— Margo kills Skylar for having an affair with the same man *she* is having an affair with. Maybe she found out about the baby! Hell hath no fury, so she poisons Randall, and now he's dead. It all fits! But why kill Brixi? Brixi's vase was in Margo's car...a neighbor hears what we assume was Margo talking to Brixi inside the apartment just before Brixi is found dead. Maude said Brixi knew too much and was afraid Margo had done something to Skylar. So, exit Brixi!"

Calvo paused and studied her thoughts for a moment. She looked at Hilliard with wide eyes.

"Good lord! Did Margo try and poison Tulie because Tulie knew about the sashes? Maybe Tulie approached Margo at the party and asked her if she got her sash back, and Margo needed to silence her. We know Tulie did get her sash back because she turned it in with the dress at the costume store. How did she get it back? She said she found it on the ground, which is not gelling. Maybe she saw something when she went back for the sash herself!"

Both Hilliard and Calvo sat in silence for several moments: the enormity of the crimes stunning them both.

"In my book, I see three people with motives for killing Skylar," Hilliard said, rubbing a thumb above his eyebrow. "The connecting piece is Skylar's pregnancy. Randall would not have wanted that to get out, let alone take on a new baby and ruin his marriage. Margo would have been ballistic if she knew Skylar was pregnant with Randall's baby, and ditto for Rachel. I believe something happened that night in the folly. Did Skylar tell Randall then that she was pregnant? Did one or more people overhear her?"

Calvo paused and then looked at the detective with haunted eyes. "You're forgetting someone," she said sadly. "Tulie. I hate to say it with all my heart, but if Tulie overheard something about her father and Skylar's pregnancy, how would she deal with it? She was so protective of Rachel. She would have known that kind of information would push Rachel over the edge."

The silence that filled the small room pulsed with tension. Minutes went by.

"Any news from the vase?" Hilliard finally asked, his thoughts back to the maid's murder.

"That's what I went out to check on," Calvo said. "They said they should have the results back any minute, along with the fingerprint analysis from the waterski. I have never worked so many deaths at once in my life!" A thought suddenly came to the lieutenant.

"There's something else," she said excitedly. "Skylar's necklace! The boys saw Margo with Skylar's purse, hiding it! Why would Margo have Skylar's purse unless she knew Skylar wasn't going to be around anymore? And the muddy shoes in Brixi's closet that Maude said were in Margo's garbage can. Skylar was found buried in the pecan grove. It had been raining a lot...hence, muddy shoes. It's all fitting together!"

Hilliard thought for a moment and then said, "Or, it's mud from the shoreline at the lake." He looked at the lieutenant with furrowed brows.

The detective pawed through the photos he had practically memorized by now. They were the pictures taken by the photographer at Skylar's and Landon's engagement party. He suddenly pounced on one and held it up. He peered out through his glasses and looked over at the lieutenant with a gleam in his eye.

"Look!" he said, turning the picture to show her. "This looks like it was taken before Skylar changed into her ball gown. She's standing with a group of young women, and they're looking at all the presents in the parlor. None of them are in costume, so this had to be taken before the party began, since we know Skylar never returned. Look at her necklace," Hilliard said, letting Calvo take the photo from him. The lieutenant nodded, her lips pressed together. Around Skylar Harris' neck was the necklace with the gold heart, her name barely discernible, but there.

"She probably took it off and put it in her purse when she put on the diamond necklace for her ball gown," Calvo said sadly. "Margo hid the purse, probably hoping to make it look like Skylar disappeared from the party under her own volition, taking her purse with her. I don't suppose any of those pictures show Skylar with her purse? That would cement the purse that the boys saw Margo hide was hers."

"I haven't seen one," Hilliard said. "One more thing," he added, snatching up several pictures at a time and shoving them across the desk. "In all of these pictures, Skylar is wearing her engagement ring. When her body was found, she was not wearing it. Calvin said he didn't see it when he saw Skylar's body. Of course, we can't rule out that Calvin didn't take it to replace the ring Skylar kept from Dennis. If not, where is it? And, what happened to Skylar's purse? My guess is Margo has dumped it by now. It wasn't behind the cookbooks when I had Baldwin check for it. Luckily, Margo and Reed were out that morning. She still doesn't know we know about it."

Dawson Kingston stood in his small kitchen and ran warm water over his inflamed hands. The itching was getting worse, and small blisters had formed on his palms. His head throbbed. He couldn't figure out what was happening to him. He was waiting for a return phone call from Detective Hilliard. He had left two messages saying he needed to talk to the detective immediately.

Hilliard glanced at the stack of messages waiting for him near his phone and decided he would get to them later. Calvo had stepped out to check on any other incoming reports. He snatched up his phone and dialed the number from the yellow sticky note in front of him.

After several rings, Reed Tillson picked up. The detective was relieved that he had answered and not Margo.

"Mr. Tillson," Hilliard began, mentally scurrying to form the correct words. He was walking a tightrope of timing. "I had a few more questions for your wife," he said awkwardly. "I know she's tired of our intrusions, but we are still looking into Brixi Carter's death, and as Margo employed her, it would be helpful to understand a few more things about Brixi's routine. Would you mind bringing her here to the station? I would deeply appreciate it."

There was a disgruntled sigh at the other end of the line. Finally, Reed said, "I can try."

"I'm afraid I'll need you to do more than try," Hilliard said, suddenly reaching his limit with the deferential treatment Margo Tillson had received. "I can come and get her. I just assumed she'd rather not be seen riding through Orleans Parish in a squad car."

"Subtle," Reed said sarcastically. In truth, he was more upset at the thought of his wife's anger when he relayed the message than he was with the detective. He fervently hoped they found the poor maid's killer. "I will give it all I have," he said finally. "I'll try for two o'clock, will that work?"

"Just dandy," Hilliard said. "Thank you." He hung up.

Angela dried her hands on a kitchen towel and answered her ringing phone. She was surprised to hear Brenn's tearful voice on the other end.

"I need your help," Brenn said rapidly, sniffing repeatedly. She sounded agitated and frantic. "I know

424

you don't like me, but I've never planned a funeral before. My mother's best friend, Margaret Topper, oversaw my mother's funeral arrangements. You have to help me with Daddy's. I don't know when Rachel is coming back or where she is, and Tulie is…well, you know."

The sniffling was getting to Angela, who barely contained the contempt she felt for her young cousin.

"You haven't even asked how Tulie is," Angela said. "In case you're interested, she's doing much better after the treatments they gave her at the hospital. She'll be fine."

Her words were met with silence. She wondered if Brenn had hung up until a small sniffle sounded.

"Where are you, by the way?" Angela asked. "I haven't seen you at the house."

There was a pause. Brenn stopped sniffling. "I, well, I didn't want to go back there, with Daddy dying and all. It's creepy being there all alone. I talked Reed into letting me stay with them for a few days. They have all those guest rooms."

"Margo is allowing you to stay with them?" Angela asked, shocked, knowing Margo hated the girl as much as she did.

"What else could she do?" Brenn said angrily. "Daddy *was* her brother-in-law."

Angela knew Brenn was aware of the rumors of her father having an affair with Margo, but she said nothing. She found it interesting that Brenn had turned off the waterworks so quickly. As if on cue, they began again.

"So, will you help me with his funeral?" she said, the sniffling more pronounced than ever. "Aunt Margo is having a meltdown since he died. Uncle Reed is about to shoot her."

Her words went through Angela like a shock wave. Only Brenn would say something as inappropriate as someone wanting to kill another member of this cursed family.

"I'll contact the funeral director," Angela said acidly. "This should have already been done, Brenn. It's been two days."

"It's different when they are looking into his cause of death," Brenn shot back. "I think they think something suspicious happened to Daddy. They only just released his body."

Once again, the crying had stopped. Brenn had gotten what she wanted.

"Thanks," Brenn said bluntly, and hung up.

Angela looked at Calvin who was seated at the table. "I'm not happy about this," Angela said quietly. "I feel like everything is about to blow sky high. One thing is for sure, I'm not letting Tulie out of my sight."

31 SPINNING PLATES

Officer Blevins tapped on Hilliard's doorframe. He found the detective and Lieutenant Calvo poring over photographs atop his desk. The two looked up at him eagerly, eyeing the sheaf of papers in his hand.

"Got your reports," Blevins said without preamble. "Who did you give Saint's season tickets to, to move these to the front of the line? Also, you've got a weird-looking woman out front who wants to see you, and a young guy who says he's left several messages and it's urgent he sees you."

"Names?" Hilliard asked. He was pretty sure the woman was not Margo Tillson, as the lady was usually dressed to rival a runway model.

Blevin's looked down at a note in his hand. "The guy is Dawson Kingston. The woman is Madame Sangers." He grinned and handed Hilliard the reports he was carrying, along with a purple business card with a crystal ball on it. "Are you turning to a psychic to

427

manage all your unsolveds?" The remark was met with icy silence. "Do I send 'em in?" he asked finally, feeling the need to retreat..

"Let me see Mr. Kingston first," Hilliard said, thumbing through the messages he had ignored all morning by his phone. He cringed when he saw two from Dawson.

Officer Blevins nodded and walked back out into the hallway. Reluctantly, Hilliard set the new reports aside until after he talked to Dawson and the "weird-looking woman."

"Buckle up," Hilliard said, sighing elaborately as he fixed his eyes on Calvo. "I don't know what's so urgent. I swear, if it's another death other than a woodchuck meeting its demise, I'm transferring to Salt Lake City. Dealing with Mormons has got to be easier. This whole thing is like keeping a row of spinning plates going all at once, but they keep crashing!" He placed the small voice recorder on his desk and pushed the record button as he heard footsteps just outside the door.

Dawson Kingston appeared in the doorway. Calvo and Hilliard looked at him in surprise. The young man was wearing short white cotton gloves. In his hand was a large envelope.

"I'm sorry I didn't get back to you," Hilliard said, standing and retrieving a metal chair from the corner of the room. He placed it next to Calvo, who slid hers over to give Dawson room. Hilliard scooped up the photos scattered across his desk and stacked them into a pile, and placed a binder over them.

Dawson sat down, keeping his hands close to his body. His face looked pained.

428

"What's with the gloves?" Hilliard asked.

"I'm not sure what's going on," Dawson said. He gently peeled off the glove from his left hand, winching as pain shot through him.

Calvo gasped. "What in the world did you do?" she asked. Dawson's hand was swollen and red, the back of it puffy as if it had been blown up with a pump.

"I'm not sure," the young man said. "My mom put some salve on it and made me put on these gloves. It helps a little. I'll be okay. I have something I need to talk to you about. I think it's important, and I probably should have talked to you sooner, but I wasn't sure yet."

He reached into the pocket of his denim shirt and pulled out the foil gum wrapper. His fingers were so swollen and sore that he almost dropped it. He placed it on the desk.

"Brenn had this in a tin can that she grabbed from the house two days ago…the day Randall died," he said. "It was right after the police cars left. I rang the front doorbell because I wanted to talk to her. I saw her car hidden in the trees, so I knew she was there. When she didn't answer, I went along the porch to the back and ran into her. She was carrying a big tin with red flowers on it. I had seen it before in Rachel's cabinet. I was there one afternoon when Brenn was making tea for Tulie and Rachel. The tea she used came from that same tin can. Tulie and her Mama used to sit out in the sunroom almost every afternoon after supper and have tea and talk."

He paused, the memories weighing on him. "Anyway," he said, "I always wondered why Tulie and Rachel seemed out of it all the time. For about a week, they seemed better. It was the best I had seen them. It was just before Margo's engagement party for Landon. I didn't put two and two together until I bumped into Brenn and saw all that tea fall out of the tin she was hurrying out of the house with. It was like she didn't want anyone to have it. She yelled at me and hurried to scoop it up. I deliberately put my shoe over some while I helped her pick it up. After she left, I put it in this wrapper." He nodded to the foil.

Hilliard reached to open the wrapper.

"Stop!" Calvo said suddenly. "Don't touch it! If that tea is what Brenn was giving Tulie and Rachel, it may be poisonous. What if it's the same thing found in the tea cake frosting? Dawson, that's probably what happened to your hands. You said you picked up some spilled tea and put it back in Brenn's can. You can absorb poison through your skin. We need to get you into the hospital," she said urgently.

Dawson remained seated, ignoring Calvo's concern for him. He cast his memory back to two days prior.

"That's why she used the lid to the can to scoop it up when it spilled," he said, dazed, "so she wouldn't touch it. This all makes sense now. What I was going to say is that for about a week, Tulie and Rachel seemed better. When I saw Brenn running away with that tin, I remembered something. There was something going on at the same time, and Rachel and Tulie seemed to improve. Rachel hired painters to paint the kitchen cabinets in new colors. She was really excited about it. She and Tulie emptied all the cabinets and threw stuff away. I helped take out the bags of trash from the kitchen. I think they dumped the contents of that can in a trash bag along with some stale crackers and stuff.

That's why they got better. They tossed Brenn's stash of tea."

"I'll be damned," Hilliard said. "Just when I thought we had this tied up with a neat bow."

Calvo stepped into the hallway and called out to a passing officer, telling him to have an EMT step in if one was around. She returned and took her seat.

"Why would Brenn want to poison Rachel and Tulie?" Calvo asked. "The inheritance?"

"I'm not sure," Dawson said. "She never liked either of them, but that's why I didn't come to you sooner with my suspicions, because I couldn't answer that exact question. But that leads me to the other thing I brought you," he said.

He placed the large envelope on the desk. Hilliard took it and opened the unsealed flap. Inside there were two photographs. The first was the one Dawson took of Tulie and Ryder at the dock the day Ryder died. The other was an odd shot of a blackboard with green letters scrawled upon it in a darkened room. Hilliard raised his eyebrows and looked at the young man for an explanation.

"The first picture is the one I took of Ryder and Tulie the day Ryder drowned," Dawson said sadly. "Rachel had me taking pictures for insurance reasons, and I thought it was a great shot of them playing pirate."

"Yes," Calvo said. "We have a copy of that. It was in a frame in Tulie's room."

"I made it for her for her birthday this summer," Dawson said.

"And this one?" Hilliard asked, cutting him off.

"I was at a séance that Rachel wanted after Ryder died. She hired this psychic to come to the house and try and reach out to Ryder. Rachel was having a really hard time. Anyway, some strange stuff happened during the séance. I thought it was all fake until a couple of things happened that seemed to throw the psychic off. She looked genuinely freaked out.."

"What happened?" Calvo asked, turning to face him, her face eager.

"Miss Angela's cat jumped at the window and got his nails caught in the screen, which made us all jump. When we looked back at the table, some strange words were written on the chalkboard that hadn't been there just a couple of minutes before. I was next to the psychic, and I still can't figure out how she did it that fast. I would have heard her writing with the chalk."

Hilliard looked at the strange photograph and passed it to Calvo. She studied it, frowning. The letters seemed to glow against the black chalkboard. She read the five strange words aloud:

GOLD
TREASURE

TORN
SECRET PATH
MURDER

"What do you make of it?" she asked Dawson.
"Well, if you look at the picture, you see Madame

432

Sangers at the far left of the picture. She didn't see me take the photo. She is looking at the blackboard, and she looks totally frightened. That really stood out to me. The first two words probably have to do with the treasure hunt we were going to play that day. Tulie was spraying the gold rocks, and she asked Brenn to make a treasure map because Brenn likes to draw. I don't know what two of the bottom words mean," he said.

"Two of them?" Hilliard asked. "Which one do you understand?"

Dawson shifted uncomfortably in his chair. "SECRET PATH. There's a tunnel," he said, feeling guilt wash over him. "It was an old rum runner's tunnel. My grandfather made it for Brett Broussard long ago. It ran from a secret door in the folly down to the river. They would haul illegal rum onto the dock and up the tunnel, where they stored it during Prohibition. I knew about it, and I realized the day Ryder died that Brenn had discovered it. I saw her at the top of the cliff with her map. But I had just taken the photo of Tulie and Ryder, and he was *holding* the map. It was while Tulie was screaming that I saw Brenn calling down to Rachel, asking what happened. The only way Brenn could have taken the map from Ryder and gotten up there that fast was if she went through the tunnel. Plus, she would have passed me on the trail through the pecan grove if she had gone that way. I was right there digging the hole, and I didn't see her. That might be the 'SECRET PATH' on the chalkboard."

"Who else knew about the tunnel?" Calvo asked.

"Not many. Me, my mother, and Mr. Randall. He saw me come out of it one day and wanted to know all about it. I'm not sure how Brenn found it unless he told her about it. But using the tunnel and being up on the cliff gave her an alibi as to where she was when we think he fell into the lake."

Hilliard whistled and leaned back in his creaking chair. He laced his fingers behind his head and stared at the ceiling, his mind racing. A tap sounded at the open door, and he turned to see a young EMT standing there.

"Can you take a look at this young man's hands?" Hilliard asked, nodding toward Dawson. Calvo scooted her chair back and stood, moving out of the way.

EMT Scott Waters donned purple latex gloves and gently removed Dawson's other white glove from his hand. He turned the young man's reddened hands over to see white blisters covering his palms in clusters.

"Looks like poison oak, or something else like it," the medic said. "Have you been handling any chemicals or substances that are new to you?" he asked.

Dawson looked to Hilliard for a sign as to what to say. The detective jumped in.

"We believe it may be a garden plant," he said. "A member of the nightshade or belladonna family. Possibly Angel's Trumpet."

"Aw, Datura Stramonium," Waters said sagely, reaching into his medical backpack.

Hilliard smiled, clearly impressed. "I won't pretend to know what you just said," he said, grinning.

"Also known as Jimsonweed, Devil's Trumpet, Angel's Trumpet, stinkweed, mad apple... Unfortunately, it's an ornamental plant that people around here love to add to their gardens. It's ridiculous how careless people are with these poisonous plants. Look at me," Waters said to the young man, playing a small pin light into Dawson's pupils. "Headaches? Dry mouth?" he asked.

"Yeah, I've had a bad headache for a couple of days. I *have* been really thirsty. Am I okay?"

"You would have had stronger symptoms by now if you had gotten a good dose of it," Waters said. He brought a silver tube of ointment from his bag and gently applied it to Dawson's hands. Dawson flinched, biting his lips.

"Sorry," Waters said, studying the blisters. "These are going to be painful for a few more days. I'll bandage you up, and it's a good idea to keep the gloves on. You can take ibuprofen for the pain. Just try to give your hands a rest if you can. You're lucky. It could have been much worse if you had prolonged exposure to that stuff."

He wrapped Dawson's hands with layers of gauze and taped it off. He gifted him with the ointment and a Ziplock bag of bandages. "If you see someone growing those damn flowers, tell them they're playing with fire," Waters said, hoisting his bag. The officers thanked him, and he left the room.

"Thanks," Dawson said sheepishly to Hilliard and Calvo. He felt they should be mad at him for withholding knowledge about the tunnel rather than helping him find relief for his hands.

"Back to this," Hilliard said, holding up the picture of the blackboard. It says MURDER."

"You need to talk to the lady in the waiting area," Dawson said, playing his trump card. "I asked her to meet me here."

"One more question, before we talk to her," Hilliard said. He selected a photo and passed it to Dawson, who looked at it without picking it up. It was a photo taken at the engagement party. In it, he was standing at the dessert table, placing a piece of pie onto a plate. Other desserts sat nearby, along with glass bowls of whipped cream nestled in crushed ice.

"You helped pass out pie at the party, correct?" Hilliard asked him, studying the young man's face. Dawson merely studied the photo and looked up, nodding. His face showed no emotion. "There was pie found in Skylar Harris' stomach," Hilliard continued. "Did you serve her any pie?"

Dawson thought back to the party and slowly shook his head no.

"She was playing up the southern belle thing," Dawson said, "and had all these guys around her. I do remember one guy racing over to me just as I was placing a piece of pie on a plate. He said, 'I need pie for Miss Skylar!' and he grabbed up the plate and ran off, all excited. It was rather pathetic, I thought. I looked over at Landon, and he was seething."

"I understand your mother made the pies," Hilliard said gently.

Dawson reacted to the question with the first real emotion they had seen. Nostrils flaring, he asked, "Just what are you implying?"

Hilliard held up a hand to head off the assault. "I'm just clarifying," he said. "Right now, the only thing we have is a tox report showing an overdose of a drug that can be fatal, and stomach contents with peach pie. It doesn't appear she ate anything else at the party. Drank a lot of champagne, but didn't eat anything other than pie."

Dawson looked back down at the photo, striving to calm down. Finally, he said, "I don't know anything, other than my mother would have nothing to gain by hurting Miss Harris. And before you put that bead on me, yes, I helped my Mom with the pies, but I didn't even know Skylar Harris and would have no reason to kill her!"

"Did you see anyone hanging around the dessert table? Anything now that you're thinking about it might seem odd?"

"Several people wanted pie," he said, thinking hard. "Two were the young women with Skylar's group. Brenn got a piece. I remember the whipped cream dish was empty, and she brought another one from the kitchen and put a big glob of it on her pie. Margo got a piece, but each time she tried to take a bite, someone stopped to talk to her. I thought it was funny at the time. That's all I remember."

At the mention of Margo's and Brenn's names, Hilliard and Calvo perked up.

"Think hard!" Calvo pressed. "Did anyone else eat a piece of pie from the same pie you were serving? You get what...six pieces or so from one pie?"

"Yeah, I saw the two young women I mentioned eating theirs with Skylar. I think they got the pie just to impress her that they liked what she liked. But they ate it and they're not sick."

"Do you know the name of the man who took the pie to Skylar?" Calvo asked.

"Yeah, I know Southgate," Dawson said. "He was a big shot in High School. Made it even bigger in petroleum. His family owns a huge refinery by the river outside Baton Rouge. Galveston Southgate, that's his name."

Minutes later, Madame Sangers entered in a swath

of layered silk scarves and the cloying smell of Frankincense oil. Calvo motioned to her abandoned chair, and the medium sat, accompanied by the jangling sound of her myriad bracelets striking each other. She looked nervously at Dawson, who nodded to her reassuringly. Calvo remained standing off to the side.

"Mr. Kingston here said you might be able to help us with a case we're working on," Hilliard began. He placed the photo of the blackboard in front of the medium and watched with interest as she recoiled. "You seem upset by this picture," Hilliard said kindly. "That is you in the photo, correct? You appear frightened there as well. What can you tell me about the words on the chalkboard? I assume you wrote them, but why?"

Madame Sangers flashed a look of anger at the detective that quickly dissolved into panic. She played with an enormous ring of purple amethyst on her right ring finger, twisting it around and around.

"I...I know you think I'm a phony," she said. She held up a hand with two-inch-long fingernails to stop Hilliard as he began to speak. "I do not care! I'm used to it. But this...this séance with Mrs. Barrows was not right." She swallowed and looked at Dawson for reassurance. Again, he nodded.

"It was to be a simple thing. I was to speak to the young dead boy and give the grieving mother some clues to his death. But some things happened that were not of my doing." Her breathing escalated. "The bell is a trick, I will admit to that. I have a small Tibetan bell that sits on the table to ring once for 'Yes' and twice for 'No' answers to the questions the customers ask. I have a second bell on an elastic between my knees that I

438

control by stretching the elastic in and out with my thighs, causing the bell to ring. They can't tell that it is not coming from the bell on the table. People tend to see and hear what they believe to be true. And the people who come to me *want* to believe!" she said emphatically, hoping to justify her fraud.

"But that night," her tone changed, and fear played across her face, "that night, the bell, it was not of my doing. It began ringing and grew louder, more frantic. I wasn't doing it! Then it changed to another kind of sound, like a ship bell clanging. It was almost deafening!

"Thunder broke out, and a cat screamed. Someone went to free the cat from the window screen. I reached to my left and hurriedly flipped the blackboard over. It's on a swivel, and it's quite easy to do without leaving my seat. I was told to write GOLD and TREASURE on the board ahead of time. I did that before we began with glow-in-the-dark chalk. But as I waited for the woman to free the cat, I felt this piercing cold breath waft across my face. It moved to my left. When I turned to look, there were three other words added to the chalkboard that were not there a moment before. I didn't write them!"

The room was silent for several seconds. Hilliard looked over to Calvo, who was leaning against the filing cabinet, her face confused. Finally, Dawson spoke.

"I was sitting right there," he said. "No one stepped over to that chalkboard. I could see everyone, and they were focused on Angela getting her cat free."

Hilliard stared at the medium for a moment and then back down at the photo. "So, you wrote GOLD and

TREASURE. But not TORN, SECRET PATH, and MURDER," he intoned. "Do you have any knowledge about what those words mean?" he asked her.

"No! I don't. You may think I'm making this up, but I honestly did not write those last three words! When I saw them and felt the cold spot pass me just before, I was frightened. It had never happened before." She looked at the detective pleadingly.

"I would assume not," he said, his voice taking on a harsh tone. "My guess is your parlor tricks are nothing more than that...tricks....meant to rob innocent people of their money."

Calvo cringed at Hilliard's criticism of the woman. After all, she did come in to talk to them.

"Maybe Madame Sangers did bring Ryder back from the dead," Calvo said, bracing herself for Hilliard's outburst. "Someone wrote the other words on the blackboard. It seems that maybe Ryder was trying to tell us who his killer is. Maybe most of Madam Sanger's performances are tricks, but even a broken clock is right twice a day," she said, smiling at the medium.

Madame Sangers abruptly rose from her chair. "I came here out of the goodness of my heart," she said, glaring at Hilliard. "Once I knew this was more than just a boy accidentally drowning and a mother who is suddenly missing, I had planned to come to you even before this young man phoned me. Something was not right at that séance! That was not what I was paid to do."

Hilliard leaned forward, his face inches from the recorder. "Who paid you and to do what?" he asked firmly.

Madame Sangers wavered. Dawson could read her thoughts. Hilliard had insulted her. Why should she help them? Dawson looked up at her with pleading eyes. She softened and said, "I was asked to ring the bell with the appropriate answers. And, I was asked to write the two words GOLD and TREASURE on the blackboard ahead of time."

"And who paid you?" Hilliard repeated.

Madame Sangers pressed her eyelids shut and took a deep breath. "Brenn Barrows," she said.

32 "TIME PASSES, BUT DEATH REMAINS"

Dawson remained seated after Madame Sangers departed in a cloud of Frankincense and irritation.

"She won't put a curse on us, will she?" Hilliard asked sarcastically. "Seriously, Brenn paid Madame Laveau to fake a séance?"

Calvo grinned at the detective's reference to the famous Voodoo priestess of New Orleans during the mid-1800s. Dawson managed a smirk. He was still panicked by the whole séance thing.

"So you're convinced it was a fake?" Dawson asked. "I was there. I'm not so sure all of it was faked. I did find the fake pitcher of water trick. You can buy it online."

"Ok, let's say part of it was faked, will that make you happy?" Hilliard asked him.

"She said she wrote the first two words," Dawson said, "so she admitted to faking that. But I believe her that she didn't write the last three. And no one else

442

could have. I was sitting right there. There wasn't enough time, and I would have seen or heard them. If Brenn paid her, then Brenn had an agenda; I think we can agree on that. So, I'm thinking she was hoping the séance would throw suspicion on someone for Ryder's death. Why else do it? So, let's look at the top two words that Madame Sangers admitted to writing, at Brenn's request: GOLD and TREASURE. If you're thinking like Brenn, those two words would point to Tulie, who was painting rocks with gold spray paint for pretend gold in the game. It was also Tulie's idea to have a treasure map made. This tells me, Brenn wanted Tulie to take the fall for Ryder's death. She makes sure she's seen at the top of the cliff as an alibi that she couldn't have been near Ryder when he went into the lake…there wouldn't have been enough time. We now know, if she went through the secret tunnel, she did have time to hurt him."

Calvo smiled fondly at the young man. "You've missed your calling," she said. "That's very logical. Problem is, we have no proof."

"We know Ryder is seen holding the map in this photo," Dawson said, pointing to the picture he took of the boy and Tulie. "We know we next see the map in Brenn's hands when she calls down from the cliff."

"Calvo and I measured the distance from the dock up to the cliff," Hilliard said. "We timed it at 15 minutes. How much faster could she have gotten there if she took the tunnel?"

"She would have shaved off at least five minutes," Dawson said. "Brenn never really liked Ryder and Tulie. I will tell you right now, Tulie would never hurt that boy in a million years! Ryder was her twin! She adored him, and she and Rachel never got over his death."

Calvo looked down at the blackboard photo again.

"But, according to Madame Sangers, she only wrote the top two words: GOLD and TREASURE. So, who wrote the last three words, and what did they mean? If SECRET PATH means the tunnel, that points to you, your mother, and Randall. You said you were the only ones who knew about it. We don't know for sure if Brenn knew about it or used it that day. Then you have the word MURDER. That's pretty specific. I don't know what TORN means."

"I have no idea," Dawson said. "All I know is that I would never hurt Ryder, and Randall was his father. I don't understand what happened at the end of the séance, but something was strange."

The room was silent for a minute, and Dawson squirmed in his chair.

"Is Tulie okay?" he asked, afraid of the answer. "She's at Angela's, right? She's going to be okay?"

"She is regaining her strength," Calvo said. "I called to check this morning. Angela won't let anything happen to her."

"I need to tell you something," Dawson said, his voice low and guarded. "I didn't tell you earlier because I...I wasn't sure what it meant." He looked miserable. "I saw Brenn at the folly the night of Skylar and Landon's engagement party. She was standing in the bushes near the door. When she saw me, she took off. I thought it was strange. I was gathering up empty glasses and stuff. I heard some voices coming from the folly, but it didn't surprise me. There were guests everywhere. That was right before the engagement announcement. Later, after the cake ceremony, I went back to the garden and the folly for any other glasses or trash. The garden was empty. I looked in the folly and saw Skylar lying there." He glanced at the detective guiltily. The two officers looked at him in shock.

"I'm sorry. I just didn't know what had happened! I thought she had passed out drunk. But then, I saw Tulie's blue sash around her neck and I panicked. I knew it was Tulie's. It kept falling off all night, and I heard her tell you when you talked to all of us that Margo went to get it back for her after she traded sashes with Skylar. Tulie was acting so strange that night, and I had heard the rumors about her father and Margo. I wondered if maybe Randall had been fooling around with Skylar, too. I saw Randall and Skylar go into the garden earlier. So...I took the sash from around Skylar's neck. I heard someone coming, so I went out through the secret door and down the rum runner's tunnel. I hid the sash until I could give it back to Tulie and booked it back to the party. I got back just as Calvin was wheeling his chair out of the garden, which I thought was strange."

"That solves the mystery of the traveling blue sash," Hilliard said, sighing. "For someone who just swore Tulie could never hurt her brother, you seem to have no problem finding her capable of strangling Skylar Harris," the detective said, fixing the young man with his steely blue eyes.

"I thought it impossible to believe," Dawson said, tiredly. He slumped back, all the wind knocked out of him. "But Tulie was acting so strange at the party. I saw the blue sash and panicked."

"How did you manage not to leave your footprints in

the pollen?" Calvo asked.

"I was just careful to step where it had been…"

"Disrupted," Hilliard said, grinning. Neither of the other two got the joke, even though it was the second time Calvo heard him say it.

"Was Skylar alive when you took the sash?" Hilliard asked.

"She looked dead to me," Dawson said, his stomach in knots. "I know I did wrong. I was just so surprised to see her lying there with Tulie's sash around her neck."

"Think hard, Dawson," Hilliard said. "Was the sash knotted tightly around her neck, or was it just placed there to look like she had been strangled?"

Dawson looked down, trying to picture the horrible scene that night.

"It was pretty tight around her neck," he said. "I had to undo it. Then I saw how red her neck was…I messed up! I'm sorry."

"We'll figure it out later," Hilliard said. "You look tired. Go home. Take care of your hands. Please, do not try to interfere with this. We'll take care of it. Don't talk to anyone about what you know. I'd hate to see another call come in for a disappearance or, heaven forbid, a mysterious death. You are not out of the woods on this," he said sternly to the young man. "You tampered with a dead body and evidence, and, in all honesty, I can't rule you out for some of these unsolved cases."

Dawson looked surprised as he rose nervously, collected his ointment and bandages, and paused near the door.

"There is one more odd thing," he said, sounding depleted and scared. "At the engagement party…two women were talking to Tulie. I was standing only a few feet away at the bar, gathering up glasses. One was Margaret Ruthers. I know her because she is always asking my mom for her pies for fundraisers. Pretty pushy lady. The other woman I don't know. Anyway, the other woman took Tulie's hand and seemed upset about a ring Tulie was wearing. I heard her say she lost one just like it at Barry's waterskiing party all those years ago. Tulie seemed lost about what she was saying, and Mrs. Ruthers pulled the other woman away, but it was clear, the other lady was upset. I don't know what that was all about. Like I said, strange stuff was happening with Tulie that night."

"Thank you, Dawson," Calvo said. "I'll give Mrs. Ruthers a call. In the meantime, don't go anywhere. Stick close to home."

Dawson nodded and walked out, closing the door behind him.

"We need to nail down a few things, and fast," Hilliard said, as soon as he felt Dawson was out of earshot. "I'm very afraid there are other people in danger. We need to find out how the drugs got into Skylar's system, who tried to strangle her, who killed Brixi Carter, and finally, what happened to Ryder and Rachel Barrows? It looks like someone also tried to poison Tulie. And…we can't rule Landon out for Skylar's death. Dawson just said Landon 'was seething' at the attention Skylar was getting at the party."

An enthusiastic voice answered Lieutenant Calvo's cell phone on the second ring.

"Galveston Southgate!" he pronounced proudly. "How can I help?"

"Mr. Southgate, this is Lieutenant Calvo with the Orleans Parish Police Department. May I have a moment of your time, please? It's about Skylar Harris' death."

The other end of the line was quiet. Finally, a less enthusiastic voice answered, "Of course, but I have little to offer. I'm afraid I didn't know her."

"I believe you were kind enough to bring Miss Harris a slice of pie at the party," Calvo said without wasting any time. "Do you remember that?"

"Sure. She wanted one, and I got her one. Twice, I believe. That was all," he said, his voice becoming guarded. "Is there something wrong with that?"

"Not at all," Calvo answered smoothly, her Creole accent as soothing as a hot toddy. She glanced across the desk to see Hilliard reading some reports. "Can you please just tell me what you did after Miss Harris requested a piece of pie?"

Confused as to the importance of his small gesture to ingratiate himself with a beautiful woman, Galveston finally laid out his movements succinctly.

"I believe I said I would be glad to get her a piece; I don't remember the exact words. I went to the dessert table. The guy who works around the properties was placing pie on some plates. I picked one up and took it back to her. I had gotten her one earlier. Oh wait. I mean, I was going to hand it to her...the second time... but I dropped it. Someone bumped into me. I turned to run back for another one, but the Barrows' girl was standing there and offered me her piece that she had just gotten. So, I handed that to Skylar. No big deal."

Calvo strove to maintain a calm demeanor, despite her mind screaming. "Which Barrows' girl?" she asked calmly, but her voice quavered.

"Not the scatterbrained one, the other one…the chubby one," Galveston said unkindly. "I almost didn't take it because she had put quite a lot of whipped cream on it, but I didn't want to keep Miss Skylar waiting or to know I dropped her pie, so I went with it."

"And you saw Skylar eat it?" Calvo asked, glancing at the digital recorder with its voice indicator jumping.

"I'm getting the feeling there was something wrong with the pie," Galveston said, all attempts at friendliness gone. "I think I would rather not answer any more questions without my lawyer."

"Mr. Southgate," Calvo said firmly. "You are not under any suspicion whatsoever. But that is an important question that I need answered. Your cooperation would be greatly appreciated."

"I already cooperated," Galveston said. "I gave my consent for buccal swabs, had my picture taken, and I was fingerprinted two days after the party. But, I'll answer your question. She pretty much wolved it down. She said she had hardly eaten all afternoon. I took the empty plate she handed to one of the girls and gave it to a passing waiter."

"Thank you," Calvo said. "You have been extremely helpful. Just so you know, everyone at the party was fingerprinted and gave DNA samples. We did not single you out. Thank you again." Calvo hung up and pressed the Stop button on the recorder. "Holy crap!" she breathed. She looked at Hilliard, who had been listening to the cell phone Calvo had placed on speaker.

"I think we got her," Hilliard said.

"Got who?" Calvo asked with exasperation. "I thought we were leaning toward Margo for Skylar's death!"

"Speaking of Margo," he said, reaching for a pile of papers and handing one across the desk to Calvo. "It's the results from Brixi's vase," he said solemnly.

Calvo had almost forgotten the new reports during the flurry of information pouring in from Dawson and Madame Sangers. She scanned the document eagerly, mumbling the words in short clips. She jerked her head up as she came to the pertinent section.

"Minute amounts of human blood found within the crevices of two of the beveled diamond shapes on the lead glass," she said, her voice elevated. She looked back down at the forensic report for the vase and mumbled on. "Holy crap!" she screamed, her finger pressed next to the final line. "The blood DNA matches that of Brixi Carter. It *was* the murder weapon!" Her green eyes glistened.

"It gets better," Hilliard said, popping a caramel into his mouth. "Page Two."

He handed her a second report from the fingerprint division. It also pertained to the vase.

"Latent prints were found on the glass in several areas," she read aloud, her heart pounding. "The following exemplars match as to print contributors to the exterior of the vase:

Brixi Carter
Maude Gleason
Gladys Pritchard
Unknown Male

"The interior of the vase neck near the top shows a match for one contributor:

Brenn Barrows."

Calvo sat thunderstruck, staring at the last name in bold black print. Hilliard grinned, appreciating the moment of the great reveal.

"Continue on," Hilliard said.

Calvo flipped to the second stapled page, which was a report on the fingerprint findings for Barry Broussard's waterski. Her breath coming in bursts, the lieutenant read it aloud.

"A few partial prints were found on the ski's rubber bindings. The age of prints contributed to diluted findings. Contributors were from three matches:

Roger Henderson
Barry Broussard
Archer Hilliard
Brenn Barrows

The screw still encased in the front rubber binding showed one latent print. The contributor was Brenn Barrows. Another latent print matching Brenn Barrows was found on the *underside* of the same binding."

"We got her," Hilliard said, rolling the caramel across his bottom teeth. "There is no good reason in the entire world for Brenn's fingerprints to be on that short screw and underneath the binding. She bent the binding back to remove the original screws and replace them with shortened ones that would give way under pressure. It truly is evil. The screwdriver showed my prints. The other prints were too old and hard to lift."

"And the vase?" Calvo asked, flipping back to the first page. "Margo's prints aren't listed. Who's the

'Unknown Male?'"

"I'm guessing Brixi's uncle who mailed her the vase. We can get his prints and double-check. Here's what I think happened: Brenn took those flowers to Brixi, pretending Margo sent her to show her sympathy for Brixi's grandmother's passing. Brixi let her in, probably turned away to fill the vase with water for the flowers, Brenn grabbed it and hit her repeatedly over the head with it. It had to be more than one blow. The first strike never causes blood in blunt force trauma; it's the second, third, and so on that transfers blood onto a murder weapon or creates blood spatter.

"She may have worn gloves, but I doubt it. It would have looked strange to Brixi. She probably was careful to grip the vase in one area on the outside and wipe that portion off, which is why those other people's prints were still there. She put the vase in Margo's car on the passenger floorboard in the garage. She made one mistake—she didn't wipe the *inside* of the vase where her fingers touched the neck when she handled it."

Calvo leaned back, the report still in her hand.

"I have to admit," she said in a husky voice, "I am shocked! But why kill Brixi? Why set up Margo?"

"Maude said Brixi knew too much," Hilliard said. "She was afraid Brixi had been snooping and was talking too much. Maude said the muddy shoes found in Brixi's apartment were Margo's, and Brixi found them in the garbage at Margo's house. Brixi knew about the broken statue and the strange note that was with it at Margo's birthday party. Maybe she knew something else, and Brenn needed to silence her, and set up Margo for her murder in the bargain."

"That thud on Mrs. Pritchard's door that afternoon,"

452

Calvo said. "I've always wondered what that was."

"A bag of caramels says Brenn deliberately hit the old lady's door as she went by so that Gladys *would* look out and hear the part of the conversation Brenn wanted her to, which is exactly what happened. Gladys heard the name "Margo" and "flowers for me?" Maude said Brixi often complained about how snoopy Mrs. Pritchard was. What we're seeing is that Brenn must have overheard Brixi talking to Maude at Margo's on more than one occasion. My guess is, Brenn had a gold mine of information at her disposal."

Calvo looked up at the grinning detective. "Holy crap on a fajita!" she choked. "I have no words!"

"Hard to top 'crap on a fajita,'" Hilliard smiled.

"My Creole grandfather had a saying: 'Time passes, but death remains.' Can you believe it? A waterskiing accident from almost 18 years ago held onto its secrets and pointed out a cold-blooded murder scheme. Brenn rigged it so her Uncle Barry would fall. Did she mean for it to kill him? I don't know. But we do know, she was willing to take that risk. This is beyond sociopathic. She's dangerous. We have to arrest her...now!" she said, pushing her chair back from the desk. "Before she hurts anyone else. We have enough! At least for Barry's death. And we have her fingerprints on the vase for Brixi's murder."

"And, if she doctored the pie or the whipped cream, she killed Skylar!" Hilliard said, hurriedly gathering together all the documents and photographs covering his desk. "We need the paperwork ASAP. You corral Judge Nethers, show him we have probable cause, and it's a matter of life and death. We get her in jail and hold her for the arraignment. That will get the ball rolling. We also need a search warrant for the Barrows' house. I'll call Angela and tell her to keep Tulie under lock and key! We'll head out to Rachel's as soon as we get Nether's John Hancock. Hurry!"

Calvo ran from the room with a folder of documents. Hilliard snatched up the phone, thumbed through his contacts, and punched in Angela Peterson's number. The phone rang as he drummed his fingers impatiently. Calvin picked up on the fourth ring, sounding agitated.

"Calvin!" Hilliard said, his voice urgent. "I need you and Angela to keep a close eye on Tulie! Do not let her out of your sight! Keep her in the house. I'll explain later. Do you understand?"

A snort came from the other end of the phone. Calvin cleared his throat, and the disgusting sound of phlegm assaulted Hilliard's eardrum.

"Well, your timing is bad," Calvin said flatly. "Angela is outside looking for her. We can't find her."

33 WHEN SHADOWS WALK

"Tulie's not outside," Angela said breathlessly as she burst into the house, the screen door slamming behind her. Calvin faced her in the kitchen, his face showing concern that he rarely conveyed.

"She has to have gone back home," he said. "Go over and check."

Angela nodded. "At least Brenn is at Margo's," she said. "I swear, if I have to deal with that girl one more time, there will be another disappearance to deal with around here!"

Angela walked to the front of the house and out the door. She stopped when she heard the sound of men's voices coming from the lake. Walking past the stand of pine trees, she looked down at the water to see a Search and Rescue boat floating across the inlet.

Angela's heart raced, and she ran for the edge of the lake. "What are you doing?" she called, panicking. "Is someone in the lake?" In her mind, she was praying, 'Please don't be Tulie, please don't be Tulie.'

A man at the helm turned to look across the water at her. He turned and said something over his shoulder to a second man who was leaning over the boat, his back to Angela. He turned and looked over his shoulder at the frantic woman on the cliffside above and shook his head no. After that, the two men ignored her.

"Oh God!" she breathed. "Please, no more! No more!"

She hurried on to Rachel's house; prayers for Tulie's safety repeating over and over in whispers from her lips. A patrol car came screeching down the Barrows' driveway and pulled onto the grass near the back porch steps. Detective Hilliard and Calvo exited and hurried toward the sunroom just as Angela ran up.

"What's wrong?" she wailed. "What's going on? Is it Tulie?"

"You still haven't found her?" Hilliard asked in alarm.

"No! Why is there a rescue boat in the lake? Please talk to me! I'm going crazy here!" Angela begged.

Hilliard stepped a few steps over to get a better look at the far shore, where a boat was anchored. He deliberated on how much to tell Angela. He was keeping Randall's deathbed confession to himself. He knew the rescue team had divers in the water looking for Rachel's body. He wished they had come in a nondescript boat that didn't announce who they were.

"It's not about Tulie," Hilliard said finally. He needed Angela to calm down. "It's some other police business that I can't talk about right now, but it is not Tulie."

Angela studied his face, a million thoughts going through her mind. She landed on the one most pressing for now.

"Are you here to look for Tulie?" she asked. "I was

just coming over to see if she's here."

Calvo jumped on the excuse. "Yes, yes, we are. We'll check inside for her, and you can wait here," she said, not wanting Angela overseeing their arrest of Brenn. They also planned on searching the house for evidence and didn't need Angela interfering. Angela fumed. She was always being kept away during police investigations.

"The hell I will!" Angela barked and pushed past them. She stomped up the steps and into the sunroom before they could stop her.

"If we keep her out, we'll have to tell her we are here on police business, and I don't want to show our cards at this point," Hilliard whispered angrily to the lieutenant who was following the woman into the house to remove her. "I'll handle Brenn, and you take her to Tulie's room and give her some innocent task, like seeing if it looks like Tulie may have been there today."

The two officers hurried into the house. Angela was already in the front hallway calling Tulie's name at the top of her lungs.

Silence followed. The house was eerily still.

"Where's Brenn?" Calvo whispered to the detective. He shrugged. She looked out the kitchen window. "I don't see her car," she added.

"On the one hand," he said. "If she's not here, it will make the search a lot easier. On the other hand, we still need to arrest her, so let's hope she hasn't run for the border."

"She'd have to *swim* for the border," Calvo said. "Right through the Gulf of Mexico! We'd better hurry, either way."

Calvo entered the hallway and walked over to

Angela, who was about to take the stairs. "You can help me," Calvo said, as she caught up with Angela and took her elbow. "Let's check Tulie's room. You can see if it looks like she came here today, maybe to pick up something to bring back to your house."

Angela looked suspiciously at the short officer. "How would I know if she took something today?" she asked. "I don't know her room! I've been in it maybe once."

Calvo scrambled for an excuse as Hilliard waited a few feet away. "You never know," the lieutenant said, trying to sound casual. "Something might jump out at you."

Angela flung the officer's hand from her elbow and hurried up the stairs. "Tulie!" she screamed. "Tulie!" She ran to Tulie's room, with Calvo hurrying after her. Hilliard crept up the stairs, keeping out of Angela's eye line. When the woman burst into Tulie's room, he hurried on to Brenn's room and entered through the open doorway. He closed the door silently behind him.

The room was in disarray; underwear was discarded on the floor, and soiled t-shirts were flung over a desk chair. The bed was unmade, and the pillow was missing. Hilliard frowned. Something seemed off. Why was the pillow gone? He looked on the floor on the other side of the bed, but there was nothing there. He walked to the desk, covered in artwork, markers, and pastel pencils. He picked up a drawing of a fairy that he had to admit showed real talent. Other drawings of woodland creatures in various stages of completion lay strewn about the desktop.

He opened two of the three desk drawers only to find more art materials. The bottom drawer stuck as he pulled on the wooden handle. It opened a few inches and refused to budge; the wood swollen by the Louisiana humidity and heat. He jerked hard, and it suddenly slid all the way out, landing on the floor. A few glossy photographs tumbled out, along with a sketchbook. He picked up the photos and gave them a cursory glance. One was taken at Skylar's engagement party. It showed Rachel, Tulie, Angela, and Calvin near the cliffside by the bar set-up. They seemed unaware it was being taken as they looked out at the party.

The next photo was Tulie walking through a parking lot carrying two platters of what looked like small desserts. Other women were crossing the same area carrying flowers and food. A gold cross adorned the brick façade of the building near a glass door that was propped open. The last picture was Tulie baking in the kitchen with flour everywhere and her hands caked with batter.

Hilliard stood for a moment, contemplating the pictures. Tulie was in each picture. *Why take a photo of her walking through a church parking lot?* he wondered. He thumbed quickly through the sketch book but found nothing of interest. It was mostly pencil sketches of trees and the old tire swing outside. He put the art book back into the drawer but hung onto the three photos of Tulie. He squatted to align the drawer with its runners and shoved to push it back into place. It went a few inches and stopped. He shoved again, and it shot into the desk; a cracking sound came from the back.

"Great," he sighed. "I broke it."

He yanked the drawer again and heard something fall with a rattling sound from behind it. Pulling hard, he forced it out and got down on his knees to peer into the opening. Reaching his hand into the shadowed void, he pulled out a prescription pill bottle, cracked from the impact of the drawer hitting it. He turned it around until he could read the label. It was a prescription for Flunitrazepam. 'To be taken once daily at bedtime for insomnia,' the small, typed instructions read. The doctor's name was Clarkson, and the patient to whom the prescription was made was Rachel Barrows. It was dated over two months ago. The final line read: 'No refills.' The detective shook it gently, noting there weren't many left in the bottle.

Hilliard felt his head swimming. This was the drug found in Skylar's toxicology report. This was the date rape drug Calvo had read in the report called Rohypnol.

"Bloody hell!" he said beneath his breath. He regretted that he had handled it, probably obliterating valuable fingerprints with his gloved hands. He held it gently by its cap and dropped it into his suit pocket.

Calvo's raised voice sounded in the hallway, alerting him that they were coming out of Tulie's room. "I appreciate your help, Angela," Calvo said. "It was worth a shot. We'll find her! I promise. You go on back home. Maybe she showed up since you've been here."

Hilliard heard the sound of the two women walking down the creaking staircase to the main floor. He quickly bent to peer into the cavity of the desk to align the drawer once more. Something white was shown in the back, barely discernible in the shadows. He reached in and pulled out a bent envelope. It wasn't sealed. He opened it and slid a 5" x 7" photograph from its interior. He frowned as he looked at an image of Tulie seated at the sunroom table, a cup of tea in front of her.

A silver tea service sat in the center of the table. Across from Tulie were two chairs, each with a teacup placed in front of it. Both were full of brown liquid. It appeared to be sunset: orange and yellow hues played across the sky and reflected on the lake outside the mesh windows to Tulie's left.

Another strange photo of Tulie, Hilliard thought. *What was Brenn up to?*

Hilliard replaced the picture in the envelope and slid it into his other jacket pocket. He shoved the drawer back into place and rose, dusting off his knees. He made a quick search of the closet and turned his attention to the locked drawer of the bedside table that had tempted him once before. This time, he had a warrant. He pulled a small tool kit from his inside jacket pocket and selected two pointed metal lock picks. He deftly applied them and pulled open the drawer.

A plume of sweet-smelling perfume wafted up from the open drawer. Inside was a bundle of blue envelopes addressed to 'Randall.' Hilliard selected the top one and opened it. He pulled out a faded letter in blue ink. Perusing it quickly, he realized it was a love letter to Randall, signed, 'Your Southern Belle.' The other letters were of the same content. He wondered why Brenn had them. At the bottom of the small pile was an empty blue envelope that had just the name 'Tulie' written on it. The only other thing of interest in the drawer was a bottle of Tea Rose perfume and a small handkerchief soaked with the scent.

Hilliard pocketed the letters but left the perfume and handkerchief. Before he exited the room, he glanced again from the window above Brenn's art desk. His gaze was met with a partial glimmer of the lake. The rest of the view, including the dock, was obscured by a giant elm tree's branches. The other window to the right of the bed had views mainly of trees, with a small portion of the cemetery showing to the right.

Hilliard met Calvo coming out of Rachel's room. She had performed her own searches after getting rid of Angela. They both went downstairs into the kitchen. She seemed anxious. "I have something to tell you," she said, her voice urgent. "But first, did you find anything?"

"I'll tell you in the car," he said, smiling. "Did you check the cabinets in here?"

"Yeah. Looks like they took it all in for testing, even the cleaning agents from under the sink. Tulie's room didn't give up much. Angela said the little suitcase and some clothes were at her house while Tulie stays with them. I did peek quickly in Rachel's room. Nothing. Bed made, curtains drawn. I didn't bother with Randall's since our guys did a pretty thorough sweep of that room." Calvo led the way to the sunroom, her steps urgent.

"Did Angela say if she knew when Brenn was coming back?" Hilliard asked. "I'm not leaving until we have her in handcuffs in the back seat of the car."

Calvo stopped and faced him, standing near the table Hilliard had been looking at in the photo he had just found hidden behind Brenn's desk drawer.

"That's the important thing I need to tell you," she said, frowning up at the man over a foot taller than she was. "Brenn isn't living here right now. Angela said she's staying at Margo's for a while. Said she was scared to stay here alone."

Hilliard stopped, his expression shocked.

"She's at Margo's? You're kidding! Why Margo's?"

Calvo shrugged, stepping out through the sunroom door onto the back porch. "Brenn told Angela that Reed said she could stay for a few days until Randall's funeral is over. We can still arrest her there," she said, glancing back at the detective for his reaction.

"That's not the point," Hilliard said, his voice filled with panic. "That places two suspected murderers in the same house at the same time!"

Reed Tillson opened his front door, his facial expression that of a man ready to explode.

"You don't have to ring the doorbell off!" he yelled at the detective standing there, sweat pouring from his forehead. "What is the matter with you people?" he barked. "Do you have any sympathy for us at all? Our son's fiancé was just found murdered…in *our* pecan grove! They finally released her body, and now we have to face a funeral, which is going to destroy our son. The reporters have been merciless, and Margo is having a breakdown! Her brother-in-law just died, and we're dealing with his distraught daughter, who just moved in with us while we finish up funeral arrangements that Angela dumped on us. Rachel is still not back. Our maid was found murdered. Anything else we can offer you on our private tour of hell?"

Hilliard paused. Reed's angry outburst put the insane situation in neon letters. He stopped himself before mentioning the dead cat found in their garden.

Lieutenant Calvo took a step forward. "We apologize for the intrusion," she said gently. "There is a lot going on, and as you may imagine, our plates are full as well as we try and find out what happened to Skylar, Brixi, and Mr. Randall. We actually need to speak with Brenn, please, and we'll leave you in peace. I'm afraid we will have some follow-up questions for you and Miss Margo concerning Randall, but that's not our mission right now."

"What do we have to do with Randall's death?" Reed shot back at her. "I thought he died of some viral infection."

"It's just some routine questions about how the surviving family members plan on helping out with Tulie and Brenn," Calvo lied. "Randall's will, will have to be gone over, and you and your wife would be helpful with that, at least until Rachel returns."

The mention of a will seemed to calm Reed. He hesitated, and his face relaxed. "Yes, yes, I see," he said. "Hadn't thought of that. Of course, Rachel will get the bulk, I would think, but there probably are codicils and such to go over."

Calvo could almost see the man's hamster wheel turning in his mind as he pictured coming into some money.

Reed cleared his throat. "I'm sorry I didn't bring Margo in earlier. It's been a rough day. I'll let Margo know," he said. "She's pretty much taken to her bed since Randall died. She, uh, says she's sick." His face colored, and in that moment, Calvo was positive he had heard the rumors about his wife and the recently departed Randall Barrows. "As for Brenn," he said, "she is out running some errands...for the funeral, I think. I can have her call you if you like."

Hilliard bristled. He wouldn't relax until he had Brenn and probably Margo behind bars.

"No need," Hilliard said. "I don't want to cause her any stress when she has her father's funeral to deal with. Please don't mention we dropped by."

Reed looked at him suspiciously but said nothing.

"You haven't by chance seen Tulie, have you?" Calvo asked innocently.

"No," Reed said. "Brenn said Tulie is staying at Angela's for a few days. You should check there. Anyway…." he said, beginning to close the door. "Let me know what surfaces in Skylar's death. I don't think I will go near that grove again. I hope the developers tear it all down."

He shut the door, leaving Hilliard and Calvo standing on the columned front verandah. They turned and walked toward their car. Hilliard held up a hand and walked around the corner of the house to the back lawn. He strode to the cliffside and looked down to the lake where the two men in the rescue boat were pulling a diver in over the side. The detective could tell from their body language that they hadn't found anything. Moments later, the boat engine roared to life, and they headed farther over near Reed's damaged dock.

The two officers pulled out of the mansion driveway. Hilliard reached over and set the air conditioning to full blast.

"Do we head to the funeral parlor and see if Brenn is there, look for Tulie, or what?" he asked, as Calvo closed her vent halfway. Her face was beginning to crack from the glacial air. "I think Margo will sit tight for now. The fact that Tulie is gone and so is Brenn is of great concern. Where do we start?"

Before Calvo could answer him, her cell phone rang.

"It's Margaret Ruthers," she said. "I left a message

asking her to give me a call. Hurry and get out onto the main highway so my call doesn't drop!

"Mrs. Ruthers," Calvo said as she answered her phone. "Thank you for calling me back."

Margaret Ruthers sounded guarded but hospitable. "My pleasure, Lieutenant. What may I help you with?"

"It's just a small thing," Calvo said casually. "I was told that you and a friend were talking with Tulie Barrows at the Tillson's engagement party for their son. Do you recall that exchange?"

Her question was met with silence. The phone crackled, and Calvo feared the call would drop. It was followed by a strange sound like someone smacking their lips together. Finally, Margaret Ruthers answered her.

"I seem to recall us chatting with Tulie, yes," Margaret said. "I believe I mentioned wanting some more of her marvelous tea cakes for an upcoming event. She had kindly donated desserts before to our worthy church causes."

Calvo jerked her head in Hilliard's direction, who had been listening to the call on the phone's speaker.

"Tea cakes?" the lieutenant repeated.

"Why, yes. Tulie's cakes are in high demand around here," Margaret said. "We all thought her Mama was making them, but Brenn Barrows let the cat out of the bag long ago, saying Rachel had been too sick to make them and it was actually Tulie in the kitchen wearing the baker's cap. It didn't matter to us! They are simply to die for!"

Calvo openly cringed. It took her a moment to recover.

"No complaints...about the tea cakes?" she asked. "I

mean, no one could tell the difference if they were Rachel's or Tulie's?" She didn't know how else to broach the subject concerning any signs of sickness or poisoning among all the tea cakes Tulie supposedly cooked up.

"No one had a clue!" Margaret said, sounding more relaxed. Tea cakes seemed an innocuous topic. It soon changed gears.

"Back to your conversation with Tulie at the party," Calvo said. "I understand a woman with you seemed upset about a ring Tulie was wearing. Can you tell me about that, please?"

The strained voice returned on the other end of the line.

"Daphne Hobart had an extremely expensive ruby ring go missing at a party hosted by Barry Broussard a long time ago. It's worth a great deal of money. It was in her purse that she left in a guest room at the Broussard home while she helped with making desserts. Someone stole it during the party. I noticed Miss Tulie's ring one day when she brought tea cakes to our fundraiser at church. It looked just like Daphne's. I had admired it several times when Daphne wore it to my little soirees. I mentioned it to her, and she and I walked over to Tulie at the party so Daphne could see it for herself. She's certain that it's her ring."

"Why didn't she report it?" Calvo asked.

"Well, I mean, all the news of Skylar Harris missing from her own party threw us all. Then we had those awful policemen and agents showing up, shoving Q-Tip's into our cheeks and taking fingerprints, and all. It didn't seem the right time. Now, we have Skylar's body showing up and Mr. Randall's death, and...my Lord!

Have you ever?"

"No, ma'am, I've never," Calvo said. "One last question, please. These cakes that Tulie delivered to various events, was she always alone, or was anyone with her?"

"I never saw anyone but her," Margaret said. "You'd have to ask the others. I do know she was alone when she brought them to the church fundraiser and to Mrs. Friggers' shower for her new daughter-in-law. I was in attendance at that party, and I saw Tulie in the doorway...alone. What's all this about the tea cakes?" Margaret asked, her voice quivering with interest.

"We're just looking at the Barrow's ledgers," Calvin said quickly. "With Randall gone, their financials will have to be gone over. That includes all family members, including Tulie. We're just getting an idea of the scope of her business."

There was another long pause. "And Rachel's, of course," Margaret said. "She's the one with the money. Tulie's little side hustle wouldn't make a dent in the Broussard money. I would think you'd be asking Rachel these questions." A suspicious tone threaded its way through the final statement.

"And we shall," Calvo said lightly. "You've been most helpful! Thank you so much, Mrs. Ruthers. We'll look into the ring Mrs. Hobart is missing as well. Have a lovely day."

"You too," Margaret said, but her voice was less than cordial. She hung up.

"So, Tulie *does* make tea cakes," Hilliard said, "just like Brenn said. Every time I think we have this damn case sewn up, a sink hole opens up!"

"Right now, we have to find Tulie," Calvo said,

"especially after you just showed me the stuff you found in Brenn's room while we were driving over to Margo's. That prescription bottle with Rachel's name on it has got to be how an overdose of fentanyl got into the whipped cream on Skylar's pie. Someone crushed the pills and added them to the cream. We are assuming it was Brenn since she bumped into Galveston and handed him pie, and you found those pills in her room. It was pure genius. The coroner thinks Skylar was already dead when someone put Tulie's sash around her neck and squeezed. It had to have been almost immediately after Skylar succumbed to the poison. The heart would have had to just finish pumping to leave that reddened area around her neck. That makes Brenn, Skylar's murderer."

Hilliard was quiet for a moment. Finally, he said, "We can't rule out that they were Rachel's pills. Rachel had a bigger motive to kill Skylar if she knew she was fooling around with Randall, let alone pregnant with his child."

"Yes, but the pills were in *Brenn's* room, and she handed Southgate a pie piled with whipped cream that was probably loaded with the drug," Calvo said. "Still, I can't see Rachel doing it, and the last thing she would do is use Tulie's sash to strangle her and leave it behind. Dawson saw the sash around Skylar's neck."

"Look at those photos again that I handed you from Brenn's room," Hilliard said, as he sped down the highway toward Borgdorf's Funeral Parlor. Every Broussard-related funeral for the past 100 years had been handled by the ritzy funeral home. He prayed Brenn was there.

"Ok," Calvo said. "What am I looking for?"

"They all have Tulie in them. Now, follow me here... What if those were deliberately taken to set Tulie up? A photo of Tulie at the engagement party with her mother, Angela, and Calvin. Why? Why that moment in time? To show Tulie wearing a blue sash...a blue sash found wrapped around Skylar's neck? Dawson found Skylar's body before someone else could report it, and he took the sash away, ruining that part of the setup. Did Brenn poison Skylar with the Rohypnol in the whipped cream, follow her to the folly, where Skylar is failing fast? She starts to fall, grabs the chair, knocks it over, and falls to the floor, dead. Brenn takes the blue sash from Skylar, knowing it's Tulie's, and wraps it around her neck, pulling it just hard enough to look like strangulation.

"The next photo shows Tulie walking through a church parking lot with platters of what looks like small cakes. We now know that according to Margaret Ruthers, Tulie did bring tea cakes for a church fundraiser, and made them for other ladies as well. So, why would Brenn take a picture of something so irrelevant as Tulie carrying food across a parking lot?"

"To set her up," Calvo said in hushed tones. "Tulie in a picture wearing a blue sash that Brenn used to stage Skylar's murder, and Tulie with tea cakes. Tea cakes that were found to have poison in the frosting, which killed her father. A picture of Tulie in the kitchen *making* the cakes. She was going to frame Tulie for both murders! Which means, Brenn was planning to kill her father for months with the poisoned tea cakes."

"Three murders," Hilliard corrected. "Brenn also paid Madame Sangers to rig the séance to point to Tulie as Ryder's murderer. It's four, if you count Skylar's unborn baby.

"My guess is, she was going to put the pill bottle in Tulie's room at some point," Hilliard continued. "The picture of the four of them at the party also clearly shows the ruby ring on Tulie's finger…strike 3. If it looks like Tulie stole Daphne Hobart's ring, she's capable of other nefarious things. I'm not sure what the last photo is for. It's just a picture of Tulie at an empty table in the sunroom at home."

Calvo studied the picture for several seconds. Angela Peterson's words ran through her mind.

"Angela said she found Tulie having tea and talking to an empty chair as if Rachel were sitting there. She told me today at Rachel's house that she thought she smelled Rachel's favorite perfume in the sunroom that day. Angela was worried that Tulie was acting strangely and was out of it. We see a full cup of tea across from Tulie in the picture and another one next to it. Maybe Brenn had been sitting there with them and got up and took the picture to use later as proof that Tulie was talking to an empty chair and was out of her mind."

"I'll be damned!" Hilliard exclaimed. "There is a handkerchief reeking of perfume in Brenn's nightstand, along with a bottle of Tea Rose perfume. That little psycho probably placed it where Tulie could smell it and make her hallucinations concerning her mother all the more real. I've had it with that brat!" Hilliard said. "Let's find Brenn and arrest her."

Hilliard shot through a red light to the sound of blaring horns and screeched to a halt at the front door of Borgdorf's Funeral Home. He jumped from the car and ran for the double glass doors. He jerked on the handle.

The doors were locked. Looking up in surprise, he saw the small sign attached to the slender side window.

CLOSED DURING BURIAL SERVICES FOR JACKSON CALDWELL. WE WILL RETURN AT 4:00 PM.

Hilliard slammed the car door so hard that Calvo was afraid he had broken it as he propelled himself into the driver's seat.

"Dammit to hell!" he screamed. "Where is she? And where is Tulie?"

"Thank you so much for the ice cream," Tulie said. It was the first time she had felt even a small amount of happiness since her father's death. The world had seemed to stop in mid-axis. Nothing felt real anymore. The freezing taste of Rocky Road ice cream had awakened memories of happier days.

"No problem," Brenn said, as she steered her Mustang toward Lake Broussard. "We sisters have to stick together now. I figured you needed to get away from Angela and Calvin for at least a little bit. You didn't mention my texting you to them, did you?"

Tulie shook her head no and dug her pink plastic spoon into the last glob of ice cream in the disposable bowl. "They were in the kitchen, so I did what you said and slipped out a different door and met you at the end of the driveway. You were right...Angela wouldn't have let me leave the house."

Tulie missed the grin that spread across Brenn's face. She gripped the steering wheel as she maneuvered the car down the backroads of Orleans Parish; the trees' canopies of leaves flashing patterns of light and dark across the windshield.

Brenn cast a furtive look at her passenger and said, "Tulie...I suppose you've heard the rumors going around about Calvin." She paused and glanced again at Tulie who looked over at her in surprise.

"What rumors?" she asked.

"You know...that he was in the garden the night of Skylar's party. I saw him myself come out of the path by the bar. You know how obsessed he is with murders and the Bayou Slayer and all that. What if he killed Skylar? Just to see what killing really felt like? I could see him doing that. I mean, he's writing a book about murder, right? Maybe he was going to blame it on the Slayer."

She looked over at Tulie, who was staring at her with her eyes open wide.

"Cousin Calvin wouldn't do something like that!" Tulie said, her voice shocked. "I'm sure you're wrong."

Brenn turned onto Broussard Lane, taking the right-hand turn-off that led to Margo's house.

"Aren't you taking me back to Cousin Angela's?" Tulie asked, seeing the Broussard mansion through the trees.

"Yeah, I will. I just need you to do something for me real quick," Brenn said. "It will only take a minute."

Tulie set the empty ice cream bowl on the car floor as they pulled into Margo's driveway. She thought it odd that Brenn didn't pull all the way up to the house but instead parked farther back where the driveway turned. Brenn killed the engine and opened her door.

"Come on," she said.

Tulie reluctantly opened her door, got out, and shut

it. She followed Brenn, who was walking to the side of the house where the garden and its main archway sat off to the left. But she didn't turn into the garden. She kept walking toward the back of the yard.

She stopped near the cliffside and turned to wait for Tulie to catch up with her.

"Show me where Calvin was sitting the night of the party," Brenn said. "I just want to see how close he was to the gardener's path."

Tulie frowned. Brenn had been near them several times during the party; one time fixing Tulie's sash. She must have seen where Calvin was sitting. But Tulie obliged her and walked to the flower bed, hugging the cliffside.

"He was right here," she said, stepping to the exact spot where Calvin's wheelchair had sat. She looked at Brenn for further instructions. But the face she had seen moments earlier was gone. In its place was a face she did not recognize. Brenn's eyes had turned dark, and her face was clenched in tight bands of muscles. She was breathing heavily. Tulie felt pure hatred seething from every pore.

"You killed Skylar!" Brenn said, her face working in spasms. "You strangled her because you heard her in the folly with our father that night, telling him she was pregnant with his baby!"

Tulie reeled backwards, almost falling. Her mind fractured as she tried to rebound from Brenn's transformation and the lies coming from her mouth.

"You murdered her!" Brenn said. "You strangled her with your blue dress sash! You knew Rachel was depressed over his long absences, and now you realized it was because he was having an affair with Skylar. So you choked her to death in a fit of rage! You killed Ryder, too! You were on the dock when I saw you from the cliff. You pushed him out of the boat." Tulie looked around her for a place to run.

"You were showing him your gold rocks," Brenn screamed, her eyes blazing. "What happened? Did he say they were stupid or something, and you got mad and shoved him? I saw you! You untied the boat and pushed it away so he couldn't use it to pull himself out of the water since he can't swim! And you killed my Daddy! You poisoned his tea cakes! They will find out that he was poisoned. And all of Orleans Parish knows you make tea cakes! You're a murderer! I won't let you get away with killing my father!"

Brenn made a rush for Tulie, grabbing her upper arms and pulling her through the flowerbed to the cliffside. Tulie tipped to her right, her foot sliding into a row of begonias, their red petals falling like teardrops to the ground. The jagged rocks of the lake shoreline lay forty feet below.

Suddenly, the sound of a man screaming reached their ears, and Brenn stopped, her grip tightening on Tulie's arms. They both looked below to where one of the divers was pulling himself up onto the shore, shouting to the two men in the rescue boat that was hidden in the cliff's shadow.

"There's an arm here," the diver screamed, clearly in shock at the sudden discovery. Brenn froze, momentarily forgetting Tulie. "There's a body wedged under this broken dock by the boat house!" the man yelled.

Brenn took a step forward, still holding tightly to Tulie, who was sobbing. She could see the broken dock and a badly decomposed forearm and hand. The arm showed a partial femur bone with fragments of gold fabric encasing it. A deteriorating green sash was wrapped around the wrist. Tulie recognized the gold dress. It was the one her mother wore to the engagement party.

"Mama!" Tulie screamed out. The only thing holding her up was Brenn's firm grip on her arms.

Tulie's scream jolted Brenn back to the moment. "Shut up!" she screamed. "Shut up!" She jerked Tulie toward the cliff as hard as she could. "You can join her," Brenn said. Her face was red with hate. She planted her left foot and put all her weight against the trembling girl who was sliding through the muddy flowerbed, losing her footing. "Help me!" Tulie screamed.

Suddenly, a man's shouts from across the lake echoed loudly. "Brenn! No!" Brenn looked in shock toward the sound of the male voice she knew all too well. She looked out across the lake to see Detective Hilliard and Lieutenant Calvo racing from a running car toward the lake, their heads tilted up towards her. "Don't do it!" Hilliard screamed.

Brenn paused, looking down at them and the diver who was now staring up at the scene above him. A smile of pure evil crossed her face. She turned to look into Tulie's frightened eyes, savoring the moment, and then lunged forward to hurl her from the cliff.

A fury of wind came howling across the lawn, engulfed in a black mass of swirling shadows and long black hair. Reaching out with spectral arms, it flew headlong at Brenn Barrows, careening into her with a force that sent plants and foliage flying. Tulie fell backwards into the flower bed, knocking the wind from her. In horror, Hilliard and Calvo watched from below as Brenn fell from the cliffside, her screams of terror cut short as her body shattered against the first row of jagged boulders. Calvo covered her eyes.

Hilliard watched as Reed Tillson dashed across his lawn and stopped abruptly at the top of the cliff. He looked down at a scene straight out of a horror movie. Brenn lay lifeless on the rocks. A few yards away, he could see a partially skeletonized arm reaching up from the mangled ruin of his boat dock. He sank to his knees next to Tulie.

The following week was a blur of activity. Two funerals were held for members of the Barrows' family. Randall Burrows' services were at 11:00 am, followed by Brenn Barrows' at 2:00 pm. They were interred in the family cemetery at the Barrows' home; their bright marble crypts sitting in juxtaposition to the weathered ancestral tombs next to them. Rachel Barrows' funeral service was held a few days later, after her body had been autopsied. It was determined that her cause of death was a broken neck. Her lungs were too deteriorated from the aquatic organisms that had made their home inside her to check for water to see if she was alive when she went into the lake. She, too, was brought home, and her tomb of pale pink marble was placed next to Ryder's, where they would spend eternity reunited.

In a macabre succession of funeral processions, Skylar Harris's body was laid to rest in her family plot. The area florists ran out of flowers as the last of the deaths surrounding the Broussard clan came to an end.

34 NIGHT WHISPERS

Detective Hilliard's small office played host to the people who could finally answer his questions about the various deaths he and Lieutenant Calvo had been covering.

Margo Tillson walked in alone; her gait unsteady but resolved. She took a chair across from the detective. Calvo pulled a chair to the left of the desk so that she and Hilliard could both face the woman. They were struck by her appearance. She wore an expensive two-piece linen pantsuit with a champagne-colored silk camisole. A strand of simple pearls encircled her neck. Her hair was perfectly styled and pushed away from her face just enough to showcase the matching pearl earrings that dangled from each lobe. The coral lipstick was the same shade as her bangle bracelet. Margo wore oversized sunglasses with tortoiseshell frames, which she kept on as she waited for the interview to begin.

"We appreciate your cooperation in this," Detective Hilliard began. "I know you would rather be anywhere but here and talking to anyone else."

"Almost anyone else," Margo said, her tone dry. Hilliard didn't ask for clarification.

"Mrs. Tillison…" he began.

"Oh, why so formal?" she interrupted, "after all our time together?" She tilted her head to where he saw himself reflected in her tinted shades.

"May I ask you to remove your sunglasses?" he asked amicably. "I like to see who I'm talking to."

She hesitated and then slowly pulled them away from her eyes. She folded them carefully and placed them inside her handbag. Hilliard was touched by her haggard appearance. Her eyes looked haunted and dull, as if no modicum of pain could affect her anymore than what she had already endured.

"Basically," Hilliard began, "we need to clarify a few things, and in return, we can offer you some closure as well as to the tragic events surrounding your family. Fair?" He waited, but there was no response.

"We had tests run on the gown you were wearing the night of the engagement party. The tests showed orange pollen stains, which leads us to believe you were indeed inside the folly. Would you tell us in your own words what happened that night regarding Skylar's death?"

Margo's eyes wandered to a calendar hanging behind the detective's head and remained there for a few moments. She finally looked back at him, lifted her shoulders, relaxed, and began.

"You already know Randall and I had been having an affair for some time. It's not something I'm proud of. Rachel and I competed for everything since we were kids. I was the prettiest; she was the smartest. She had a heart; I had none. So, when Randall came sniffing around, I didn't discourage him. Reed isn't exactly a stud in bed. Our age difference has always been a challenge in our marriage.

"The night of the party, I saw Skylar looking down at a note and then going into the garden. Randall followed soon after. I knew what that meant. He and I met often in the folly, and I was furious. I tried to follow them, but that damned caterer kept stopping me. By the time I got to the folly, they were both gone. I saw Tulie standing at the fountain with a green sash that I immediately recognized as Skylar's. I saw the pollen stain and knew what *that* meant! She told me Skylar took her sash, left her with the soiled green one, and was going to meet Tulie back at the folly after the announcements to switch the sashes back. I offered to do it for Tulie. I was going to confront the little tramp. She was about to marry my son and get her foot in the door for a fortune. I guess I was also praying that she would tell me that nothing was going on with Randall.

"After the cake cutting, I saw Skylar go back into the garden to return the sash. I followed her a few minutes later. I found her in the folly. She was lying on the floor. My first reaction was that she had passed out because she looked so drunk at the party. But then I saw the red marks around her neck, and she looked dead. I panicked. I thought maybe Randall had killed her. I couldn't think of any other person who might want her dead. My first thought was that Randall fooled around with her, had his fun, and brushed her off. Skylar may have threatened to tell Rachel, or something like that, and he snapped. I went back to the house for the key to the folly to lock it before anyone else could find her lying there. I came back and locked the door.

"When I returned, I went to Skylar's body. I

remembered Tulie's sash, but it wasn't there. I dragged her body to the secret door in the folly and put her in the tunnel. I had to figure out what to do. I left her there, locked the door, and hurried back for the parents' announcement, which we didn't end up doing. I came back later with a shovel, but her body was gone. I swear! It's the truth. I figured Randall found her in the tunnel and finished what I was going to do. When I heard they found her buried in the grove, I was sure he put her there.

"I hid Skylar's purse, hoping people would think she ran out on her own party and ditched my son, like she did Angela's boy. I would rather suffer that embarrassment than have the truth come out. You see, I still loved Randall..." she said, her voice cracking. She looked down, her face twitching. With eyes brimming with tears, she looked up and said, "I know it's stupid. I knew who he was. That he would always be a cheater, but I loved him! I wanted to protect him. I really did believe we would be together someday. He hadn't loved Rachel for a long time."

Calvo pressed her lips together, saddened that a sister could feel so little for her own blood.

"We have information stating that the blue sash was around Skylar's neck," Hilliard said evenly.

Margo looked him squarely in the eye. "It was not there," she repeated. "Why would I lie about that?"

"Speaking of Rachel..." Hilliard said, resisting the urge to retort to Margo's last question.

Margo blanched. This would be harder to tell. She went over the argument in her bedroom that she had with her sister the day after the party. Rachel had accidentally fallen from her window. Through ragged breaths, she admitted to burying her in the lake to cover it up and that she wrote a fake note saying Rachel was going away for a while to appease Tulie. She missed the sudden reaction from Hilliard at her mention of the note. Margo continued, admitting she called their Cousin Jenny on Rachel's cell phone that Randall provided her, as a further cover-up to make it look like Rachel was still alive.

"But then, it all went wrong," she said, tears running from her eyes. "Someone saw me. The blackmail notes started coming. A wet green sash kept appearing for me to find that looked just like the one that was wrapped around Rachel's wrist when she went under the water. It was awful! I paid out a lot of money! I thought it was Brixi because she was always looking through my things. But, I had nothing to do with Brixi's murder! Absolutely nothing! I seem to always be in the middle of someone getting killed, but I didn't kill her or Skylar! I did take my son's engagement ring from Skylar's finger when I hid her body in the tunnel."

She paused when she saw the looks of disgust on the officers' faces.

"Why not?" she said angrily. "I mean, she didn't need it anymore, and it cost a fortune! I'll give it back to my son when I can figure out how to explain how I got it. That won't be easy. This has all been so stressful. Reed wants to sell the house and move away. I *want* to go! There has always been something wrong with that house. I do believe it's haunted. And that lake is nothing but death. I do...I do want to move now."

She broke into quiet sobs. Across from her were two faces trying to mask the revulsion they were feeling.

After several tense moments, Hilliard took a deep

breath and in a restrained voice, said, "You will have to face charges about your involvement in handling Skylar's body and your sister's. It's against the law to impede a death investigation and move a body. Do you understand? These are not light charges, Mrs. Tillson. Tampering with a deceased body is a class 3 felony. You may be facing some prison time and charges. I'm sorry all these deaths have caused you so much inconvenience and stress."

There was no mistaking the harshness or sarcasm of his tone. Margo jerked up her head and glared at him.

"I didn't kill them! That's the important thing here, not what happened after! Do you know who you're talking to?"

"I'm beginning to," Hilliard said. "Put up your For Sale sign, but you aren't going anywhere for a while," he said evenly. "Reed can move on if he likes. By the way, we did check to see if your maid Stephanie was with you the evening Brixi died. We called Tilliard's. It seems you did lie. At the time someone was bashing Brixi over the head, Stephanie was out picking up your dinner order. Lucky for you, your prints weren't on the vase that killed her."

"What did you do with Skylar's purse?" Calvo asked.

The shocked look on Margo's face was worth the price of admission. She sat staring at the lieutenant for several seconds. Calvo could visualize the wheels turning in her head.

"It's gone," she said, finally.

"Let me guess," Hilliard said. "Bottom of the lake?"

Margo rose, snatching up her purse. She glared at him as she opened it and flung a packet of white index cards across the table to Hilliard.

"Here!" she barked. "Here's the blackmail notes. I certainly wasn't blackmailing myself! You can check my bank account and validate the huge amount of missing funds. I have to live with my sister's death for the rest of my life, but I did not murder anyone!"

Hilliard opened a drawer and brought out a stack of blue envelopes. He laid them on his desk and watched as Margo's face went pale.

"Speaking of notes," he said evenly. "Perhaps you *did* write these. I only realized it when you just admitted to writing a fake letter to Tulie from her mother. I found these in Brenn's drawer. They are written on the same blue stationery used to write love letters to Randall as the fake one you handed to Tulie that was supposedly written by Rachel. Rachel didn't write those letters to Randall all those years ago…you did. Brenn's mother found them and realized her husband was having an affair. She assumed it was with Rachel since Randall married her after the divorce. She never recovered from reading those letters or the betrayal, and she hung herself."

Margo stared at the letters Hilliard had spread out across the table. The envelope with Tulie's name on it was last in the pile. She stood frozen to the spot, her fingers gripping her purse. She finally lifted glazed eyes to face the detective.

"Must have been a bitter pill to have Randall end up marrying Rachel instead of you," Hilliard said, his tone icy. "And yet, you kept after him all those years and were willing to hide a young woman's body in a tunnel to save him. Here's your parting gift, Margo. Randall didn't kill Skylar. You did it all for nothing…and I do mean all!"

484

The room pulsed with tension. Hilliard watched her facial muscles twitching in spasms of anger. She snapped her purse shut as she glowered at the man. Her chest was heaving, and tears rimmed her eyes. She started to say something, thought better of it, and walked out. Hilliard and Calvo sat in stunned silence for a moment.

"The only time she cried was for herself," Calvo said in disbelief. "Margo Tillson is a textbook narcissist. Not even when talking about her own sister's death and sinking her into the lake...not one tear." She shook her head. "She didn't even ask who killed Brixi when we told her she was off the hook because of the vase and the fingerprints. Brixi was nothing to her."

"She's a sociopath," Hilliard said, looking over the pile of blue letters. "I'll get the paperwork filled out for her hearing on tampering charges. I think her mind fractured long ago. It would have to. Did you hear her say she thinks that house is haunted? Good grief," Hilliard sighed.

His outburst was met with silence. Puckering his face, he turned to look at Calvo and squinted.

"No! Please don't tell me you believe that house is haunted! I can't take this spooky kick you're on much longer!"

Calvo smiled, undaunted, and said, "I don't need to convince you. You believe what you want, and I'll do the same. But I'm the one who read all of Calvin's newspaper articles about the Broussard cases. Lavinia Broussard fell down the main staircase in 1944, and her death was always considered a mystery. Many believe she was pushed, by who or *what?*"

"Oh my gosh!" Hilliard spouted. "Was Caspar

sliding down the banister, too?"

Calvo hurried on, ignoring him.

"All the people who stayed there afterwards reported the same thing: tapping on their door, piano music in the wee hours, lights in the garden... It was her husband, Brett, who flooded the Indian burial ground. Just sayin.' That is a boatload of accidents and deaths surrounding that lake and that family! And what of the wet green sash that kept showing up to scare Margo? Rachel's dead body had Skylar's green sash wrapped around the arm."

"I thought you were intelligent. I guess I was wrong," Hilliard said hotly.

"Obviously, I am not, or I would have chosen a different partner." The two looked at each other and finally grinned, calling a truce.

Tulie Barrows sat quietly in the small police cubicle and answered their questions. She told the detective and Lieutenant Calvo that it was Brenn who came up with the idea of buying tea cakes and passing them off as Rachel's, and in the end, her own. She denied putting cakes onto Randall's tray. It was Brenn who brought him his meals while he was sick. Tulie said she hadn't bought tea cakes in months. When Calvo told her they suspected Brenn of causing her and Rachel's hallucinations and confused states by poisoning their tea, Tulie looked genuinely pained.

"Why would she want to hurt us?" she asked, her face swollen from tears. She searched Calvo's eyes for an answer, yet she feared what she would learn.

"We think Brenn was filled with hatred from Randall's abandonment of her and her mother, and that he caused her mother's suicide. You and Ryder were born, and she became invisible: basically a guest in what should have been her rightful home. She hated the entire Broussard family. They had everything she never had. We will never know if she meant to kill Barry, but she did rig his waterski to fail, resulting in his death. Based on what you told us she said to you on the cliff before she fell, Ryder was pushed from the boat, and the boat untied and moved so he couldn't climb back in. I think everything she said to you was a confession only flipped to make you the killer. Ryder must have done something to make her mad that day.

"It looks like it was Brenn that overheard Skylar confronting your father in the folly, telling him she was pregnant. Brenn ran home and got Rachel's pills and crushed them into a powder that she secretly added to a scoop of whipping cream. She placed it on a slice of peach pie after she heard Skylar asking for a piece earlier, and deliberately bumped into Galveston Southgate, causing him to drop his pie on the ground. She handed him hers with the poisoned cream and it was just a matter of minutes. Skylar's huge consumption of alcohol exacerbated the drug's reaction. She was probably dead within seconds of entering the folly to give you back your sash. Brenn took your sash and wrapped it around her neck to look like you strangled her. But Dawson found it first and removed it."

Tulie's head hung down to her chest as tears streamed from her eyes. "And she poisoned Daddy with the same drug?" she asked brokenly.

"No," Calvo said gently. "She put a high dosage of the poison into his tea cake frosting that she was feeding you and your mother to keep you both confused and dazed. We believe she was making it from the Angel's Trumpet flowers, your Cousin Angela is growing at her house. We found the same chemicals in little Tommy Simons' bloodstream when he was poisoned by blowing on one of its flowers. Brenn was keeping it in a tin can in your kitchen. She probably boiled it and added it to the frosting on your father's cakes. She then made sure we found out from the women you took cakes to that you were known for making tea cakes."

"Now I know why Brenn always paid in cash for the cakes. That way, nothing would show up on our credit cards showing they were bought, not homemade." Tulie shook her head. "She always stayed in the car when I delivered them…so everyone would think I was baking them all by myself and no one could tie her to them."

After a few moments, Tulie looked up at the detective and in a voice filled with pain, asked, "Did Brenn kill my Mama?"

"No, Tulie," Hilliard said softly. "That was a tragic accident. We finally had a long talk with Margo. Your mother fell from your Aunt Margo's window during an argument. Your aunt panicked and put her in the lake to cover her death. She was afraid people would think she or your father did it on purpose because of the rumors of their affair. I think she was protecting him. Her maid, Brixi Carter, knew too much and it cost her, her life. We think Brenn killed Brixi and tried to frame Margo. Brenn must have been there the night your mother fell and saw Margo put her into the water. Margo finally confessed that she was being blackmailed. Since she thought at first it was Brixi, and Brixi was found murdered, she kept quiet about it. Brenn got away with hundreds of thousands of dollars by blackmailing your aunt. Based on the blackmail notes Margo showed us, Brenn knew a lot…enough to leave clues in the notes."

"What kind of clues?" Tulie asked, still stunned.

"Clues about a broken neck and something green. Words about a dead baby and a ring. Your stepsister is the most evil person I have ever encountered. Those notes prove she was working Margo for two murders! Skylar's and your mother's death. She was setting her up for Brixi's as well."

Tulie sat stunned. Her mind was shutting down under the weight of it all. Hilliard continued gently.

"She probably killed Brixi because the maid was blabbing her mouth off to Maude and the other maids about the muddy shoes and her suspicions about Margo," he said. "If Rachel or Skylar's bodies are found, there goes her little blackmail scheme. It would all be over. She needed to shut Brixi up."

Tulic appeared dazed, too shaken to cry. Her eyes blinked repeatedly as she tried to retain all the information.

"Madame Sangers knew Mama was gone," Tulie finally said sadly. "I didn't want to believe it."

"Brenn hired her to fake the séance about your brother's death," Calvo said, wondering if telling Tulie Brenn had rigged it to look like Tulie killed her brother would push the trembling girl over the edge. "She paid the medium to write GOLD and TREASURE on the blackboard so it would look like you had something to do with his death. But what we found was that the last three words weren't written by Madam Sangers. That is still a mystery."

"What were they?" Tulie asked, suddenly rallying. "I've forgotten. It was so long ago."

"SECRET PATH. TORN. MURDER," Calvo said.

Tulie thought hard, casting her mind back to Ryder's séance. She had felt him all around her that night, but she remembered being very frightened. Suddenly, her face froze, and a look of horror came over her.

"Torn!" she said breathlessly. "I remember now! There was a torn paper in the bottom of the boat. It had a big skull on it! I was so frightened when I couldn't see Ryder that I blanked it out. But I remembered a skull. It was there…it was torn…"

Lieutenant Calvo looked at Hilliard, and she could tell he had arrived at the same answer.

"The photo Dawson took showed Ryder holding the map only minutes before you went to spray the rocks," Calvo said. "The next time we see Brenn, she is up on the cliff holding the map…or what was left of it after it tore. Ryder must have taken it into the boat and when Brenn wanted it back, he refused. When she grabbed it, it tore. And in a rage, she shoved him overboard. If she had saved him, it would have been an accident. But she untied the boat and moved it out of his reach and let him drown."

"No more!" Tulie begged. "Please, no more. I will never know why my own stepsister would do such evil things to us…her own family! Why?"

"I think you will find the answers in these," Hilliard said. He took the blue letters from his drawer and passed them to Tulie. He and Calvo watched her face as she read them. She looked up, bewildered. She pulled the envelope to her with her name on it that her mother had left her when she went away.

"I don't understand," she said. She looked at the dates scrawled across the top of each letter and her face froze. "These are love letters to Daddy before he married Mama," she said, her voice small. "Mama had an affair with Daddy while he was married to Brenn's Mama?" Her voice cracked and the tears flowed.

"No, Tulie," Hilliard said gently. "The writing looks like your mother's, but it is actually your Aunt Margo's. *She* had an affair with your Daddy while he was still married to Brenn's mother. It caused Brenn's family to fall apart, and her mother...well...died. Your mother didn't write that goodbye letter to you either...Margo did. This is why Brenn hated you all so much, especially Rachel. She thought Rachel was having the affair that ruined her life and caused her mother to commit suicide. She wanted to destroy you all."

Tulie buried her face in her hands.

"Tulie, Brenn had dealt with too much trauma and her mind wasn't right. It may also have been about the money. With Ryder, Randall, and Rachel gone, Rachel's money would have gone to you. Even though Brenn had nothing to do with Rachel's death, it must have felt like a 'lagniappe'...a gift."

"So she was going to throw me off a cliff?" Tulie asked, stunned. "Just for money?'

Calvo pressed her lips together and reached into a folder. She reluctantly handed Tulie a folded piece of stationery. Tulie unfolded it with shaking hands. She looked at the typewritten words in total disbelief.

"Please forgive me. I could not bear for my mother to suffer the shame of everyone knowing Skylar Harris was having my father's baby. After Ryder's death, I had been living with the guilt that I pushed him into the lake and let him drown. I think I went crazy after that. When I heard Skylar in the folly telling my father she was pregnant with his baby, I snapped and killed her. I poisoned my Daddy and Aunt Margo with my tea cakes for all the pain they caused my Mama. I miss my Mama. I feel so alone. She has abandoned me, and I am lost. I have nothing left to live for. When you find my body, please bury me next to Ryder. I'm sorry.

Tulie Barrows"

"We found that in Brenn's car," Hilliard said. "Brenn was probably going to leave it where it would be found after your body was discovered at the bottom of the cliff. She was so far gone at that point that it didn't even register there were three men below in the lake searching for Rachel's body who would witness her throwing you from the cliff."

Tulie handed the letter back to the lieutenant. Her face was filled with pain.

"Yet, she was still going to push me," she said, her voice trembling.

"Tulie, your stepsister was sick. Her mother's suicide and your father's abandonment of them never left her. Rage fueled everything she did. That ring she gave you was stolen from the woman who confronted you at the engagement party. Brenn set you up to look like a thief as well. I think it all amused her. It was a sick, evil, twisted game that satisfied her need for revenge."

Tulie suddenly looked over to the lieutenant with her forehead furrowed.

"The suicide note she wrote for me said I poisoned

Daddy *and* Aunt Margo with my tea cakes. Aunt Margo is dead?" she cried out.

"No…no, Tulie," Calvo said, placing her hand on her arm. She took a deep breath. "We found a new box of tea cakes in Margo's kitchen. It had a typewritten note taped to the top that said, 'Aunt Margo. Love you, Tulie.' It looks like she was going to give those to Margo, and it would look like you killed her with the same poisonous cakes that killed Randall. One was missing, and Reed said Margo had it that morning with her tea. He told us at the door earlier that day that she was in bed, sick. I didn't realize she was actually ill. My guess is they will find enough poison in the frosting to have killed Margo just like your father if she had eaten more of them. It's why Brenn wanted to move in with them…to place the tea cakes and make sure Margo ate them. She didn't care that someone else might eat them by mistake."

"This can't be true!" Tulie cried.

"I found those blue letters and the envelope with your name on it in Brenn's desk," Hilliard said. "Brenn knew Rachel was dead when your father handed you the fake goodbye letter from your mother. She knew someone else had to have written that note. It wouldn't have taken much to realize it matched the letters she had kept all those years that sent her mother over the edge. She realized at that moment, when she saw the goodbye letter from Rachel, that it had to have been Margo who wrote all of them. Margo was the one having the affair with your Daddy, not Rachel. It was Margo, not Rachel, who was cheating with Randall behind her mother's back. It started with blackmailing Margo, but it looks like she was prepared to kill her now that the bodies of Rachel and Skylar were found, and the blackmailing would end. All the secrets were revealed."

Tulie rose on unsteady legs.

"I need some time. Thank you for all you've done for me," she said, shakily. "Cousin Angela said she will take care of me until I can figure out what comes next. But now I know my Mama never left me. She wouldn't have, I knew that." She gave them a heartbreaking look. "Don't forget me," she said, sounding like a small child.

Calvo stood and enfolded the young woman in her arms.

"You're a brave young lady, Tulie Barrows," she said fondly, tears rimming her eyes. "You'll be just fine. Let me give you a ride to your cousin's house."

"I have a ride," Tulie said, a sad smile skimming her face. "Dawson is outside waiting for me. Thank you again." She smiled at Detective Hilliard and left the room.

"Unbelievable!" Calvo said, sinking back into her chair. "Even when the words were coming out of my mouth, it was hard to believe it all! And Margo! She admitted to finding Skylar dead in the folly, hiding her in the tunnel, and putting Rachel in the lake. Like you said, that's tampering with a dead body. There will be ramifications for that. Plus, she hid Skylar's purse so people would think Skylar ran off. That's tampering with evidence, which is a class 6 felony! Oddly, Margo refuses to admit she buried Skylar in the grove. Why not admit to that if she admitted to the other? The stains on the dress prove Margo was in the folly, but that's all we have. So, who buried Skylar? Maybe it *was* Randall.

He knew about the tunnel. At least she is back home in her family plot where she belongs."

Calvo paused. She reached for one of Hilliard's caramels and popped it into her mouth. Her mind returned to Brenn. "All those deaths!" she exclaimed. "All that planning and evil! It had to have been her who killed Angela's cat. She knew about Angel's Trumpet being poisonous. It's not a stretch to believe she knew pollen was deadly as well. Did Brenn really think she could just kill and kill, and claim all that money from Rachel's will?"

"Sure," Hilliard said. "After Brenn's Aunt Susan died, she had no one. I think her original plan was to keep drugging Tulie so that she appeared touched in the head, and then set her up for Skylar's, her father's, Margo's, and Ryder's deaths. Tulie goes to prison. You can't inherit if you're convicted of murder, so, with Randall, Rachel, and Ryder gone, Brenn was next in line. She wouldn't have gone to all that trouble with the tea cakes over the summer if it weren't to prove that Tulie made the cakes that killed her father.

"I knew the minute I looked out from Brenn's bedroom window all those years ago she was lying," Hilliard said. "She said she saw Ryder sitting in his boat that day that she was making the map in her room. I looked out the window. Due to the large elm tree there, you can't see the dock. Oh, one last thing. I checked with Dr. Clarkson. Brenn never called him when her father was succumbing to the poison. She just hoped he would die. I'm not sure why she called 911, unless she felt he was too far gone, and it would make it look like she tried to save him."

Calvo shook her head.

"If Reed's black dog hadn't run at Brenn on the cliff," Hilliard said, "it would be Tulie dashed to pieces on those rocks instead of Brenn. Maybe she decided to kill Tulie rather than risk her getting out of a prison term, or it was the heat of the moment, and she snapped."

Calvo looked at him, brows knitted together.

"You think that was a black dog that flew at them from across the lawn?" she asked, her tone filled with irony.

"Well, of course," Hilliard said. "You saw it happen. What else would it be?"

"You don't want to know what I think," Calvo said, smiling.

"Oh no! Enough! I mean it! There's no such thing as ghosts, or curses, or aliens, or Moth Man, or Bigfoot!"

"I believe with all my heart that Rachel saved her daughter's life in the only way she could. From beyond her watery grave," Calvo said solemnly. She reached into the same folder where she had returned Tulie's fake suicide note and pulled out the photo Hilliard found in Brenn's bedroom. Tulie is seated at the table in the sunroom, a full cup of tea sitting across from her before an empty chair. Calvo slid the photo across the desk to the detective, a sad smile on her face.

"Look closely," she said, pushing the picture closer to him. "Look at the silver teapot in the center of the table."

Hilliard grinned at her and bent his head over the picture. He pushed his glasses up on his nose and leaned closer. The smirk disappeared. He pulled the picture to him, peering at it in shock. He looked over at her sharply.

"You doctored this!" he said accusingly. "There is *no* way!"

Calvo leaned back and folded her arms. "There are more things in heaven and earth, Hilliard, than are dreamt of in your philosophy." She smiled fondly at him, relishing the look of pure panic on his face. He looked down again at the photo. Reflected in the silver surface of the teapot was the faint image of a woman with raven black hair, sitting across from Tulie, before a full cup of tea.

Tulie and Dawson sat on her back porch in weathered rocking chairs and watched the last vestiges of the sunset leak into Lake Broussard. Angela was yelling something at Calvin inside their house on the other side of Lake Grove Estates. Her shrill voice spilled through the screen door, past the lit jack-o-lanterns, and bounced off the lake water. Lights shone from Margo's house across the inlet. The new solar lawn sconces reflected down the shiny rocks of the cliff past where Brenn's body had lain to a newly built boat dock. A For Sale sign at the end of Margo's driveway swayed in the breeze.

Tulie looked off to her right at the pecan grove and felt a shudder.

"Poor Skylar," she said. "To be buried like that in the dirt. If the storm hadn't uprooted that tree, she might never have been found."

Dawson rocked quietly and said finally, "Sometimes you have to bury something to let something else survive."

Tulie looked at him quickly, but she couldn't read his face. He stared out at the water. Minutes passed.

"Ryder tried to tell us who killed him," Dawson said finally, his voice low. "He tried all along. The King of Spades had Brenn's name on it. He showed it to us over and over again. He wrote the clues on the blackboard. He was the only one other than Brenn that knew something was TORN and that it pointed to MURDER: Brenn's torn map. He rang the ship's bell. The bell was ringing that day because the boat rocked when he was pushed overboard. And his ghost knew Brenn took the SECRET PATH as an alibi. They were all his way of letting us know."

Tulie sat with tears in her eyes. Finally, she said, "I gave Daphne Hobart back her ring that Brenn stole. I still can't believe how much Brenn must have hated us all. It's so sad. She and I had so much in common. We both took care of our mothers when they were too broken to function. We should have been kindred spirits. She had so much pain buried inside."

"Are you going to be okay?" Dawson asked kindly.

"I'm taking it one day at a time," Tulie said. "Cousin Angela is a little too protective, but it's nice to have them there. I think the money will be okay. Daddy's lawyer is still going over the wills and stuff."

Dawson looked over at her. So much had changed since those idyllic summers of pirate games and magic shows. He reached into his jeans pocket and pulled out a red handkerchief wrapped around something. Tulie glanced down at it and looked at him with a smile.

"Snacks?" she asked.

"Do you remember the old rumors about your Mama's great-grandpa burying pirate treasure around the property? That he was buddies with Jean Lafitte, and there was hidden treasure around here?"

Tulie nodded, her heart rate increasing.

Dawson laid the handkerchief in her hand and waited. She peeled away the cotton fabric and gasped. An emerald the size of a walnut twinkled up at her in the moonlight. She looked at him with bulging eyes.

"I found it the night of the storm," he said. "I went out after I heard the lightning strike something. There were trees uprooted everywhere. That was shining up at me in one of the holes. There's probably more." He smiled, shaking his head. "Brett Broussard planted pecan trees over buried treasure and probably didn't even know it. I figure it belongs to you now. After all, Margo sold off the grove to those developers, and she's moving away. You're a true Broussard descendant."

Tulie stared unbelievingly at the gem in her hand. *How excited Ryder would have been to know there was real treasure just feet away*, she thought sadly.

They sat in silence for a time. Tulie held the gem in a closed fist and looked out at the water. Dawson allowed her time to takc it all in. A light breeze blew across the lake's surface, sending ripples of small waves toward the shoreline. The cicadas sang, their rhythm low and constant. Tulie looked over to the pink marble of her mother's tomb, not far from where she sat, and the tears came.

"I hear them at night," she said softly to Dawson, who had pulled his rocker closer to hers, their weathered wooden arms touching. "She and Ryder whisper to each other. I was afraid at first to live here alone, but I'm not alone."

Dawson put his hand on hers. It felt rough and dry, the broken blisters on his palms scratchy against her skin.

"You don't have to be alone," he said.

She looked at him in the fading light and smiled.

The breeze lifted her hair and dried the humidity from her face. A broken cobweb fluttered overhead.

"Summer's lacing," she said, smiling.

Rebecca F. Pittman is a bestselling author of 17 titles in the paranormal and true crime genres. She is regularly featured on TV, radio, and podcasts internationally. Her love of mysteries was fueled when she discovered Nancy Drew early on, then enflamed with her first Agatha Christie reading. Shirley Jackson's *"The Haunting of Hill House"* cemented the love affair with mysteries, ghosts, and clues, and she never looked back.

Her non-fiction books cover the most haunted locations in the world. She was the only author permitted to write about the paranormal events at the Palace of Versailles in Paris. Her love of puzzles and clues segued easily into the true crime field with her books on the infamous murder cases of Pam Hupp and Alex Murdaugh.

Ms. Pittman is also a game creator, escape room entrepreneur, former talk show host, model, and motivational speaker. But if you ask her where her pride lies, it's in her four sons, three daughters-in-law, and 15 grandchildren.

She makes her home in the foothills of the Rocky Mountains in Colorado, but can be found on beaches on each coast as often as possible.

Check out her free newsletter, books, games, and upcoming events at: www.rebeccafpittmanbooks.com.

Other books by Rebecca F. Pittman

Non-Fiction:

The History and Haunting of the Stanley Hotel
The History and Haunting of the Myrtles Plantation
The History and Haunting of Lemp Mansion
The History and Haunting of Lizzie Borden
The History and Haunting of the Palace of Versailles
The History and Haunting of Salem: The Witch Trials and Beyond
The History and Haunting of the 1771 Enfield House
The History and Haunting of the Smurl Family Horror
The History and Haunting of the Bell Witch (June 2025)
Countdown to Murder: Pam Hupp
Countdown to Murder: Alex Murdaugh
How to Start a Faux Painting & Mural Business
Scrapbooking for Profit
Troubleshooting Men: What in the World Do They Want?

Fiction:

T. J. Finnel and the Well of Ghosts (Juvenile Fiction)
When Shadows Walk

Coming Soon in Murder Mysteries:

The Puzzle Box
The Diamond Peacock Club
Hourglass

Games:
The Lizzie Borden Paranormal Card Game
(On sale at www.rebeccafpittmanbooks.com)

www.ingramcontent.com/pod-product-compliance
Lightning Source LLC
Chambersburg PA
CBHW071629260626
47170CB00001B/17